TEARS AND FEARS AT BLACKBERRY FARM

ROSIE CLARKE

Boldwood

First published in Great Britain in 2026 by Boldwood Books Ltd.

Copyright © Rosie Clarke, 2026

Cover Design by Colin Thomas

Cover Images: Colin Thomas

A CIP catalogue record for this book is available from the British Library.

Paperback ISBN 978-1-80557-513-9

Large Print ISBN 978-1-80557-514-6

Hardback ISBN 978-1-80557-512-2

Trade Paperback ISBN 978-1-80656-252-7

Ebook ISBN 978-1-80557-515-3

Kindle ISBN 978-1-80557-516-0

Audio CD ISBN 978-1-80557-507-8

MP3 CD ISBN 978-1-80557-508-5

Digital audio download ISBN 978-1-80557-511-5

This book is printed on certified sustainable paper. Boldwood Books is dedicated to putting sustainability at the heart of our business. For more information please visit https://www.boldwoodbooks.com/about-us/sustainability/

Boldwood Books Ltd, 23 Bowerdean Street, London, SW6 3TN

www.boldwoodbooks.com

1

BLACKBERRY FARM – APRIL 1944

The wireless was droning on about the state of the war. A voice was saying that General Eisenhower was turning Britain into a big armed camp as part of his plans for the invasion of Europe, most of it still under Hitler's command. All visits to the coast had been banned and all overseas travel had been cancelled due to tight security. It went on to say that more bombs had been dropped in a single night than ever before and it was described as a birthday gift for Hitler.

Pam Talbot shuddered at the thought, because, after all, it meant people being killed and she couldn't help feeling sorry for the ordinary German folk who were probably as sick of the war as she was.

It looked bright and sunny as Pam glanced through her kitchen window, which made a change after all the misty mornings they'd had recently. Living on a farm in Fenland Cambridgeshire, you got used to mist lying over the land in the early mornings, but today it was clear and the sun was not hiding behind a bank of cloud. Pam sighed because the pleasant weather did nothing to lift the cloud that had seemed to hang over her life for the past year or more.

Her once glorious honey-blonde hair, caught up in a twist at the nape of her neck, had streaks of grey now, but in her early fifties her face was still unlined and youthful, though her eyes were shadowed with grief, their bright blue dimmed and without the sparkle she'd had in her youth. Her dress was a navy and white spot, with a collar of white, fastened with a small gold and pearl brooch, a present from her late husband, but over it she wore an enveloping apron of starched white cotton. She looked neat and efficient and capable, and she was all those things, but she no longer sang as she worked.

'Oh, Arthur,' she said aloud, her throat catching as she thought of the husband she had so recently lost. 'Why did you have to die so young? We had so much more to do...'

Sometimes, it seemed to Pam that everything had started to go wrong after her husband died – or no, perhaps it was the war. This wretched, hateful war that dragged on and on had taken two of her sons from their home, leaving just Artie to carry on the work of the farm. She suspected that it was first Tom's injury, and then worrying over John, that had exacerbated Arthur's heart condition. Or maybe that was just because she needed something to blame for all the sorrow that had built up so that it felt unbearable at times.

This was no good! Pam struggled to pull herself together. She had work to do and standing about, worrying about things she couldn't change wouldn't help her do the baking or iron the sheets. She was on her own today, because Jeanie, Artie's wife, was out in the fields with him. Pam's daughter-in-law had taken her baby son with her. They were hoeing weeds between the potato rows and Winston Talbot would be in his carrycot. Artie said she should leave him at home with his granny, but Jeanie knew that Pam had enough to cope with looking after Jonny, her eldest, motherless, grandchild, who was now a mischievous toddler into everything. However, at the moment, Jonny was with Lizzie, wife to Pam's first son Tom; she'd taken him and her own boy off for the morning, to give Pam a rest, because she'd thought Pam looked tired.

Pam had a large family: three sons, Tom, Artie, and John, and two daughters, Susan and Angela, two daughters-in-law, Lizzie and Jeanie, and now three grandsons: Jonny, Arthur, and Winston, but only one was in her charge. Jonny's mother, Faith, had died tragically at his birth and Pam had taken him into her care. She also had her nephew, George, living with them and two land girls, Olive and Izzy, which meant a lot of work for her: washing, ironing, cooking and cleaning. Pam's youngest son, John, was now lying badly burned in a military hospital overseas; Tom was in the Army and Artie struggled to keep the farm going.

Choking back the foolish, sentimental tears, which came because she'd been thinking of her late husband, Pam turned away from the window, but then she heard the postman's knock and went to the door to open it.

Jock, her usual postman, beamed at her cheerfully, his weather-roughened skin red and mottled with fine lines. 'Letters for you, Pam,' he told her. 'This one is from overseas. Can't read the postmark – I reckon they do that on purpose, but I know it is Cyprus. That will be about your John... and this one...'

He got no further, because Pam snatched the letter from abroad and ripped it open. She read the first few lines eagerly, hoping it was from John, but it was from that nurse again – Sister Jane Forster.

'Oh!' she cried in surprise and relief. 'John is being transferred to England. It says here that I can't visit him yet, because he has asked that no one does for a while...' Tears blurred her eyes.

Jock nodded sympathetically. 'They feel sensitive, them that's been badly burned,' he said, showing his understanding. 'Makes a proper mess of their face sometimes, and they need time to heal before they can look at anyone they know. It happened to a cousin of my mother's... months afore he wanted visitors.'

Pam wanted to shout at him to shut up, but she knew he meant it kindly, so nodded, mumbled her thanks and retreated into the kitchen to read her letters.

The nurse had told her that they were coming a little earlier in the year but had been delayed for reasons she was not at liberty to disclose. Pam continued reading:

I realise this is a terrible time for you, Mrs Talbot, but we have to think of John for the moment. His wishes and feelings must come first, as I am certain you understand, and he mustn't be upset by other people's emotions. He has written to you at last. John wanted to see the damage for himself before writing and now he is able to see quite well again, so that is one blessing. However, he was terribly shocked and said it would horrify his family to see him this way so he has asked for space to become used to his own face and to give it time to heal. I am certain it will look much better soon, though he may never be the John you knew. This will be hard to accept, and I support John's request that your visits should be delayed for a few months longer.

Pam sat with the letter in her hand for a while, her emotions veering from grief to vague annoyance. She was racked with sorrow for her beloved son's pain and his injuries, a little annoyed with the nurse for thinking she would upset John in any way. Of course she understood that John's feelings came first – but she was his mother! All she wanted to do was touch him and hug him, tell him that her love would never alter; she was just glad he was alive after all the months of worrying, thinking him dead when there was no news, except that his plane had been lost.

Tears trickled down her cheeks as she wondered if he knew that Lucy, his girlfriend, had got tired of waiting for news and married someone else. Pam hadn't been certain about the girl he'd planned to make his wife from the start; she'd sensed a reluctance in her when she'd put Jonny in Lucy's arms. It was natural perhaps that she might be a little jealous of John's first love, Faith, who had born him a son out of wedlock, but a child was innocent and deserved unquestioning love.

It was uncertain whether John would ever marry now and that made Pam's heart ache. She would have welcomed Lucy had he married her, but although she'd thought her in love with John, she'd had her doubts – but she would have put them aside if only John was uninjured and coming home to wed the girl he'd chosen. Pam wasn't sure how much he'd loved Lucy. Somehow, she didn't believe it was the same as the head-over-heels feeling he'd had for Faith... Poor little Faith. She hadn't deserved to die in such tragic circumstances – that uncle of hers! He'd hurt her so grievously she'd given birth prematurely and alone. However, fate had prevailed and he was dead now in an accident. Pam wished she might have had a go at him before he met his comeuppance. She'd have had his eyes for what he'd done to Faith. Pam's fingers curled like claws at the thought of how much pain her John had been forced to bear these past years. This bloody war! Had it not been for the war she was sure they would all still be happy and healthy. Damn that Hitler!

They had all been devastated by Faith's death, though thankfully, her son Jonny had lived and brought joy and laughter into their lives. It was needed!

So much tragedy. It was hard for one family to bear, almost a curse, she thought, but dismissed it instantly.

Pam took a deep breath and looked at her next letter. She realised it was from her eldest daughter, Susan, and her hand trembled as she tore it open, but the next minute she was smiling. Susan's letter was filled with the joy of a young girl having the time of her life at college in Cambridge. She was learning to be a teacher and she was loving every minute. She'd been to films, dances, debates and trips on the river. Goodness knows how she ever got any studying done!

Pam's spirits lifted as she folded the letter and popped it back in its envelope. Arthur would have loved to read that!

She had two small bills – and the third letter was from her eldest son, Tom. He wasn't Arthur's biological son, but he was a born farmer and Arthur had treated him just the same as Artie and John. In fact, Pam thought Tom might have been her husband's favourite, because they thought so much alike. Tom was dependable and he never expected anything, was always content to work for what he got – unlike Artie, who had been so angry over his father's will.

Artie was a constant concern. Because he'd been so resentful that he wasn't to inherit his share of the land until after Pam died, she had tried to compensate for his disappointment and given him the pig land along the Chatteris Road without thinking about it. She'd thought it just ten acres of land, not particularly valuable, imagining that he would farm it for himself – but Artie had sold it for ten thousand pounds, a huge sum, making his share of everything so much more than all the others. He'd invested it in acres of land in Sutton Fen, and given himself so much work that he was finding it hard to cope and neglecting other work.

Arthur wouldn't have wanted that, but he'd never told Pam that bit of land could be worth a small fortune. She'd had no idea it might hold sand and gravel deposits: valuable commodities used in building. Tom had known, but she hadn't consulted him before giving Artie the land. It was her own fault, but she felt guilty, because her daughters, Susan and Angela, ought to have shared in that windfall. Tom wouldn't bother, he would make his own way, and John might never want anything... but she would have to try to make it up to the others one day.

Pam shook her head. This was getting her nowhere! She had to get on or she wouldn't have docky ready when they came back in from the fields for their food midday. She returned to the sink and started to peel the potatoes she'd washed earlier. They were last year's crop and had still been encrusted with the rich dark earth they'd come from. It was the best way to keep them in the sack, though some were beginning to get eyes and sprout shoots, long past their best, and would probably be better replanted than eaten, but it was all she had left. She would boil and mash them and make them tasty with pepper, salt, margarine and a little milk; then whip them up so no one would know they weren't the best quality.

Food was becoming more of a problem as the war dragged on. Rations had got smaller and smaller, and Arthur's little store of tins in the attic had run out long ago. These days, the family at Blackberry Farm ate what they grew; mostly stews, often containing more vegetables than meat. Artie sometimes managed to shoot game, but every other farmer did the same so there wasn't much about – and, of course, you couldn't kill game birds in the breeding season or there would be none the next year. Rabbits were still around in plenty, and the occasional hare. Pam longed for a good old steak and kidney pie, but that was once a week these days, if you were lucky, and used everyone's meat rations. Thankfully, she still had her chickens and the meat left over from Sunday roast was cold chicken, which she would mince and cook in pastry, moistened with gravy, and mixed with onion from her garden; together with the mashed potatoes and vegetables, it was a filling meal. But oh, she could eat a nice big steak if she got the chance!

Pam chuckled at the thought. Her mood was lifting as she worked and by the time her son and daughter-in-law walked in, a couple of hours later, she was smiling.

'Where are the girls?' she asked, because they still had two land girls. Olive and the new one – Izzy. The girls came and went, many of them unable to cope with bitter cold mornings during the winter in the fen. They preferred to go back to the brighter life in the towns.

'They went for a drink at the pub,' Jeanie answered, carefully depositing her carrycot on the sofa. 'Izzy says she'll get some crisps and a pork pie if they have any. Olive said she will have her pasty cold for her tea.' Jeanie smiled. 'Winston slept all morning...' She looked around her. 'It's quiet, Mum. Where is Jonny?'

'Lizzie took him to the doctor's with her lad; she said Arthur had a bit of a chill. She intended to visit some friends afterwards. Yes, it is quiet without him, bless him...'

Even as she spoke, the back door opened again, and Tom's wife entered with the two children, Jonny running ahead of her into the warm kitchen, young Arthur in her arms, but fighting to get down.

'We had seed cake, Gan'ma,' Jonny said, clutching at her skirts. 'Jon-Jon like Gan'ma's cake best...' His eyes were as blue as his father's and Pam's heart lifted at the sight of his beautiful face. 'Cake please, Gan'ma.'

'You've had plenty to eat this morning,' Lizzie said, putting Arthur down. He went and sat on the mat, playing with a toy train engine he carried everywhere with him. Arthur was as dark as his namesake and his father; unlike his cousin Jonny, he was quieter and spoke less. 'Dot gave them both a slice of toast and dripping – and a big slice of her seed cake.' Dot Goodman was the wife of a local butcher; she had no children of her own and had volunteered to look after Lizzie's son when she was at work.

'You can have cake later, Jonny,' Pam promised, bending down to ruffle his fair hair, which was so like his father's it hurt to see it. 'Would you like a piece of my pasty? We're having docky now, darling.'

'Can I sit on your knee?' he asked and Pam smiled. He liked to sample her lunch sitting on her lap. Jonny seldom ate a proper meal in the middle of the day.

'What did the doctor say about Jonny's chest?' Pam asked Lizzie. Jonny had had a persistent cough since the winter.

'Nothing to worry about. He gave us some mixture for him and another for Arthur. He says if one gets it the other is usually bound to, because they spend so much time together.'

Pam nodded. 'When the boys were young and Artie got the measles, I put them all in bed together so they all had it at once. Best to get it over as youngsters.'

'Are you feeling any better, Mum?' Lizzie asked, looking at her anxiously. 'I've got the day off if you need any help...'

'No, I'd rather be busy,' Pam replied. 'When I'm on my own, I think too much.' She smiled at Lizzie. 'I got my letter from Tom. You said he would write; Susan did, too. Tom seems cheerful – says he is back training new recruits. I think he's had enough of the war, Lizzie.'

'Oh yes, haven't we all,' Lizzie said. 'I am hoping he will get a nice long leave soon. Tom says we are on the offensive now and that once General Patton gets dug into it, he'll soon have the enemy on the run.' Now that the Americans had entered the war, after Pearl Harbor, they seemed, according to the newspaper headlines, to have taken over most of the planning.

'Thank God!' Pam replied. Then, as the babble of voices around her were suddenly still, 'I also had another letter. John is being transferred to a sort of hospital-come-home for the disabled. According to Sister Jane, he doesn't want visitors for a while.'

'No, I don't suppose he does,' Lizzie said and went to hug her. Pam trembled and Lizzie drew back to look at her. 'He's alive, Mum – and he's coming back to us. Perhaps not to the farm yet, but he will be in England and safe.'

'Yes, I know, and I should be thanking God for it,' Pam said, a smile breaking through. Lizzie was such a dear girl! 'I just wish he could come home and – and Faith would be waiting for him...'

Lizzie nodded sombrely. 'We all wish that, Mum,' she said. 'With everything that has happened, we just have to be thankful that we've come through as well as we have.' She crossed her fingers and Pam nodded, knowing that she worried Tom would be sent off on a dangerous mission again.

'I know,' Pam agreed. 'Take no notice, Lizzie. It was just...' She shook her head, because she knew she was lucky that John hadn't died of his horrific injuries. For months they'd all had to live with the idea that he was gone. 'I'm being daft...'

'No, you're being a mum,' Jeanie said and came to put her arm around her waist. 'Shall I serve the food, Mum? It all looks ready.'

'You can help,' Pam said, looking at her affectionately. She was lucky, really lucky, in her family. Lizzie and Jeanie were so supportive. Some women had lost everything and had no one to comfort them.

2

John Talbot stood looking out of his bedroom window at the hospital, or residential home, which would be his hiding place for a while. It was situated in Sussex and surrounded by beautiful scenery. His room – a large, pleasant one, furnished as a sitting room with a bed – was on the second floor and gave him a good view out across towards the sea. He couldn't glimpse the beach or any of the activities he knew to be taking place as the preparations for invasion in Europe went ahead; it was too far off, but he'd been told it was stony, except when the tide was way out, though he could see the high cliffs of the promontory and knew it was there, imagining the waves crashing against an outcrop of rocks.

He'd been at Primrose House for just two days. The home for convalescent soldiers was situated not far from the seaside town of Hastings, but in a pleasant country setting, with extensive front gardens that stretched out towards the clifftops, and a big wood at the back of the property, though he'd only glimpsed it as he was helped out of the ambulance. The first day here, he'd spent sleeping, exhausted by a long sea voyage and then the ambulance ride. He hadn't left his room yet, preferring to sit on the bed or stand at the window and look out at the view.

It was drizzling with rain at the moment. Accustomed to the blue skies of Cyprus, where he'd been stationed before that last fatal mission that had left him horribly scarred, John thought the outlook dismal – as bleak as his future.

Not for the first time, he cursed those willing hands that had dragged him from the sea. Had he crashed on land, his plane, already blazing in the cockpit, from the direct hit they'd taken, would have exploded and he'd be dead. Why wasn't he dead? He would rather be dead than look and feel like this...

John had, some weeks earlier, asked Sister Jane to write a letter for him. It was to Lucy – the girl he'd intended to wed. He'd wanted a mother for his son, Jonny, but Lucy had become far more to him – he loved her and he couldn't bear for her to see him this way. Without vanity, John knew that he'd once been handsome, but now he felt he was a monster, the skin around one eyelid puckered, red and blistered, most of his right cheek was misshapen with blotches and craters where it had festered, and his mouth swollen like a trout's. Sister Jane told him his mouth was getting better all the time.

'The scabs have gone from your mouth and from your cheek.' When John couldn't see, she'd given him the truth, in her calm practical way. 'It is still very red and swollen and will be for a while. The scars round your eyes may never completely heal, and when they do, the skin will probably be mottled and brown. Your right eyelid has been badly burned, but it protected your eye, so you will have sight, but you've no eyelashes, and there is a deep scar across your forehead. I'm not sure if your eyelid will ever recover its normal shape, John – but most of the injuries will heal. You will have discoloured skin and some scarring is inevitable. With luck, the eyelashes may grow back. You will never look as you did, but you are not a monster, as you seem to believe.'

John blessed her for her straight talking; it was so much better than lies, because he knew he had to face the truth. His appearance would improve, but he would always bear deep physical scars, as well as other, perhaps more painful mental ones. It was the mental scars that had made him feel life was too much to bear. John knew it was selfish to wish that he'd died or to think of taking his own life, because he had a son – but sometimes, when the pain was bad and he dwelled on all he'd lost, he couldn't help wanting it to be over.

'Lucy would scream if she saw me like this...' John had told Sister Jane after he'd seen the ruin of his face.

'Lucy was a nurse and saw a lot of burn cases,' Sister Jane had told him. She'd never raised her voice once to him, even when he was withdrawn and sullen, but was unfailingly calm and kind, reassuring. John believed he wouldn't have made it without her. However, she'd done what he asked and John had managed to sign the letter to Lucy. His hands had been very painful back then, but now, some months later, the pain had eased. They were still stiff, even though he exercised his fingers all the time. However, he could now use a knife and fork and was gradually finding ways to do most tasks for himself.

John knew that his life as he'd known it was over. He'd been a highly skilled plasterer and loved his work – but it was hard, physical work and he knew it was beyond him now. Sister Jane said he would recover his strength in time, at least some of it.

'You almost died,' she'd explained carefully. 'It takes a long time to get over something like that, John. You will be able to work again, but perhaps not doing what you did before the war. It may be best to seek something less strenuous...'

Despite knowing she never lied, John was torn by doubts. If he couldn't go home, couldn't have the woman he'd loved, couldn't even do the job he'd been so good at... what was the point of it all?

He'd told Lucy it was over. She hadn't replied and perhaps it was best that way. John didn't want her to see him like this, didn't want to see the horror and revulsion in her eyes. Yes, she had seen burns cases before, but they were not the man she'd loved; it was different, no matter what others might say.

So the life he'd known was over. John felt that he never wanted to go home. His mother would look at him with love and pity and then she would try to smother him and protect him. He couldn't imagine what Artie would say – they'd never been close as brothers. John might talk to Tom when he felt able. Tom was the only one he intended to see, because Tom wouldn't flinch or scream or cry. Yes, when he could, he would ask for Tom to visit.

John intended to ask his eldest brother to become Jonny's guardian. Pam loved him and she would look after him, but he would need a man to guide him. His throat caught at the thought of his young son – Faith's son. It was like a knife twist in his guts. He'd adored his beautiful Faith, thought her too good for him, a princess... a wry smile touched his swollen mouth. He'd thought himself the luckiest man in the world when she'd promised to wed him. How long did they have together? He could count the months on one hand – barely more than a year from falling in love to a promise to wed, and then the war had parted them...

How had he ever thought war exciting? Faith had, too. She'd wanted to help and she had done some nursing, but then she had discovered that she was having John's child... and they were not even wed. John always thought of her as his wife, but of course she wasn't. They hadn't had a chance to marry... His poor darling Faith. John shuddered to think of what she'd gone through, her loneliness and fear, cut off from her family, because her mother disowned her – but then Lizzie had helped her. Tom's wife had taken Faith in and it should all have been fine; it would have been once he returned to wed her – but her uncle had harmed her in a rage.

John's eyes closed. How many times he'd been through this in his mind. It drove him close to insanity to think that he hadn't been able to save her – he'd been far away, fighting this bloody war that he now hated.

He would never have thought of Lucy if Faith had lived. Her memory was enshrined in his heart – a thing apart. All gone now. What did John have to live for?

Some distance away, the clifftops invited. He could stand there, buffeted by the rain and wind, looking down at the sea, losing himself in it until he let go. Spreading his arms like the wings of the planes he'd flown in, he could just dive down – down towards that yellowish-grey spray of churning water and the release that death would bring as he crashed into the jutting rocks below.

'It is time for your exercises, John.'

Her voice behind him brought a sigh to John's lips. Whenever he felt like taking his own life, she appeared, nagging at him, pushing him, forcing him to go on by the sheer strength of her will. Sister Jane: his guardian angel and his tormentor.

He turned to look at her, so neat in her uniform, her shining moonlight-fair hair caught up under her cap so that you could only see little wisps appearing at the temple and her nape. She smiled as he turned, her manner unfailingly cheerful.

'In the dumps again, are we?' she said brightly. 'Well, after we complete your exercises, I'll help you to walk in the gardens.'

'Walk me to the edge of the cliffs and push me over,' John said, glaring resentfully. Why was she so intent on making him live, forcing him back to a life he didn't even wish to contemplate?

'Don't be so selfish. Think of your poor mother – and your son.' Sister Jane looked at him thoughtfully, then, 'Stop feeling so sorry for yourself, John Talbot. I have other patients who would be glad to be in your shoes – they've lost far more than you have: arms, legs, hands, feet, even sight. You can see most things now; your movement is much better, and you have all your limbs – all you've lost is your vanity.' Her harsh words brought him up sharp. It wasn't vanity, not truly – he just couldn't face people he knew staring at him. More than that, his memories never gave him peace and the nightmares plagued him.

John moved towards her. For a moment, he felt like taking that slender neck in both hands and breaking it... but then he saw the look in her eyes and his anger drained away. 'I don't know how you've put up with me all these months,' he said, giving her a reluctant smile, even though that still hurt as the skin stretched.

'I don't know either,' she admitted and laughed. 'Now, do you want to do your exercises or not?'

'I may as well...' He returned to the chair beside his bed and sat. She produced some ointment, which she rubbed into the skin on the back of his hands and in-between the fingers so that he could flex them more easily. 'I don't know why you bother – I'm never going to be able to do the work I did...'

'Perhaps not – but you might be able to stroke and feel a child's cheek – or a woman's,' she replied, not looking at him. 'I think you'll do more than you imagine – though plastering is hard, back-breaking work. I doubt if you'll do hard manual work again, John. Not because of your hands, but for damage that went on inside and your back... you know the spine was damaged on impact. It is why they had to drag you out. We are lucky you can walk. Work will come – but something easier than what you did before. When you feel able, you might try some gardening. Not digging, but a little weeding on your knees... or something clerical...'

'I started work at fourteen and a bit,' John told her. 'Dad was a farmer and well off. He didn't think his sons needed to be highly educated. Maths is easy for me and I can read and write, but I'm not a scholar. Dad thought that was enough – and it was for the job I loved.' He held up his hands, flexing the fingers awkwardly in the way she'd shown him. 'These were to be my fortune. I was an artist in my own way.'

'Then perhaps you could paint in time,' Sister Jane said and caught his look of dismissal. 'Don't shut out the possibilities. You will need something to fill your days, John. An artist can get lost in his work; you could try, just for your pleasure.'

John shook his head and she didn't pursue it. He knew she was just encouraging him to think about what he would like to do with his life. He had been told he could stay here for as long as he wished; some of the injured men might never leave, but John still had the use of his arms and legs. It was still difficult for him to walk far, though his back was healing; he hadn't broken anything; just badly bruised. Time had healed many of his injuries and he knew that he'd been lucky – if you could call this living hell luck.

His exercises done, John was bullied and coaxed into putting on his jacket. The drizzle had stopped and, although it was still dull, it was warm enough as Sister Jane encouraged him into the lift at the end of the hall. His steps were slow and forced at first, but as they went outside, he felt the fresh air and breathed deeply. It still hurt a little to walk, but he gritted his teeth and got on with it. If he wanted to be more than a useless lump of flesh confined to his room, John had to go out in the air; he had to walk more each day, building his strength.

It was good to be out. John felt his depression easing as he held Sister Jane's arm and allowed her to guide him slowly around the garden paths. The perfume from the rose beds just coming into bud was glorious, but behind that was a salty tang that you only experienced at the coast. Here on this broad plateau of the cliffs, the breeze was sharp, though down in one of the sheltered coves along this rocky coastline it would probably be less so. John stood for a moment to gather his thoughts, breathe deeply, and, as the sun appeared from behind the fast-moving clouds, to feel its warmth on his face.

'I'd forgotten how good life is,' he said and looked at her, a rueful smile on his lips. 'I'm sorry, Sister Jane. I've been a selfish pig, haven't I?'

'Oh, dreadful,' she said briskly, but her eyes were laughing. 'Is it over then, John? Are you looking forwards now?'

'Not much point in looking back,' he said and then he grinned. 'Not saying it won't happen again, but I'll try...'

'Good, that's what we like to hear.' She was the professional nurse again, but he felt the slight tremble of her arm as he tucked his through it.

'Do you think we could sit on that bench?' he asked. 'I'm bloody knackered – pardon my language, but I feel as if I've walked a marathon.'

'You have come a long way,' Jane replied, but he knew she wasn't talking about the distance. It was only half what he would need to do if he wanted to get to the cliffs, but he wouldn't go there – to take his own life. Not now.

'I want to see my brother Tom. I know there is a lot going on at the moment, but if Tom can get leave, he will,' he said. 'If I write the letter, will you post it for me? I have no idea where he is, but there is an address that will send letters on for us.'

'Of course I will,' she promised as they reached the bench and sat down. 'I have it on good authority that we have crumpets and strawberry jam for tea this evening. I think you might like some when we get back.'

'And where did you manage to get crumpets?' he asked with a mock frown. 'Don't you know there's a war on?'

Sister Jane could have told him that the people of the area were being amazingly kind, bringing special food for the young men who had given so much for their country. Instead, she laughed, and he thought she looked attractive. Not pretty like Lucy. Not beautiful like Faith. Just nice and warm and attractive. He supposed she must be in her thirties and wondered about her life but didn't ask. One day he might, but not yet. First, he had to get stronger and begin to build his life again...

'Is your brother in the Army?' she asked, reaching out to smell a rose.

'He is – but for the moment he is training youngsters. That's what he wrote to me. I read his letter...' John's throat caught. 'He is the only one I can bear to see. Tom will talk to Mum, make her understand why I don't feel able to see her just yet.'

'Yes, I see,' Sister Jane replied, looking thoughtful. 'You are close to him?'

'He's always been the one I can talk to – and he wants to come.'

'Let's hope they give him leave,' she said lightly, playing with the rose. John reached out and picked it for her and she laughed. 'Don't let Lal see you do that. He is our gardener and he tells us to ask if we want flowers for the wards. He doesn't like his flower beds messed up...'

John laughed. 'I'll tell him you wanted it. He's a brave man if he tries to bully you, Sister Jane.'

She laughed, smelled her rose, then shook her head.

He stood up and offered his hand, assisting her to rise. 'Shall we go and get those crumpets?' he asked.

* * *

Jane sat brushing her hair that night before she retired. It looked much better now that it was growing again, but in Cyprus she'd had it cut short because it was hot on her neck and it wasn't easy to keep it right when she was working all hours. Michael had loved it long. She sighed as she remembered the happy times when she and her husband had lived life to the full. He was wealthy; she came from a good family. They had everything: a wonderful home, cars, one for each of them, money to spend, and love. It was perfect. Then the war came and it was gone in a flash.

Yes, there was still money in a bank somewhere, but Jane had let the rest of it go when she rejoined the nursing service. She hadn't been able to face the thought of returning to a place where she'd known the perfect life. She couldn't turn back time, couldn't bring Michael back from the dead – couldn't face her old life without him.

So she'd thrown herself into her nursing and the horror and pity of what she had seen had burned her own grief away. Yes, the memories were still there and the pain of loss, but dulled, buried under a thousand other pains and other people's grief. For a long time, her own feelings had been numbed. She felt pity and concern for her patients and worked long hours, going far beyond her duty to help them. It had been enough; it was a way of getting through. Then, she'd begun to look forward to each day, to appreciate the seasons once more, to smell the perfume and taste the small pleasures of life. Her heart had healed slowly, but it had happened – and then a young pilot had been brought in badly burned and, all at once, Jane was feeling grief and pain again – his grief and pain.

She shook her head as she looked in the mirror. John Talbot was perhaps twenty-one or even twenty-two. She was more than ten years older. Her fresh beauty had gone; it had gone like the wind, taken by the shock of grief when Michael was swept away to a place she could not follow. Too many nights of weeping and long hours without sleep had taken their toll. She was passable but no more...

Jane trilled with laughter at her own thoughts. She wasn't vain, had never been vain, but she would have liked to be beautiful for John. He'd told her his story, told her about Faith, how she'd died giving birth to his son... and Jane knew that Faith was beautiful. Lucy, his second love, was pretty. Jane couldn't compete with either, but it was ridiculous that she should try or want to.

John was her patient, nothing more. She had put so much of herself into bringing him through the dark days that she had become invested in his life – his future. Yet she knew he saw her only as someone who poked and prodded, making him do difficult things that caused him pain – and that was as it should be. She had dedicated her life to all her patients. John was not the only one needing her – he was just the one she'd been foolish enough to love.

'Be sensible, Jane,' she told herself. 'He likes and trusts you – and he is getting better. One day he will move on and you will stay here.' It was true and she knew it, but love didn't just vanish because it was inconvenient. She'd let down her guard for John and she would just have to live with the consequences. He wouldn't be leaving for a long time yet, but she longed for that day, because he needed it. Above all, she wanted him to be happy – and she would be fine here. She was needed and respected. Jane had her life and, surely, she didn't need anything more.

As Jane pulled back the covers and scrambled in-between lightly scented sheets, she was already thinking of the next day, and what her patients required from her, her little flight of fancy forgotten – or almost. It never occurred to her once that a man who was so badly scarred would not care that she was not beautiful or even that she was older. It didn't cross her mind, because Jane never noticed the scars at all. That smile John had given her earlier! No wonder the girls fell in love with him. No, she didn't see the scars. She looked into John's blue eyes and she saw the man inside and he was beautiful. Oh, so very beautiful, so loving, and caring – and for the moment he needed her and she was happy to be there for him.

3

Tom Gilbert sat on the edge of his hard, unyielding Army cot in the wooden hut that was accommodation for him and his men in this secret location known only to a select few, and looked at his brother's letter. He'd read it three times already. It was what he'd been waiting for since they'd first heard that John was badly hurt. He'd understood it would take John a while to reach out, but as the months had passed, he'd begun to wonder if it would ever happen. Now it had and Tom felt relieved and thankful that he'd asked for him. It would be far better if he were the one to visit first, because he could tell his mother what to expect, prepare her for the worst. Tom had seen some of his comrades burned, and he knew that it could look horrific. Even when eyelashes grew back and skin became less puckered, it often looked dead white, taut over cheekbones and the scarring was sometimes mottled brown. For someone who loved the patient, it could be horrific and more than one young woman had run crying from a hospital room, to the stark reality that the man she loved no longer looked the way he had and never would.

Looks were not everything, it was commonly said, and most folk tried to ignore disfigurement, to be kind, but it was difficult in some cases. One man Tom had visited had lost half his nose and his top lip, and that wasn't easy to take, even for him, though he'd managed to hide his shock and pity. However, he'd heard months later that his former corporal had taken his own life the very day he was released from hospital for a home visit.

Tom's heart was filled with pity for his youngest brother. John was by far the most good-looking of the family – though young George would make the girls giggle when he was older. John had his looks from his mother, but Artie and Tom took after their blood fathers – though they had different ones. Tom's had died in the First World War – the war to end all wars, they had said. And that was an irony because this second war had been a bloody and devastating one.

The sharp angles of Tom's face looked harsh, his generous mouth twisted wryly at that thought, because for some war was a way of life. Some of the men he was training loved it. They loved to kill, not just to shoot an enemy but to creep up on an unsuspecting man and slit his throat. Tom had done it on a mission, but he didn't enjoy it – some of his latest recruits did, and it made him wonder what they would do when the war was over.

It had to end sometime. Even the great German war machine, magnificent in its way at the start, had begun to grind to a halt. They were running out of supplies, money, and probably the will to continue as the Allies gathered strength. The tide was turning. Yes, there was a lot of fighting still going on and it would continue for a while – but time was running out for Germany and its allies. General Patton was making a difference, gathering his troops, ready for the storm of retribution he and his fellow leaders were planning – and Hitler had a lot to answer for. His seemingly mad desire to conquer the world had caused too much grief and misery.

John had been handed more than his fair share of pain and loss. His first love dead after giving birth to his son, and another girl he'd planned to marry had got tired of waiting and married someone else. Now John was lying in a hospital bed, badly wounded and scarred. It seemed he was gradually recovering, but Tom didn't know if his brother would ever be able to have the care of his son.

Tom, too, had been wounded more than once, but the last injury to his right leg had left him unfit for active service. He now had a noticeable limp, and he was permanently seconded to the training of eager young recruits. He enjoyed it and hated it in equal measures. Some of the youngsters were so bright and clever, and it went against the grain, knowing that he was sending them to probable death or injury, when he reported that they were ready for the dangerous missions that still remained mostly secret. Only some of them hadn't been, because somehow the enemy had known they were coming.

He was luckier than his youngest brother, Tom thought. He would be able to return to his old life when the war was finally won. He never doubted it would be. He smiled as he thought of his Lizzie waiting patiently at home with his beautiful son. Tom had never feared opening his letters as some young soldiers did; he knew his Lizzie would never go off with another man, even though like all the others in the armed forces, he was often away from home for months on end. Nodding to himself, he decided he was due for some leave – overdue really, as he'd wanted to get this last batch of recruits ready for service.

Folding the letter, he prepared for duty. After this training session, he would approach his senior office and apply for compassionate leave; he could spend some time talking to his brother and perhaps persuade John to either allow his mother to visit or even go home for a couple of days.

As he approached the group of soldiers he had moulded and forced into a tightly knit band of ruthless killers, he saw one staring at him hard. It was a man he'd released from prison – Lieutenant Regan, the man who had been accused of murdering Lieutenant Armstrong, a fellow officer. Armstrong had ended his life in a ditch near Tom's home, his head striking a forgotten plough shear. It was widely believed that Regan had tinkered with the brakes on his fellow officer's car, thereby causing the accident that had hurled him into the ditch. Tom knew different; it was a secret that he'd forced to a dark corner of his mind, but now and then it popped out to haunt him. It was he who had pushed the car into the ditch, after Artie had shoved the man in and they'd realised he was dead. Artie had been fighting him because he'd attempted to rape their sister Susan, and Artie had been trying to punish him – but he'd been losing. It was only as Tom shouted, distracting his opponent's attention, that Artie managed to knock him backwards into the ditch. Neither of them could believe the ill luck that had caused the RAF officer's sudden death.

Artie had been shocked and stunned. Afterwards, he'd complained that he'd wanted to go to the police, because that push hadn't been meant to kill – it was just fate that had decreed it. Tom had known he couldn't allow that for the sake of his family and his Army training had taken over. He'd managed to cover up what had happened, to prevent Artie being arrested and tried for manslaughter, if not murder – and another man had been arrested for a crime that wasn't his. Even though the brakes on Armstrong's car had been tampered with, and it was probable that Lieutenant Regan had intended to kill him, he hadn't actually succeeded.

Yet Tom felt guilty every time he saw Regan, who had made it plain he was here only because he could be shot for what he'd done, if found guilty in a court martial. Recently, he'd seemed to be enjoying the dirty tricks he was learning – possibly too much, in Tom's opinion. He wasn't exactly an innocent by any means.

'Right you, lazy lot,' Tom said as the men came to attention. 'This is your last chance. Fail it and you're back to prison...'

'Win the prize and get a bullet in your head,' Regan sneered. 'A tempting choice – sir...' He was deliberately late with the sir and his salute was openly provoking, but Tom ignored him. He'd probably given Regan too much rope, but as yet he hadn't hanged himself.

* * *

After a ten-mile hike, over rough, hilly terrain, in drizzling rain, which Tom followed on his motorcycle, the whole batch of recruits passed. In truth, they already had, but Tom never veered from the training routine he'd been given as a new recruit himself; it was tough, but it sorted the strong from the not-quite-strong-enough. This last batch had proved better and more skilled than some of the soldiers taken from the ranks. Perhaps the threat of a return to prison had encouraged them to seek excellence, but whatever, Tom thought them one of the most highly skilled bunch of killers he'd had a hand in training.

After the good news was announced and the usual mocking cheers and groans had died down, Tom invited them for a drink later, as was his custom, and went off to see his commanding officer. His interview with Major Carlton was cordial. Permission for compassionate leave, granted.

'You deserve it, Captain Gilbert,' Major Carlton said, standing up to offer his hand. 'You won't be going with your men this time. The last injury made that impossible, which is fortunate since I don't imagine many of them will be coming back.'

'Is it as rough as that?' Tom frowned, because sometimes it made him feel guilty, knowing that he was training men for what amounted to suicide missions. Usually, the men were volunteers, but only a handful had actually come forward this time. Tom had offered ten hard men an escape from prison, knowing that they might be exchanging brief freedom for almost certain death. 'They are a tough bunch, sir. I think it will take a good officer to keep them in check.'

'I am putting forward Sergeant Robinson's name. You trained him and he was promoted from corporal after the last show...'

'Yes, Stuart Robinson is a good man and loyal,' Tom agreed. 'Young... I'd thought someone older, more experienced.'

'We've had several missions go wrong of late,' his officer told him with a frown. 'We're running a tight ship, Captain Gilbert. Sergeant Robinson is the best on offer. At least he is loyal. We know that some missions have been leaked, but we don't know how or why...' He hesitated, then, 'When you return to duty, Gilbert, you will have a new assignment.'

'Another group of new recruits?' Tom asked, intrigued, because with the war now turning in the Allies' favour, he'd thought his work might be ending soon.

Major Carlton shook his head. 'No. We're standing you down from that for a while. The future of our unit is under discussion; it may be that we've done our job – however, something big is coming up, but that's hush-hush for now. We have a tricky mission for the immediate future, and it will be dangerous. We need to make sure the details don't go astray this time, and that is where you come in, Gilbert. You'll be attached to my staff – but as far as the men are concerned, you're on punishment detail. We're going to throw you in the cooler for a couple of weeks for disobeying an order...'

Tom stared him unflinchingly. 'Why? Are you suggesting I become a spy?' The very idea was like vomit, stuck in his throat, and it was on the tip of his tongue to refuse point blank, but something in the officer's eyes made him pause.

'We have a traitor in our midst, Gilbert. This isn't a game I'm playing. I trust you implicitly, but you're known to be a bit of a rebel. I want to arrest you for going AWOL on your return from leave. The story is that you asked for compassionate leave; I refused and you took it anyway – so two weeks in solitary. You will be temporarily demoted to private... and should make your displeasure known.'

'You are hoping that if everyone thinks I'm in disgrace I'll hear rebellious talk and discover who is getting details of secret missions to an outside source.'

'Got it,' Major Carlton said. 'I knew you would do it, Gilbert. Men you've trained were betrayed – including, we think, your friend Shorty...'

Tom nodded. Shorty had been his closest friend in the Army – and Major Carlton's son-in-law. His death had been a severe blow to them all. There had been rumours way back then that somehow the enemy had got wind of some missions and been waiting for them. It made Tom burn with anger to know that the traitor could be amongst them – even a fellow officer.

'I understand the need, sir, and, much though it goes against my instincts, I'll do it – but I want my orders in writing. If – God forbid! – anything untoward happened to you, I don't want a stain like that to remain on my record.'

'Good point. It might happen that if anyone even suspects I've ordered an investigation, I could be found out on the moors with my throat cut.' Major Carlton frowned. 'This has to be a secret, Captain Gilbert. If anyone got wind of it, they would stick a knife in your back, to say nothing of mine, and we'd be no further forward.'

Tom nodded. 'I'll hand the letter to my wife for safekeeping, tell her that she is not to open it unless I die under unusual circumstances. Lizzie wouldn't dream of opening the letter if I tell her not to.' He saw the doubts in his superior officer's face. 'It is the only way I'll do it, sir. I'm not prepared to be branded as a deserter permanently.'

'I've been thinking of this idea for a while. I knew you would insist on something of the sort, and I've prepared this in case it became necessary.' Major Carlton laughed wryly, handing Tom an envelope. It wasn't sealed and Tom read the orders inside quickly. It stated the facts quite clearly. He nodded, sealed it himself and placed it in his inner pocket.

'I'll begin this evening. When I take the men for a drink. I'll moan about you a bit – and tomorrow I'll leave...'

Major Carlton extended his hand, then shook Tom's. 'Don't take this lightly, Gilbert. It may be one of the most dangerous missions I've given you yet. Whoever this traitor is, he won't hesitate to dispose of you, if he suspects you've sussed him out.'

'I won't thank you for the mission,' Tom replied. 'It is dirty and it's dangerous – but I understand it is necessary.'

'Good. Dismissed, Gilbert...' Major Carlton raised his voice as one of his underlings knocked and entered. 'Permission for leave refused. You are needed here, Captain...'

Tom scowled at him, saluted smartly, then turned on his heel and walked out, a look of anger that wasn't all feigned on his face. He was uncomfortable with what had been asked of him, but there really was little choice. If they had an enemy spy in their camp, they had to know who it was and eliminate him, before he caused the loss of more lives. Out here on these lonely moors, isolated from other troops and civilisation by the need for secrecy, they had to trust one another. The missions these brave men in this special unit undertook were dangerous enough, but if the enemy had prior knowledge, they became nigh-on impossible.

* * *

Tom left camp very early the next morning. He flashed a pass for twenty-four hours at the guard and was allowed out without even a cursory glance at what was an old pass, never surrendered. Tom hadn't bothered to take his kitbag with him, just a small rucksack. It would look more authentic if he left his kit behind, though his paybook was in his breast pocket, because every soldier had to keep it with him at all times. He had his uniform and a supply of civilian clothes at home. All he needed was a few bits and pieces he'd shoved into his overcoat pockets and the rucksack.

He rode his motorbike, a good supply of petrol coupons in his pocket, feeling that it was better than using the trains. First, he had to see his brother John and then he would go home, but he'd post the letter to Lizzie immediately – he'd written to her, enclosing the one he'd been given, with instructions not to open it.

Tom's natural caution had made him demand the official orders, because things had a habit of going wrong, and he didn't want to end as a deserter – or to be cashiered with a blemished reputation or even shot for being a coward. If he hadn't known Major Carlton to be honest and decent, he would have refused the mission. It was a rotten deal and it stank. The last thing Tom needed was a knife in his back from a traitorous spy. His fall from grace had to be convincing. He'd begun it the previous evening by pretending to get a little drunk and letting a few complaints about his superior officer escape...

Tom stopped in the village to post his letter home. His gaze swept the still deserted streets to discover if he was being watched, because even though a part of him trusted his superior officer, another part of his mind was warning him to be cautious. However, no one was about and he remounted his bike and roared off as the sun appeared from behind the clouds and the daylight came.

4

John steeled himself as he heard voices outside the small room and knew that his brother had come, as he'd asked him. He pushed himself up the bed, pretending to be reading the newspaper as Tom entered; then, looking up suddenly, he saw his brother regarding him, an unfathomable expression in his eyes. It wasn't pity and it wasn't disgust or shock – but then, John had known that very little would shake the rock that was his elder brother.

'They've broken through at Anzio,' he remarked, as if the news was all that mattered. 'The men that drove the attack had it rough, but it looks as if they have the measure of the enemy at last.'

'Yes, it looks that way,' Tom agreed. 'They are marching on Rome, I believe – but it has cost a lot of lives.' His eyes met John's steadily. 'How are things now?'

'I'm getting there – but my face looks a bit of a mess, doesn't it?' John forced himself to speak lightly.

'Yes, must have been damned painful,' Tom replied and the calm way he spoke brought a laugh from John.

'Bloody hell, Tom,' he cried. 'Aren't you going to tell me it isn't too bad and will get better?'

'I dare say you've already heard that a hundred times,' Tom said. He sat on the chair beside the bed and handed John a punnet of raspberries. 'I've seen burns before – and in time it tones down a bit, but I'm better looking than you now, little brother.'

John choked with laughter. 'You bastard, Tom. It hurts to laugh.'

'It looks sore, John. You might not believe it, but I've seen worse.'

'That is what Sister Jane tells me,' John muttered. 'She might have – you might have – but Mum won't. I don't want them to come, Tom – any of them. Not for a while. Perhaps not ever. I don't want pity from the women – and I don't want Artie to patronise me, either.'

'He wouldn't,' Tom said. 'I think you'll find Artie has changed a lot since you last saw him, John. Besides, Lizzie told me they are moving into their new house soon. Artie is rich now. He has good fenland in Sutton and a big house with the land, but it is a way out of the village, nothing much around for miles. I'm not sure how Jeanie will like living there. He still looks after the family land, of course, and they eat with Mum most days – but they won't be living on the farm much longer.'

'Mum will miss them,' John said. 'With Susan away at college and Dad gone.'

'Yes, but they will be in and out – and she has George living with her. He refused to go and stay with his other aunt when she asked him at Easter. Told Mum that he prefers to be with her – and he's a big help on the farm now. It's all he wants to do when he leaves school. Mum says he is determined to leave at fourteen and work for her. She thinks he may as well, because Artie will be increasingly busy with his own land. I just wish I was able to help more...'

'I noticed your limp is worse,' John said. 'Why don't they give you an honourable discharge, Tom? You've earned it.'

'Maybe they will,' Tom nodded thoughtfully. 'I am going to ask for it after... Well, soon.'

'You and your secrets,' John said. 'I don't want to know anything – but Mum could do with you at home, Tom.'

'I know. She would like you there, too, John. Surely you know she wouldn't judge you?'

'More likely to smother me with tears and sympathy,' John retorted but smiled. 'I know she loves me. Maybe, when it is as healed as it is going to be. She could come for a visit, but I shan't go back to live there, Tom. I just couldn't... Faith and everything...' A note of bitterness crept into his voice. 'I was going to be a partner in Jack's building business; he promised me. I couldn't work at plastering now. It would kill me. I'll only do light work; it isn't just the scars you can see. My back was badly bruised and went into shock and there are other things. I'm lucky I can walk, but I'm no use for the farm either...'

'You don't have to be. I remember your school reports. You've got a good brain if you want to use it, John. Artie was never much good at figures. You could keep things right for us...' Tom gave him a straight look. 'You won't stay here forever, John. One day you will have to do something. There's a house with your name on it in Sutton – and, most important, your son. Think of him.'

'Jonny...' A look of pain entered John's eyes. 'Don't you think I want to see him? He is Faith's son and I love him. It took me a while to get over the way she died, but then I did, and I knew I loved my son – her son. Yet, how can I look after him? I shan't marry...'

'Did Mum tell you about Lucy?'

'No, but Sister Jane did, when she didn't reply to my letter,' John said. He closed his eyes for a moment, then looked at his brother. 'I am glad she found love and is happy, Tom. I can't marry anyone; I have nothing to offer...'

'Not yet perhaps, but in time. After the war, I will build the farm up to what it was – and there are other plans. Perhaps a spot of building. I know you can't do the physical stuff, but you could advise me, do the bookwork, phone people, stuff like that. You'd be with people who love you and others would get used to the scars in time. I've got friends who lost limbs and have facial scars and after a while – well, you just don't notice them. A man is what he is inside, my brother, and I know you better than most.'

'You almost persuade me,' John said and reached out to take Tom's hand. His were scarred and still red, but not really painful any longer, though his grip was still not as strong as he'd like. 'Thank you for coming. You've helped – but promise me you will explain to Mum that she can't come, not for a long time yet.'

'I'll tell her,' Tom promised. 'She won't like it – but she will accept it.' He looked into John's eyes. 'You ought to see your son as soon as you feel able. He is young and he's hardly seen you – you don't want to be a stranger to him all your life.'

'No, I don't want that,' John said, looking sad. 'I'm afraid he'll be frightened when he sees me...'

'Children adapt easily,' Tom replied. 'He might shy away at first and he might say something hurtful – but you need him, John. He is your son – yours and Faith's. She would expect you to look after him, somehow. You're not going to let her down, are you?'

'You really hit hard, don't you?' John said ruefully. 'I'll think about it – perhaps Mum and Jonny, but no one else – and not for a few months. I might get an operation. My eyelid... they think they can ease that so I don't look so squinty...'

'Yes, that could help,' Tom agreed. 'The scarring will get less red in time...'

'Sister Jane says my eyelashes are coming back on this eye at last, but she doubts they will on the swollen one.'

'You'll have to wear false ones like the girls do,' Tom said and John swore at him. 'Stop feeling so sorry for yourself. So you aren't as pretty as you used to be – so what? You are still John Talbot and you have a family. Be proud of that. Step up like a man, not a weak coward hiding away.'

'Bastard!' John muttered. 'If I had the strength, I'd punch you in the face, Tom.'

'You might be able to do it now,' Tom said, exercising his injured right arm. 'I've never got the full strength back in this one. I can't throw a nine-darter any more. I'll be lucky if I can hit the board.'

John muttered something under his breath and then grinned. 'I could never best you in a fight and nor could Artie. I'd bet you could still beat him if it came to it.'

'Maybe,' Tom said. 'I'd suffer hell for it afterwards. The arm is fairly mobile again, but it aches like the very devil – and my leg is the best weather forecaster you'll ever meet.'

John nodded, his grin disappearing. 'This bloody war, Tom.' He took a deep breath. 'Tell Mum I will write when she can come – after I have that op, next week I think they said. She can bring Jonny, but she'll have to take him away if he screams at the sight of me.'

'He's a child. He may be frightened, but he'll get used to it – if you give him the chance – and you must.'

'You ask a lot, Tom.'

'Nothing you shouldn't want to give,' Tom replied. 'Take time if you need it, but don't leave it too long.' He stood up to go as a nurse entered the room. 'Shall I come again later?'

'No. I'll write to Mum, but tell her how I feel – and thanks for coming, Tom. It had to be you.'

'I know.' Tom smiled at him as the nurse waited patiently, clearly wanting him to go. 'Just remember that we all love you – even Artie in his way...'

John nodded and Tom went out. The nurse began to tidy around him and John sighed. 'Where is Sister Jane?'

'She is busy. She said she will come to go through your exercises later.'

'Right, thanks.'

'Would you like a cup of tea and a piece of cake?'

John agreed and thanked her and she went away. He lay back and closed his eyes. His right eye felt sore and itchy and he wanted to rub it, but resisted the urge. Sister Jane had told him he must not do that, so he didn't, but sometimes it was nearly unbearable. He would be glad when the operation was over. The doctors had talked of various things, but the eyelid was the only one they were preparing to do for him at the moment. Highly qualified facial surgeons were in short supply and John wasn't the only one needing this kind of surgery. He knew in his heart he'd been lucky; he could see and he could walk, talk, and think. In time, he would get stronger. He would never be the John Talbot who had won Faith's love, but she wasn't around any longer. She'd been so beautiful; the loveliest girl he'd ever seen, and her loss continued to haunt him. He'd been upset over Lucy's desertion, but for some reason that no longer mattered. Perhaps it hadn't been a deep love after all, just a rebound thing after Faith's loss. Suddenly a wave of rage went through him and he cursed as anger overtook the grief he'd been harbouring so long. It wasn't bloody fair! Damn this rotten war that had taken so much from so many!

Tom was right. John knew that he would have to see his son if he wanted to include the boy in his future life. The longer he left it, the harder it would become. Jonny must think Pam was his mother. He wouldn't want to be parted from her – which meant John would need to go home one day. Yet a part of him couldn't accept that; it was too painful. Knowing how Faith had died. Knowing that folk would stare at him. He couldn't face it, not yet. Perhaps he never would...

* * *

'Oh, Tom,' Pam cried, hugging him fiercely as he caught her up in his arms and kissed her cheek. 'It is so good to see you! Have you been home – but, of course, Lizzie is at work.'

'Yes, she is,' Tom said. 'Besides, I wanted to give you the news first, Mum. I've seen John...'

'Tom...' Pam caught her breath. 'Is it bad – really bad?'

'Pretty nasty, Mum,' Tom admitted. 'One eyelid is badly puckered and he has no eyelashes yet. His right cheek is still red and the skin is pitted and puckered – and white around his eyes. He has other scars, but those are the worst – however, he can see to read, and he can walk and talk, so we must be grateful.'

Pam closed her eyes for a moment, swaying a little on her feet, but when Tom took her arm in concern, she shook her head. 'It's all right. I'm just feeling his pain. It's not fair, Tom. He's had too much hurt... far too much for any man.'

'I know,' Tom agreed. 'But he is alive. He is still our John – and he has to think about his son. We mustn't show pity. If he allows you to visit with Jonny, you mustn't smother him with love or show—'

'Do you think I don't know that?' Pam interrupted fiercely. 'He's my youngest son, Tom – and he was so beautiful. I know he was proud of his looks...'

Tom nodded. 'John was the best of us, but we can't give him back what he has lost, Mum. We just have to make him face up to the future or... he'll shut himself away in that place for the rest of his life.'

'You sound so hard,' Pam said, looking into his face as if searching for the son she'd known before the war; then she sat down on the nearest chair, her shoulders sagging. 'That wasn't fair. I know what you are saying is right – and thank you for speaking out, Tom.'

'Perhaps I am harder than I was,' Tom admitted. 'But I know how I would feel if I were in John's shoes – besides, Jonny needs him, and so do we. Artie is going to be tied up with his own land more and more. Even when I get home, we'll need help, and John could help with the bookwork. You know that isn't my strongest point.'

'Arthur did all that for us...' She laughed. 'I think Lizzie is better with figures than I am. You'll have to ask her.'

'I want John home if he will come,' Tom said. 'He needs time and I'm not free yet but... I'm going to ask for a discharge when... soon. I think I've earned it and you could do with having me around.'

'I certainly could,' Pam said, meeting his eyes. 'I'd like all my family here, Tom – but...' She shook her head. 'It can never be as it was...'

'I know you miss Arthur,' Tom said. 'It's one of the main reasons I want to get home as soon as I can manage it – but there are others.'

Pam nodded, smiling wearily. 'You've always been the strong one, Tom. I don't know what we'd do without you. Surely this war can't go on much longer? Please, don't go off on any more dangerous missions if you can help it...'

Tom smiled but didn't answer. How could he make a promise he couldn't keep? Yes, the tide was slowly turning in the Allies' favour. General Eisenhower had many of his troops over in Britain now, massing for what would be a huge push. Italy was almost in Allied hands and the next step would be the liberation of Europe, but when that would happen, Tom had no idea. Until it did, he might still be needed...

5

Tom's visit was all too brief for Lizzie's peace of mind, but he told her that they had one day before he had to head back to his camp. They spent most of the night talking and making love, and were late up the next morning, the sun already peeking through a crack in the curtains. If it hadn't been for young Arthur yelling his head off, they might have stayed in bed for longer. Lizzie had told her assistants she wouldn't be in, so they would have to share her work at her hairdressing salon. She thought they weren't too pleased, but despite the fact that Lizzie's business was booming, when it came to a surprise visit from Tom, she was inclined to shirk her duty.

'I hate it when you have to go,' she told Tom, clinging to him for one last passionate kiss before getting up. 'It's time this war was over, my love. I want you home with us. You are missing so much of your son; he is growing up and you need to be here to see it. He is three years old and misses you when you go back, and he cries for his daddy.'

'Oh, don't tell me that,' Tom groaned. 'It's hard enough to do my duty as it is, Lizzie.'

'I'm sorry. It's just I want you home so much.'

'I want it every bit as much as you,' Tom told her huskily. He looked into her face, touching her cheek with one finger. She was beautiful, her English peaches-and-cream complexion soft and delicate as ever, but the years had added a bloom and she'd changed from the young girl he'd known; she was a mother and had her own business, a successful woman in her own right. 'You'd be all right if anything happened to me, Lizzie. You've got the house and your business – and I made a will so the land that comes to me one day would be yours when Mum is gone.'

'Don't!' Lizzie put a finger to his lips. 'I hate it when you say things like that. Money, land, property! They mean nothing, Tom. It's you I want. Surely you know that?'

'Of course I do, my dearest Lizzie,' he said softly, kissing her lips. 'You know I want to be here, too – but I have no control over what they demand of me.' He hesitated, then, eyes darkening, 'There is something coming up – no, not another mission, but it could still go wrong for me. Read my letter if you hear bad news, Lizzie. Not before then... but never believe ill of me, my love. As soon as I can persuade them to let me come home for good, I shall. I've had enough – more than enough.'

'I put your letter in a safe place. I realised it was important and I haven't opened that envelope, Tom. I shan't unless...'

'You'll know if you need to,' Tom told her and then kissed her again. 'I have to go back, love. Believe me, I'd rather stay here with you and Arthur and get back to working on the land.'

Lizzie nodded, looking into eyes that looked strained and anxious, his lean features taut, brow furrowed in thought – Tom was concerned about something. He'd told her as much as he could and she wouldn't press for more, because Tom's secrets were not his own, but she did wonder what had brought that look to his eyes. It wasn't fear as such, but reluctance... Yes, whatever he had to do next, he didn't want to...

Tom was always strong, dependable, never hesitating to perform his duty, but this time she could see the conflict in him. What was he being forced to do? Something that went against the grain, but if it was his duty, he would do it – and do it to the best of his ability.

A little shudder of fear went through Lizzie, because Tom had been injured so many times – how many lives did he have? He'd been lucky enough to get home when others had not, time after time, but luck wasn't infinite. John had been so unlucky and Lizzie knew that Tom had felt a bit guilty that he'd had so much in life and John so little, but surely his luck wasn't about to run out?

Tom laughed, suddenly throwing off his mood and pulling the covers off Lizzie's naked body. 'I might only have a few hours of freedom left,' he said, 'but

I intend to make the most of it. Up you get, lazybones. Let's go down by the river and take Arthur for a picnic...'

* * *

Lizzie always wanted to howl her eyes out when Tom left, but she didn't. It helped that they'd had a wonderful day by the river, paddling in the shallow, brownish and freezing water and enjoying the early-summer sunshine. The fields were a fresh green and the hedges bright with hawthorn, a sprinkling of tiny deep blue wild flowers here and there. A family of ducks, complete with nine fluffy young ducklings, came to share their picnic, squabbling over the bread Arthur threw for them. It had been a day to treasure to add to her precious store. They'd had few enough holidays; the war had stolen the first precious years of their marriage and Lizzie sometimes resented that. Who gave the people that started such things the right to take away a man's freedom to live as he wished? Oh, she was patriotic enough and knew the war had to be fought, but that didn't stop her being angry that she had to sleep in a cold lonely bed night after night, when she should have had Tom beside her. Why couldn't people just get on with their own lives and stop fighting?

It was useless to struggle against the reality of her life because it only brought frustration. Lizzie was one of thousands of women managing at home without their husbands, struggling with meagre rations and shortages, a dull boring routine that was necessary just to survive – and Tom was right: she did have a good business, two in fact, because her little dress shop was doing all right and her hairdressing salon was usually booked solid, especially at week-ends when the single girls went dancing. Some of them had to dance with each other, but there were usually a few servicemen home on leave and the girls all got dressed up, in their finest clothes, and did their best to make their evening special.

Lizzie sometimes listened to the girls who came to her salon talking about the young men they'd met and danced with, but she didn't envy them their freedom, even though it was lonely spending night after night alone in her house. She visited Pam often, helping her as much as she could, and Pam did the same, caring for Arthur when needed, although Dot Goodman had him some days to ease the load on Pam.

Lizzie's own mother lived in March and was never much interested in her daughter, though she did love her grandson. Lizzie normally visited her once a fortnight on a Sunday morning; she then went home and had her dinner with Pam. When Susan was at home from college, she spent time with Lizzie, and, now and then, she and Jeanie had a trip to the pictures or took the train into Cambridge, the nearby university town, and went shopping for clothes. Lizzie remembered her time in London. Her life had been exciting there, because of the big shops, the hairstyling competitions she'd entered, the theatres and cinemas, and the people she met. It was a different way of life, vibrant and busy – but she'd still been lonely for Tom. The truth was that however much she filled her life with work and other people, without Tom she was alone. No one could take his place and she missed him more than she ever let him guess.

It wasn't surprising, Lizzie thought, that a lot of young women went astray when their husbands or boyfriends were serving overseas and they had to spend every day and night alone. She felt the loneliness, but she was wise enough to know that for her no other man would do. When they'd quarrelled and she'd gone to London, before their marriage, she'd never been able to put him out of her mind. She believed Tom felt the same about her and she clung to the fact that war couldn't go on forever – but each year that was stolen from them could never be replaced.

Supposing Tom never came home? Lizzie shuddered. She mustn't let herself think such thoughts, even though they all knew it could happen. John had almost died – in some ways he was dead to his family, because he was too ill to see them. It couldn't happen to her Tom! It mustn't, because she would find his loss unbearable – and so would Pam. Artie had more work than he could do now and Lizzie knew it would be the Talbot family land that got neglected. Artie had made it clear that he was more interested in his own fortune than that of his family.

Lizzie hadn't said anything to Tom, because it would only frustrate him, but the land, newly grassed, that was supposed to be used for grazing, to make the work lighter for Artie had not been used for cattle grazing either. Artie had sold the last of the bullocks off at Christmas and the cows were still being milked, but only one young heifer was in calf. That meant there would be no bullocks next Christmas and Pam relied on that money to get her through the year. Artie said he'd been too busy to arrange for a bull to be brought round when some of the cows were in season, and was now saying that perhaps it would be better to have sheep on the land rather than buy calves in to fatten. Lizzie was sure his father, Arthur Talbot, would never have wanted that – because without calves the milk cows would dry up and there would be little milk or butter for Pam, and another source of income would be lost to her.

Perhaps Lizzie ought to have made Tom aware of his brother's neglect, but she hadn't wanted to waste a minute of their precious time together. Pam could have told him if she'd wanted, but Pam didn't seem to realise what was going on with the farm. They were still growing some arable on the Chatteris Road land, but the loss of the cattle would reduce Pam's income by half and was not what Artie had agreed with his brother. Lizzie frowned as she prepared her clothes for work the following day. She would wait and see if Artie changed his mind and bought in some calves to rear, but if he continued to leave the home fields without grazing animals, she would write and let Tom know. Perhaps he could get another leave to talk to his brother.

Lizzie sighed. None of these things would have happened if Tom had been here – and in a way it was Pam's own doing. She'd given Artie that piece of land that they'd kept pigs on, not knowing she was giving away a small fortune. Artie had used his windfall from the sale of the land to buy rich dark fenland in Sutton Gault, and now spent more than half his time there. Unless Tom came home for a longer period to sort things out, it was only going to get worse.

Perhaps she ought to talk to Pam herself, Lizzie thought as she peeped in at her sleeping son, and then sought her own bed. It might be that wrapped up in her grief over Arthur and John, Pam just hadn't noticed what was going on with the farm.

6

'Did you speak to Tom, tell him that you neglected to see to those cows in season and have only one heifer in calf?' Jeanie asked, looking at Artie. She was annoyed with him for various reasons, because he seemed to have forgotten all his mother had done for him, and Jeanie loved Pam; she thought of her as another mother and she didn't see Vera, her own mother, often these days, because she was too busy helping Artie to go gallivanting off to London, where her family lived.

'What he doesn't know won't bother him,' Artie said with a shrug. He was angry with Tom but didn't want to tell Jeanie the reason, which was still the guilty conscience over what had happened to that airman he'd thrust into the dyke. For goodness' sake, he hadn't meant to kill the man – but by covering it up, Artie felt he'd been made to look guilty, and try as he might, he couldn't forgive his half-brother. Tom had done him one big favour with the land that he'd sold for ten thousand pounds, but even though they'd got on better for a while, Artie felt estranged from Tom. Who the hell did he think he was, taking over like that? With an effort to sound natural, he went on, 'The land lying fallow for a while won't hurt. When he gets back and ploughs it up, it will be all the better for it.'

'What about your mum?' Jeanie said. 'Won't she suffer a loss of income at Christmas? Your dad always sold the bullocks and that money was Pam's to keep house through the year. How will she replace it?'

'There's a decent crop of potatoes coming on the Chatteris fenland,' Artie said. 'She'll still have some milk money – and I'll either put a few sheep in or make sure the cows are taken to the bull next time.'

'That isn't good enough. Why can't you buy some calves and fatten for her?'

Artie rounded on her, temper flaring. She was nagging and he didn't like it. 'For goodness' sake, Jeanie. Give me a bit of peace, will you? Don't you think I've got enough to do with all the land. That fenland I bought needs more attention than I bargained for – never dreamed I'd have to dig half a dozen ditches out and no one to help.' He made a growling sound in his throat. 'Never seen such neglected dykes, full of weeds and damned great tree trunks in some of them. If I don't get them free of obstructions, the land will be too wet and we'll get poor crops...'

'I know you're busy,' Jeanie said calmly, because she did love him, but he was such a difficult man at times. Moody and forgetful, he made her cross, but then he smiled and laughed and kissed her and she remembered why she had married him – but he wasn't getting away with this if she could help it. 'Calves aren't that difficult. I could help with them and so would Pam if you asked her. I'm sure she gets fed up in the house on her own all day... we don't always go back for meals now and the land girls like going to the pub for lunch a couple of times a week. I think she must be lonely and it will be worse when we move to Sutton Gault, Artie.'

'Easier for us, though,' Artie said, 'and you loved the house, so don't pretend you didn't.'

'I do and I want my own home but... we might have waited until Tom gets home. She'll be all right then...'

'I don't want to live there,' Artie grunted, his handsome face twisted with a sullen but suppressed anger. 'I'll run the farm the best I can and I will get those calves if you insist – but... well, I want to be on our own, Jeanie. I don't always want Mum to be there when we're together in the evening... we can't, well, you know.'

Jeanie sighed. It was time they had their own home, but at the moment Pam seemed so lost and lonely, because she was grieving for Arthur still and because of John's terrible injuries. Jeanie had got some of what she wanted, so she gave in. She didn't want to quarrel with Artie; she loved him, but she knew something was on his mind and he wouldn't tell her what was bothering him. It made her wonder if... But he wouldn't look at another woman! Artie had played the field, as folk said, when he was single, but surely he wouldn't stray now they were married and had their son? Much as she wanted and loved her husband, Jeanie was aware of his moods and his resentment of his elder brother, too, though she had no idea of the root cause. Artie could be carelessly cruel and not realise it, but he could also be tender and loving: a man who thought too much for his own good, perhaps.

Winston was a constant joy to them both. They took him with them when Jeanie helped on the land; sometimes she strapped him on her back as she worked, and she always took his carrycot into the fields. If there was a cool wind blowing, she stacked straw bales round him to help keep him warm, but Pam had taken her children into the fields when they were young and it hadn't hurt any of them, so Jeanie took Winston with her rather than leaving him with a minder, as Lizzie often did her son.

Artie said that as soon as he got the land sorted and they started to earn a decent income, she was going to stay home and have more time for herself, but Jeanie loved her work and didn't want to give it up. Besides, there weren't many casual workers for hire these days, and until Artie's profits came in, he couldn't afford to hire a man full-time.

Perhaps a part of Artie's moodiness of late was because he'd invested almost every penny of his windfall in the fenland, which was good dark soil and would be fruitful once he got it in order, but he didn't have a lot of spare cash, and perhaps he'd discovered that he'd taken on more than was wise. Jeanie had tried to get him to wait, but he'd said if he didn't snap all the land up it would be gone.

'After the war, the price of land will rise again,' he said. 'It is cheap now, Jeanie – and I want all I can get.'

Jeanie knew his ambition was for her and their son – and future children – but she would have preferred he'd bought a little less and taken things a bit easier, because he was stressed and snappy more often these days. If, as she suspected, she was already carrying their second child that wouldn't make things easier. Jeanie might not do a man's full day's work, but she was strong and laboured hard. Once she got big with child again, Artie would have even more work. As yet, she hadn't dared tell him what she suspected...

She remembered Artie's panic when their son was on his way, and the calm reassurance Pam had given her as she struggled to give birth. If they had their own house in Sutton Gault, Pam would be a long way from her and so would the doctor and midwife.

That was months away! Jeanie put the worrying thought from her mind. Pam would come and stay when the birth was imminent or she could go there. It would all work out, and she wasn't actually sure she was pregnant yet.

* * *

Artie stood looking across the grass fields, bright with yellow cowslips and buttercups, waving in the slight breeze that stirred the air, but empty of cattle, a faint trickle of guilt at the back of his mind, because he had promised Tom that he would graze bullocks on these fields and raise more money for his mother – but if the cows gave birth regularly, that made more work here in the yard, milking and mucking out, and calves were sometimes sickly, needing attention. He'd sort of forgotten to arrange for the bull, but at the back of his mind, he'd thought it wouldn't matter for a while. If he had his way and enough men to help, he would sell off the cows and put all the land to arable. Once it was set up for the year, it was less work, and livestock was an everyday thing. They needed feeding even if snow was a foot deep.

The land girls were a big help, hoeing between the rows in the potato fields, ploughing, harrowing, spraying the crops when necessary and keeping the dykes clean near the farm, and shepherding. That meant biking down to the washes to count the bullocks they still had, and filling their water trough; they had just half a dozen at the moment, instead of the fifteen they normally reared. Olive was good with the cows; she did all the milking, mucking out and feeding in the mornings now. That took most of the morning, and then she had to do it all again in the evening. Then, of course, there was the harvest, when they all worked flat out to gather the wheat, oats, barley too, before they went down in heavy rain. Once a crop went down, perhaps in a sudden thunderstorm, it was the devil to harvest and a lot of the yield would be lost.

The latest land girl was another shirker. Artie had seen Izzy watching him and he knew what that look in her eyes meant. Once upon a time, he would have taken her across the fields and obliged her, but not now. He was married and he loved Jeanie, but the girl was always brushing up near him in the cowsheds, fluttering her long lashes, more than likely false ones – and she wore perfume, nail polish and bright red lipstick for work!

Swearing to himself, Artie made up his mind that he would take a morning off that coming Thursday, go into Ely market and buy those blasted calves that Jeanie was on about. The land girls could look after them – and perhaps the extra work would stop that little tart making eyes at him every time he came near her. It was another reason he didn't want to spend much time at his mother's farm, but he couldn't very well tell Jeanie that – nor that he'd been tempted a couple of times: Izzy had a voluptuous body, the kind that made a man want to explore it and he was no different from any other man faced with a wanton who never stopped giving him the green light.

It would be bloody daft. Izzy wasn't worth the risk to his marriage. He'd met that sort before. She would have her knickers off for any man who would buy her a few drinks or give her presents. She couldn't hold a candle to his Jeanie for looks either, though his wife didn't always look her prettiest these days. Jeanie worked as hard as he did, but also had her child to look after, which meant that she got so tired that some nights she was fast asleep by the time he got to bed – and, although they made up for it at the weekends, their sex life wasn't as good as he'd like. Artie blamed it on living with others – his mother and young sister, George and Jonny – and the land girls. He couldn't walk around without his clothes off and nor could Jeanie – and she still had a fabulous figure, despite having had her first child only a few months ago. Mind you, she was a bit plumper than she had been, but he didn't mind that and she was getting her waist back to normal again...

Artie smiled as he thought of her snuggled up against him and he turned to go into the house, thinking that he hoped Jeanie wouldn't be too tired tonight, because he really wanted... As he turned, he bumped into something soft and put his hands out to steady himself, catching hold of what felt like a woman's hip. It was too dark to see properly and he hadn't known she was there.

'Jeanie?' he said and the woman gave a little giggle. Then, at the same moment, he caught a whiff of the perfume. *Evening in Paris*. Jeanie didn't wear that! 'Izzy,' he said. 'I didn't see you there – sorry.'

'That's all right,' Izzy replied, moving closer. 'I don't mind. I wouldn't mind if you wanted to touch a bit more of me... you only have to say, Artie.'

'It was an accident,' he snarled, angry now with himself for responding to her. 'Just stay out of my way if you know what's good for you!'

'Oh, my, we do need it, don't we? What's wrong – isn't she giving you enough?' Her mocking voice made him grit his teeth and he had to keep a firm grip on his temper. Artie could have slapped her, but he didn't trust himself. He was afraid of violence these days – it could be dangerous. Besides, despite everything, he did fancy her a bit, and he hated himself for it.

Striding off towards the house, Artie knew he was more angry with himself than Izzy. He ought to feel sorry for her instead of resenting her. She couldn't have much of a life if she felt compelled to have sex with men she hardly knew, and she had been throwing herself at him for weeks now. He, on the other hand, had everything a man could want – and to feel aroused by her wasn't right or decent. He was a married man. He loved Jeanie. He loved his son – but Jeanie seemed to nag him over things these days and there were moments when...

Thrusting open the kitchen door, he was met by the smell of baking and herbs, and, as he saw Pam and Jeanie looking with love at Winston waving his tiny fists at them, Artie's mood softened, and he thanked his lucky stars he hadn't given into an unworthy urge.

Jeanie looked at him and smiled. 'Your mum says that John is going to write to her soon – that's better news, isn't it?'

'Yes, it is,' Artie agreed and smiled at his mother. 'John must be feeling a bit better. I expect Tom's visit did him good. I'm going to buy some calves on Thursday at the market to fatten for the Christmas market – do you and Jeanie want to come for the ride, Mum?'

'Oh, no,' Pam replied. 'You take Jeanie and perhaps have a meal out. You don't get much time off, Artie love. It will be nice to have some calves again. I used to love feeding them when they were young.'

'Then I'll definitely buy some for you,' Artie told her. 'It's my fault the cows aren't producing this season.'

'You've been too busy,' Pam said, forgiving him as she always did. 'But the ones you get will be fine. We can feed them up all summer and autumn, and sell them at Christmas – and you might get me some more chicks to rear if you see any for sale... I wouldn't mind some ducks, but I doubt there will be any going.'

Jeanie came to Artie, put her arms around his waist, and lifted her face for his kiss, her gaze soft and approving. As his mouth joined hers, Artie was glad that he'd resisted that momentary temptation. He would make sure to stay well clear of Izzy in future. If he didn't need the help so much, he would tell her to pack her case and leave, but he'd never get another land army girl. They were in short supply these days, the first rush of young women wanting to do their bit had faded and most of them preferred the Women's forces these days, if only for the glamorous uniforms – much better than dungarees and wellies.

_____

7

Tom was arrested when he returned to camp after being absent for six days – most of which he'd spent travelling; it had taken the best part of a day to get to Hastings, longer and several changes to get from there to Ely and then on to his home in Mepal by bus. He was accused of going absent without leave on his arrival and marched to the prison. Because of the major's plan to disgrace him, he had no pass to show and had no defence. During wartime that could mean a court martial and even a death sentence, though as he'd returned of his own volition, it would most likely just be a short spell in military prison. He was placed in solitary confine-ment, where he alternated his time yelling profanities and pacing the small cell. All part of the plan to make it look as if he'd turned against his superior officer.

It wasn't the first time Tom had been in the cells; he'd been unfairly impris-oned once before for fighting with another soldier, when he'd really had no choice. As before, he kept to a routine of exercise to keep himself fit, but his mind wasn't at rest. He hated what he was being forced to do and his mind played tricks on him, making him wonder if it was all a clever plot to ruin his reputation, and brand him a deserter, though why Major Carlton would wish to do that, Tom couldn't imagine.

On his release from the cooler a week later, he was marched to Major Carl-ton's office and given a severe reprimand in front of witnesses.

'You've served your country well, and you're no coward,' Major Carlton said, glaring at him after dressing him down for several minutes. 'Therefore, you are to be spared a court martial but reduced to the ranks immediately with a corresponding cut in pay.' Major Carlton came up to Tom, staring him in the eyes in a hostile manner. 'You disobeyed an order, Gilbert. I thought I could rely on you. I've gone out on a limb to save you from a court martial. Don't let me down again!'

Tom looked straight ahead and saluted, 'Sir,' but gave glare for glare.

'Dismissed...' the major said and Tom was marched out into the camp compound.

'Bastard!' he muttered, causing the MP to look at him oddly. 'All I wanted was a pass, to visit my brother in hospital. I asked for a week's leave, and that bugger refused it.'

'Think yourself lucky you aren't still in the cooler,' the military police officer said. 'We had an alert on here and you were looked for. You could be shot on sight for deserting, soldier. You'd better report to Captain Connors – you're with his men now.'

Tom groaned inwardly. It was the real dirty squad, the men who got picked for all the worst jobs about camp, every one of them lazy scroungers who were forever trying to get one over on their superiors. None of them had ever been sent on the kind of missions Tom had led, nor had they wanted to be here. It was the punishment they got for causing the Army trouble one way or another; they hadn't committed a crime that would get them court-martialled or shot, but they were no use for proper soldiering. In peacetime, the Army would have simply kicked them out, but that would leave an escape route for any shirker who didn't want to fight. So they were on permanent punishment detail, at least for the period thought justified; they would then be returned to the ranks and given another chance to fight the enemy. Some of them would end up deserting, others would simply keep their heads down, obeying orders if forced but refusing to play the hero.

Spitting on the ground, Tom strode off towards the office of the man he'd been assigned to, feeling really angry. This wasn't what he'd joined up for and he didn't like it. Nor did he like Captain Connors. Connors was one of those men who thought themselves better than anyone else, or that was the impression he gave Tom. He hadn't had much to do with him, because since his first days in the Army, when he'd known his share of punishments, Tom had been a damned good soldier. He'd become accustomed to command and demand respect and this humiliation stung like hell.

He couldn't avoid noticing some of the looks he got as he walked through the camp, rows of wooden huts with tin roofs for the main part with a few solid brick buildings; beneath his feet, earth compounded by many boots with areas of recreational grass where some men were kicking a football around. The camp, at first in Norfolk, had been moved a few months back because of security issues. Now, tucked away in this lonely valley in Wales, they were surrounded by hills, the tops shrouded in clouds that day.

There were some sly grins and a few jeers as he walked past groups of soldiers, because Tom had not always been the most popular of officers and there was a fine line between respect and resentment. It had been necessary to put the men through a hard routine if they were to have a chance of survival; only the fittest and the toughest would get through the kind of missions his men had been asked to perform. Any soldier had to be prepared for fierce fighting. If you signed up to the Army, you knew you were putting your life on the line and many of them would never go home, many more would be badly injured or bear some scars for the rest of their lives. So Tom put his recruits through the most punishing routine he could think of, and it brought rewards. It also brought resentment against him, though most of them thanked him in the end – but there were others that hated him.

A few might seek to get their revenge once word spread that he'd been demoted to the ranks. Tom had never sought promotion, merely doing his duty as he saw it, but it hurt to be humiliated and returned to the ranks after all his hard work. He was proud of what he'd done and he refused to be shamed, but it still stung, even though it was all a sham. However, if his humiliation led to the capture and execution of the man who had betrayed comrades – men Tom had trained! – it would be worthwhile. If the missions were being leaked to the enemy, men were being slaughtered without a chance – men like his friend Shorty. Tom would take this humiliation on the chin if it meant getting the bugger who has caused the missions to fail.

Feeling a hand on his shoulder, he turned, half expecting a sneering insult, but one of the men he'd just finished training was looking at him with sympathy. It was Corporal Zeeman, a man he had taken from prison for this mission and he knew to be very handy with a knife.

'I knew you hadn't deserted,' he told Tom. 'Some of the buggers were sneering, but I knew you'd be back.'

Tom nodded. 'I visited my brother in hospital. He's had it rough, really rough. I asked for leave but was refused so I just went...'

'Not fair to refuse after all you've done, sir,' the young soldier said. 'You've got quite a reputation here and some of the men think you were unfairly treated.'

'You could say that. Thanks, Corporal Zeeman,' Tom replied wryly. 'You don't have to address me as sir any more. I've been reduced to the ranks.' He turned his head and spat. 'If the bastard thinks he'll break me, he won't.'

Zeeman nodded. 'As far as me and some of the lads are concerned, you're one of the best officers. You'll get a rough passage from some of the buggers – pardon my language, sir. Just wanted you to know you still have friends here...'

Tom looked in the direction Zeeman had indicated, seeing about six of the men he'd recently trained. He nodded and grinned, to show that he was unbroken, then saluted. All of them saluted back.

'Thanks,' Tom said, then, 'I might ask something of you one day – will you do it if I ask?'

'I would, anything,' Zeeman replied earnestly. 'I reckon we'd follow you anywhere.' He looked towards the other lads, all of whom nodded their heads.

'Right. Keep the faith and don't believe all you hear,' Tom said and winked at him, then strode off. He started to whistle, shoulders back, head up, defiant to the end.

Tom had a job to do and no matter how much he disliked it, he would do it. If he was fortunate enough to discover the identity of the man he was trying to find, he would probably need help, and maybe he'd just found it.

Outside Captain Connors' office, Tom wiped the grin from his face, then stepped up and knocked. He was ordered to enter and did so. Two men were inside, Captain Connors and... Lieutenant Regan; the one man he didn't want to brush up against, for his own reasons. The back of Tom's neck suddenly prickled and, sensing danger, he knew he had to be very careful.

'I was told to report to you, sir.' He saluted smartly, avoiding the leering stare from Lieutenant Regan.

'Ah yes – you can go, Regan.'

Regan saluted correctly and left, showing Captain Connors more respect than he ever had Tom. Silence ensued, and Tom knew he was being weighed in the mind of his new officer. A thin, wiry man with a prominent nose and hard eyes, he studied Tom for a considerable time without speaking.

'What made you do a damned foolish thing like that, Gilbert?' Captain Connors spoke at last in a slightly amused but sarcastic tone, surprising Tom. 'I thought you were Carlton's blue-eyed boy?'

'Appearances can be deceiving, sir.'

'So it would seem. I wonder what you did to upset him, apart from disobeying an order?'

'No idea, sir.' Tom hesitated, then, as Connors offered him a cigarette from a silver case, 'The bastard has had it in for me from the beginning. Sent me on all the rotten missions he could – hoped I wouldn't get back, I daresay.' He accepted the cigarette but didn't light it, tucking it in the top pocket of his blouson. 'I was entitled to that leave, sir. My brother asked to see me – and he has been burned. Badly. I had to go.'

'Yes, I quite see that...' Connors said smoothly, making Tom think of a spiv he'd known as a lad in Ely and instinctively felt distrust for the man. He chuckled. 'Well, I am afraid you won't be going on any glamorous missions or getting promoted in my squad, Gilbert.' He paused, then, 'You'll have to be punished, of course, but things might just get better for you if...' He paused, blew a smoke ring in Tom's face, and then laughed unpleasantly. 'I'll consider whether I want to use you or humiliate you.'

Tom repressed a shiver as he looked into the calculating eyes. Connors was like a bloody cockerel crowing on top of a dunghill when he'd just clawed a rival half to death! Tom had instinctively disliked this man, but until now he'd been able to ignore him. Tom Gilbert wasn't afraid of any man, but he found himself wishing he had the full strength of his right arm, because he had a feeling he was going to need it.

'Right. Latrine duties for two weeks, Private Gilbert. We'll see how you shape up. Dismissed!'

Tom saluted, turned and walked out. Inside, he was seething now. Damn Carlton! He could have assigned him any duty he wished, but he'd chosen to place him with Connors, where his humiliation would be complete. Why? Why should a man who he'd served so faithfully do this? For a moment, he doubted the man he'd trusted implicitly.

It took Tom half an hour to work it out, as he assumed his new duties, but then he knew it had to be the answer. Major Carlton must have an idea where the leak was – and he'd placed Tom where he was most likely to catch the whispers. It made sense. Every man in Connors' squad had a reason to hate the Army, but it wasn't the Army they were hurting with their treachery; it was men Tom had trained and others who were highly skilled and valuable. It was their country they were betraying.

The next two weeks were going to be unpleasant, but Tom had risen every morning of his life and gone to muck out the cowsheds. The latrines might stink, but they couldn't be that much worse than a cow with a loose bowel.

He grinned and started to whistle. If he could sneak up on an enemy when the slightest noise could betray him and set all hell loose, he could get through two weeks of a filthy job. After all, someone had to do it...

8

Artie looked at Jeanie in disbelief as, that evening, she told him that the doctor had confirmed her suspicions. She was carrying their second child and that meant there would be just over a year between the two. Artie wanted more children, but he hadn't counted on them coming this fast.

'Are you sure?' he asked, his heart sinking as Jeanie nodded. 'It's a bit soon after Winston, isn't it?' Jeanie had had such a terrible time when Winston was born and he knew a moment of fear. He didn't want to lose her!

'Yes – but it means they will grow up together,' Jeanie said and he could see the hurt in her eyes and cursed himself. 'I know it is quick and I know it means I can't work, just when you really need me, but I hoped you'd be pleased.'

'Of course I am,' Artie said swiftly. 'I love Winston and we decided we would have at least three – but I'm a bit worried for you, Jeanie. I mean – you had a really rough time, so are you completely over it? I don't want to lose you.'

'You won't lose me, Artie. I know it was bad for a while last time, but the doctor thinks it will be easier with the second – he says I'm perfectly healthy.'

'It is just I love you too much...'

That brought a smile to her face and she stepped towards him. Artie took her in his arms and held her, but even as he kissed the top of her head, his mind was busy thinking about what he would do when Jeanie had to stop work. He knew he ought to have bought some of the land and kept back a certain amount of money, but he'd wanted it all. Artie was tired of working for a pittance, which was all he'd been paid for his job on his father's farm. Yes, Arthur had given them all extras when he had the money, but that was a gift and you couldn't rely on them. Artie expected to own his share of the land after his father's death, but Arthur had changed his will to protect Pam, giving her the income from the farm while she lived. Artie had found that difficult to take, but his mother had given him a few acres to sweeten the pill, and it had been worth so much more than anyone realised. Artie had seen the chance to make his dream come true and he'd grabbed with both hands, but he was going to find it hard to get round all the land on his own. Jeanie had been with him these past months, driving tractors and hoeing potato rows, helping to gather hay and stack it. It was all going to take longer without her.

'I'll have to apply for another land girl,' he told Jeanie as he let her go after hugging her. It wasn't her fault she'd fallen again so soon; Artie enjoyed their lovemaking and he hadn't done anything to prevent her getting pregnant. He'd imagined it would take longer before she fell again, but either she or he was good at making babies. They were probably going to have a large family. After all, his mother had given birth to five healthy children, though she'd had one miscarriage. He wouldn't mind a big family; he just wished the second wasn't coming so soon.

'I can work for a while yet,' Jeanie told him. 'Olive is very good, Artie. She could do a lot of the things I do – I'm not sure about Izzy.'

'She'll do the work if you keep an eye on her, but you can't rely on her.' Artie's smile caressed her as he moved closer and stroked the back of her neck with his strong fingers. 'We've had a few land girls, Jeanie, but you're the best of the bunch by far. You do the work of a man and never complain – but you'll have to cut back soon. I wouldn't have minded if this hadn't happened for another year or so, but I don't want to lose you – or the baby, so when you don't feel like work, just tell me.'

Jeanie promised she would and they went to bed. Holding his wife's soft, warm body to him and smelling the special scent that was hers alone, Artie felt a surge of desire. He did love her so much and he wanted her. Artie couldn't imagine ever wanting anyone in Jeanie's place, even though he might fancy other women from time to time. She was his Jeanie and he couldn't lose her!

'Promise me you won't work if you find it becoming too much,' he whispered as he drew her closer, nuzzling her neck. 'I might moan and get in a temper if I have too much to do, but I love you and I can't lose you, Jeanie.

Remember that when I don't do and say the things I should. I know I can be a bit of a sod at times.'

Jeanie laughed and snuggled into his hard firm body. He worked long hours and he was strong and fit, not an ounce of fat anywhere. 'Do you think I don't know you, Artie Talbot? You are a bugger sometimes, but I happen to love you. I won't risk our child – but perhaps you might have to leave some of our land fallow this year. You have to look after your family's farm, but your new land can be brought round gradually. Don't kill yourself for money, Artie. I'd rather have you than posh clothes and a diamond ring.'

Artie laughed as he admitted, 'I have taken on a bit more than I can handle, I'll confess it to you, Jeanie, but I want to get it all ready for next spring. We shan't make much this year, but next should be a lot better.' He sighed. 'If Tom got his discharge, I would only need to give him a hand at harvest time.'

'Is it likely?' Jeanie asked. 'He is doing an important job. I can't see them letting him go until the war is over – and goodness knows when that will be. One day the papers talk about the tide turning, and the next there is a setback. I sometimes feel it will never end.'

'We can always hope,' Artie said and then kissed her. Jeanie responded warmly but yawned. 'You're tired,' Artie said. 'Go to sleep then, love.'

Jeanie nodded. Snuggling into his body, she was asleep in minutes. Frustrated and wanting more, Artie wished that he could sleep as easily as his wife. His mind was like a racing track, the thoughts going round and round, chasing each other.

Bugger it! He needed to sleep. It would be another long day tomorrow. He groaned, his unsatisfied body craving the relief his wife had been too weary to give him. Easing out from her side, Artie went to the bathroom, and then down the stairs to the kitchen. He was restless and decided to make himself a cup of cocoa. The range was still hot and he fetched a saucepan from his mother's pantry. Pouring some milk and adding water, Artie placed the saucepan on the range. It was hot enough to heat it, but it would take time.

He was just whisking the cocoa into the milk when the door to the stairs opened. Artie asked without turning, 'Did you want half a cup of cocoa?'

'Yes please...' The sound of Izzy's voice made him swing round. She was wearing just a thin nightdress and it showed her nipples and the slight curve of her stomach.

Artie was acutely aware that he was wearing just his pyjama pants and nothing more. He'd got up in frustration and forgotten to put on a dressing gown as he normally did if he came down in the night. Izzy was staring at him and the hunger in her eyes gave him a swift reaction. He turned abruptly, afraid that she might see his response to her, picking up his cup and retreating to the staircase.

'I've left some for you,' he said, and went up the stairs quicker than he'd come down. His traitorous body had betrayed him and he was very much afraid that she'd seen. Damn it! He didn't want her, he wanted Jeanie – but she was pregnant again and too damned tired...

* * *

'Another child?' Pam looked at Jeanie as she gave her the news the next morning. 'That's lovely, Jeanie. Your two will grow up together. I always feel sorry for my Angela. She was born last and there was a big gap between her and Susan. I am sure she feels lonely sometimes.'

'She has lots of friends,' Jeanie said. 'Angela loves the animals. Why don't you get her a pet of her own?'

'She had a kitten once, but it got knocked down by a lorry a couple of years ago, don't you remember?' Pam said and Jeanie nodded. 'I didn't give her another because it took her ages to get over losing the last one.'

'What about a little dog? It would be company for you when we're all out, Pam.'

'Yes, it would, but I'm not sure about Jonny. You know he is into everything?'

A shout from upstairs told them that Jonny had woken. Jeanie volunteered to fetch him, but before she could get to the stairs, Olive came down, holding his hand and talking to him.

'He wants his granny...' Olive said as Jonny ran to Pam and was swept up in her arms.

'Want bickkie,' he said. 'Jonny hungry, Gan-gan...'

'Yes, you can have a biscuit,' Pam said and took one of her home-made oat crumbles from the tin. She sat him in his chair and he proceeded to eat with evident enjoyment. 'I don't think I need a dog,' she told Jeanie. 'I have plenty to keep me busy – but I'll ask Angela if she wants a pet. She might have her own ideas.'

Angela came down then, dressed for school, her long hair in one neat plait at the back and tied with a blue ribbon. Pam smiled at her. She was growing up and already very pretty, her mouth soft, her green eyes wide-set and filled with innocent joy. It hardly seemed any time at all since Angela needed help to dress and do her hair, but now she was always neat and tidy and seldom needed calling in the morning. Her hair was always lighter in the summer, blonder than Pam's own had been as a girl. It was strange how the girls and John took after her and her elder sons after their fathers.

'What would you like for breakfast, Angela?' Pam asked her fondly. 'A piece of toast and jam – or an egg?'

'Toast, please, Mum,' Angela said and looked at Jeanie. 'Can I take Winston for a walk on Sunday, Jeanie? My friend Annais has a little brother and she takes him down by the river. Mum won't let me take Jonny by the river.'

'Because he is too quick at running off,' Pam told her. 'He'd end up falling in the water and you would have to go in after him.'

'I can swim. I learned at school, at the pool in Chatteris.' Angela was at the secondary school in Chatteris now. She hadn't passed her eleven-plus examination, probably because she didn't want to go to the high school in Ely. Pam had stopped worrying about it. Angela wasn't studious like her sister Susan; she didn't want to go to college and become a teacher. She would probably work on the land until she got married and became a farmer's wife.

'I know – but I don't want any accidents,' Pam said and gave Jeanie a warning look.

'I might come with you,' Jeanie said. 'If it is nice and warm – but Winston is a bit too young for you to take to the river on your own, Angela.'

'I'll ask Lizzie...' Angela said and walked to the back door. 'I'll be back for my breakfast in a few minutes, Mum.'

'Lizzie won't let her take Arthur, will she?' Jeanie asked. 'I know she wouldn't do anything daft – but accidents happen.'

'I doubt Lizzie will let Angela take her son to the river. Susan used to take him for a walk in his pushchair, but she was older.'

Jeanie laughed. 'I can remember asking my neighbours if I could take their babies for a walk at her age. I couldn't wait to grow up and have my own.'

'Well you've got Winston now – and another on the way.' Pam nodded her approval. 'We'll arrange things when the time comes, Jeanie, so you aren't alone. What are you hoping for this time?'

'I'd like a girl, but I think Artie would like another boy – more sons to grow up for the empire he's building.'

Pam laughed. 'That lad is a worker, I'll give him that, Jeanie. You tell him to slow down a bit or he might overdo it. Arthur was just the same at his age...' A look of sadness entered her eyes. 'Worn out before his time.'

'I've told him, Mum, but you know what he is – goes his own way. I think the new land needed a lot more work than he'd expected.'

'He will have to take someone on – even if it is another land girl. Olive does most of the milking now there isn't as much to do, and I've been feeding the calves myself. He could take Izzy with him sometimes, give you a little rest.'

'I suggested that, but he says she isn't trustworthy. I think he will try to find someone he gets on with...' Jeanie sighed. 'It would solve it all if Tom got his discharge, Mum. He really ought to ask. He limps quite badly now, doesn't he?'

'Yes, and I think his leg causes him pain, but Tom is as stubborn as the others – he'll do it in his own time or not at all.'

9

'You're a stubborn chap, aren't you?' Captain Connors looked at Tom as he reported for duty one warm late June morning. The heat had been building these past few days and it was becoming sultry. 'Had enough of latrine duty yet?'

'Sir!' Tom saluted smartly but with attitude. His duty of two weeks had turned into three, but he'd done whatever he was told, merely glaring at the sergeant who gave the orders and muttering curses under his breath.

During that time, the Allied troops had stormed ashore in Normandy and the longed-for invasion of Europe had begun. Tom had heard it from the BBC and he'd read all about D-Day in a newspaper, and the bloody fighting that was taking place in the ensuing battles. It had helped to make his work less tedious. At last it was happening! Some of his men had been among the invading force – though not the ones he'd been training before being reduced to the ranks; they were being saved for something special behind enemy lines, because their missions were to create havoc and uncertainty, leaving the spear heading of invasion to others.

'How would you like an easier task, Gilbert?' the officer asked, looking at him, eyes slanted in curiosity. 'I can't make you out – why did Major Carlton turn against you? What did you do that made him hand you over to my loving care – hmm?'

'No idea, sir.'

'Don't talk much, do you?'

'Nothing to say, sir.'

'So – shall I put you back on latrine duty or shall I give you a break?' Captain Connors deliberated, his long pale fingers tapping the desk. He was a lean man, narrow-set eyes, thin-lipped. 'Guard duties? Or perhaps you'd like to be a steward in the bar? I understand you used to play darts rather well. We've been putting together a darts team...'

Tom kept a straight face. 'Arm's a bit stiff for that now, sir. I could try – but...' He shrugged. 'It's your choice. You are the officer.'

'Yes, I am,' Connors grinned. 'We'll see... Back to the latrines for now.'

Tom gritted his teeth. Connors was playing with him, taunting him. He swore softly, but the officer heard and laughed.

'That's better, Gilbert. I know the resentment is there – let it out. Tell me why Carlton has it in for you and I'll see you get easier duties.'

Tom saluted and was dismissed. His anger was grinding inside him as he reported for the duties he'd hoped to see the back of, but Captain Connors was wary of him – and there had to be a reason for that. Tom had always thought that officer a bit of a bastard, but there was no reason for him to have singled Tom out for the worst duties. It made Tom wonder why he was so insistent on knowing the reason for Major Carlton's behaviour towards him. Yes, Tom had gone absent without leave, but he'd returned within a few days and he'd had a good enough excuse. It was unreasonable of Major Carlton to refuse him compassionate leave, especially since he'd finished his current training session. So Captain Connors smelled a rat – and Tom had to convince him, because he was beginning to suspect that the traitor might be nearer than he'd thought.

He pondered over the problem as he scrubbed filthy toilets and cleaned floors that had urine and vomit on them. The habits of some men were pretty disgusting, though you couldn't always control when you vomited and men who were drunk weren't particular about where they passed water. Tom was accustomed to cleaning up after livestock; this job wasn't going to break him – but perhaps he should let Connors think it had...

Tom's brain buzzed as he struggled to think of a reason why Major Carlton had it in for him, but there just wasn't anything that made sense... unless he was jealous of Tom's success and the popularity it had brought him with the men? Those undergoing his training might hate his guts, but afterwards they respected him – and he'd been on good terms with most of the officers at the camp, his reputation as a good fighter marking him out as a decent officer.

Jealousy was as good an excuse as any. Tom decided on a course of action. That evening, he would get drunk and break some stuff in the officers' mess – he'd just barge in and swear a bit, knock a table over or something. He would be back in the cooler for a while, but then, when Connors sent for him next time – he would accuse Major Carlton of being jealous because he had been in action many times, while he was stuck in his office. Tom felt it was a weak excuse, but it was all he could come up with and thus far he was getting nowhere with his investigations. He'd thought some of the men on latrine duty might know something – might be the source of the leaks, but they were a lazy bunch and most of them just swore and slopped about with their bucket and mop, doing as little as possible. He didn't think any of them could be bothered to get involved in spying; too much like hard work.

* * *

Tom tipped the whisky bottle to his mouth and finished the contents; he'd drunk half of it and splashed some on his clothes, because he wanted to appear drunk and reek of the stuff but not actually be intoxicated. He threw it at the window of the officers' mess and it smashed against it, cracking the glass but not breaking it. However, it had the desired effect and a couple of officers came out, looking for the source of the disturbance.

'Bloody bastards the lot of you!' Tom yelled and lurched towards them. 'Call yourselves soldiers, sitting on your arses while good men die...'

'Steady on, Gilbert. You're drunk,' one of the men said.

'Don't mind if I do,' Tom replied, deliberately misunderstanding them. He pushed the officer aside as he went into the mess. 'I'll have a double whisky...' He went up to the bar, swaying for a moment and then crashing sideways into a table. 'I want a bloody drink...'

'You can't come in here,' one of the older officers said. 'Get rid of him, someone...'

'That's Tom Gilbert – he was unfairly reduced to the ranks,' one officer muttered. 'Poor devil has been on latrine duty for weeks. Don't blame him for getting drunk after all he's been through.'

Tom lurched towards him. 'Too bloody right,' he shouted. 'Bloody Carlton is jealous of me because I saw action and he didn't, stuck in that office... refused me compassionate leave to see my brother... not bloody right...'

And then, he simply pitched forward into the table and knocked glasses flying so there was a terrific splintering of glass and a clatter of the table going over. Lying on the ground in the midst of the mess, Tom closed his eyes and pretended to snore.

Someone brought a jug of ice-cold water and threw it over him. Tom jerked, his eyes opening; then he was seized by two military police, hauled to his feet and dragged off to the cooler.

'Damned fool,' one of the MPs said. 'What good do you think that's going to do you?'

Tom cursed but ignored him. He would probably be in solitary for a couple of weeks again, but hopefully, his little display of drunken temper would reach the ears of Captain Connors and maybe – just maybe – he might start to discover something useful, because up to now he'd heard nothing remotely like treason. All the men he'd come in contact with had been fond of swearing but not one word had he heard about any secret missions.

* * *

Three days later, sooner than he'd expected, Tom was marched to Captain Connors' office. Once again, the officer was smiling. He offered Tom a cigarette. This time, Tom accepted a light. Connors nodded.

'So you think Major Carlton is jealous of your reputation as a war hero, eh?' Connors smiled and nodded, mulling it over. 'He hasn't seen action since he has been here – and you've covered yourself in glory a few times. Thought he'd take you down a peg or two, did he?'

Tom grunted and Connors gave a sneering laugh.

'It fits with what I know of him – good family, thinks his place is to command without risking himself, but then doesn't like it when you get the medals...'

'Sir!' Tom said, but the gleam in the officer's eyes told him that Connors had swallowed his story – perhaps because it had come out when he was drunk and not in answer to his questioning. So far, so good.

'Right...' Captain Connors nodded his satisfaction. 'Want to get even with him – and all his sort?'

'Don't understand you, sir.' Tom was wary but the back of his neck tingled.

Carlton's eyes narrowed to steel points, sending a flicker of ice down Tom's spine.

'I might have a little job for you...' Connors said. 'I think you've been badly treated, Gilbert. Reducing you to the ranks was harsh, sending you to me to discipline was brutal. You earned your promotion. The trouble with these jumped-up Jonnies is that they can't bear to see a good man get on. Carlton thinks he is one of the elite, but one day he and all his ilk will be given the kind of treatment they've handed out for generations – and it is coming soon.'

'Bastard,' Tom muttered, letting his upright stance relax as he drew on his cigarette. 'Doesn't know what work is – just sends men out on bloody dangerous missions and when they don't get back... he bloody doesn't care. I told him and it pissed him off...' He checked himself. 'Shouldn't have said that, sir!'

'I agree with you, Gilbert,' Captain Connors said smoothly. 'Just between us – I can't stand the bastard. I've asked for training and to be sent on a mission, not once but several times. He turned me down flat; said I wasn't the right material...' His eyes glittered. 'I'd like to see him come down a peg or two... what about you?'

Tom hesitated, then inclined his head.

Connors smiled, looking at him thoughtfully. 'If a few of his missions went awry, the top brass would replace him. I've heard there are whispers about it... good to see him sent back to the dark hole he crawled out of, eh?'

'Yeah... but what about the men he sends? I trained the poor buggers – don't want them to suffer.'

Connors shrugged. 'Scum from the prisons – casualties of war, but if you don't want to be a part of it...'

'I'm British, don't want to betray my comrades or my country...' Tom replied. 'I won't be a traitor, sir.'

'Who said anything about helping the enemy?' Connors said, gaze narrowing suddenly. 'I merely thought a few blunders, send the wrong orders... the men get back and never see action.'

Tom's spine tingled. Was Connors the traitor he'd been sent to find; he couldn't be sure – this could be just petty spite against a fellow officer.

'I'd like to see Major Carlton being reprimanded,' Tom said with a show of reluctance. 'But not at the expense of my country or my men...'

'Patriot?' Connors sneered. 'Don't you get it that you're being used by pompous fools in high office? Same on both sides – men with inflated egos started this war and the sooner it is over, the better.'

'Agree with that, sir,' Tom said, puzzled as to what was coming next.

'These secret missions are only prolonging the agony,' Connors told him. 'If they were stopped, it would help the peace effort...'

'Peace effort?' Tom repeated, because he had no idea where this was going. 'Hadn't heard of that, sir.'

'No? Well, Carlton and his sort don't want you to. They want the glory that comes from the heroic deeds of others... he will get a cushy job after the war for his part in it. Probably a knighthood or some such... money for him but nothing for the poor devils who did the fighting.'

Tom nodded, appearing to agree. 'Is there a peace effort going on, sir? Are they secret negotiations?'

'Yes, well, supposed to be,' Connors said. 'I happen to know that certain officers in the German High Command have had enough of this war and they are willing to overthrow Hitler and take control of the German forces and will then come to terms for an end to the war – but these secret raids have to fizzle out first. It makes them look foolish and they won't talk peace unless they are in a strong position – don't want to be humiliated...'

'That makes sense,' Tom said, nodding as if he believed this cock-and-bull story. What made more sense was that, now that the invasion of Europe had started, some enemy factions were beginning to worry about their own skins. Connors was up to something, but Tom couldn't let him see that he suspected him of lying. 'So if the missions stopped being successful, they would stop fighting and come to the negotiating table... that is what you're saying?' Connors nodded. 'You know this for certain, sir?'

'Nothing is certain in this life, Gilbert, but – and I'm trusting you with this – I've had reliable information from someone in our government, but it has to remain our secret – there is to be another attempt to kill Hitler.'

'I see, the war comes to an end – and in the meantime Major Carlton's group is disbanded, and he is demoted in disgrace... I like it.' Tom grinned. 'Anything to bring him down and the war to an end.'

'Good. I thought you were the man for the job – though Regan didn't agree. He thought you'd run straight to Major Carlton with anything I told you.'

'That rat?' Tom scorned, senses alerted. So Regan was involved too. That eased Tom's conscience; he deserved everything that was coming to him. 'I'd see hell freeze over first!'

'Good. I need details of his next two missions. I know there are two big ones coming up. Do you know anything about them?'

'No, sir. I was briefed just before we went each time. There was never a chance to get the information out...'

'Well, it happened a couple of times, but you're right, it is hard to get anything because the men leave right after the briefing. However, the present mission has been delayed for reasons unknown.' Connors' gaze narrowed. 'Carlton has his papers locked away in a big safe. Two attempts to open it have come to nothing – it's a key, not a number lock, but intricate and tricky, so unless we blow it, we can't get into it without the key...'

'If you blew the safe, you would be surrounded instantly and you'd never get away with it.'

'Which is why we haven't,' Connors replied. 'Carlton keeps the key on a chain under his shirt. I've been told he sleeps in it... only someone he trusts could get that key, unless they killed him, of course.'

'He no longer trusts me,' Tom replied. He looked at Connors. 'Are you saying you want me to kill him?' He shook his head. 'I'm no murderer...'

'Come on, Gilbert. You're a skilled killer. If anyone can get close enough to kill him and get the key, it's you... Besides, you know that I can't let you live if you refuse. You know too much now.'

Tom stared at him, mutiny in his eyes as he realised how skilfully he'd been drawn into the trap. He was a part of it now, whether he liked it or not, and he wondered how many others had been blackmailed into doing this man's bidding by similar means.

'You said you wanted him disgraced...' he said slowly, as if capitulation was being dragged from him unwillingly.

'Get the key without killing him then – but get it...' Captain Connors smiled and then blew a smoke ring. 'Otherwise... and, Private Gilbert, don't think of going to the MPs or anyone else. You've been sent to the ranks for desertion, and you made your feelings about Major Carlton very plain the other night. If someone else kills him for the key, you will be blamed – but if you do it, I'll give you an alibi...' He shrugged. 'You're with us or you're dead.'

Tom stared at him hard for a long moment, then inclined his head. 'Seems I don't have much choice – but there had better be something in it for me afterwards.'

'How about an honourable discharge so you can go home?'

Tom inclined his head. 'I'll keep you to that – and remember, I am a skilled killer just as you said. If I kill once, I can do it again, sir!' With that, he saluted and walked from the office without waiting to be dismissed.

Outside, he let out a long whistle. Captain Connors was a dangerous man – but was he the only one? Who gave him his orders – and did that person wear a British or a German uniform?

A shudder ran down Tom's spine. He was trapped. Whatever he did, he would be unlikely to get out of this alive...

10

Lizzie woke feeling sick and made a dash for the bathroom. Sunlight was slanting in the window, throwing colours over the plain white bath and tiles, the floor black and grey linoleum with a neat little white mat. It was the third morning she'd been sick in a row and she was pretty certain now that she was having their second child. She sat on the toilet after vomiting, wiping her mouth on a flannel and feeling sorry for herself. Lizzie didn't often give way to such feelings, but this sickness was taking its toll and she felt tired a lot of the time. She was happy to have a second child, had thought it might not happen until Tom was home for good, but she needed her husband here to hold her and kiss her, so they could celebrate the news together.

It wasn't to be. Lizzie sighed because she knew Tom had something important to do. He hadn't hinted at what it might be and she could only hope it wasn't too dangerous, but she had an unpleasant feeling in her tummy and not just morning sickness.

Hearing a cry from the room next door, Lizzie knew that her son Arthur was awake and wanted up. He was just a few months younger than Jonny and into anything these days. Sure enough, when she entered his room, he'd climbed over the bars of his cot and started playing with his colourful bricks on the floor. He loved to build a tall tower and then knock it down with a clatter and did so as she arrived, giggling as Lizzie got her feet showered with play bricks.

'You are a mischief, young man,' Lizzie said and smiled as she picked him up to kiss his face. He looked so much like Tom, dark hair and eyes, and his smile could light up her heart. She had bathed him the previous evening and he still smelled of baby powder. 'Shall we take a picnic down the river with Auntie Angela?'

'Angela... Angela...' Arthur chanted, throwing his bricks about to show he was excited as he was set back down on the floor.

Lizzie had decided that she would let Angela take him in his pushchair, but she would go too and have a picnic. Angela's friend and her little brother could come, if they liked – and Jonny, if Pam would allow it. The weather was forecast to be beautiful and it would be pleasant to sit on a blanket by the water and relax in the sun. It was too difficult to take the children to the sea with just one adult; besides, back in April, everyone had been warned to stay away from the coast, and all overseas travel by diplomats had been banned, because of the invasion plans. Anyway, the river had memories of happier times, becoming her favourite place when she had a day off. They would go when she'd finished her housework.

Beginning to polish her sitting-room furniture, most of which already shone from hours of hard work, she frowned as she thought about the consequences of her having a second child. She would need more time off from work. Lizzie was a little anxious about what that would mean, as she had built up a solid customer base who asked for her. She now had a qualified hairdresser working with her and an apprentice – but, if she couldn't go in each day, even for a few hours, she might have to take on another apprentice and make Janice an improver. That would mean more money for Janice, but Lizzie wasn't sure the girl was ready to work on customers unsupervised yet. That meant another qualified stylist rather than the apprentice, and the wage would be double. That would be fine if the new stylist worked up her own customer base, but if she simply took over Lizzie's that would bring the profits down with a bump.

If Tom was home, it wouldn't matter. Lizzie knew he had lots of plans for the future, which should mean their income was sufficient that a small loss of profits wouldn't be felt – but until then, Lizzie was holding the fort. Yes, Tom had some of his pay sent directly to Lizzie, as most of the men did, but she thought they'd made some sort of mistake, because last month she'd received about a quarter of what she had been getting. If for some reason Tom's pay remained at the reduced rate – and she couldn't imagine why that would happen – but if it did, she couldn't afford to give up work. Lizzie had become used to having her own car, and to having the convenience of a telephone at home – both of which she'd been able to run from her own profits. If they were reduced, too, some of the luxuries she was accustomed to might have to go.

Lizzie wouldn't enjoy waiting for a bus on a cold night. It was so much easier to just get in her car and drive – and to visit the wholesaler for her supplies. If she ordered them from a salesman and waited for the delivery, it cost a lot more. It was like running round after your own tail, she thought, but then shook her head. Tom's paycheque was probably just a mistake and would be rectified. It hadn't mattered before, because Lizzie was earning a wage for herself plus a small profit – but another skilled hairstylist would eliminate any extra she might have earned, at least until the new hairdresser built her own client list.

Lizzie boiled an egg for Arthur but couldn't face more than a slice of toast for herself. At least she wouldn't need to buy maternity clothes this time, as she still had the dresses she'd worn when she was carrying Arthur. It wasn't easy to buy new clothing these days as rationing was tight. Usually, Lizzie got a remnant of material from the market and made her own dresses, buying something stylish just once in a while, but fashion was regulated and everything had to be utility these days. The clothes she'd had before the war were better than anything that was available now.

Just as well that she'd invested in her own little dress shop. It meant she sometimes found something she really liked at wholesale prices for herself, and it was making a tiny profit each month. Lizzie didn't think it would ever bring her riches, but even a few pounds made things easier, especially with Tom away. Once he was home and free to do as he pleased, he could get himself more land – or invest in building a property. She knew he had ideas for building another house behind theirs. They had a huge garden, which meant a lot of work for Lizzie, though she had it set with vegetables, which saved her some money – but they could divide some of the land off and build another house with its own entrance. Tom planned on doing a lot of the work himself, which should bring in a profit when he sold – unless he let it out to someone. Lizzie wasn't sure what he intended yet. All that had to wait until Tom came home. Her life was on hold for now.

Tom would come home, she knew he would. He'd been wounded several times and he'd been awarded medals. Surely Tom had given enough? Lizzie knew that her husband had been changed by his experiences in the war; he was harder, though underneath he was still the man she loved and wanted with every fibre of her body. Yet she wished he would request his discharge. It ought to have been offered him before now, though she knew he felt he was still contributing to the massive war effort. Britain was just a small country, but they'd taken on a big job and it had almost been too much for them; without their allies, Canada, Australia, New Zealand, now America, and many others from the Commonwealth, they would have gone under by now. Hopefully, things were going the right way at last. The newspaper reports spoke of fierce fighting in Europe. Rome had been liberated just before the invasion of Normandy, the people cheering the soldiers in the streets. Lizzie's spirits lifted. Perhaps Tom would be home by the time she had the baby. She would write to him and tell him of the new life growing within her – though not before it had been confirmed by her family doctor.

Jeanie was having another baby, too. There would be quite a tribe of little Talbots and Gilberts soon, Lizzie thought with a smile.

'Breakfast time,' she said as she finished her polishing and scooped up young Arthur. 'It's a pity your namesake isn't here to see you, Arthur. He would have loved you.'

Lizzie smiled as she set her son down, then held his hand as they went into the kitchen together. Her work done, she could linger over breakfast with her son, which was always a rushed affair when she was working. Later, she would tell Pam of her suspicions, because she knew that her mother-in-law would be happy and proud. Pam loved a big family around her and if things went well, her house would be full of youngsters for many years to come.

11

Pam smiled and looked pleased, just as Lizzie had known she would. 'Tom will be over the moon when you tell him, Lizzie. I keep thinking it isn't like him not to write or telephone. He must be very busy. Perhaps when you write, he will get a short leave – or even a longer one. Artie is snowed under with work. George will help out in the school holidays, but we really need Tom back by harvest. I wonder if I could apply to someone to get him an honourable discharge? I heard of someone who wrote to the War Ministry and told them they couldn't manage without their son; he was needed or they couldn't continue to farm all the land – apparently, he got an immediate discharge.'

'Tom would hate that,' Lizzie told her. 'He promised he would investigate the possibility as soon as he'd finished his latest training session – so maybe we'll have good news soon.' Lizzie shivered, feeling cold all over.

Pam looked at her in concern, because it was a warm day. 'Are you all right, love?' she asked anxiously. 'If you don't feel up to it, you should cancel the picnic. Susan will be home in a few weeks, at the end of term, and then you could all go together.'

'I'm all right,' Lizzie told her. 'I promised Angela, so we'll go – but we can go again when Susan comes home on holiday. Have you heard from her recently?'

'Yes, she writes at least once a week,' Pam said. 'She is having a lot of fun, going out with groups of friends. They stick together because it is safer for them at night. I thought she might find a new boyfriend, but she hasn't as far as I can make out.' She smiled. 'I had another letter from John, too. He sounds as if he is feeling better and I shall visit soon.'

'That is wonderful,' Lizzie said. 'Don't worry about Susan. I think she knows just what she wants of life.'

'No, I don't – I just wonder why she seems to have gone off going out with male friends.'

'Susan suggested there was someone she liked a lot who went away,' Lizzie said thoughtfully. 'She was playing the field, going out with a lot of young men for a while – but she seems to have lost interest in courting for the moment.'

'Yes.' Pam nodded and frowned. 'I've wondered why; it may be that she is studying hard. Just wants to pass all her exams and get herself a good job as a teacher; it is what she has always worked towards – and her dad wanted it for her as well. Angela doesn't seem to know what she would like to do.'

'I think Angela wants to come and help me at the salon weekends,' Lizzie said. 'She is a bit too young at the moment, but I told her she can start after her fourteenth birthday if she likes. I'm not sure she wants to learn to be a hair-stylist, but she likes the idea of earning a little money for herself.'

'Yes, I know.' Pam sighed. 'I haven't been able to give her as much pocket money as I did, Susan. Things have been a bit difficult since Arthur died. He left us property and land, but neither are producing much income just now... the cows aren't giving milk as they should and the home fields are lying fallow. Artie promised to get some calves, but he could only get four – we used to have a herd of at least twelve bullocks to sell before Christmas, and there were more arable crops, as we hired the washlands for the grazing.'

Lizzie nodded. 'I think it is just temporary, Pam. Artie made a mistake and most of the cows ought to be in calf...'

'Two just came into season, so hopefully they will have calves,' Pam said. 'Artie has just had too much on his mind with one thing and another – that is why he wants Tom back.'

'Would another land girl help?' Lizzie asked, but Pam looked doubtful.

'We've had several over the years. Some are good, but others get bored and apply to enter one of the Women's services – or they just go off and get married like Francis did. And Jeanie, of course – but I'm glad she married Artie; she is good for him.'

Lizzie agreed. 'Olive is a nice girl. She fits in well, but I am not sure about the other one.'

'Izzy?' Pam frowned. 'I don't think she will stay long. I'm surprised she stayed this long, to be honest. There isn't much here for girls who were used to a big town; she doesn't really fit in, does she?'

Lizzie shook her head. 'We've got three picture houses in Ely and there's a dance on at the Corn Exchange most weekends... but I suppose that isn't a lot if you're young and single. I think Izzy is looking for a boyfriend. If she met someone she liked locally, she would probably settle down for a while.'

'Oh, well. If Artie wants another land girl, he will have to apply for it himself. I've got the quota they allowed me...' Pam broke off as the girls in question entered the big kitchen. 'Finished your chores for the day?'

'Thank goodness for Sunday,' Izzy said. 'I'm going to get washed and catch the train into Cambridge. I'll be there before lunch...'

'Not sure there's much going on Sundays,' Pam warned. 'The shops will be closed – probably the cinemas too.'

'I don't want to buy anything. I am sure I can find something to do – go on the river in a punt or something...' She looked at Olive. 'Do you want to come?'

Olive shook her head. 'I am going to wash my hair this morning and finish the hem on my new dress and...' She stopped and blushed. 'This afternoon I am walking out with a young airman... Zeke is a New Zealander from the base, and he is lovely. He came across the field to me the other day and we got chatting. We might have tea out somewhere, Pam. Zeke has his own car.'

'That's lovely for you, dear,' Pam said and smiled approvingly. 'I think that is the first time you've been out with a young man since you came, isn't it?'

'Yes, it is,' Olive agreed. 'I've been asked before but I said no... but Zeke is... well, he is different.'

'Love's young dream,' Izzy sneered mockingly.

Pam gave her a severe look. 'That wasn't very nice, Izzy. Olive is entitled to go out with a young man if she likes him.'

'Yeah, I know. Sorry – I'm off to get washed...' Izzy disappeared up the stairs to the bedrooms, her shoes clattering on the wooden steps.

'Well, I think that is lovely,' Pam said, turning back to Olive. 'Did you want a cup of tea, dear? It will be a little while for the water to warm up again if I know Izzy – she always uses more than she's allowed, but I'll heat some kettles for you so that you don't have to wait too long.'

There was a line on the bath, called the Plimsoll line, and you were not supposed to let the bath water rise above it to ration the fuel everyone used for heating water, but some people ignored it, and Izzy was definitely one of them.

'Thank you. I wouldn't mind a cup of tea – and a slice of toast if that is all right? I'll make it myself. I know I had breakfast earlier, but the fresh air always makes me hungry these days.'

Pam laughed. Olive was plumper now than she had been when she arrived, but it suited her. Working with people who appreciated her had made her more confident; she was dressing better now that Pam had shown her how to make her own clothes, and Lizzie had cut and permed her light brown hair so that it now fell in waves, softly about her face, making her look really pretty. Her eyes were hazel, more green than nut-coloured, and she had very long lashes, though she never used much make-up to enhance her looks.

Angela came bounding into the room, a big smile on her face as she saw Lizzie. 'When are we going for our picnic?' she asked.

'After lunch,' Lizzie said. 'It will be sandwiches, an apple and cake – and there is enough for your friend, too, if she doesn't bring any. What time is she calling for you?'

'Half-past two,' Angela replied and looked at her mother. 'What shall I do until then, Mum?'

'You can peel the potatoes for lunch or feed the calves for me,' Pam said and laughed as Angela nodded enthusiastically at the second offer. 'Make their feed up in the pail then. You know how – and then go and call them into the shed. It's easier than carrying it out to them, and they get to know it's feed time.'

Lizzie laughed as Angela went off to do as her mother instructed. 'She'll make pets of them and won't want to let them go when it's time to sell.'

'Two of them turned out to be heifers, so we may keep them and rear them as milking cows. It's just two bullocks to sell then – but a milk cow is worth more in the end. Most farmers keep the heifers, but Artie says the farmer who owned them was selling up. He'd had enough of working all day and half the night for little profit...'

'Things are really difficult then?'

'Yes, they are, Lizzie,' Pam admitted. 'If it wasn't for the rents on Arthur's properties, I'm not sure I could manage until we sell the harvest.'

'It's as well he bought them as investments then,' Lizzie said with a little frown. 'I knew the war was making things more difficult, Pam – but I didn't realise it was quite that bad.'

Pam sighed. 'Part of it is my own fault. I gave Artie the pig land and he sold it. I had the money for the pigs, but now there isn't any more to come – what with the reduction in the milk and not enough bullocks...' She shook her head. 'Artie isn't managing as well as his father. I wish Tom was here. He would sort it all out...'

'Yes, he would,' Lizzie agreed, resolving to tell Tom in her next letter that he was needed at home if he could possibly get his discharge...

'There is one piece of good news,' Pam said, suddenly brightening. 'John says I can take little Jonny to visit now. He has had a successful operation on his eyelid and he says it looks better than it did – so I hope to go next week...'

'You'll need to stay in a hotel at least one night,' Lizzie remarked. 'Let me know when you are going, Pam, and I'll hold the fort here...'

'I don't think you will need to,' Pam replied. 'Artie and Jeanie are moving into their new house, so they will have something to eat at home, and the girls can go to the pub for lunch; they usually do that at least once a week. They can get their own breakfast for once – but if you could make sure George and Angela are all right, please. Angela will probably stay with you if you let her – but George says he'll stay here to look after the house and the livestock.'

'Do you trust him to stay here alone?'

'He is thirteen now, going on forty,' Pam said with a smile. 'Quite the man of the house these days. He does anything on the farm, including cutting the grass for hay. He can drive a tractor as well as Arthur used to...'

'Good. He will look after you then,' Lizzie said. 'As soon as he can leave school, things should improve.' She saw the doubt in Pam's face. 'What is bothering you?'

'Tom can keep Artie in place,' Pam replied. 'George is too young. Artie is neglecting the farm, leaving it to the land girls... I know he has his own land, but that wasn't what I expected when I gave him those few acres of pig land... as I thought it was.' She smiled wryly. 'It's a problem of my own making, Lizzie.'

'No, it isn't,' Lizzie said, angry now. 'Artie owes you – and he should take care of your land first. I am surprised Jeanie lets him get away with it.'

'She tells him – but you know Artie...' Pam smiled oddly. 'Arthur always went his own way and Artie is just like his father...'

Lizzie nodded, because she knew Arthur, a kind-hearted and generous man, had always done exactly as he thought fit. Artie took after his father in many ways and that meant he wouldn't respond to any little reminders either she or Pam gave. Only when Tom came back could they expect things to be more the way they had been before the war. It was another reason Tom ought to apply for a discharge for physical disability. Yet she knew he wouldn't – at least until this next job was over... whatever that was.

12

———————

What the hell was he going to do? Tom knew he'd found his little nest of traitors, but he was being watched all the time. There was no way that he'd been able to work out a way of contacting Major Carlton, because if he simply told him the truth, there was no proof – and then he would be a marked man. Yet he had to contact his superior officer and warn him that it was intended to take his life – or at the very least his secrets, and then his reputation.

Tom hadn't wanted to involve anyone else, but he knew he had no choice. If he wasn't to become entangled in this murky plot without hope of getting free of it, Major Carlton had to know what was going on – but who to trust? Corporal Zeeman had offered unquestioning loyalty, but was it right to embroil him? Tom had little choice.

Once his mind was set, Tom chose his moment. He saw the soldier enter the latrines and followed, pretending to clean until the corporal was the last man inside. Then he grabbed him, by the arm.

'If anyone comes in, fight me,' he hissed, and seeing the startled look in his eyes. 'I need your help, Zeeman – still want to help, even if it means we both end up for a couple of days in the cooler?'

'Sure thing, Captain.' Zeeman grinned and drew a line across his throat. 'Want me to kill someone for you?'

Tom laughed and shook his head. 'I am trying to prevent a murder and worse, but I don't have much time. I need to get a message to Major Carlton and I'm being watched – and it has to remain a secret.'

'I'll take it,' Zeeman agreed and Tom passed him a sealed envelope, which he pocketed the instant another man walked in. Immediately, Zeeman launched at Tom and threw a punch at his chin, rocking him back on his heels. Tom gave a convincing yell of surprise and anger and hit back. They shouted insults and went at it hammer and tongs, ignoring the little group of spectators that built up swiftly.

'Stop that this instant!' An officer had arrived. 'Not you again, Gilbert. Right, cooler for you – and you... What's your name?'

'Zeeman, sir.' Corporal Zeeman saluted. 'He started it – called me a bastard...'

'Don't care who started it. You're both in trouble...' He looked pityingly at Tom. 'Haven't you had enough of it yet, Gilbert?'

Tom shrugged defiantly, but said nothing. The MPs had arrived. The officer told them to march Zeeman to Major Carlton's office, because he was under his direct command now that Tom had been decommissioned, and Tom straight to the prison cells.

'I'll let you cool off before you see Captain Connors. He is going to love punishing you, Gilbert.'

Tom didn't answer. He didn't expect to be in the cooler long. Connors wanted him free to kill and steal...

He heard a few jeers as he was marched off to the prison once again, but he also saw some sympathy in certain faces. It looked as if he might be able to count on more than Corporal Zeeman if he needed help. His plan to bring down the traitors might work, if his letter got to Major Carlton, but there was still a risk, because Tom only had two names so far and he believed there had to be more. He wasn't prepared to throw his own life away, but he couldn't just stand by and see Major Carlton murdered and his work destroyed by a traitor.

* * *

Corporal Zeeman was brought in about twenty minutes after Tom was locked back inside his cell. He saw his face and it looked bruised, perhaps one of the military police had roughed him up a bit, but as he was thrust past Tom, he winked.

Good! That had to mean the message had been passed successfully. Tom went to his bunk and lay down. Now all he had to do was to keep himself as fit as possible and wait.

* * *

It was three days later that both Tom and Zeeman were released. They were given a lecture and told to report back to their commanding officers. The releasing officer told them to shake hands and apologise, but they just glared at one another. He shrugged and told them they were stupid bastards and next time it would be longer.

Tom went to Captain Connors' office. He was kept waiting while the officer signed some papers and then dismissed his adjutant. Then he looked at Tom.

'What was that all about?' he asked, brows rising.

'I didn't start it...' Tom said, glaring at him. 'What do you expect when you keep giving me the worst duties? The men have lost all respect for me. I had to fight back.'

'Getting to you, is it?' Connors sneered. 'Why don't you do something about it? You know what I want...'

'Been trying to think of a way,' Tom said. 'Might need a bit of help.'

'You're on your own,' Connors said, confirming what Tom had known all along. He was going to be the fall guy. He would be the one to be shot for killing an officer who had demoted him unfairly.

'What guarantee have I got that you will stand by me, if I kill him as you say you want? I can't see why he has to die. You just want those secret papers and an end to his group. Why do you want him dead?'

'Did I say I did?' Connors looked at him suspiciously. 'What are you up to, Gilbert?' He looked round the office as if he thought their conversation was being overheard.

'Just asking for orders, sir,' Tom said. 'I want to be certain that I got it right...'

Captain Connors came up to him. 'You know what I told you. Do it or you won't live to regret it.'

'Sir!' Tom saluted smartly.

'Oh, you're on bar duty now,' Connors said. 'It might make you smell sweeter – and give you a better chance to do what you have to do...' He gave Tom a menacing look, his eyes granite hard. 'Make it snappy or you're dead...'

'Yes, sir,' Tom saluted again.

'Dismissed!'

Tom turned and walked from the office, a little smile of satisfaction on his face. Connors had been rattled there for a while. It was a part of Tom's plan to make him unsettled. He needed to be involved in some way, though how was another matter. Tom's thoughts went round and round, chasing their tails. If Major Carlton went along with Tom's suggestions, things would soon start to move swiftly – and he still hadn't decided how he could get Connors to show his hand. At the moment, it was just his word against Tom's, even though he might just have said a little more than he intended in his frustration.

It all depended on whether Major Carlton was prepared to go along with Tom's plans.

* * *

Tom enjoyed the bath and the pleasure of wearing clean clothes. It was pleasant to feel like a human being again instead of something that got dragged out of the gutter. He was aware of a few curious looks as he took his place behind the bar of the officers' mess, one of the few brick-built buildings, with comfortable armchairs and small oak tables. It was obvious he was the subject of some speculation but kept a straight face, giving nothing away as various officers asked for drinks. They were wondering why the change, because this job was one that a lot of the men wanted; a privilege. Certainly it beat what Tom had been doing the past few weeks.

'About time, Gilbert,' one of the officers said and smiled as he ordered a whisky. 'Glad to see you here.'

'Thank you, sir,' Tom replied but didn't smile. The officer had never been more than a casual acquaintance, but it was nice to know that not everyone had been pleased to see him in disgrace.

It was halfway through the evening when Major Carlton entered the bar. He looked round the room and then saw Tom and his expression of disgust said it all. He marched up to the bar and glared at Tom, his face a picture of outrageous anger.

'What the bloody hell are you doing here, Gilbert? The last thing I heard about you was that you were back in the cooler where you deserve to be.' He

ordered a whisky from the other bartender. 'We don't want your sort in here –
I'll have something to say to Connors...'

Tom slammed down the tray of glasses he'd collected, causing some of them
to go flying and smash on the floor. 'You bastard!' he roared. 'You rotten
bastard... I don't know why you've got it in for me, but I'm damned if I'll put up
with it.' He lunged forward, but the other bartender grabbed his arm and pulled
him back.

'Don't be a fool, Tom,' he said. 'Strike an officer and you'll be in trouble...'

'I'll swing for the bugger,' Tom muttered furiously. 'This is all his fault...'

Major Carlton drank his whisky, set his glass down and swore. 'You are a
bloody fool, Gilbert,' he said, winked, and then walked out of the bar.

Tom muttered something beneath his breath, then strode out after him. He
went to his barracks, where Corporal Zeeman and six others were waiting
for him.

'Has it started?' Corporal Zeeman asked and Tom nodded; the corporal had
been briefed and he believed he could trust him to do exactly as he'd asked.

'If my plan works, they will come to arrest me shortly,' Tom told them. 'You
know what to do?'

'Yeah – good luck, Captain,' Zeeman said. 'We'll back you all the way...'

'Right. Now I have something to do,' Tom said. 'I'll see you – or I won't...'

He slipped out of the back window, looking to either side to see if he'd been
followed, but after that scene in the bar, Connors must be wondering what was
going on – and, hopefully he would try to find out...

* * *

Major Carlton was waiting in the place Tom had requested. He saw Tom and
stepped forward while keeping in the shadow of the hangar.

'Was that enough?' he asked tersely. 'Will he take the bait?'

'I think so,' Tom replied. 'He doesn't trust me to do it despite his threats, so
now that I've put myself squarely in the guilty zone, he may try to take it into his
own hands, because if you are found dead, I'm going to be the obvious suspect.
The only way to protect you is to have the MPs come after me tonight – but first
I need those papers, to convince him that I've done what he wanted.'

Major Carlton thrust a packet into his hands. 'These were all missions we
discussed and aborted. Let his little friends run around trying to prevent attacks

where they are never going to happen – the traitor.' He clapped Tom on the shoulder. 'I know this has been hard on you, but we couldn't be sure. He goes by an Irish name, but he had a German mother... but there must be others.'

'Regan is just a rat. I wouldn't mind betting Connors promised to get him a pardon and out of your group if he helped him – but there may be others I haven't found.'

'We must hope Connors or probably Regan can be persuaded to tell us once we have him,' Major Carlton replied. 'Now, you'd best get back to your barracks... and good luck.'

'Thanks. I'm going to need it...'

Tom walked away. Major Carlton waited for a few minutes and then walked in the other direction. He had not gone more than a few steps before he was grabbed and bundled into the boot of a car that was passed through the barracks gate a mere ten minutes later by a saluting guard.

* * *

'You are certain these are the ones?' Captain Connors asked when Tom passed him the papers. 'How did you get them?'

'With the key,' Tom replied. 'It opened the safe and there they were – these were all that were inside, apart from a gun and some money.'

'Did you take those too?'

'I might have done,' Tom replied. 'May I go now, sir?' He used a deliberately insulting tone.

'Yes – but you're back on latrine duty. After that little show tonight...' Captain Connors broke off as the door of his office was thrust open and two MPs entered. One of them pointed a gun at Tom.

'Private Gilbert, you are being arrested for the brutal attack and attempted murder of Major Carlton.'

'Is he still alive?' Captain Connors asked quickly. 'What happened to him?'

'He was beaten and kicked in the head,' the military police officer replied. 'He has been taken to hospital and is not expected to live the night.'

'You will be arrested and court-martialled, Private Gilbert,' Captain Connors said, looking at Tom in disgust. 'I gave you a chance this evening – and this is how you repay me...'

'I didn't hit him that hard...' Tom protested, but his arms were seized and dragged behind his back and he was marched out of the office. Glancing back, Tom saw the gleam of satisfaction in Connors' eyes. He wasn't going to lift a finger to help him. He'd got what he wanted all along...

Tom steeled himself for yet another spell in prison. He'd done all he could. It was up to Major Carlton now. Hopefully, he would soon be released and Connors would be the one finding himself on a charge of treason. It just depended on what their traitor did next. Would he pass his information on to his friends overseas, or would he try to make sure that Major Carlton did die? If he succeeded, then Tom could end up being shot as a traitor and that didn't bear thinking about...

13

Pam took a deep breath as she looked at the military home for convalescing soldiers. She had arrived in Hastings late the previous night and taken a taxi from the railway station to the hotel Lizzie had arranged for her, feeling a bit disorientated, alone in a place she'd never been to with a small child, and a little nervous. Jeanie had offered to come with her, but despite some anxiety, Pam had refused. Artie needed Jeanie on the land while she could work, and, after all, Pam was a grown woman. Yet she'd never been further than Cambridge since her marriage, except for a couple of holidays at the seaside of Hunstanton, when the children were young, but Arthur had taken her and fetched her back at the end of their stay. Besides, she was younger then; it was surprising how your confidence waned when you got older, and Hastings was a much bigger place than the small Norfolk resort. She hadn't seen much of it yet, because it was dark when she'd booked into her hotel, but she'd felt a welcoming breeze after the sticky heat of the long train journey, made more difficult by an impatient child who wanted to run and play, and kept asking when he would see his daddy.

The hotel people had been friendly when she'd arrived and cooed over Jonny, their sympathy flowing over her and the child when Pam told them she was there to visit her son in Primrose House. She'd felt better after a good night's sleep and the nice woman in reception had told her where she could catch a bus that would take her almost to the nursing home itself. Pam was impressed when she discovered that John was staying in what had been an imposing country house before the war, set in large and very beautiful gardens. The borders were glowing with the bright colours of summer flowers: pinks, misty blues, and mauves on one side, bright orange, red and yellow on the other, and the smell of the roses was wonderful.

Pam could have quite happily sat on a bench in the gardens all morning, listening to the sound of birdsong and the bees humming, but she walked up the gravel drive, holding tightly to Jonny's hand as he skipped beside her, and entered the house without stopping more than a few moments to admire some graceful trees at the far end of what must be extensive grounds. Inside, the floor had a mosaic of black and white tiles and a magnificent oak staircase that bent to the left at a small landing, with a table and a vase of flowers, and then carried on to the floor above. It must have been a magnificent home once upon a time, she thought; but as Pam paused at the reception desk, she heard raucous laughter, and a door at the far end of the hall burst open and then a group of men entered, for the most part wearing pyjamas and dressing gowns, some hobbling, others on crutches, two in wheelchairs pushed by pretty young nurses.

'Yes, madam, can I help?' a young woman at the reception desk asked and Pam's wandering thoughts were recalled.

'My grandson and I have come to visit my son John – John Talbot,' she said, her words breathy and anxious.

'Oh yes, Mrs Talbot. Sister Jane asked me to tell her when you arrived. Would you like to take a seat over there and wait? I'll let her know you are here...' Another burst of laughter came from the men and their nurses and the receptionist smiled. 'They are in high spirits today. Sister Jane – she is our matron really – has arranged a sports day and they've been practising for the wheelchair race and the three-legged races...'

'Oh...' Pam was taken by surprise. She'd expected all the patients to be desperately ill, and miserable, but as they came towards her, they were laughing and jesting amongst themselves. She saw that nearly all of the men had burns on their faces. Some were very disfigured and some just a bit scarred, but all had other injuries; legs or arms were only half there in some cases. Yet all of them seemed to be enjoying their lives, at least in this moment.

Pam had been steeling herself for this visit, wanting desperately to see John, perhaps to hug him if he would let her, yet terrified of what she might see. She was glad that she'd seen these young men first, because now she had a better idea of what to expect and it wasn't really so very terrible after all. She'd made it worse in her mind than it was in reality.

'Funny man!' Jonny piped up as one of the men came a little closer. He pulled at Pam's skirt. 'Got one leg, Gan-gan...'

Pam felt as if she wanted to fall through the floor. 'He is a brave soldier, see his uniform,' she said quickly, giving the soldier, one of the few fully dressed, a look of apology. 'Like your daddy...'

'Not my daddy...' John said and turned his face into her.

'I am sorry...' Pam began, but the man smiled and shook his head.

'He's only a little lad. Mine was twelve and he screamed his head off when he first saw me – but he's getting used to the idea now. My wife cleared off and left him with his grandmother...'

'I am sorry.'

'I'm not. Best gone if she can't take it. You're the little one's granny?'

'His mother died,' Pam said, feeling the need to defend Faith, who she knew would be here if she could. 'I've looked after him since he was born.'

'Lucky little chap to have you,' the soldier said, made a grimace that she knew was meant to be a smile and went past her and up the stairs, using his crutches with practised ease.

Pam jumped when someone touched her shoulder and she turned to see a young woman of about thirtyish, watching her with interest. 'Hello, are you Sister Jane?'

'Yes. You are John's mother – I can see the resemblance and in the boy.' She smiled warmly. 'Thank you for coming to visit us. I wanted to have a few words before you see John...'

'Is he ill, again?' Pam asked anxiously, because at one time, it had been touch-and-go whether John would recover from his internal wounds.

'No – no more than usual,' Sister Jane replied. 'Come into my office and we'll talk in private...'

* * *

Standing outside John's room sometime later, Pam took a deep breath. Sister Jane had described John's injuries, both inside and out, but she'd seemed more concerned for his mental state.

'Sometimes he is brighter and I think he is getting to a stage that we can call normal for him, but then he slips back. His brother persuaded him that he should see you and start to think about returning to his home and John agreed – but since then he has been brooding again. It would be best not to exert any pressure, Mrs Talbot. If John is ever to come home, it must be for him to decide. Otherwise, he might do something desperate. I've known men with lesser injuries take their own lives, simply because they couldn't face the thought of returning to their families.'

'I see...' Pam's heart had sunk. 'I was hoping we might get him home. Just for a few days to see everyone...'

'No, I don't think he is ready for a home visit yet. Allowing you and his son to come was a huge step for John. He will need a few months before we can think of a home visit. It may be that a consultant can help to improve his looks a little more – but that won't be for three months, which is the next time he visits us. There are not many with the skill and thousands needing help...'

'I understand,' Pam had said. She'd looked at Jonny. 'What if he gets upset?'

'Why don't you go in first? I will keep Jonny here and then come in a quarter of an hour. If he gets upset, I'll take him away and give him some cake.' She had held out her arms to the child.

Pam had hesitated, but Jonny was responding to Sister Jane, climbing on her lap. She took a packet of fruit gums from her pocket and offered him one.

'Sweetie...' he'd chortled and took it, sucking loudly.

'He loves those...' Pam had said and Sister Jane nodded.

'Yes, John does too.' She'd offered the packet to Pam. 'Give him these and, when Jonny comes perhaps John can give him a sweet. If they share something it may help...'

Pam had agreed. This nurse seemed to know John very well, but she supposed that happened over several months of personal care and attention.

Sister Jane had given her directions to John's room and Pam went alone, leaving Jonny with the nurse. A little to her surprise, he seemed content to remain, which was unusual, because he often screamed if a stranger approached him. Even Dot Goodman had sent him running to hide his face in his granny's skirts the first time he'd seen her.

Now, outside John's door, Pam paused and took a deep breath. As she went in, she saw John sitting on the edge of his bed, looking out of the window, and from the left side his face looked almost normal with just a bit of redness at his brow, but when she spoke and approached, he turned towards her and her breath caught. His right cheek was still very puckered and red and there was a scar at his temple; his right eyelid was slightly askew, but his eyes were open and looking straight at her.

'Hello, Mum,' he said. 'Sorry it's a bit of a mess – but it's not as bad as when Tom came.'

'You are still my John,' Pam said. 'I am sorry it happened to you, my son, but it makes no difference to my love for you. I just want you well and...' She stopped herself before she said the words. 'When you're ready. You know you'll always have a home with me, John. No one has your room; it is waiting for you.'

'I'm not sure whether I'll ever come,' John replied. 'Not everyone will be as accepting, Mum. I know looks aren't everything – Tom tore me off a strip for self-pity, but it isn't that...' He shook his head, because his feelings were too deep to explain. 'You didn't bring Jonny?'

'Sister Jane will bring him in a moment or two. I wanted a word with you on my own. Don't worry for the future, John. I know you can't go back to plastering. Tom says they could do with you to look after the accounts; you were the best with books and stuff at school – but you can do whatever you want. Your dad had a house lined up for you; it's mine for the moment, but if you need it, I could sell it and give you whatever it makes...'

'I don't need anything here,' John told, her a little smile playing at the corners of his mouth. 'I've helped in the garden a bit, not much yet, but I'm getting stronger – and I fixed a door lock for Sister Jane. I'm not useless and for now this is my home.'

Pam wanted to deny it, but couldn't. 'It's certainly a lovely place – and the gardens are beautiful. I could sit and look at them for hours.'

'I do just that and I think,' John said. He hesitated, then, 'You know Lucy got married?'

'Yes. Her letter arrived the day after we learned you were in hospital – until then we all feared we'd lost you. I am sorry...'

'Don't be,' John said. 'I wouldn't have married her now. I don't have the right to marry anyone, Mum. I'm not much good for anything and I don't exactly make a girl's heart miss a beat...' He smiled wryly. 'I won't inflict that on anyone. I am glad Lucy is happy.'

'You might...' Pam let the words die as she saw the warning in his eyes. He was still hurting too much to think of loving again, no point in telling him that would ease in time. 'No, perhaps you won't marry again, John – but you do have a son.'

'I know and I've been thinking about that...' John said and then the door opened and Sister Jane popped her head in.

'Are we ready to see our son, Daddy?' she asked; then bent, whispered something and gave Jonny a little push towards the bed, remaining in the doorway herself.

To Pam's surprise, Jonny ran straight to the bed, clambered on and crawled up to look at his father's face. 'Daddy...' he said and then flung himself on John and started to kiss his face. He giggled and looked at John. 'You look funny, but Janey says you is a brave soldier with a medal... and I loves you.' He chortled with glee as John gave a strangled sob and hugged him. Pam watched as John's eyes flew to Sister Jane and she saw the warmth and gratitude there – and an answering warmth in the nurse's eyes. It was only then that she became aware that tears were running down her cheeks.

Pam didn't say a word. She just handed the packet of Rowntree's fruit gums to John and watched as father and son shared the sweet treat. Then her eyes moved to Sister Jane's and her own conveyed gratitude, though she said nothing.

'What you's get medal for?' Jonny asked through a mouthful of gums.

'I flew a plane...' John said and held his arms out straight at either side, making them dip up and down while jiggling the child on his knee. Jonny had a fit of the giggles and tried to imitate the noise John was making, spitting out bits of chewed gums at the same time. John grabbed a piece and popped it in his own mouth and that made Jonny laugh even more.

'I'll leave you for a while,' Sister Jane said quietly, but only Pam heard as the nurse left them to themselves.

Pam watched as father and son got to know each other again. John seemed to lose all inhibitions playing with his son and Pam could hardly believe what she was seeing. She'd worried Jonny would cry or show fear, or turn his face away as he had when the soldier had spoken to him downstairs. She'd wondered whether he would remember his daddy, but he had instinctively known him. Sister Jane had clearly said something to him when she had him alone in her office and it seemed to have worked. Whether it would have been the same had Pam brought him straight in, she had no way of knowing – but it was obvious that Jonny knew his daddy. They had been together only a handful of times in his little lifetime, but the bond was there, a natural instinct the inborn love of a child for its father... or Faith was looking on from above and helping them to overcome what might have been a traumatic meeting.

Pam didn't know what to think. Since his death, Pam had felt Arthur's spirit with her a few times when she'd been low, heard his voice in her head, felt that his love surrounded her. Perhaps Faith was here now for these two. Perhaps it was God. Pam wasn't sure what to believe, but she thanked God in her heart, because she had been so worried that Jonny would reject his father. He hadn't. She was just so grateful that her chest hurt with the grief she had to hide; emotion that was part pain, part relief and part joy almost overwhelmed her again. Whatever the future held, John had something to live for – and perhaps it would bring him home.

* * *

Pam took Jonny for a second visit the next morning before availing herself of a taxi to the railway station. When it was time to part them, Jonny had a few tears and didn't want to leave, but John kissed him and told him he could come again when he'd had another operation. Jonny hadn't really understood, but he'd gone with Pam, turning round to look back and pulling at her hand when they went outside.

'Want my daddy,' he said and burst into tears, the excitement of it all finally becoming too much.

Pam felt in her pocket and gave him a small bar of Fry's chocolate. It stopped the crying from becoming a screaming fit, but he was quiet and, on the train, he refused to look out of the window or at a Rupert Bear comic she'd bought at the station.

'Please don't be upset, Jonny,' Pam said, reaching for his hand. 'I'll take you to see Daddy again as soon as I can.'

Jonny pulled his hand away, looking at her stubbornly. She realised he had a mind of his own that hadn't appeared until now. Always, he'd seemed content with his gan-gan, but it wasn't until they reached the farm and Pam washed his face and hands before putting him to bed that he turned to her with a little cry of despair and buried his face in her bosom, sobbing his heart out.

'Want Daddy,' he hiccupped as the tears dried. His little woeful face tugged at Pam's heart. 'When we see Daddy again?' he asked.

'As soon as we can,' Pam promised. 'Daddy is still a little unwell, Jonny – you know when you feel sick and it hurts?' He nodded. 'Daddy feels like that sometimes so he needs to stay there for a bit longer – but we'll see him soon.'

Jonny sucked his thumb. Pam didn't stop him. She hadn't understood how much he knew of his father and how much he'd missed him. Jonny had been too young to understand or express his feelings on John's previous visits, but now he was fully aware that he had a daddy and he wanted him close.

We all want him home, Pam thought, her own heart aching, but she wasn't sure if it would ever happen. John seemed content where he was – and he relied on Sister Jane. Pam knew the look that had passed between them was special. The nurse felt more for John than just the sympathy she might have for a patient – but did John know? Did he feel anything more than gratitude for her?

Pam had no idea. She didn't want to explore that avenue of thought, because she knew instinctively that if John returned the nurse's love, he would never come home. They would probably stay there for years, Sister Jane caring for her patients, and John doing whatever he was able. Perhaps that would be best for him – but what of her family? What of little Jonny?

Surely John couldn't give him up? Pam had seen the bond and love between them. John hadn't made his plans clear, simply thanking her for continuing to care for Jonny – 'until I can,' he'd said. Would that time ever come? Pam didn't know. What happened if John wanted his son with him at that place?

Pam felt the tearing pain in her heart. It would kill her to part with Jonny now – and yet she had no right to keep him. How could she when Jonny so obviously loved his daddy? If Sister Jane won John's heart, they would take the boy and she would see him only if she visited...

'I can't...' she whispered. 'I can't...' Yet she knew she must. John had so little left. If he asked for his son, she had no choice.

Smothering her desire to weep, Pam kissed Jonny goodnight and received a wet kiss in return.

'Night, night, love,' she whispered. 'Don't let the bedbugs bite.'

Jonny giggled and she kissed the top of his head, his hair shining and clean, then left him to sleep. Life could be so bloody unfair, she thought as she went back downstairs.

George was laughing and talking to the land girls as she went into the kitchen. He grinned at her and launched into some tale of a dog that had followed him home.

'Can I keep him, Aunt Pam?'

'If his owner doesn't claim him,' Pam said. 'Lord knows how we'll feed him – he'll have scraps, unless you give him your meat ration.'

'I'll share it with him,' George offered.

'I will too,' Olive said. 'I love dogs – and it looked so sad until we brushed it and gave it a sausage.'

'Those cold sausages were for your supper...'

'I'll have just mashed potatoes,' George said instantly.

'You can have half my sausage,' Olive said and smiled at him.

'I dare say Artie will shoot a rabbit or two if we ask him – and he could shoot game birds once the season starts in the autumn...'

'Rover will eat bread,' George said. 'Thanks, Aunt Pam... I'll go and tell him. He is in the shed but... can I bring him in?'

'As long as he doesn't have fleas...' Pam shook her head as he went out, smiling at Olive. 'Most folks had their pets put down when the war started, because they knew we couldn't feed them – but my butcher might save some scrag ends and bones that I can stew the meat off for him. He'll have to eat what we can manage, same as the rest of us...'

'You'll love him, Pam,' Olive said and Izzy sniffed. 'He was a bit dirty and smelly, but we gave him a wash outside and cut bits out of his fur. I think he'd been a stray for a while and he doesn't look much but...'

'I don't care what he looks like,' Pam said. 'George will love him and so will Angela.' She looked round. 'Where is she?'

'She went home with Lizzie. She begged Lizzie to do her hair, so she said she is going to put some waves in it for her...'

Pam nodded. Her grief lifted a little, because she still had a wonderful family and she was lucky. Life hit you and knocked you down, but you had to get up again.

'How was John?' Olive asked, looking at her anxiously.

'Much better than I expected,' Pam said. 'He was playing with Jonny. I had a bit of trouble with Jonny when we left. He wanted to stay with his daddy.'

'Of course he would,' Olive said warmly. 'Daddies are special, aren't they? I just wish I'd had one to play with me...'

Pam nodded. Olive had spent a lot of her childhood in an orphanage. Pam would have hated that for Jonny. She'd jumped in to help when Faith died – but she'd never thought about the day when she would have to part with a child that had become as dear to her as any of her own children.

14

Three days passed with Tom in solitary confinement and no word from anyone. His mind was on fire with possibilities, including the one where he got shot for assaulting a superior officer with intent to murder, but on the fourth day his cell door was opened. An MP stood there looking at him strangely.

'You are requested in Major Carlton's office, sir.' He saluted Tom, which was rather different from his manner when Tom had been dragged here and thrust so forcibly into the cell that he'd fallen on his knees.

Tom saluted him back. 'Thank you, Sergeant.'

'Captain!' The MP clicked his heels as if expecting some kind of reprimand, but Tom merely nodded his head. Military police had a job to do, and as far as this one knew, he'd gone AWOL and then assaulted the officer who had sent him back to the ranks. Clearly, he knew now that it had been some kind of ruse, because he was showing respect.

'You did your job,' Tom said, smiling. 'And I did mine...'

'Yes, sir! We've been told.'

Tom walked away from the prison block, hoping never to see the inside of it again, and made his way through the compound to Major Carlton's office. It was a very hot day without a breeze and had been stifling in the cell. He breathed deeply. Fresh air. He might go for a walk on the moors later, needing the freedom that had been denied him for a while. The major was sitting at his desk, but he got to his feet the instant Tom entered and saluted him.

'That was a splendid bit of detection on your part, Tom,' he told him. 'We not only got Connors and Regan. You were right in your estimation of that one. Once we had Regan in custody, he told us everything – names, dates, the lot. He was recruited the minute he arrived and has been in cahoots with Connors the whole time – and there were two others we now have in custody elsewhere.'

'I'm glad you got them – and also that you're safe, sir. I know Connors wanted you dead; it wasn't enough to discredit you and get the group disbanded – he wanted you out of the way. I hope you will forgive my little surprise.'

'I thought I was a dead man when your fellows grabbed me, but they explained the rest of the plan – that you'd neglected to tell me – and one of them took my uniform. He was roughed up a bit by your fellows and admitted to hospital as me...' Major Carlton laughed. 'I played cards for two days with your men, and they fleeced me for every penny I had on me, but I heard what happened when Connors tried to kill the man he thought was me – and all I can say is thank you.'

'It was too much of a risk to let you be the bait,' Tom said. 'I suspected that if both I and Regan were out of the picture, and Connors had the papers he wanted, he would have one last go at killing you – but I asked for volunteers to take your place and had six. I gave the others the job of keeping you hidden until it was over.'

Major Carlton nodded. 'Connors knew when Regan was arrested that the game was up. He had already passed those false papers. Knowing he couldn't continue at the base, he absconded, then attempted to kill me in the hospital, and was then planning to disappear...'

'He will be shot as a traitor I hope?'

'He would have been, but he used a cyanide pill before we could bring him to trial.' Major Carlton frowned. 'We didn't get the names of his outside contacts – but at least we've eliminated his little network inside the camp.' He frowned. 'We just have to remain vigilant – and change a few things...'

'And I am Captain Gilbert again?' Tom asked, just to make sure.

'Yes. I've given orders to rectify the mistake with your paycheque and restore your good name, Captain Gilbert.' The major smiled. 'And now I think you deserve a long holiday.'

'I was thinking I might put in for my honourable discharge, sir. I'm not fit for service these days.'

'Sorry to disappoint you, Tom,' Major Carlton replied. 'Two months' leave should see you nicely through the harvest on your family farm – but then... we have another bunch of recruits arriving in the autumn. I know I did say that you'd done your duty, and you have – above and beyond – but after the comments I've had about you being one of our finest officers and the devotion of your men... Well, the truth is, I need you for a bit longer, because we have a very important mission. I don't know if you've heard a whisper about a new "miracle weapon" the Germans have perfected?'

Tom shook his head and Major Carlton looked grave. 'They will use it on London and other important cities and it will be worse than the Blitz. We need to find and destroy the factories, Gilbert; they are in Germany itself – and these men will need specialist training before they go.'

'I understand, sir. Imperative to have at least a couple of men amongst them that speak German...'

'Yes, exactly. Despite the gains the Allies have made since the invasion, these weapons continue to cause untold harm, and Hitler will try to cripple us, destroy Allied bases and terrorise the people. I am hoping the next bunch will be the last to be sent on a mission like this, which is quite honestly a suicide mission. After that, they will probably disband us – as far as the rest of the world knows, we don't exist.' He laughed, highly amused by this. 'You've helped to shorten the war, Tom. You should be proud. It would be a shame not to see it to the end. I'm certain it can't last more than a few months – but this last mission is vital, because unless we can stop them, these rockets will cause chaos.'

Tom sighed inwardly but accepted the order. He'd enlisted for the duration, even though his wounds surely qualified him for a discharge, but at least he would have two months at home with his wife and family. 'Yes, sir. If it is necessary, then I accept your decision.'

Major Carlton's broad but stern face relaxed a little. 'We've lost a lot of good men, Tom. I can't lose you just yet...' He held out his hand and Tom clasped it firmly. 'Enjoy your rest and...' He laughed as Tom turned to go. 'You'd best have this – or you might be arrested for going AWOL again.'

He handed Tom his pass and orders, then saluted. Tom did the same and left his office. A feeling of relief swept over him. Two months would be a wonderful break from this place and a big help to his family. He knew that Artie would be struggling to gather the harvest alone, but now he could sort a few things out and, hopefully, get things back on track.

As he walked away from Major Carlton's office, Tom was saluted many times. Some of the other officers came to him and apologised if they had offended him, expressing their admiration for what he'd done. It was common knowledge now that Tom had exposed a spy in their midst and was considered a hero.

'I really believed you had gone bad,' one officer told him. 'You'd make a damned fine actor, Gilbert. I can't believe we had a traitor in our midst all this time...'

'He was the reason some of our missions went wrong. Connors sent the information out and the enemy was waiting... one of my best friends was killed that way.'

'I know. I was sorry about Shorty. He was a good man.' The officer saluted Tom. 'Well done, Gilbert.'

He wasn't the only one to make his feelings known, but when Tom neared his own mess, he saw a group of men waiting; it was the men he'd recently trained. They cheered loudly and saluted, crowding round to congratulate him. Their mission had been postponed until the traitor was exposed, but they would be leaving soon and he could only pray that at least some of them made it back. Going into enemy territory was always a huge risk, but now they had got rid of the traitor, there was a good chance several of them would return in one piece.

Tom grinned. 'I couldn't have done it without help from some of you. Thank you for keeping Major Carlton safe – and Corporal Zeeman that was brave to volunteer to take his place in the hospital. You might have been killed in his place.'

'Ha! He used a baton – was going to club the major as he slept, only I wasn't asleep and, with a knife at his throat, he didn't struggle much until the MPs came and dragged him off...' Zeeman grinned; clearly, he'd enjoyed playing his part. 'Connors sent a message for you, sir. He said if he ever sees you again, he'll shoot first and question later – and if he doesn't, others will.'

'I shan't be seeing him,' Tom said confidently. 'He took his own life rather than be shot as the traitor he was... and thank you for what you did, Zeeman – all of you.' He paused, then, 'It was a little taste of action for you all and perhaps because of it the mission you're about to go on will be safer. You might even get back, if you remember what I taught you.' Tom chuckled as the men jeered and laughed. 'Even you, Corporal Zeeman...'

'Sergeant now,' Zeeman told him proudly. 'Haven't got my stripes sewn on yet, but Major Carlton promoted me...'

'Good. You deserve it,' Tom said. He smiled at them. 'I have two months' leave coming up. You'll be gone before I come back – good luck, all of you.' He wondered just how many would make it back and hoped it would be most of them. It was only the missions that had been betrayed that had gone badly.

They saluted him again. Tom returned to his barracks and packed his kitbag. He would take his motorbike to the station and leave it there. Lizzie wouldn't be happy that he had to return after his leave, but there wasn't much he could do about it. It seemed he was in the Army for the duration, limp, or no limp...

* * *

Lizzie gave a scream of delight when she saw Tom standing at the door of their home. She'd been to Sutton to fetch Arthur from Dot Goodman's house, after a long day at work, and she'd been feeling tired, but now she felt as if she had wings, flying into his waiting arms.

'Tom! Oh, Tom my love...' she cried. He embraced her and kissed her, little Arthur squashed in-between them until he squawked his disgust. Then Tom took him and swung him up on his shoulders and he squealed with delight.

'Dadda... Dadda... Dadda home...' he cried and, putting his arms tight around Tom's neck, almost choked him.

Tom spluttered and pulled him round to look at him; his eyes bright with mischief, he kissed his nose and then threw him in the air, catching him safely as he giggled with delight.

'Again, 'gain, 'gain,' Arthur chanted hopefully as he was swung up in the air once more, safe in his father's strong arms. All that latrine cleaning had done some good, because Tom's wounded arm had improved with the exercise. Though not as strong as it had been, it was certainly becoming less painful to move.

Lizzie was unlocking the back door of their home. 'Have you seen your mum? How long have you got this time, Tom?'

'No. I wanted to see you first,' Tom said, following her inside. He set Arthur down on the floor and drew her into his arms once more, kissing her softly on the lips. She felt the renewed strength in him, and a lightness that had been missing for a while. 'Lizzie, I love you so much and for a while I was afraid I might not see you again...'

'Oh, Tom, what happened?'

He hesitated. 'I wasn't sworn to secrecy – but this is for you, your ears only, Lizzie,' he said, and then told her the story as she made a pot of tea and brought out some biscuits.

Lizzie gasped with horror. 'I'm glad I didn't know when you were here before, I should have been so worried for you, Tom. Thank goodness you are home and all right... Are you home for good?'

'Two months.' Tom looked apologetic as he sat down. 'I did ask for my discharge, Lizzie, but the major says he can't manage without me. We've lost a lot of good men lately – and he needs me for one last training group.'

'He said that last time...' Lizzie remarked wryly.

'I know.' Tom looked at her. 'Don't let it spoil things, love. I have two whole glorious months – and that will help Artie and Mum, but what of you?' His gaze narrowed as he really looked at her, noticing her unusual pallor. 'You don't look as bright as usual, Lizzie. Have you been unwell?'

'Not unwell... a bit sick in the mornings, but that is usual...'

'Lizzie...' Tom met her eyes. 'You're having our baby? Wow! That's a home-coming surprise!' As she nodded, he jumped up and took her in his arms, gazing at her with tenderness and love. 'I'm glad, if you are?' Lizzie smiled and he kissed her gently. 'A boy or a girl this time?'

'I don't know...' Lizzie laughed. 'Dot says it is another boy, but your mum thinks I've having a girl this time... we shall have to wait and see.'

'Mum will be right,' Tom said confidently. 'It's wonderful news.' He gave her another hug. 'Gosh, I'm hungry. What are we having for supper?'

'I don't have a lot in,' Lizzie replied. 'I'm not eating very much – and Dot fed Arthur his tea. He had sausage and egg with bread-and-butter soldiers! I was going to have cheese on toast... but I could pop back to Sutton to see if the butcher is still open...'

'No, I can think of a much better idea,' Tom said. 'I'll ask Mum to look after Arthur this evening and we'll go out somewhere – but I wouldn't mind a bit of toast for now. I didn't stop for a meal. Once I was free to come, I just got on the train and came...'

'Yes, I'll get us a slice of toast now with our cup of tea.' Lizzie looked at him excitedly. 'Where shall we go?'

'Either the Lamb Hotel in Ely – or get on the train and go into Cambridge,' Tom replied. 'We might do that, Lizzie. Make a night of it. We haven't had much to celebrate for a while – but now we have...'

Lizzie laughed, her eyes shining. 'Yes, let's go tonight, before you get caught up with all work on the farm, Tom.' She flung her arms about him and kissed him again. 'It is so lovely to have you home, my darling, wonderful Tom. I do love you so very much.'

'I love you,' he replied, bending his head to plant a kiss on her nose. 'I guess I am just lucky, Lizzie. I never realised until I understood that I would be fortunate to get out of that mess with my life how lucky I am. Yes, I've been under fire a few times, but that was different. You don't have time to think when you are at war, and I always believed I would get back – but I thought I was a dead man a few days ago.'

Lizzie shivered. 'Well you aren't, because you are lucky – and you're clever. You think and you plan – and that's why you're still here.' She hugged him. 'Let's forget the war for the next two months. I need you; Arthur needs you – and the farm certainly does...'

Tom nodded. 'You'd better tell me, because Mum probably won't – not if it is Artie's fault...'

'He neglected to have the bull to the cows, so only one was in calf – another three should be now, but those fields you put down to grass have been almost empty for months.'

Tom frowned, then, a look of determination on his face: 'I'll try to get some kind of livestock. If there are no calves going, we'll have some pigs or sheep. I think Artie kept the sheds when he sold the pig land. We need the cows to be calving regularly to keep the milk coming, but we can fatten pigs for Christmas to give Mum an income.'

'Pam has a new cockerel,' Lizzie said. She laughed. 'It makes such a row first thing in the mornings – but she has high hopes for it. She wants to rear more chicks, to supplement the meat rations – and they've got a dog now. It was a stray and followed George home...'

'I'll have to trap or shoot some rabbits,' Tom said, smiling. 'Probably be some game around soon – a nice pheasant or a brace of partridge, but not for the dog...'

'Poor little birds,' Lizzie said. 'I know we have to boost the rations however we can, Tom, but make sure you kill them and don't let them suffer a lingering death. I saw one that Artie winged but didn't kill...'

Tom muttered something under his breath. 'If I shoot them, it is instant,' he promised.

Lizzie nodded. She was a farmer's wife and couldn't afford to be sentimental over livestock, but little birds in the fields were different. Lizzie wouldn't eat them herself, always refusing if Pam offered them to her, but she knew others enjoyed them – they enjoyed any meat they could get these days. Even offal was prized now, and coley – a kind of fish that Lizzie's mother had boiled up for her cat – was sought after, though Lizzie hated the smell of it cooking and never bought it herself. Personally, she preferred to eat vegetable pie with some gravy made from bones and a nice crusty pastry, but she turned a blind eye when others ate things she couldn't. No one could really be fussy at this stage of the war if they wanted to eat and not feel hungry all the time.

* * *

'I'm so glad you're home for a while, Tom,' Pam said when he popped up to see her. 'It will be lovely for you and Lizzie to have a night out. You've had so little time together – and I am always happy to have little Arthur. I know Lizzie thinks it is too much for me, because I have Jonny, but I love my grandchildren.'

'Of course you do, Mum,' Tom said and kissed her. 'Did you get to see John?'

'Yes, I did – and so did Jonny. He didn't take much notice of the scars, just seemed excited to see his daddy, though how he knew him, I don't know – but it was lovely to see them together.' She hesitated, fighting her emotions. 'It wasn't as bad as I'd feared.'

'Did John say anything about coming home?'

'I don't think he will,' Pam said sadly. 'I think he will make his home there – perhaps not in the hospital wing, but they have some private rooms in the rest of the house. Well, mansion, really. I think the sister in charge of the place has her own little apartment...'

'She is the matron, isn't she?' Tom said. 'I know John still calls her Sister Jane – but she became the matron when she took that place over. I expect she will be there for years to come, even when the war finally ends.'

'If it ever does...' Pam sounded despairing.

'It will, Mum. It can't go on much longer.' Tom put his arm about her shoulders. 'If John is happy there, perhaps we should leave him? You can visit now and then.'

'I know – but he will want Jonny as soon as he is better. I think Sister Jane is in love with John – and she is pretty and kind, though older...' Pam swallowed a sob. 'It would be wonderful if he found love despite his burns, Tom. I am just a selfish old woman for wanting to keep Jonny.'

'No, that is the last thing you are,' Tom said and gave her a bear hug. That made her smile through her tears. 'John was lucky you took his son. If Faith's family had wanted him, he wouldn't have stood a chance of getting him.'

'I know.' Pam's head came up and she gave him a little push away. 'It's just... I love them both. I want them to be happy...'

'But you wish they would come here and let you continue to share Jonny?' Tom nodded. 'We would all like that, Mum, but if John wants to find his own way – all we can do is help where we can and wish him luck.'

'Thank God for you, Tom,' Pam said and sniffed into the big slightly used handkerchief he offered her. 'I know you are right. It just hurts to lose those you love.'

Outside, a cockerel crowed, and the sound was so normal and comforting, but all they'd lost as a family was still there like a grey cloud obscuring their sunshine. Yet the smells of home lifted Tom, bringing a surge of new confidence that he tried to impart to this dear woman he loved and respected so much.

'I know. You've lost too much already,' Tom said gently. 'But you've still got us, Lizzie, little Arthur and me, and Artie, Jeanie, and Winston, Jonny for the moment – and there will soon be more grandchildren for you to fuss over... Life has to go on, dearest, and you have to live for all of us. We need you.'

Pam sniffed hard. 'I was so pleased when Lizzie told me her news, Tom. All we need now is for you to get your discharge.'

'Not yet, I am afraid. I've got two months' leave. Enough to sort things out for you here – but the war can't last much longer. Until it ends, I am needed and that's all there is to say about that...'

'Yes, I suppose you must do your duty,' Pam replied sadly. 'I sometimes think that both you and John have given more than enough already.'

'I don't disagree with you,' Tom said. 'I am glad John is out of it now and I'll do my best to get home as much as I can...'

'We were worried for a while,' Pam told him. 'You didn't write or phone for ages, Tom. I thought you must have been sent overseas again, but Lizzie said she didn't think so.'

'No, nothing like that,' Tom replied with an easy smile. 'Just some red-tape stuff – bit of a faff on at the camp, but it is all over now.'

'Thank God for that,' Pam said. Then, as she heard a yell from upstairs, 'Jonny has woken from his nap. You get off and dress up in your glad rags, love. I'll be delighted to have Arthur. I don't have him enough.'

15

John was on his knees by the flower beds when Jane saw him. It was a beautiful soft warm summer day without the hint of a breeze; the birds were singing and bees were humming about the stocks and marigolds. She walked towards him, his head turned so that she could see only the left side of his face and it made her heart catch to know how very handsome he'd been before the crash that almost killed him. It must be so hard for him, she thought, aware of all the suffering he'd been through, both physical and mental. To lose his first beloved Faith the way he had, then to be badly injured for a second time and lose the affection of the young girl he'd hoped would be a mother to his son. The son Jane knew was very important to him.

As she neared John, he said, without looking round, 'Is it time for my pills or something?'

'How did you know it was me?' Jane asked with a little laugh.

'Because I couldn't see for weeks when the bandages were on and so I recognised you by your smell.'

'You mean disinfectant and soap!' she cried. 'That could be any nurse.'

'Oh, no.' John turned his head to look at her, mischief in the blue eyes that were as bright as ever. 'You don't smell of carbolic – you smell of roses...'

'Flatterer!' Jane said and sat on a wooden bench nearby, watching as he carried on with his job of weeding the flower bed. 'You like the flowers, don't you?'

'I like the feel of the soil on my hands, especially when it is a little damp. My father wanted me on the farm with my brothers, but I never thought of working on the land – but I like gardening. It's peaceful. Farming is all rush and tear in harvest time, then there's the animals; they need looking after every day, and there's always a job cleaning ditches and cutting hedges in the winter.' John got to his feet and wiped his hands down faded RAF breeches, held up by braces and worn over a sleeveless vest; his arms had turned a pale gold in the sunshine. His gaze sought Jane's, a little self-consciously. 'I didn't mind the work – but the animals...' He gave an odd little laugh. 'They get taken away to market and I never liked that... I know we all need to eat, but I was a kid and they were my pets. Or I thought they were...' He sat on the bench beside her, the memories spilling out of their own accord. 'My brother Artie found me crying once because a cow I called Mary had been taken to slaughter; she was too old to produce calves and milk and so she had to go. I loved that cow; she was so gentle and always gave the best milk. Artie jeered at me for crying, and told me that was what farmers did...' John looked straight at Jane. 'After that... well, I didn't want to be a farmer.'

Jane nodded. She knew that John was a very sensitive, caring person. She'd nursed him from the first day he was brought in to the hospital in Cyprus, when they hadn't been sure he would live. At first, it had been touch-and-go whether he could survive his injuries, but gradually, he'd responded to her care. Then, when she'd been asked to escort some wounded patients to this convalescent home and given the job of managing it, John had been amongst the patients to be transferred. Her feelings for him had developed and strengthened over the months she'd been his nurse. John was just one of the men who needed special care, but something about him had touched her heart. His lean, scarred face reflected his every emotion, which he could never hide from her. 'What made you join the RAF?' she asked him.

'I was young and ignorant; I thought it would be so peaceful to fly in the sky, up above the clouds...' He smiled wryly. 'I imagined it would be better than being in the Army... and it was patriotic and I wanted to kill the enemy... but the bombs killed everyone, destroying families as well as enemy factories and bases.' John shrugged. 'I always tried not to think about it. My job was to get us there and back, nothing more. I told myself the bombs were nothing to do with me.'

'You did what you were ordered, John,' Jane said. 'It's war. A lot of terrible things go on. The whole idea of war is barbaric, but it happens – and we were all caught up in it.'

John nodded; now that the floodgates had opened, he wanted to know: 'Were you always a nurse – is it what you wanted? What happened to you?'

They hadn't spoken quite like this before. It had always been patient and nurse, but now, in this peaceful garden on a warm day, it was different somehow, and they were talking as two people who liked and understood each other, on equal terms.

'I started to train as a nurse when I left school. Then I married, but after a few years war came and my husband joined the Army.' Jane looked thoughtful, a little wistful. 'He was killed within weeks – and then I volunteered to become a nurse again and they were eager to have me, because I'd taken most of my exams before my marriage and they needed us.' She hesitated, and it was clear to John that the memories still hurt. 'I expected to have a quiet life as a country doctor's wife, occasionally helping out in his surgery if needed, but having a family... it wasn't to be, so now I have my family here... I couldn't have a child, you see.'

'You look after us all,' John said, smiling at her. 'What will you do when the war is over?'

'I shall stay here while I am needed,' Jane replied. 'After that – who knows?'

'Perhaps you'll marry again,' John said, but she didn't answer. He was silent for a while, then, 'Mum wants me to go home. I'd like to stay here – in one of the private rooms, but I want my son with me. Do you think that is possible, Jane?'

'Would you be able to care for him?' she asked. 'When he goes to school, he'll need his father – or someone – to take him. There will be many occasions when he needs a parent to help him, just be with him... can you cope with all that? You would need to live in the real world again. For his sake, John. You can't shut him up here forever – he needs friends and a life as he grows up.'

'I don't know if I could,' John replied honestly. 'I could manage to wash and dress him, to get him something to eat... but that isn't enough, is it?'

'I don't think so,' Jane said, looking into his eyes, so clear and honest and thoughtful. 'It is Jonny you have to think of, my dear. Can you be both mother and father to that little boy? It is a big responsibility.'

'I was hoping...' John sighed regretfully. 'I don't think I was very fair to Lucy. I did love her, more than she thought – more than I knew – but I was thinking of Jonny. I'm not sure what to do, Jane.' He felt lost when it came to the question of his son, wanting him, needing his unquestioning love, but unsure of what he could give in return. 'I want my son – but is it fair to him?'

'Give yourself more time,' she advised. 'Perhaps when you've had a bit more treatment on your face, you might think of going home, John. Your mother seems very capable and she obviously loves Jonny. It is the obvious solution.'

'That only makes it more difficult,' he sighed. 'I know Mum will be upset when I take him, and I'm sorry for that, but he's...' John broke off and shook his head.

'All you've got?' Jane said and saw the answer in his eyes. 'Has it occurred to you that if you let it happen you might find love again? I know you've been hurt, terribly hurt, and more than once in many ways – but there is always hope if you allow it into your heart, my dear.'

'With this face?' John shook his head. 'I've loved and been loved. I don't want sympathy...'

'Well, Rome wasn't built in a day,' Jane said and stood up. 'I have things to do. Your tablets are due in half an hour. Don't overdo things, John. You are much better, but take it in small steps.'

'Thanks, Mum,' John said cheekily. 'You fuss over me just the way she did when I was a kid.'

* * *

Jane shook her head and walked back to the house. If John thought of her as another mother, her case was hopeless, she thought, checking the urge to go back and tell him not to be a fool. Love was there under his nose if he could only see it, but she wouldn't do that. John didn't want sympathy. Jane didn't want gratitude. He either loved her or he didn't – and it served her right for letting her heart rule her head! As a nurse you couldn't afford to fall in love with your patients, and she didn't – not all of them. Just this one.

* * *

John sat on in the sunshine after Sister Jane had gone into the house. He'd intended to finish the flower bed that afternoon, but it would wait until the morning. Sister Jane was right. His back did ache. John would have pushed on, thinking he had to suffer to get his strength back, but she was right – his guardian angel.

A little smile played about his mouth then. All the men called her pet names, some of them cheeky, some endearing. For him, Sister Jane had been an angel; there on the darkest nights when he'd battled against his illnesses and his black moods, because it was the despair that had almost killed him. He'd had nightmares about Faith's death, over and over, and the nun who had died because she'd helped him in France, when she'd tried to protect him from the enemy soldier. The bastard had killed her with a knife and he'd been too late to stop it.

It was always those dreams that haunted John. He never thought about the crash that had nearly ended his life; he didn't remember it; he recalled nothing of that time, until he'd woken in the monastery being cared for by monks. His journey back to Cyprus was hazy, because he'd been ill again, but the one memory he truly treasured was the touch of cool, caring hands and a soft voice that made him cling to life somehow. Many times he'd wanted to die, but each time she'd saved his sanity with her calm common sense and her sweetness. She was almost certainly an angel and not just the nurse she appeared to be. His guardian angel. Faith had told him once that she believed everyone had one... perhaps his beloved Faith had sent her to him in his time of need?

That was daft, of course it was, but John had felt Faith close several times of late, urging him on to do something – but he didn't know what.

'What do you want me to do?' he asked softly. 'Tell me, my love. Please tell me.'

There was no answer. John shook his head. He didn't know why he'd told Sister Jane about his experience as a young boy; he'd never told anyone else, even Faith. It had just popped out, because out here in the garden they were talking, not as nurse and patient, but just as a man and a woman. John knew that he couldn't live on the farm all his life. He loved his mother and thought a lot of Tom and the girls – but he'd never got on with Artie. It was as if Artie just had to get at him – and to let him see his face the way it was now... John couldn't do it. He knew he would see disgust, followed by pity, and he wasn't prepared to put himself through the emotions that would rouse.

John knew he was too sensitive – he had the soul of an artist; Faith had told him that once, when he'd shown her the backs of the colleges in Cambridge and gone into raptures over the beautiful grounds. He'd loved the artistic side of his pre-war work as a plasterer. To start off with a rough brick wall and end with a perfectly smooth surface – and the delicate roses he'd done around the light fittings, the scrolled plasterwork he'd done in special properties, some of them ancient; it was a work of art... A sigh left him because he knew he would never do that again.

John looked at his hands. The gardening was helping them become more supple, giving him far more strength. Could he do something artistic – paint or draw? At school, his art teacher had once told him he had talent, but he'd dismissed the idea – painting was for sissies, and he'd been as rough and tough as any other lad. Yet now... now he needed something to fill his emptiness, to make him want to get up in the mornings.

He knew there was a recreation room where drawing and painting materials were on offer at the house. The people here were marvellous, always trying to help their patients to improve fitness and mental stability through various activities. Maybe he would try... it would be a start, John thought. It might lead to something he could do, something useful that would earn a living for him and his son. Jane was right. If he wanted his son, John had to live again. He had to find work of one kind or another. Tom had offered the accountancy work for the farm. Well, John could do that. All they had to do was send him the receipts and it would take a few days once a year. No, he wouldn't go back for that... but he knew he must find something. Something he could use his hands for and his quick brain, but didn't need the hard slog of a manual job like plastering...

Smiling, John collected his tools and took them back to the shed where they were stored. Time for his medicines and then... he nodded to himself. He knew exactly what he wanted to do first – he would try to paint a portrait of Sister Jane...

16

Jeanie hadn't been feeling up to much all day. She'd worked throughout the morning beside Artie as he stacked the hay they'd cut, raking it into small piles so that he could bale it and tie it with string. They had a nice little stack of fodder for the animals now into winter. Tom had gone down the washes, where the river overflowed in winter; they hired the land for the cattle and he was cutting the hay there. He'd said they might as well get what good they could from the long grass that had grown because no stock had grazed much of the land. Artie had grumbled, because he'd had other things planned, but he'd done what Tom suggested. Jeanie had helped because it was quicker if she did and Artie would work on his own land when this was finished.

'I'll take you home and then get on with my own work,' he told her. 'Unless you want to stop with Mum for the afternoon?'

'I think I would,' Jeanie said. 'I don't see as much of her as I'd like now – and she loves Winston.'

Artie nodded and smiled, because, Jeanie thought, he was fond of his mother in his own way – of all of his family; he just wasn't good at showing it. He forked the last of the hay up onto the stack; they'd built it in the corner of the field nearest to the farmyard, because that made it easier to use for the feeding. Tom would bring a load back from the washes and add that to the stack.

It was good having Tom back to help with the work, Jeanie thought as she watched her husband, his muscles rippling as the sweat built on his back. He'd taken his shirt off because it was such a lovely day and his skin had turned a pale gold in the sunlight. He might be lean, but he had strong muscles and a good body. Jeanie always kept her blouse on, because, like most redheads, her skin was too sensitive and burned easily. She used calamine lotion on her face, smearing it over before she worked in the sun. Artie laughed and said she looked as if she had war paint on, but it saved her from feeling sore at the end of the day.

He turned and smiled at her. Jeanie smiled back. She loved working with Artie, they both enjoyed being in the fresh air, especially on days like this. It was nearly August and the heat was building. They were late with the hay; it ought to have been done in June or sooner. Artie had kept putting it off until Tom turned up, but it was done now. There would be some hoeing of potatoes to do but not much more heavy work now until the wheat, oats and barley were ready to harvest. Artie had some potatoes on the fenland and they would have to come up soon if they wanted the best price. That was a back-breaking job and he would need to get some women and youths to help out as part-time workers...

'Come on, daydreamer!' Artie said. 'I'll carry Winston. Mum will give us a cup of tea before I go back to the fen and continue clearing that five-acre piece near the house. I'd like to get a crop in this year – it will have to be market garden, but even if I just grow some lettuce, it's better than nothing.'

Jeanie nodded and gave Winston to him. The child was growing well and getting heavy or perhaps it was just that she didn't feel quite right. It was probably the sun; it must have been hotter than she'd thought, though with the slight breeze, it had seemed just nicely warm.

Artie marched off towards the farmhouse, Winston in his carrycot in one hand, a hayfork in the other. His long legs strode out strongly on the newly mown grass, Jeanie following slowly in his wake. Her head felt a bit strange, sort of light, and the ground wasn't where it was supposed to be... Sighing, Jeanie gave a strangled cry and then sank down by degrees, first to her knees and then collapsed onto her side as her senses swirled and then it all went black.

* * *

Jeanie wasn't aware of being carried, but she stirred as she was placed tenderly on the old and slightly lumpy sofa in Pam's big kitchen. 'Good thing you spotted her fall, Olive,' Pam said, placing a cool cloth on Jeanie's brow. She shot an annoyed look at Artie. 'This one wasn't even aware there was anything wrong...'

'She didn't say a word all morning,' Artie said defensively. 'I asked her twice if she was OK because it was very warm, but she just had a drink of water and said she was fine.' He looked at Jeanie anxiously as she opened her eyes and focused on him. 'You had us worried, love. What happened?'

Jeanie sat up gingerly and sipped the glass of water Pam offered. Her head ached, but not as much as her back. 'I fainted...' she said. 'Oh, Mum, my back really hurts.' She looked at Pam anxiously. 'You don't think... Am I having a miscarriage?'

'I don't think so,' Pam replied. 'I looked when Artie carried you in, but I couldn't see any blood – but I believe you may have to stop working in the fields, Jeanie. This was a warning – and if you carry on, that is what will happen. I've seen it before with other young wives...'

'I worked right until the last minute with my first,' Jeanie protested, shooting a look at Artie. He wasn't able to hide his feelings; he was worried and she knew it would be a severe blow to him if she had to stay home. 'I am sure it was just the sun. I'll be fine soon.'

'I need to get off,' Artie said. 'If you're all right, Jeanie, I'll be back for you later, when I've finished.' He glanced at his mother. 'Make sure she rests for a while, Mum.'

Pam nodded. 'You get off then. Jeanie will be all right with me.'

Artie bent and kissed Jeanie's cheek. 'I'll be back as soon as I've finished that bit.'

'Promise?'

'Promise,' Artie said. He glanced at his mother and then went out without another word. His manner one of suppressed frustration.

'He isn't very pleased,' Jeanie said, eyes teary, because she felt unwell. 'Artie is used to having me and Winston with him. We work well together. We always did, right from the start.'

'Well, he will have to manage by himself or take one of the land girls with him,' Pam said. She looked at Olive, who had come in for a cup of tea. 'You are the best with the cows, so Izzy can help Artie do whatever he needs. Tom is here now and he'll do a lot of the jobs on the farm.' She looked at Jeanie severely as she protested. 'I am not having you kill yourself or your baby, Jeanie. We lost Faith. I won't have it happen again. You can come to me whenever you feel like company. Maybe small jobs like feeding hens and collecting eggs – but you're to stop doing the work of a man, my love.' There was a break in her voice, 'I couldn't bear to lose you, too, Jeanie, or the baby.'

'Oh, Mum,' Jeanie said and burst into tears, because she knew in her heart that Pam was right. She couldn't go on working so hard if she wanted to carry her baby full term. Artie might be cross, but he would just have to accept Izzy in her place, at least until she felt better again.

* * *

Artie hacked at a stubborn tree root that was blocking the dyke, all his anger and frustration going into the attack. It was the last one, so next he could dig out the accumulation of sludge that had blocked the dyke over years of neglect, and then the field would drain properly, instead of lying wet all through the months when he'd needed to plough and set his crops. He would only be able to work a small area of it this year, set it with winter cabbage and veg that kept growing well into the autumn. It would not bring in much money, but he could supply his own kitchen and his mother's – and perhaps that would make up a little for what he knew was neglect of her land.

He was a bloody fool! That was the plain honest truth. He'd grabbed at the fortune that was offered him and splurged almost the whole lot on land, fertiliser and seed. The crops he'd managed to get in were growing well and he would get an income from that, but this five-acre field and another eighty acres he'd bought had all needed far more maintenance work than he'd expected, but this ditch was the last of it. The other sixty acres were all in good heart and growing well. After this, it would just be the normal routine of ploughing, sowing and harvesting, with various small jobs like hoeing and harrowing, but none of them the kind of back-breaking work this damned dyke had been. Even so, it was too much for one man.

Artie dragged the huge trunk free of the dyke and hauled it up onto the trailer with the rest. He would take it to the farmyard he'd bought along with the land; it might dry out and be useful for logs in time. Loaded and ready to leave, Artie stood looking about him with satisfaction. His land, all of it, and it would be rich land too once he'd got it right. Nearly two hundred acres in all, if he counted the pasture land at the back of his house. Never had he thought he would own so much and he was proud of it, determined to make it the best farm in the district. He was on his way and the future would be worth all the hard slog.

Not if he lost Jeanie, though.

A frown creased his brow. It had scared him when Olive came running into his mother's kitchen and told them that Jeanie was lying in the field and she couldn't wake her. He hadn't noticed she wasn't behind him; he was just so used to her being there and working as hard as he did that he'd forgotten she was vulnerable just now.

Damn it! Artie hadn't done all this work just to see the most important person in his life snatched away. He remembered what had happened to Faith and how they'd all condemned the man who had caused her to go into premature labour and die of a wound he'd inflicted. Everyone had been so angry – and now Artie had been guilty of almost doing the same to his wife. It wasn't the same, of course it wasn't. He hadn't lifted a finger in anger to Jeanie and never would – but he had been insensitive and neglectful.

It was a habit he had. Artie frowned. He knew he'd said and done things in the past – things he regretted. As a youngster, he'd mocked John unmercifully, aggravated by his younger brother's weakness – as he'd seen it. John had been sensitive and caring, always bringing their mother gifts when he'd started earning his own money: even before that, when he had pocket money. Maybe it was jealousy. John was his mother's favourite, always had been – and Artie knew that his father favoured Tom. Artie had been the hard one, always going his own way, saying what he thought – but inside he'd been jealous of both his brothers. It was wrong and stupid and he regretted things he'd said and done to John. Tom was tougher. Words just bounced off him and Artie had never been able to best him in a fight – might be able to now, though Tom was getting stronger again.

Shaking his head, Artie turned away and mounted his tractor. It was John he felt bad about. All the things he'd said to him when he was courting Faith – and then she'd died. Now John was in that blasted home and wouldn't come back to the farm. Was it his fault? Did John think he would say hurtful things about his face? Artie felt guilty. He wished that he could turn back time. Had he been more vigilant, perhaps Faith would still be with them. He should have noticed that devil hanging around the place, but he'd had his mind on other things. Artie just wished that John hadn't had to suffer so much. It was rotten luck for him and Artie would change things if he could – but what could he do that would make his life any better?

* * *

Jeanie was looking better when Artie got back to fetch her and Winston home. His mother had cooked tea for them all and insisted that he and Jeanie stop and eat before going home. Tom had shot some rabbits and a hare earlier in the week, and a jugged hare was a particular favourite of Artie's. So he gave in, merely going upstairs to the bathroom to wash himself before sitting down at table, because he'd been sweating like a pig and must stink like one, too.

As he came out of the bathroom, his face glowing from the cold water, he almost bumped into Izzy. She looked at him and laughed, a come-hither gleam in her eyes.

'I hope you've left some hot water for me,' she said, her eyes seeming to invite. 'I was going to have a bath.' She ran the tip of her tongue over her bottom lip and Artie felt a pang of sharp desire. He cursed himself mentally and turned away. She was a Jezebel if ever he'd met one!

'I used cold,' he said curtly and brushed on by as she stood deliberately in his way, flaunting herself as always.

'I'll see you in the morning. Where do you want me?' Izzy called as he walked down the hall.

'What do you mean?' Artie turned and glowered at her. 'I don't want or need you.'

'That's not what Pam says. She told me I am to help you on your land while Tom is home. He can manage all the jobs in the yard I used to do...' Izzy smiled invitingly. 'I'm all yours whenever you say, Artie Talbot.' Her words had double meaning and they both knew it.

Artie grunted and strode off down the hall, taking the stairs two at a time. He felt as if the devil was after him, because Izzy was temptation. It would be madness to work alone with her down the fen; there were too many places where they could go that no one would see and Artie didn't trust himself around her. He would rather work alone than be tempted by her flaunting herself at him all day.

Artie faced the truth. Yes, he wanted sexual intercourse with Izzy, but he did not love her. He didn't even like her, if he thought about it. She was just like the girls he'd had brief flings with before he fell for Jeanie. Artie had always been able to get whatever girl he'd wanted, and even when he'd made his intentions clear – sex but no talk of marriage – most had been only too eager to oblige.

Jeanie was worth ten of a girl like that! Artie would be a damned fool to give into temptation. He was a man who needed physical relations often, but Jeanie would never stand for him having an affair; she would leave him if he were unfaithful. So no matter how much he needed the release of a brief fling, he couldn't give into it. It wasn't as if he and Jeanie didn't make love, they did – but not as much as Artie wanted: not at the moment. She was too tired after working all day – and now he would have to treat her with kid gloves, because the last thing he wanted was for her to lose the baby. She would probably hate him for it.

Artie went into the kitchen and sat next to Jeanie. She turned to him and the love in her eyes made his heart beat faster. His determination grew. No matter how much Izzy tempted him, he wouldn't give in. He had far too much to lose.

17

Tom had finished cutting the grass on the washes and he'd stacked his hay in the fields. It hadn't worked out too badly after all, because they now had a good supply of fodder for their herd of cows in the winter. In the meantime, Tom had managed to buy some pigs for fattening and he'd used the old materials they'd kept to make them some shelter. He'd also got a sow and a boar for them, which meant they could breed some piglets later in the year. His mother wasn't keen on the idea of pigs near the farm because of the smell, but he'd put them in the top field, as far away from the house as he could, though the noise of the planes taking off from the nearby airfield might scare them at first. Cattle wouldn't fare much better – the fields really needed to be put back to arable, but that took extra labour and Tom was only here for a few more weeks. His mother needed another source of income and the land girls could look after the pigs; it was the kind of work Olive enjoyed.

She was a pleasant girl, Tom thought, watching as she carted a barrow of muck from the sheds to the mound at the far end of the yard. It made good fertiliser and Artie had used much of it on his own land this year, because they hadn't got as many arable crops on Blackberry Farm. The three fields nearest home would normally have had crops of barley or wheat nearly ripe by now and to see them down to grass was a bit sad, but Tom wasn't here all the time and Artie had more than he could manage as it was, so the stock had been the easier option. What Tom hadn't reckoned on was Artie getting so far behind that he'd neglected to make sure the cows were serviced at the right time.

Tom frowned as he thought about his half-brother. Artie was all right. He meant well, but he was a bit selfish at times. They had a reasonable relationship because all brothers fought when they were lads, but it was a natural reaction and Tom sensed that Artie was thinking a bit more about things these days than he had once. He knew his younger brother hadn't wanted to cut hay, but he'd done as Tom suggested without much argument and he wouldn't have once.

Would it ease Artie's mind if he told him that that Lieutenant Regan was probably dead, shot as a traitor? Tom had been considering it the past couple of weeks since he got home. He wasn't sure if Artie was still feeling guilty over that incident last year where he'd accidentally caused a man's death. Tom had made sure that Artie didn't get arrested for it, and with the court martial of the man who had been blamed for Armstrong's accident, Tom felt that whole chapter was closed. He wouldn't think about it again, but was Artie still bothered by it – or was something else causing that brooding look in his brother's eyes?

Thrusting such thoughts aside, Tom went into his mother's kitchen. She was alone, apart from Jonny, playing with a wooden train and some bricks on the floor, his mother busy making pastry. He noticed the streaks of grey in her hair that had once been golden and frowned as he sensed her distress. Life had hit her hard over the past few years. He hoped it would improve now. At least, he'd sorted a few problems for her.

Walking over to her, Tom slipped an arm about her waist. 'What's wrong, Mum? Anything I can do to help?'

'I am all right, Tom,' she said and smiled. Then, as he continued to look at her: 'I was just thinking of John, wondering how he is...'

'You haven't had a letter recently then?'

'No – not since I visited.' She sniffed as if holding back her emotion. 'He used to write all the time until he was so badly wounded. I know he couldn't for a long time but...' Pam shook her head. 'I don't suppose he has much to say really, sitting around in that place with nothing to do.'

'I think John keeps busy,' Tom replied. 'At least, he does what he can, Mum. It isn't possible for him to work, at least not yet. He did write and tell me he would do the accounts if we get the receipts and bits to him – you keep them all in Dad's desk, don't you?'

'Yes – not that there have been many lately,' Pam said. 'I know money will come in after the harvest, but it's getting a bit tight...' She hesitated, then, 'Would you take a look in the attic for me, Tom? If you have time...'

'I always have time for you,' he said. 'What am I looking for?'

'Your dad stored some bits up there. I'm not sure what really – his letter said silver and jewellery. He says they are for me if times get tough, but I didn't want to touch them... I think the girls and John need a bit more than Arthur left them so...' Pam sighed. 'If there is something I could sell... I just need about thirty pounds or so, Tom.' She looked up from her work. 'Take a look for me and see what is up there, please.'

'I'll do it now,' he promised and went out into the yard, fetching a ladder. In the hall, he propped it up against the hatch in the roof, went up and pushed the trapdoor back, then hauled himself up. There was a switch just inside the hatch and he pressed it, the one hanging light bulb came on. It gave light but not much, so Tom felt for the torch he knew his father had kept up here. When he pressed the switch, it came on, flickered and went out, the battery exhausted. Tom laughed wryly.

Oh well, he could see enough to make out the shapes of some boxes and a tea chest. He walked carefully on the joists, not wanting to put his foot down in-between and perhaps crack the ceilings below. Arthur really ought to have boarded the attic floor if he wanted to store stuff up here. He couldn't have started putting stuff up here much before the war, Tom thought, remembering he'd come up for some Christmas decorations in 1938 – but he'd not really been looking then and perhaps he hadn't noticed.

He wondered where to start. The tea chest was nailed down with a lid, but the cardboard boxes were easier. Poking about in the first one, he saw several porcelain bits and pieces so abandoned that one; the next had silver items wrapped in newspaper. Tom found what he thought might be a coffee pot and a milk jug, then a couple of teapots and some candlesticks, also a big heavy tray. He was just wondering whether that was part of a set and whether it would fetch the amount Pam had hoped for when he saw the tin cash box. It was quite large and, when he picked it up, it felt heavy; it was also locked. Tom decided to take it down to the kitchen. His mother might know where the key was...

She'd just put her latest batch of pies into the oven when Tom entered with the box and wiped her hands on her apron. 'This looks promising,' he said. 'Do you happen to know where the key is?'

'In your dad's roll-top desk, I expect,' Pam said and followed him into the sitting room. She took a key from a spill vase on the mantle and unlocked the desk, rolling the curved top back; it was old and rattled a bit but still opened and shut. Some keys were in the drawer at the right side and they easily found the one that opened the cash box. 'Well, I never...' she said as a wad of white five-pound notes was revealed on top. 'Wouldn't you just know Arthur would do something like this?'

'Back pocket money, I imagine,' Tom suggested with a grin. 'I bet this little lot never went through the accounts.' He flicked through the notes. 'There's a hundred of them, Mum. How much do you want now?'

'I only need thirty, but I'll keep the rest in my desk just in case,' Pam replied. 'What else is in there, Tom?'

'Some gold sovereigns, watches and chains; that's what made it so heavy – a ring and what looks like a diamond brooch. I think that might be worth a bit, Mum.'

She looked at it and nodded. 'I recognise that – it belonged to great-grand-mother Talbot. Your dad wouldn't sell it and neither would I. Susan will have it one day and it's a diamond ring – that will be for Angela.'

'What about the gold? Do you want to sell it, Mum?'

She paused, considering, then shook her head. 'Arthur wasn't sentimental about most things, but this cash is enough. Put the box back where you found it, Tom. We'll keep it for a rainy day – or perhaps for John if he needs help.'

'Good idea,' Tom said. 'I found some silver as well – do you want that down?'

'I think that came from Arthur's great-aunt. Several boxes of stuff up there belonged to her and I'll sell it if I get short, but I don't need any more now, Tom. Once things improve again, I shall be fine – and then the bits in the attic will be there for you all to share when I'm gone.'

'Daft!' Tom said affectionately. 'Dad wanted you to have some security. He knew things could get bad with the war and me away, and no doubt he hasn't paid tax on much of what is up there. It was for you, Mum.'

'We always had more cash than we needed while Arthur was alive. He was always buying and selling on the side, but by the sound of it, he kept more than he sold.'

Tom chuckled. 'Crafty bugger!'

'Tom!' Pam reprimanded, but she laughed because Tom had summed up her husband in two words. Trust Arthur to hoard stuff so that his family could get through the bad times and not tell anyone. 'He liked a deal. Always did, but he was honest in his own way – would never cheat a neighbour or friend.'

'Dad was a good man,' Tom replied. 'He did it all for you and us, Mum. Not for himself. He never bothered about things, unless it was for the farm or his family.'

'True enough,' Pam agreed and her eyes were smiling. 'We had some good years, Tom. Not long enough, but what we had was good.'

Tom nodded. 'I know how you miss him. I miss him, too. I enjoyed working with him, talking to him about the land and the village. He knew a lot of stuff. He used to tell me about the tithes they had to pay for the church – not just on farming land but on gardens if they grew produce.' Tom smiled reminiscently. 'A lot of stuff about what things were like when he was a lad and they only had the horses to work the land. No tractors then... and when the oats were short and the poor beasts got thin over the winter, they had to buy whatever they could to feed them.'

'I'm glad you remember him fondly, Tom. He might not have been your blood father, but he was a father to you in every way that counted.'

'I know and I loved him for it.' Tom sniffed and Pam looked at him in surprise as she saw tears in his eyes.

'I thought you'd got hard with the war...'

'I have to be, Mum,' he said and the smile left his eyes. 'That doesn't stop me loving my family. I'm just the same as I always was, or I shall be when I can come home and leave all that stuff behind.'

'I know.' She blew her nose and mopped at her cheeks. 'Put the money in the drawer and lock the desk, Tom. I'm glad it is there. I'll use what I need until we're back as we ought to be.'

Tom looked at her but didn't say anything. Pam knew more about Artie's failings than he'd thought, but she wouldn't complain. All her sons were dear to her and she wouldn't criticise them to each other – but he hoped she could stand up for herself when he went back to his base.

'Right. I'll put this other stuff back and then get home,' he said and went out into the hall. Izzy was standing outside the kitchen door and Tom had a feeling she'd been listening. 'Do you need something?' he asked, giving her a hard look.

'No, just wondered where Pam was – if everything was all right,' the girl replied, but Tom frowned as he turned away and went back up into the loft. There was something about her he didn't like, but he wasn't sure what it was. If he was here full time, he thought he would give Izzy her marching orders. He'd noticed she did as little work as possible and left most of the yard jobs to Olive – but he wasn't in charge of the girls. Pam was her employer and Artie should be capable of keeping an eye on her. Perhaps he would just have a word with his brother – because Tom didn't trust her.

* * *

Artie shrugged when Tom spoke to him about Izzy, giving him an odd look. 'It's all very well for you,' he said resentfully. 'You aren't here all the time. I know she shirks her jobs when she can, but if I'm with her, she does a fair share – and for the moment, I need her to help on the land.'

'Well, if you think you can trust her – but Mum has a bit of cash in Dad's desk now. We found it in a box in the attic and it's locked away, but there's something about that girl I don't like, Artie.'

'Found some cash in the attic?' Artie grinned. 'Good old Dad! I'm glad.' He hesitated then, slightly shamefaced. 'I know I let her down a bit, Tom, but the work got on top of me. Most of it is done now and I'm going to try to get a school-leaver in the autumn to work with me. It won't happen again.'

'Good. Dad wouldn't be pleased if we let Mum down...' Tom paused, then, 'I've got some news that might make you feel easier...' He told Artie briefly that Regan had been arrested for betraying his country and would stand a court martial. 'He will be shot as a traitor – and I am pretty sure he intended to murder his fellow officer, Armstrong. So you don't need to think about any of that stuff again, Artie. Just put it out of your mind.'

'Thanks,' Artie grunted. 'I wasn't particularly worried. You took care of it. Besides, it was an accident. I never meant it to happen.'

Tom nodded, searching for something in his eyes but didn't find it. 'What's wrong, Artie? Can I help?'

'Yes, you can get a bloody discharge and help out on the farm permanently,' Artie muttered. 'Surely you're no good to the Army now?'

'I train others,' Tom replied without rancour. Artie was only telling him half a story, but if he didn't want to confide in him, Tom wouldn't probe further. He'd offered a helping hand, but if Artie refused to take it there was nothing he could do.

Turning away, he went home to put the kettle on. Lizzie would return from work any minute and she'd said they would have fish and chips – pan fried rather than shop bought. Tom knew there was a sack of new potatoes in the shed – freshly lifted. They made wonderful chips and were easy to scrape, so he might as well get them ready.

The work on the farm was invigorating and he'd truly relaxed for the first time in months. He smiled to himself as he started the preparations for their evening meal. Lizzie would be tired and Tom felt good. The work he'd been doing had helped his arm; it ached a bit but was gradually regaining its strength.

He was probably making too much of that look of guilt in Izzy's eyes as he'd caught her eavesdropping. She was just being nosy, but she was also lazy and Tom couldn't like her. Not one little bit.

18

'Will you help me with the washing, Susan?' Pam asked her eldest daughter, just home from college for the long summer holidays. 'I've boiled it in the copper and rinsed it, but I need to start the baking – so could you hang it out for me, please, love?'

'Of course I will, Mum,' Susan replied, picked up the basket and went out into the bright sunshine in their back garden.

Pam smiled, watching her through the window as she got out her baking things. Susan was becoming a lovely girl, her honey-blonde hair longer now and tied up in a swinging ponytail. Back from college, she had the summer holidays ahead of her with nothing much to do, apart from some studying, but she'd said it was just some books she had to read, so she would find it quiet here on the farm.

As Pam watched, she saw Tom hesitate and then walk up to Susan and start chatting to her. Susan nodded and then smiled at him, before bending to pick up one end of a sheet. Tom helped her peg it on the line and Pam could see them laughing together. It was good to see them like that, relaxed and happy, but at that moment, George came bounding into the kitchen, his dog following and barking.

'Aunt Pam, Tom says he is going to take me, Angela and Susan to the pictures in Ely this Saturday – and Susan says she will take Angela and me to stay in a caravan one day soon.' His face was alight with eagerness as he imparted his news. 'She says there are lots of things to do there. It will be fun, won't it? I can go, can't I?'

'Did she now?' Pam looked at him thoughtfully. His dark hair had chestnut lights in it when the sun touched it, his young face freckled and eager, and he too was growing up fast. He needed some long trousers and, thinking about it, she had some of John's that would probably fit him. George was about the same size as her youngest son had been at his age. 'Well, if she does, I'll give you some more pocket money to spend, love.'

'I've got money saved,' George said proudly. 'You give me money for working on the farm – and George Munns gave me half-a-crown for helping him lift his early potatoes last Saturday morning. Artie's got some to lift, so I'm helping him tomorrow.'

'Well, that's good, but you can keep your money saved for something you want,' Pam said and smiled at him. She'd grown very fond of him since he'd come to the farm. 'Would you like some ginger beer?' she asked and he nodded enthusiastically. 'Come and sit down for a minute, George. I want to talk to you about the future.'

He shot a scared look at her, as if wondering what she meant to say. 'I want to stay here with you, Auntie Pam.'

'I certainly hope you will,' she said and saw the scared look disappear. 'I'm not going to send you away, love. You are my family now.' A smile crept into his eyes. 'You know I love you, George, and that's why I want to be sure of what you want – that it is right for you.'

'I want to work on the farm with Tom,' George said promptly. 'Tom's all right. I like him...'

'Yes, Tom is a good friend,' Pam agreed. 'Are you certain it is what you want, love? We've taken it for granted that you will work for me when you leave school, but is there anything else you would rather do? Some lads might like to drive a train or work in a factory, build something – or an office job.'

'I'd hate that,' George said and grinned at her. 'I can add up good and do my times table, but I don't go on books much. Don't mind a comic or the newspaper, but I don't want to work in an office – I like to drive the tractors and I can on our land, can't I?'

'It will help you when you're old enough to take a driving test, love,' Pam said. 'If you are certain, you can leave school when you are fourteen – another year, or they might make you go to the following Christmas since your birthday is late September.'

'I'll leave next summer whatever they say,' George gave her a cheeky look. 'You need me to help look after things, Aunty.'

'We'll see.' Pam hid her amusement. 'Have you done all your jobs for the day?'

'I'm going to help Tom pull wild oats out of the barley this afternoon,' George told her. 'He says it is a real good crop but there are a few wild oats. If we can pull them all out, Tom reckons it will be good enough for malting.'

'Oh, that is good,' Pam said, pleased with the news because malting barley was worth more money. 'It will be hot work, so remember to take a bottle of water with you, love.'

'Tom says he's got some orange squash and he'll bring some biscuits Lizzie made, too. She is going to have another baby – early next spring, so Tom says. He's as chuffed as a dog with two tails...'

Pam burst out laughing. She couldn't help it. The things children came out with sometimes.

'What's funny?' Susan asked, coming back in with her empty washing basket.

'Oh nothing much. George and I were just talking,' Pam told her. 'He says you've offered to take him and Angela for a day out?'

'Well, I was thinking I might go for longer,' Susan said. 'You could come too, if you want, Mum – or Lizzie. I've been offered a week in a caravan in a country park near St Ives, where they have a swimming pool and all sorts of things going on, for free...'

'You never have!' Pam stared at her. 'Who by? I don't know anyone that has a holiday caravan.'

'It is a girl I'm friends with at college,' Susan replied. 'Do you remember me asking if I could have someone to stay – and you said yes?'

'Of course.' Pam looked at her inquiringly.

'Well, Sally is coming the week after next. She will bring her ration book with her – and then, she says the week after we can have her dad's caravan... It sleeps five so she said I can take three others if I want. I thought George and Angela – and you, if you aren't too busy...'

'I wish I could, love,' Pam said, studying her daughter for a moment. Susan was a young woman now; she and her friend would be capable of looking after the younger two. 'I'm not sure about Lizzie. She is normally booked up for weeks ahead at the salon.' She looked thoughtful. 'What about Jeanie? She could do with a holiday and she isn't that much older than you.'

Susan looked surprised. 'Do you think she would? I thought she worked with Artie on his land?'

'Well, she does, but at the moment she can't do a lot of hard work. She fainted a few weeks back and we worried for the baby, but she seems much better now she isn't working on the land. I think she might like it if you asked her.'

'I shall then,' Susan said and smiled. 'Is she coming here at all?'

'I haven't seen her for a week or so,' Pam replied, frowning as she realised it. 'I suppose Artie is too busy to bring her and she normally cycles over, but of course she won't at the moment, not while she is pregnant.'

'I'll cycle up to see her then,' Susan offered. 'Do you need me to do anything else, Mum?'

'No, love, not just now,' Pam said and began to beat some eggs very fast in her big yellow mixing bowl. 'You get off and enjoy this lovely weather. They say it won't last...'

'If it rains next week, Artie will be mad,' George said, as he filled Rover's water bowl and gave him the scraps Pam had saved for him. The dog woofed them down in three seconds and looked hopefully at his young master. 'He's got some wheat down the fen that's almost ripe enough to cut. If it rains hard, it might go down and then it's a bugger to harvest...'

'No swearing, George,' Pam said automatically and then laughed. 'I know Tom and Artie do it, but you're too young.'

George pulled a face. 'I'm going to find Tom...' he said and bolted out of the kitchen door.

Pam looked at Susan. 'What can I do?' she asked her daughter. 'He is bound to pick it up from the men. I don't like to hear a youngster swear, but his friends do, so how can I expect him not to?'

'I don't think you can win, Mum,' Susan said. 'Do you need any shopping in Sutton?'

'You could pop into the butchers for me if you will,' Pam said. 'I'd like some sausage meat, if they have any, some steak and kidney – and any scraps or bones he can spare.'

'They are for Rover I suppose?' Susan said and looked at the dog who had stretched out at the far end of the kitchen, away from the heat of the cooking range.

Pam mixed some softened margarine with her eggs and then added it to the flour in her bowl. 'Well, I do use bones to make a nice soup sometimes, but if he's got a shin bone Rover can have it.' She sighed. 'Poor animal must have had a hard time before George brought it home. I think someone found it impossible to feed him and turned him out, but he'll eat anything and Tom shot some rabbits and a couple of pigeons, so he had all the innards. I couldn't let the poor thing starve, even if I had to give it my dinner.'

'That is horrid! I hate people who mistreat pets,' Susan said. Then, 'Will you give me some money?'

'Oh yes, there is some in my purse on the mantle...'

Susan reached for it and opened it, taking out a ten-shilling note. 'Will this be enough, Mum?'

'There should be two of those,' Pam said, busy beating her mixture.

'No, just the one,' Susan said and turned the purse over. Just a few coppers fell out.

'Oh, I must have paid someone,' Pam said, frowning, because she was sure she'd had two notes, but she must have spent it, though she didn't recall doing so. She left her mixing and turned away. 'I'll get you some more money, Susan.'

Going into her front parlour, she took the desk key from the spill vase and unlocked the desk. She opened the secret drawer and took out a white five-pound note, then closed it, locked the desk and returned the key to its special place and went back to her daughter.

'Leave the ten shillings and take this,' Pam said, giving her the money. 'You can buy yourself a cake or some sweets, but be careful not to lose the change; that's five pounds.'

'Mum! I'm not a little girl any more,' Susan said, laughing at her.

Pam joined in, because she did tend to forget sometimes. 'It's habit,' she said and smiled as Susan came to kiss her. 'You can still buy yourself something – the way you used to, when you were a little girl.'

'Thanks, Mum,' Susan replied. She picked up her light jacket and put it on, placing the money in her pocket, and then went out.

Pam resumed her baking. She was just putting the last of it in her oven when Angela came running in with Jonny. She'd taken him out for a walk and they both looked hot, their skins pink from the sun.

'Is there anything to eat, Mum?' Angela asked and Jonny ran to her, pulling at her skirt.

'Cake, Gan-gan,' he said, looking at her expectantly.

'Please,' Pam said automatically and he echoed her. She smiled and gave him a small rock cake. 'Mind you don't burn your tongue; it's hot...' Looking at her youngest daughter, she said, 'You can have one, too, Angela – but no more. I think there is some ginger beer left in the bottle. You both look hot.'

'We've been playing rounders in the chestnut field, with Jilly and some others. Jonny loved it; we gave him a start with his running and he scored three runs.'

'Well, that was nice,' Pam replied. 'What are you going to do this afternoon?'

'Nothing much,' Angela said. 'Olive says if she gets finished in time, she will take us down the river, where it is shallow... she says she could do with a paddle.' She gave a little giggle. 'I think she is in love with that airman. He popped in to see her as she was mucking out the sheds and she went bright pink. He seemed nice and smiled at her in a daft way.'

'Now that is being cheeky, Angela, and none of your business.'

'I was only saying. I like Olive.'

'Good. You can help her feed the calves,' Pam said. 'She'll get done sooner then. Izzy is with Artie working down the fen...'

'I love helping with the animals, but I love paddling in the river, too.'

Pam nodded. All her children had always loved the river and Jonny would be safe if Olive was there. She felt a little surge of pleasure as she thought of the young ones enjoying themselves, going to the pictures, the river and then a holiday in a caravan – and it was nice that Olive had found someone who cared for her. Some of the deep sorrow she'd been feeling was gradually lifting and the only one she really needed to worry about was John. She hadn't heard from him for a while and wondered if she should write to him and ask if he wanted another visit.

19

Susan pedalled to Sutton the long way round, via the village of Witcham, up to the old tollhouse and then turned right, into the large village. There, she stopped to order her meat from the obliging butcher, agreeing to pick it up on her way home from Jeanie's house. The butcher was a big burly man with florid cheeks and a shock of dark hair, a lock of which fell forward over his bushy eyebrows. His smile for Susan was friendly and curious and he wanted to hear how she was doing as he prepared her order.

'I'll keep that in my cold room,' he told her as she paid for it, grimacing at the five-pound note. 'You'll take all my change,' he said and held the note up to the light to check its watermark. 'The last time I saw one of these... Yes, I remember, it was your dad. He told me he'd been paid for some potatoes...' He sighed and shook his head. 'That was a sad thing – I liked Arthur and we went to school together...' Shaking his head, he added, 'Tell your mother I'll find her some scraggy bits for the dog. There's mostly a bit gets left until it's on the turn. I shan't charge for those...'

Susan thanked him, gave him a brilliant smile and left. She'd cycled past the beautiful ancient church of Saint Andrews before she got to the butcher. Now she continued along the length of the High Street, past the grocer and the smallmen's outfitters, the ironmonger almost opposite, the post office and shop, and the library, then, pedalling a bit harder up a rise past a couple of pubs and then at the far end of the High Street, she turned left to freewheel down the hill, into the fen that eventually led to the Gables, an old farmhouse with small mullioned windows, a front garden filled with roses, gillyflowers and stocks. Behind the house were the barns and paddocks of the farm, but the land was divided by the drove and off in the distance she could see two figures working – lifting potatoes by the look of it. She wasn't sure but thought it might be Artie and Izzy.

The front door opened as she wheeled her bike up the garden path, enjoying the fragrance of the summer flowers and the twittering of birds, while bees buzzed around some tall hollyhocks.

'Susan,' Jeanie cried in delight and came out to hug her. 'How lovely to see you! I knew you were home, but I couldn't get down to see you, because Artie has been working non-stop. He is across the ten acres with Izzy.' She waved at the two figures but neither saw her. 'Come on in. I am dying to hear all your news.'

'Your garden is lovely,' Susan told her and Jeanie nodded happily. 'It smells gorgeous. You've got a lot more flowers than Mum ever had.'

'I was lucky,' Jeanie replied. 'Some of it was already here. I've added roses and I grew a lot of the flowers from seeds Artie bought for me – and we found some in the house, too. They were old but they grew...' She laughed, waving her hand around to indicate the long cool kitchen with its pine dresser set with blue-and-white earthenware and a collection of pretty teapots.

'This is nice,' Susan said. A pine scrubbed-top table occupied the centre, with a hotchpotch of chairs around it, ranging from yew Windsor chairs with their hooped backs to some that looked to be oak and much older. 'Where did you get all those chairs – some of them look like things they have at the college, hundreds of years old.'

'They might be,' Jeanie agreed, her eyes sparkling. 'They came out of the attic here, as well as quite a few other bits and pieces. We managed to buy a new mattress and the three-piece-suite is new – that was a present from my mum, dad, and Terry...'

'Oh, that was nice,' Susan said, glad that Jeanie had turned away to fill the kettle from the sink and couldn't see the look on her face as she mentioned her brother. 'How are they? Your mum and dad and... Terry?'

'Mum is fine, still working as a midwife and always busy. Dad is hardly ever at home. He can't build many new houses at the moment, but he does lots of small jobs, repairs, painting, mending fences – anything really, just to keep the business going until the war ends. Terry does all his bookwork, but he is much better than he was. He recently had a new leg fitted and it is far more comfortable for him...' Jeanie stopped and nodded. 'That reminds me, he asked after you and the family. He has a holiday coming soon and says he'd like to bring Tina and spend it here...'

'Oh – when is he coming?' Susan asked as lightly as she could, though her heart raced. She'd never forgotten Terry Salmons or the teenage crush she'd had on him when he'd visited them after his release from hospital. Terry had been unfortunate enough to lose a leg early on in the war, and he had also lost his wife because of a fire at almost the same time. He'd been able to love his little girl Tina after some initial rejection of her, and it was because Vera, his mother, had wanted him to go home and help look after the business and his daughter that he'd returned to London. Before he'd reluctantly left, he'd told Susan he would come back one day, but thus far he never had.

'In two weeks,' Jeanie said and Susan's face fell, unable to hide her disappointment. 'Why does that upset you?'

'I am going to take Angela and George to stay in a friend's caravan that week,' Susan replied, desperately trying to hide how much she was feeling. 'My visit this morning was to ask if you would like to come as it sleeps five...'

'Oh, I would have loved that,' Jeanie replied. 'What a shame. Terry is here for two weeks, though, so you will still see him and Tina when you get back.'

'Oh...' Susan felt a rush of relief but hid her joy. 'It still means you'll miss the holiday. I'd change it, but it is free and the only week it's available.'

'You can't miss a free holiday,' Jeanie said. 'Is it a friend from college lending it to you?'

'It belongs to her family and it's in St Ives – there is a swimming pool on the complex and it isn't far from the quayside, so there are boats for hire on the river, too. Sally is coming to us the week before, then we are all going down to the sea together. Tom is going to drive us there – but we'll get the train back, because he will be back to camp by then.'

Jeanie nodded, turning away to pour the tea into delicate china cups that had been a wedding gift but unused until she had her own home. 'I'll take you over the house in a bit,' she said, bringing the tea tray to the table. 'Winston is upstairs in his cot, hopefully asleep. He was crying half the morning. I think he may be teething.' She smiled. 'It's so nice having you here, Susan. You are my first guest. Will you stay and have lunch with me? I've made some pasties, because Artie likes to take them to work and I did a big batch. I've got my own lettuce, radishes and salad onions in the back garden, and I've got a small green-house, too – I've got some baby tomatoes and a couple of cucumbers in there. We can have a lovely fresh salad with our pasties.'

'That's very tempting,' Susan said and her tummy rumbled. 'Thank you, Jeanie. I should love that...' She smiled at her brother's wife. 'You look very well, Jeanie. Mum said you hadn't been up to much?'

'I think it was working in the heat,' Jeanie replied. 'I've been much better since I stopped the land work, though I do miss it. This house needs quite a bit of looking after, so the two together was a bit much at the moment, but some-times I get bored here on my own. It will be lovely having Terry here for a couple of weeks – and Tina, too. I haven't seen her for a while. Terry says she has grown a lot.'

'She was so sweet when Mum looked after her,' Susan replied, smiling at the memories. She wasn't sure whether she'd fallen in love with Terry first or his daughter. She just knew she felt safe and happy with him, which wasn't the case with others she'd met, and she knew well enough the heartache it had caused her when he returned to London. Over the years, she heard very little of him, just snatches from a letter Jeanie had, though he never failed to send a birthday card and Christmas card with a small gift of perfume or nice soap – something impersonal that he might also send to an aunt or cousin. Once, she'd thought he might love her, but he'd still been grieving his wife, and Susan was hardly sixteen, far too young to marry, especially as she intended to go to college. He hadn't spoken to her of love. Instead, he'd gone home as his parents wanted. Maybe it was all in her head and Terry just thought of her as a young girl who had befriended his daughter.

* * *

Susan cycled home just after three that afternoon. Artie was in the kitchen, having come in for a cup of tea and a piece of cake, while Jeanie fed Winston, and, after greetings and entreaties from Jeanie to come again while she was at home, she'd left them. She called in at the butchers and collected her parcel of meat, noticing how large the bag of bones and scraps were. Rover would have a feast, but she supposed meat soon turned in this weather and it was probably not quite fresh – not that he would care. He'd found a dead heron on the wash recently and would have eaten it had George not taken it from him and thrown it into a large thorn bush, from which the dog had no chance of retrieving his prize.

This time, she cycled fast, wanting to get back before her mother had to start preparing the evening meal. Pam had such a lot to do and Susan liked to help her when she was at home, feeling a little guilty because she was away at college rather than helping out. She was coming through Witcham village – thinking how much easier it would be to go across the hill from Sutton to Mepal, but unable to because since much of the land was taken for the aerodrome, the road had been closed – when a car shot round a bend and made her skid off to the left and narrowly avoid ending in the dyke. The car screeched to a halt and a man jumped out, hurrying to her side.

'Are you all right?' he asked anxiously. 'I am most dreadfully sorry. I'm late... I'm new here and I got Witcham mixed up with Witchford and my patient is in labour...'

'Are you a doctor?' Susan asked, looking into his anxious face. He didn't look very old and he certainly didn't look like a doctor – or, at least, any she'd ever seen.

'A very new one,' he said and laughed. He had ginger hair, light-green eyes and freckles, and, to Susan's gaze, more the look of a schoolboy than a serious medical man.

'You want the next village down the Ely Road,' she told him, smiling. 'Carry on up to Witcham Toll and turn left and then it's a mile or so until you turn right.' All the place names had been taken down for the duration of the war and it was easy to get the villages muddled if you didn't know.

'Yes, someone told me – but are you certain you're not hurt?'

'I'm fine,' Susan told him. 'Please, don't delay on my account. Your patient may need you.'

'Yes, she does,' he said and turned to get back in his car, then stopped and looked at her. 'May I ask your name, please? I'd like to call another day and make sure you suffered no harm from my stupidity.'

'It's Susan Talbot,' she said and laughed, shaking her head. 'There is really no need – but thank you...'

He lifted a hand in recognition, but said no more as he drove away at a slower pace.

Susan laughed to herself, mounted her bike, and cycled off, wondering which practice he'd come from. Her mother hadn't mentioned a new doctor in Sutton, but that didn't mean there wasn't one.

* * *

'Oh, yes,' Pam said and laughed. 'I've been told about the new doctor. He's very young and always in a hurry. He is what they call a locum, I think – that means he is attached to one of the practices in Ely but covers a wide area in the villages around it, standing in when a local doctor is off sick or can't manage to see all his patients. So many of them were absorbed into the military at the start of the war, it left us with hardly enough medical care. Doctor Perkins is overworked, poor man. He may have taken on young Doctor Bryant to help him out. Doctor Perkins is getting on a bit and his partner at the surgery was called up for military service... because he was young and passed his medical, and he wanted to go.' Pam shook her head. 'So you met the new one then – what is he like?'

'A fresh-faced schoolboy,' Susan replied with a laugh. 'Ginger hair and freckles, Mum!'

'Oh, I heard he was very attractive...'

'I suppose he is in his way,' Susan replied, dismissing the young doctor with a shrug. 'Oh, Jeanie told me her brother is coming down to stay – the week I'm at the caravan and the next one. So she can't come.'

'That is a shame,' Pam said. 'A change of air would have been good for her – but she is fond of Terry and his daughter Tina, so it will be nice for her to have company in that big house.'

'It is big,' Susan agreed. 'Jeanie took me all over it before we had lunch – five bedrooms, a sitting room, and office for Artie and a dining room, as well as a big kitchen – as long as yours, Mum, but not quite as wide. The bedrooms are even bigger...'

'That is a lot of work for her,' Pam frowned. 'Is it all furnished?'

'One bedroom – the smallest – is being used for storage at the moment, but the others are – after a fashion. It's a mixture of old and new, Mum. Stuff that they've been given, and the rest from the attic – quite a bit of old oak they didn't know was up there when they bought the house.'

'As long as they have beds and something to sit on...' Pam said. She looked up suddenly from grating carrots for a salad. 'Still going on your holiday, love?'

'Yes, of course I shall,' Susan replied, puzzled. 'Why do you ask?'

'I thought you might want to see Jeanie's family?'

'Yes, I do, but they are here for two weeks,' Susan said and her mother gave her an odd, slightly relieved look. Susan felt the prick of tears. She'd thought her mother would have forgotten her teenage crush, but she hadn't. Susan had gone out with a lot of young men when Terry returned to London, but that had turned sour after one of them – an officer from the airfield – had attempted to force her into something she didn't want to do. Since then, she hadn't been out on a one-to-one date with any of the men who had been interested.

Pam nodded but said no more. Susan let the subject drop. She needed to know how Terry felt – if he'd forgotten the feeling between them – and if he had, well, she didn't want to make a fool of herself. If she were honest, she didn't want to let herself hope that he still felt something for her, because it hurt too much when he went away.

20

Artie nodded when Jeanie told him that her brother and his little daughter were coming to stay for a couple of weeks. 'That's good, you'll have company,' he said, noticing her heightened colour. 'What did Susan want?'

'Oh, didn't she say? Susan is taking Angela and George to stay in a caravan for a week, near the quayside in St Ives. Her friend from college is staying at the farm for a week and then they'll all go together. She asked if I would like to go, take Winston, obviously, but it is the same week as Terry comes, so I couldn't – besides, it wouldn't be fair to leave you to cope alone, Artie.'

'I'd go down Mum's for my dinner,' he replied with a shrug. 'I'd miss you, of course I would, love. Couldn't you get Terry to change to the following two weeks?'

'I expect they've had holidays booked for a while. I could ask, but that might seem as if I didn't want him here. No, I don't think I shall, Artie. Perhaps when Winston and the baby are older and you've got the land sorted, we might hire a caravan for a week?'

'Yes, we might do that but not for a year or two,' Artie said. 'It's a pity you have to miss it, Jeanie. You've worked hard for the past few years. To be honest, I don't know what we'd do without you... none of the others have been as willing as you.'

'Olive is a hard worker and very obliging,' Jeanie replied. Then, in a casual manner that made his gaze narrow, 'How are you getting on with Izzy? Is she a big help or a hindrance?'

'What do you mean?' Artie frowned, a strange, slightly guilty look in his eyes.

'Well, her heart isn't truly in her work, is it?' Jeanie commented, feeding Winston a biscuit soaked in tea, and not looking at him. 'I know she fancies you; I've seen her eyeing you when she thinks no one is looking... just the way Francis did when she first came to the farm.'

'Jeanie!' Artie exclaimed. 'I hope you don't think there is anything going on between us?'

'Not for want of trying on her part, I'll bet,' Jeanie said and turned to look at him with a teasing smile. 'I wouldn't blame you if you were tempted, Artie, just as long as you resist. I know I haven't been much fun recently...'

'You are my wife,' Artie said quickly, 'and I love you, Jeanie. I'd be a fool to throw away everything we have for a stupid roll in the hay with her.'

'Yes, you would, because I'd go back to London,' Jeanie retorted with a sparkle in her eyes. 'And I'd take Winston – but I can't blame you for looking. Izzy is very sexy – and don't say you haven't noticed, because I know you have. Most men would notice... but the sensible ones don't get involved. Don't let her get her claws into you, Artie. I think she could be spiteful if provoked.'

'As if I would,' he said, stung because he'd come so close to it recently. Working with Izzy constantly, with her going out of her way to be provocative, well, he had been pushed to the limit: very tempted to show her his male dominance, but he knew where that would lead. 'Yes, she does fancy me; I won't deny she's made that clear – but I've ignored her. I'd send her packing, but then I'd get behind with the work – even further behind than I am now.'

'Why don't you ask around for a school-leaver?' Jeanie said. 'There must be a few youngsters wanting jobs; there always is after the summer term.'

'I have spoken to John Googe as a matter of fact,' Artie said. 'His boy, Jem, is looking to work on the land, so he's going to send him next week when he gets back from his holiday with his grandmother. He goes every year for three weeks in the summer since his mother died when he was eleven. Otherwise, it is just him, his dad, and his sister: Mary Googe married Phil Haddock last year, but she goes in and cleans and does some cooking for them.'

'Yes, I know Mary. We meet in the village sometimes,' Jeanie agreed. 'I like her. I think I've seen Jem Googe, too – a big, lanky lad with black hair and blue eyes?'

'His mother was Irish,' Artie said. 'Beautiful girl when she married Phil, but she got consumption after visiting her family in Ireland and was ill for a long time. She died of a fever and Phil misses her sorely, says the house isn't a home without her.'

'No, it wouldn't be,' Jeanie said thoughtfully, then: 'I've got some stewing beef for supper this evening. When will you be ready – and would you rather have a stew or a pie?'

'I think a pie,' Artie said. 'That would be nice, Jeanie. I've got some more jobs to do – say about six this evening?'

'Yes, that's fine,' Jeanie replied. 'Have you taken Izzy home, or did she cycle to work today?'

'She cycled,' Artie replied. He couldn't quite keep his expression bland. 'I imagine she has plans for the evening – she asked to go an hour early so I let her...'

It wasn't exactly the way it had happened. Izzy had come up to him, pushing herself against him so that he smelled her body perfume – a mixture of sweat and cheap scent. She'd looked up at him, pouting her red lips, hoping for some reaction, but he'd ignored her, though he'd been tempted to give her a smack across her rump – a very enticing one that she'd been wiggling in front of him for days – but knew that if he gave into the urge it could lead to much more and he might not be able to stop.

'You really are a stubborn devil,' Izzy had cried in exasperation that afternoon. 'I know you want it as much as I do – so if you're stupid enough to deny us both, I'll have to find me a real man to oblige.'

In the past, a statement like that would have been more than enough to make Artie react and show her how real a man he was, but he'd just stared at her, refusing to answer. He hoped fervently that Jem Googe agreed to work for him when he got back from his holidays. Izzy could return to the farm in Mepal and stay there – unless she went off in a tantrum. Artie almost wished she would, though he needed her if he was to get all the ploughing done come the autumn.

Izzy was good at that job and several others that involved the tractor; she'd been spinning his early potatoes the last couple of days, while he picked them up behind her; she'd done a few baskets, always bending just ahead of him, but she wasn't quick or supple enough for the work, and after a while she'd given up, complaining of backache. Artie had managed to pick up ten long rows that day, hours of hard slog that had robbed even him of the energy to oblige Izzy, should he have been willing to risk all for her sake. It meant the crop was half-lifted and, after the field was finished, he would tell her he didn't need her for a while; if he got his school-leaver, he wouldn't have her work on his own land again.

He felt a chill at the nape of his neck. Jeanie had clearly picked up on his unease recently and noticed far more than he'd realised. She wasn't the sort to rant at him and make a scene, but she'd made her feelings clear in her own way. Artie knew it had been a subtle warning, done with a laugh, but meant just the same. Knowing he couldn't afford to lose Jeanie and his son, Artie told himself to stop being a fool. He was a man and most men would be disturbed by Izzy's obvious behaviour, but only single men were at liberty to take advantage of her lascivious invitations.

Jeanie stood up to put Winston in his playpen. Going to her, he took her in his arms and kissed her fiercely. 'I love you, Jeanie Talbot,' he told her. 'I love only you – and don't you forget it.'

'I know,' she said. 'I love you, too, Artie – now get off and finish your jobs so we can have dinner – and maybe an early night.'

'Wicked wench!' Artie said teasingly, but he saw the sparkle was back in her eyes. She'd been so tired when she'd tried to keep working beside him. Now that she had less to do, her energy was higher and her eyes told him that she was still his Jeanie, still as loving and lovable as she'd always been. Artie smiled inwardly. For a while he'd thought she'd gone, lost in the humdrum of marriage and work, and it had added to his restlessness. Now she was back, thank goodness! Now, he wouldn't feel so tempted to stray...

* * *

Jeanie sighed as Artie went back to work after his break. She'd noticed Izzy flaunting herself in front of him a few times and, knowing that Artie was susceptible to women who flirted with him, she'd worried a little. Marriages could be strong but they could also break apart. She didn't believe that her husband would hurt her intentionally, but when you worked closely with someone like Izzy, the temptation was there; her red lips, blonde hair and stun-

ning figure, guaranteed to have most men turning to watch her walk down the
street.

Jeanie busied herself with preparing their meal. She'd meant it when she'd
told Artie she would go back to her parents in London if he strayed. He wouldn't
be the first or the last, but he was hers and Jeanie wouldn't stand for it! It would
break her heart, but she wasn't like Josie Willis, whose husband was always
having affairs; Josie took him back and forgave him, again and again, but Jeanie
wouldn't. She couldn't! It would break her heart, but if Artie hurt her that way
she would leave him. She could put up with his moods and the times he forgot
his promises to take her somewhere or do something she needed, but infidelity
was out.

Jeanie thought that Izzy was one of those women for whom physical adven-
tures were a burning need – insatiable; she thought that was the word for it.
She'd known a girl like that at upper school. Even at sixteen, Sadie had been
after anything in trousers. At first, Jeanie had found it amusing that Izzy was so
evidently trying to flirt with her husband, because Jeanie knew that Artie was a
very attractive man, and she was confident of his love. However, she'd noticed
his unease whenever he worked with Izzy and realised that he was attracted to
her, despite his love for her, Jeanie. Hopefully, her laughing admonishments
would squash any thoughts he might have had of Izzy. Otherwise she might
have to confront the girl herself, but she would much prefer that Artie gave the
girl her marching orders.

21

'You go and rest, love,' Tom said to Lizzie that evening after she'd cooked them a meal of sausage meat mixed with onions, floured, rolled into balls, and fried. She'd made light and fluffy, really crispy chips with the sausage balls, and they'd had their own peas, picked fresh from their garden. Now she looked tired. 'You should cut down your working hours, Lizzie. If you need another girl, advertise for an apprentice or something.'

'I'm all right, Tom,' Lizzie replied with a smile that lit her eyes. 'I will rest after we've washed up – and I shall take on someone new, but I need another qualified stylist. I thought my improver might be ready to take over, but she isn't.'

'I suppose it takes time to learn,' Tom agreed, smiling as she took up the tea towel and wiped the dishes he'd washed. 'You must get someone, though, Lizzie.'

'Yes, I shall,' she promised. 'Have you finished for the day?'

'Yes – apart from taking a look at that heifer. She is close to her time and sometimes they have difficulty with their first calf, so I'll just look in on her later this evening.'

Lizzie nodded. 'There is no one to do that now that Jeanie and Artie have moved into their own home. I'm not sure that Pam would know what to do if one of the cows was in difficulty.'

'I've told her to ring the vet, but Olive said she would help. That girl would make a good farmer's wife – she's worth six of the other one.'

'You don't approve of Izzy?' Lizzie asked with a lift of her eyebrow.

'I think her lazy and sly,' Tom said. 'She gave me the come-on, once. I told her to behave herself and get on with her work. If looks could kill, I'd have been dead at her feet.'

'I think she is lonely.' Lizzie was thoughtful. 'I know she is a flirt, but she told me she doesn't have a family – or none that care about her. She probably just wants a man of her own – someone to love her.'

'Well, she should go after a single man then,' Tom said brusquely. 'Not throw herself at men with wives and a family.'

'Well, she wouldn't get anywhere with you.'

'I think she knows that now, but she is more interested in Artie...'

'He wouldn't!' Lizzie said, looking at Tom in alarm. 'Artie is married with a son and another child on the way...'

'I've seen his face when she flaunts herself,' Tom replied. 'I hope he wouldn't be such a fool, but there is no point in my saying anything. He'd just get in a huff and tell me to keep my nose out.'

'Well, he is an idiot then, because Jeanie wouldn't stand for it.'

'No, she wouldn't and I don't blame her,' Tom said and then smiled as she yawned. 'I'll take a look at the heifer now and we'll have an early night, shall we?'

'Yes, please,' Lizzie said and dried her hands on a towel and then put her arms about him. 'I can't believe how quickly these past weeks have gone – only just over another two weeks and you have to go back, Tom.'

'I know. I wish I didn't have to,' he said and kissed her. 'I want to be here with you, especially now.' He placed his hand on the curve of her stomach. The bump was barely there yet, but his child was growing and Tom longed to be able to stay to look after his wife – and the farm. There were always small jobs that needed doing, and although Olive did her best, she couldn't manage them all. 'If things deteriorate here, you must let me know,' Tom said and stroked Lizzie's cheek. 'With Artie away on his own land half the time, it leaves Mum short-handed. I think she ought to try for a sensible youth she can trust.'

'Why don't you ask around?' Lizzie suggested. 'If Izzy isn't to be trusted, she could leave just like that and I know Olive couldn't manage on her own.'

'Land girls aren't as plentiful as they were,' Tom said. 'Some of the early volunteers got married, others became fed up with the hours and changed to one of the women's services. So a youth would be a good idea. We'll need him in future, even when I get back. Any ideas?'

'Jack Fitch's son was asking if we needed any help,' Lizzie replied. 'I was talking to his mother in the butcher's shop the other day and he came in to find her. Said he'd been after a job on the railway, but they turned him down because he was only fourteen.'

'Bit young – but if he is willing...' Tom smiled at her. 'I will go and see him in the morning, ask if he wants to work for us.'

Lizzie nodded. 'I'm just going to take a look at Arthur. He was grizzling a bit before I put him to bed.'

Tom gave her a smile of approval. 'I'll walk up to the farm, have a look at that heifer. Then I'll pop into Mum and tell her I'm going to get a lad from school to help out – and then I'll join you.'

* * *

Pam was pleased to see her eldest son. His face looked healthy and tanned from his work on the farm and some of the harsh expression he'd been wearing had melted away as he'd relaxed into his old ways. She showed him the newspaper she'd just been reading.

'Did you see this? They are evacuating the children from London again – this new weapon of Hitler's is worse than during the Blitz, because you can't hear it coming – just a buzzing sound and then it's too late. It says here we've been trying to bomb the source factory from the air for a while, but so far it hasn't stopped the production.'

'We'll get it in the end,' Tom told her. 'One of these days you'll read that our men who do special missions have got to it – or them – and destroyed the menace.'

'Is that what you've been doing, Tom?' she asked, looking at him intently. Then, quickly, 'No, don't tell me. I know you can't...' She smiled. 'How is Lizzie?'

'She is having an early night and I shall, too. I hope she will take someone new on at the salon soon, and cut her hours back.'

'Yes, she should,' Pam agreed. 'Everything else, all right?'

'The heifer seems fine,' Tom told her. 'With luck, she'd drop her calf tomorrow and I'll be up early to look after her. If she should make a lot of noise during the night, give me a ring and wake me.'

Pam nodded her thanks. 'It has been good having you here, Tom. We shall miss you when you return to your base.'

'I was talking to Lizzie about it. I'm going to get you a lad to help out – a local lad who won't mind if he has to stay up all night when a cow is birthing.'

'We were lucky when Arthur was alive. He was so good with the stock.' Pam hesitated. 'With Artie up in the Sutton fen now... Well, it is too much for Olive on her own. It makes me wonder if I shouldn't give up the cows, Tom.' She sighed. 'The girls might find it easier if we just had arable crops...'

'Cows have always been a big part of your income,' Tom said. 'I'm not sure the farm would pay enough without them.'

'Perhaps I should sell them – and find myself a little job...'

'No, you can't do that, Mum,' Tom told her. 'Dad wouldn't like it. Artie ought to be looking after them – but... I shall speak to my commanding officer again. I might get permission to return to the farm because I am needed if I applied for it.'

Pam sighed. 'I don't want you to do anything that might spoil your record or get you into trouble. Perhaps with a school-leaver we can manage – after all, if a cow – or the sow, now we've got breeding pigs again – is in trouble birthing, I can telephone the vet myself.'

'I know – but it's a man's job,' Tom said firmly. 'Artie could pop down last thing at night after I go back. I'll have a word with him.'

'It is a long way to come...' Pam objected. 'It's my own fault, Tom. If I hadn't given him the pig land, he wouldn't have bought all that land in Sutton fen.'

'You didn't know it was worth that sort of money,' Tom told her. 'I think Dad knew that Artie would go to live in Sutton once he got his own land, that is why he changed his will. He hoped it would keep him here longer, at least until the war is over and I can get back.'

'I think Artie will give up bothering with our land then, Tom,' Pam said. 'He'll look after your dad's land in the fen – that will be his one day, but I doubt he'll come to Mepal more than he has to.'

'Just as well then, if I get a lad now,' Tom replied. 'He will be able to take over Artie's work one day. Olive will be in charge of the cows when I go back, Mum. I think we should make that official. She knows most of it and with a lad to help her, I think she will manage. Jack Fitch can learn to drive the tractor and help with the ploughing. If he comes straight away, I'll show him the ropes – but Artie will still have to do his share until I'm home for good.'

'He is doing his best – he just has too much to do.' Pam would always defend her children.

'His own fault,' Tom grimaced. 'Try not to worry – and don't even think about getting a job.' Tom gave her a hug. 'I know it gets on top of you, Mum.'

'I always thought your dad would be here until you boys took over – but with you in the Army, Artie more interested in his own land, and John in that place...' She sighed. 'It wouldn't have happened if your dad were alive...'

'I know, Mum.' Tom looked at her sadly. 'You've got George. Don't forget that he leaves school in another year. He's learning fast. He isn't up to helping with the birthing of a cow if it goes wrong, not yet, but he can run and fetch some-one. I'll speak to Ernie Faux. He's got cattle and his lad is sixteen – they would come if it was an emergency.'

'Do you think they might?' Pam looked relieved. 'Ernie is all right – and I know his wife Lou well enough – she used to work in Sutton, bring the bread round when she was younger... I had bread and cakes delivered once upon a time – until I learned to make them myself.' A little laugh escaped her. 'I was very young then and not as good a cook as I am now. No, really,' she said as Tom looked disbelieving.

'I'll believe you.' He kissed her cheek. 'I'll see you in the morning,' Tom promised. 'Don't worry too much. It's just the heifer's first time – mostly it goes like clockwork...'

Pam nodded, then, 'Oh, I had a letter back from John today. I am going to visit him with Jonny next week.'

'I know; I spoke to him on the phone earlier,' Tom replied with a warm smile. 'He says he is feeling better at last.'

'You spoke to him on the phone?' Pam looked surprised. 'I didn't know that was allowed.'

'I rang and asked for Sister Jane and she said she would fetch him. We spoke for several minutes. She said we could ring him now and then, Mum. Didn't you realise that?'

Pam shook her head. 'I thought they would be too busy to take calls from patients' families – unless it was an emergency.'

'Well, I dare say that might be the case in most hospitals, but Sister Jane seems different, friendly – and she seems to like John.'

'Yes, she does,' Pam said with a little smile. 'Well, I will ask her when I am there, because if I could talk to him, once in a while it would be lovely.'

22

John stood back and looked at the clay model he'd been working on for the past few days. When he'd decided to try the art room, he'd had it in mind to paint pictures, but he'd soon discovered that he had no real talent for it. He'd wanted to paint a picture of Sister Jane as an angel, but it had been a failure. John had captured her likeness, but there was no real life to the picture; it just looked flat and expressionless. He'd been staring at it in disappointment when one of the teachers came in. Mrs White was an art teacher at the local school, and an artist in her own right, but gave up some of her free time to work with the patients in the convalescent home. She'd looked at the picture, nodding.

'I can see it is Sister Jane, but it needs more depth,' she'd said after a few moments. For a moment, she'd studied his work in thoughtful silence. 'Have you ever painted before?'

John had explained about his pre-war work, giving a rueful shrug as he'd looked at his painting. 'I thought my work as a plasterer artistic, but the plaster had more substance – I can't get the same feel with a paintbrush.'

'Why don't you try modelling with clay?' Mrs White had suggested. 'You might find that more to your liking.' She'd given him an encouraging smile. 'Don't give up – just try something different. Start with an animal of some kind and then, when you get the feel of it, go for a bust, if that's what you'd like to do.'

'I suppose I could try,' John had replied with a shrug. He hadn't been enthusiastic after his failure with the painting, but after a couple of days thinking about it, he'd come back to the room and found himself some clay. His first effort had been a model of a cat. It had been amusing, the way he'd given it attitude, tail curled, face scowling, whiskers proud.

John had discovered the models came to life under his fingers, and he'd made several that first morning, all animals of various kinds. It actually helped his hands, making them more mobile, and he'd enjoyed modelling them and found himself laughing as the ideas came tumbling into his head. When the clay had dried out a few days later, he'd painted them and fired them in a small kiln, and then glazed them. All of the figurines had an attitude, making them appear like caricatures, but very definitely what they were supposed to be – cats, dogs, and a cow that he'd painted black and white. When he'd amassed several of the miniature animals, he decided to try something more challenging.

He'd been working on the model of Jane for some days now, and it was gradually taking shape. His fingers smoothed and pressed, forming the shapes he wanted, and he used a special palate knife to cut the sharper edges, flattening and moulding with his fingers. The beauty of the clay was that he could correct his mistakes, adding clay when he'd made lips too thin, shaping a delicate nose, smoothing it with his fingers. John had learned to make a head of hair by gradually adding smaller thin strips, coaxing them into waves that ruffled back from a smooth forehead, wide-set eyes, nose and soft, smiling lips.

It was finished. John looked at the model of the woman who had saved not only his life but his sanity and smiled in pleasure. Jane with her nurse's cap. He still had to fire and paint it, but there was no doubt it was her, and he was pleased with his efforts.

'You have a visitor, John,' a voice said behind him and he turned to see his mother, son and one of the younger nurses.

'Daddy...' Jonny cried and came rushing at him. John bent and picked him up, swinging him round, making him chuckle with glee. 'We come see you...'

'Yes, that's good,' John said and tickled him, glancing at Pam. 'Hello, Mum, how are you?'

She walked towards him, setting down her basket as she looked at what he'd been doing, his hands smeared with drying clay. 'Did you make this?' she asked, looking at the bust that was so clearly Sister Jane. 'That is good, John. Really good.' Her gaze strayed to the collection of small animals. 'And these?'

'Yes, they were my first efforts,' John told her with a smile. 'I tried painting a portrait, but it wasn't good enough for me – someone suggested clay, so I had a go. I enjoy it... gives me something to think about.'

'I love the cat,' Pam said, picking it up.

'Me see...' Jonny clamoured and John lifted him so that he could see the figurines on the shelf where he'd placed them. 'Can I have this one please?' Jonny reached for a model of a rabbit; it was a rabbit but dressed in clothes and smoking a pipe. 'It's funny...' Jonny chuckled as his fingers closed around it. 'And that one...' He spotted a dog standing on its hind legs with a walking stick in one paw and a top hat in the other. 'I like these, Daddy...'

John smiled and gave him the figurines he'd pointed out and set him down. Jonny sat on the floor and played with his new toys, chuckling to himself.

'He will probably break them,' Pam warned, but John gave a slight shake of his head.

'It doesn't matter. I just made them for fun. If he wants them, he can have them...'

Pam had been examining the various animals, which had started off simply but become more and more intriguing as he'd found his way. 'I think these might sell,' she told him. 'Were they made in a mould?'

'No, I made them individually,' he said. 'I suppose they could be made in a mould with a different kind of clay – but I like making them this way.'

'I was thinking how beautiful these miniature ones would look done in silver,' Pam said. 'I suppose that would be very expensive...'

'Probably,' John agreed and washed his hands at the little sink provided for those working in the art room.

His mother was looking round the large room. At the back of the house, it had once been an orangery and let in lots of light from the long windows that made up most of one wall. It had been fitted with shelves on two walls, and there was a small kiln, sink, easels and benches. There were woodworking tools, as well as a pottery wheel.

'This is a wonderful idea,' she observed. 'You can make all sorts of things here.'

John nodded. 'One of the chaps makes wooden rocking horses and paints them. It takes him a long time, but they're beautiful when finished. He just sold the last one. He is going to make me one for Jonny.'

'He will enjoy that,' Pam replied, looking at Jonny, who was still intrigued with his small models. 'Perhaps you could sell your models, John.'

'I suppose I might,' John agreed. 'Not for much – and hardly worth the effort; they take a while to do. I just did them for fun.'

'But if you made moulds for them, it might work...' Pam gave a little shrug.

John just smiled. His mother didn't understand; it was the actual feel of the clay in his hands that inspired him. His figurines were amusing, but John couldn't see them earning him a fortune. He found them pleasurable to make but knew that it could only be a hobby. What he could do to make a living for himself and his son was still not clear, though his desire to work had been nurtured by his modelling.

'Shall we go in the garden?' he asked. 'I've got some weeding to do and we can talk in the sunshine. I've asked if we can all have lunch in the garden...'

'That is a lovely idea,' Pam replied with a smile. 'I've brought you a seed cake, John. You used to enjoy them.'

'Still do,' he told her and smiled. 'It is nice to see you and Jonny. Thank you for coming and bringing him, Mum...'

'It is a pleasure,' Pam said. 'Shall I take him, or will you?'

'Hold my hand,' John instructed and his son placed his small one in John's, smiling up at him. He'd kept hold of the figurines in his other hand, and for the moment they remained remarkably intact.

* * *

After working in the garden, Jonny by his side, valiantly pulling up small weeds beside him, John rinsed his hands at an outside tap and they all sat at a wooden garden table to eat their lunch. It was a plate of salad sandwiches, made tastier by salt, pepper and vinegar, also scones with jam and a small topping of cream, with a bowl of fresh raspberries to follow.

'We grow them here as well as the salads,' John told Pam. 'I do quite a bit of it now. I like gardening.' He smiled ruefully. 'I have to pace myself – just an hour or so, as I did today, but after a rest I can do some more. It is getting easier.'

'I am glad to hear that,' Pam said. 'Have you thought of what you will do in the future, John? You do know there is always a home for you with me – or in the house your father intended for you.'

'I couldn't live at home,' John said with a finality that made her frown. 'It's not that I don't care about you, Mum, and the girls and Tom – but there are too many memories. I shall stay here until I can work and support myself. I'll do the farm accounts, but...'

'What about Jonny?' she asked, watching his face. John's eyes followed his son as he ran around the lawn, pretending to be an aeroplane.

'I hope to have him with me one day in the not-too-distant future,' John said and saw the flash of hurt in her face. 'I know, Mum. I know how much you love him and I'm grateful for all you've done. More grateful than I can say – but he is my son and Faith's and I think it's what she wants.'

'You couldn't have him and stay here surely?' she asked and he could see that his words were giving her pain, but they had to be said.

'I've been looking about for something – or at least, I've looked in the papers and Sister Jane told me about a small cottage just a couple of miles away – nearer Hastings. It sounds just right, two bedrooms, bathroom, a sitting room, kitchen and dining room. There is a school quite near too – I could take Jonny to school and fetch him.' He sighed. 'I'm just looking for a job I can do for a few hours each day, ideally at home...'

'That's easy enough,' his mother said. 'It might involve you studying and taking some exams – but you were always good at maths, John. The only one of the family who was – except Susan and she is good at all subjects. If you can do our accounts, then you can do other people's too. Should you qualify as an accountant, then you could run your own business from your home.'

John stared at her. At school he'd been told he should stay on and take higher exams because he had a good brain and he'd passed his exams for his job as a navigator for the RAF with ease, then he'd gone on to get his pilot's licence. John wasn't fit enough to fly now, but his brain was still as active. He'd left school to do a manual job, because he hadn't wanted to work in an office all day; the satisfaction he'd gained from using his hands far more enticing, and he'd enjoyed his work as a plasterer – but his mother was right. If he tried, he could train to be an accountant. He found maths came easily to him. Of course there was far more to being an accountant, because he would need to know all the laws concerning taxes and exemptions – but if he set his mind to it, he knew he could do it. Had he been physically fit, he would have preferred gardening, being in the open air – but he could still work in his own garden, or help out here at the convalescent home.

'Yes, I could do that, Mum,' he said, looking at her in a kind of wonder. 'I hadn't considered it – but it is a job I could manage, and I think I must look for that kind of work. I will find out what I need to do...' He smiled at her in his old way. 'Thank you for giving me the idea – it will mean a great deal to me.'

Pam raised her head and met his eyes. 'Have you considered marrying again, John? I know you've been unlucky – twice – and you may feel you could never love again, but Jonny needs a mother. With the best will in the world, you can't do everything he requires and hold down a responsible job. You will need help – either a wife or someone to care for the child part of the time. It will be easier when he starts school, but he will still need a woman sometimes.'

John's eyes dropped, his face reflecting his reaction. 'You can't think I would inflict this on any young woman,' he said, lightly touching his scars. 'How can I expect any woman to be my wife? I dare say I can pay someone to come in for a few hours when I need them.'

'Yes, you could do that,' his mother agreed, 'but Jonny needs love. He's used to being fussed over and petted, John. I think he might be unhappy...'

'You think he would be unhappy living with me?' John stared at her.

'I think you should consider marrying,' she said. 'If not for your own sake, for Jonny's. I know you have scars, my son, but – after a while you get used to them and don't really notice that much. Perhaps a young woman might feel the same given time. Think about it, John. Don't shut the idea out completely, my love.' She smiled at him tenderly. 'Love is a funny thing; it doesn't always happen where you think – and sometimes it comes unbidden when you don't.'

'That is a very deep thought, Mum,' John chuckled, because he was remembering her love as a youngster, when she had been so wise and comforting to a sensitive lad. 'I know that you love me. You are my mother – but a wife is different. There has to be some kind of spark, don't you think? Otherwise, it is a rotten life for her – just a sterile business arrangement. I hoped Lucy would be a mother to Jonny, but I did feel a kind of love for her, not the way I did towards Faith – but a physical attraction, and she for me.'

'I know – but I think if you let yourself open to love, you might find it nearer than you imagine,' Pam told him. 'In fact, I believe you already feel it but you either won't let yourself or you haven't realised...'

'What do you mean?' John asked, but Pam just shook her head and smiled.

'Look, your Sister Jane is on her way.' She indicated the nurse walking towards them. Her cap had been removed and she'd let her softly waving hair free, the breeze lifting it as she walked. 'I will say hello to her and then I'll have to leave, John.'

'Why? You can stay a bit longer if you wish...'

'I was up at the crack of dawn to be here early,' Pam replied and smothered a yawn. 'Jonny needs a sleep, too. I will come back this evening for an hour or so – or in the morning, before I catch my train, whichever suits you.'

'Come in the morning,' John told her. He reached for his son, swinging him up into his arms. 'Daddy is going to work hard and then you can come and live with me. Would you like that, Jonny?'

'Soon?' Jonny asked and clung to his neck. 'Jonny live with you soon?'

'Yes, I hope so. I just need to get my own home and then a job...'

Sister Jane came up to them, smiling. She spoke to Pam first and John watched them laughing together. They seemed to get on well – better than his mother and Lucy had got on.

Sister Jane turned to him, her eyes on Jonny, still in his arms. 'How are you?' she asked the child. 'I saw you helping your daddy with the weeding. You are a big boy now...'

'I am a big boy; I'm four now,' Jonny said and looked at her hopefully. 'Janey got sweets?'

'Please,' Pam reminded him.

'Please...' Jonny echoed and Sister Jane took a packet of fruit gums from her pocket and offered him one, which he took and popped into his mouth, chewing with gusto.

John watched them, seeing the light in Sister Jane's eyes as she looked at his son, her face softly curving in affection – and then she turned to face him and he felt something odd happen. Her smile seemed to dazzle him with its warmth and love and for the first time he saw her not just as his guardian angel but as a warm and beautiful woman. For a moment, he felt as if he couldn't breathe as his heart seemed to stop and then raced on.

Was it possible? John felt confused and uncertain. He'd felt gratitude and affection for this woman who had coerced him back to living, when he'd hovered between the murky blackness of death and life. Surely, he was imagining that look in her eyes? As he continued to gaze at her, feeling stunned, Sister Jane flushed and turned away, the moment lost as she exchanged pleasantries with his mother.

John looked at his mother – was this the source of her hints? She gave a small, almost imperceptible nod and he felt laughter bubble inside. Trust his mother to know before he did!

'Well, I should go,' Pam said. 'I need a little nap and so does Jonny. I shall visit in the morning before we catch our train, John. Sister Jane, it was nice to see you again – and thank you for taking such good care of my son. I hope he understands how much you've done for him.'

'We help all those we can,' Sister Jane said, but as she smiled, there was something very different in her eyes.

'I'll write to you, Mum, as soon as I've made arrangements...'

'Yes, you do that,' Pam replied and left them.

'You are planning to leave us?' Sister Jane said, looking at John as his mother walked away towards the long drive that led to a pair of imposing entrance gates.

'I think I'll take a look at that cottage you told me about,' John replied, watching his mother walk away. 'I want to have Jonny. I've told Mum.'

'You had to,' Sister Jane said, her voice softening. Jonny had turned round to look at them and was pulling at his grandmother's hand. 'It will be hard for her to accept, John, but he wants his daddy.'

'Yes, it will be hard for Mum, but I made up my mind and now it is done.' He turned to smile at her. 'Actually, she showed me the way. I've been wondering what I could do to earn a living so that I could look after my son – and she suggested I train as an accountant. It will take me a while, but as soon as I can find out what I need to do, I'll have him – and in the meantime I'll start making that cottage a home.'

'Yes, you must,' Sister Jane replied. 'You've been receiving some of your pay, I think – and once they finally discharge you, which I'm surprised they haven't already, you should get a pension. You won't be able to work full-time, John. Not yet, perhaps not ever, even in an office.'

'I know – but I can start my own business once I am trained and work at home,' John told her, a look of determination on his face. 'I had some small savings before the war – and my mother says there is a house in Sutton that my father intended for me. It can be sold to help me through until I build up a clientele.'

'Is it what you want to do?' she asked, her eyes meeting his.

'Not particularly,' John replied honestly. 'I would have hated it once, Jane, but now – well, I have to do something, and I know I can do it if I try. I've always been good with maths.'

'There's a lot more to accounting than adding up?' she said, teasing him now.

John laughed. 'I know I am in for some hard studying, but it is the answer. I feel it in my heart.'

'Good,' she said. 'If you feel that way, you will make a success of it, John – and when your son comes to you, you will find happiness...'

'Yes, I think perhaps I shall,' John said and took a step towards her. 'Jane, this may sound—'

He got no further because there was a shout from behind them and a nurse came running towards them. 'Sister Jane... Sister Jane... you are needed. One of the patients has had a relapse...'

Sister Jane sighed and put out a hand to touch John's. 'I'm glad you've reached a decision, my dear,' she said, then turned and walked swiftly back to the home.

John watched her go, then swore softly under his breath. His mother was a very clever woman, he thought and a little smile touched his mouth. She had seen something John hadn't and her hints had surprised him – yet, as Sister Jane had talked to his son, he'd seen the love in her face and it had still been there when she looked at him.

Of course he loved her! How could he not after all the hours she'd spent with him, nursing him, willing him, bullying him back to life? He'd known that he loved her for months, but it hadn't occurred to him that it could be more than that of an adoring patient for the nurse who had done so much for him. John had seen her as an angel, but the bust he'd made of her had shown his love for her, because he'd made her appear young and beautiful. Jane was attractive and lovely, but older than he'd made her look and there were lines of worry and strain about her eyes. He hadn't really thought of that when he was working on the model, just that she was warm and loving and wonderful. John couldn't imagine why she felt love for him and his son, but this afternoon it had shone through – and he was so very grateful.

John knew he couldn't ask Jane to marry him for a while. He couldn't even provide for himself and his son as he would want – not yet – but he would. Accounting would give him no chance to show the skill and artistry that both his plastering and his modelling had, but it would earn him a damned good living once he got the business up and running – and there was enough of his father in him to make him smile at that thought.

Suddenly, the future held hope. John had believed that his life as a man who could love and be loved was over, but now he knew that, as unlikely as it seemed, he could find love again. He could live a life that was almost normal. He could be happy again.

It was an aim to work for, because once he was trained, he would have something to offer. Sister Jane might take him as he was, with nothing, because she was such a lovely person and if she loved him it wouldn't matter to her, but John was too proud and too caring to let her. He would tell her of his love when the opportunity came, but they couldn't marry until he was able to bring home a wage – and that he would do. He would do it because he needed to and wanted to and because he was loved.

Suddenly, John felt as if he was surrounded in warmth and love, and he felt the touch of softness on his cheek like a kiss and he knew – he knew it was Faith. She was telling him it was right, telling him it was what she'd been trying to tell him for a long time now.

'You don't mind, my love,' he said to the silence of a warm summer afternoon, and he knew in his heart that she didn't mind, that she was happy for him. 'Thank you,' he whispered and his cheeks were wet with tears. Faith was saying goodbye, bidding him to let her go, and at last... at last he could feel the hurt and grief of her death softening to a blur in the back of his mind. He would never forget, but at last the tearing pain and guilt had gone.

Smiling, John turned towards the home. He had things to do. In the library he would find books and leaflets that would tell him what he needed to know – and what help he could get as he retrained. His head up, he started to whistle, a smile in his eyes. Life could still be good...

23

Back home again, Pam slipped into the routine of her daily life. She knew that it probably wouldn't be long before John sent for his son. It would be difficult to give Jonny up, but she accepted that it was right. She'd seen that Jane loved the child, perhaps because he was John's, but also because she had a maternal instinct – something Pam had feared Lucy lacked. All that had shown in her face and Pam's suspicion that she loved John had been proved right as she looked at him, her feelings all too plain to his mother. Pam only hoped that he had the good sense to see it for himself. She'd given him a few hints and when two people loved it was bound to come through in the end.

Sighing, she took her emotion out on the pastry she was pounding. Her love for Jonny was deep enough for her to give him up, because he wanted his father so badly. He'd cried after they'd left the home the next day, only stopping when Pam told him that as soon as his daddy was well enough, he would be going to live with him. Jonny had looked at her then, hiccupped and wiped his hand over his eyes.

'Will you come too?' he'd asked.

'No, I can't come to live with you, Jonny – but you will have Daddy then and perhaps... you might have Janey, too.'

'Janey?' Jonny had looked at her, eyes bright. 'I like Janey.'

'Yes, I know you do,' Pam had said. 'I expect you might have a brother or sister one day. It will be exciting and new – and you can come for holidays at the farm when you're older, and I'll visit you, love.'

Jonny had sucked his thumb, looking at her. 'When? When can I live with Daddy?' he'd asked, his tears gone.

'Soon – when your daddy is better. He is much better than he was. It might be quite soon – yes, quite soon,' Pam had told him.

Now, as she cut and shaped her pastry, Pam's thoughts were busy with the future. She would telephone her husband's solicitor and arrange for the house in Sutton to be sold. It was a large, substantial house and ought to make nearly a thousand pounds. She would ask that for it and see what happened. In the meantime, she had the money Tom had found in the attic – and some other things she might sell. Pam would give John as much as she could manage to help him get started. She would ask Tom to fetch the silver down for her and take it into Cambridge to see what it might fetch.

* * *

When Tom came to visit Pam that evening, he nodded as he listened to her plans. 'Yes, I can do that for you, Mum. I'll go up in the morning and see what I can find – there were a lot of boxes up there, so there might be other stuff that would fetch more.'

'I doubt if there are any old masters,' Pam said, laughing. 'Your dad would have bought smalls, things he understood and thought would always sell. A lot of that stuff was probably left to him, but he may have bought other things – I'd like to give John at least a thousand pounds. The house might fetch that – but if we can raise a bit extra from the silver it will help him.'

'Will you miss the rent from the house, Mum?' Tom asked, frowning. 'I've got a bit saved – you could give that to John and pay me back when the farm is in profit again.'

'No, you keep your money,' she said quickly. 'You have plans for after the war, I know. The rent won't make much difference, Tom. I have a bit of cash by me as you know – and now you've restocked with calves and pigs, I'll have an income again.'

'Yes, you should do well with those pigs,' Tom replied. 'And the cattle always bring in extra at Christmas – but we've some decent wheat and potato crops, too. I think it can't be long before the war is over now, Mum. All the headlines point that way…'

'Yes, it does seem hopeful,' she said, 'but those dreadful V1 and V2 rocket things are still killing people, and fierce fighting is still happening over in France and elsewhere.'

'Hopefully, the factories will be destroyed soon,' Tom told her, because he knew that every effort was being made to destroy the sources of Hitler's terrifying new weapon. He smiled. 'I'll see you in the morning, Mum. I'll come early, because I'm starting to cut the wheat in the fen tomorrow – but I can't start that until mid-morning, so I'll be here early to get what you need…'

'Thank you,' she said and gave him a hug. 'I don't know what I'd do without you, love. Come home for good soon.'

'As soon as I can,' he promised. 'I'll get back now, because I am taking Lizzie to the pictures. Susan and her friend are going to babysit for us…'

'Yes, that's right,' Pam replied. 'She is off on her holiday next week. I hope I am doing right, letting her and Sally take George and Angela off with just them… Sally is a nice girl and seems sensible but—'

Tom laughed. 'They are both young women, Mum. I don't think you need worry about your chicks.'

'No, I suppose I do fuss,' Pam admitted. 'Well, off you get, love, and enjoy yourselves.'

* * *

Tom brought down the box of silver the next day. There was a tea and coffee set, and several items of virtue, which were small silver trinkets, like miniature animals, scent bottles, fobs for watch chains, some set with stones, a tiny silver and gold tea set, and a lot of spoons.

'It looks old to me,' Tom said as he examined some of the pieces. 'I think that is a King George head – look at the marks, Mum. I'm not sure what George, but they aren't modern, not by a long way.'

'No, they look rather nice, especially the picture-back spoons, and those have enamelling on them…' She'd opened a box of tea spoons with brightly coloured handles. 'This lot should be worth a few pounds, don't you think?'

'Perhaps a hundred or two,' Tom agreed. 'Where will you sell them – in Ely or Cambridge? I think there are a few antique shops there that might buy them.'

'I seem to remember that your dad sold something of his aunt's in a sale room,' Pam replied thoughtfully. 'He was very pleased with the results. I might take the smaller pieces to that big sale room in Cambridge – what was it called now? It began with a C, I know.'

'I'll find out,' Tom said. 'You have to pay commission on what they sell, Mum. You don't think a dealer might be better?'

'I don't know,' Pam said honestly. 'If the dealer was honest, yes, that would save the commission. I'll try some of those little animals first – see what they make.'

'What do you want me to do with all this?' Tom asked, indicating the silver tea and coffee set.

'I'll pack it back in the box and take it to my bedroom,' Pam told him. 'You get off, Tom. I know you've work to do... and thank you.'

Tom left her to it and Pam packed the items back into the box and carried it up to her room, putting it in her wardrobe out of the way. She didn't know much about silverware, other than that it was expensive to buy new and scarce these days, like everything else. This was all old, but she didn't know whether it was valuable or not. Did people want this old stuff? Perhaps they would melt it all down, which was a shame – but Pam didn't need it and John was going to need some money by him if he wanted to learn a new trade and live independently.

Sighing, she wished she'd known the pig land could be worth a lot of money before she handed it over to Artie. It would have been much fairer if she'd sold it and divided it amongst her family. At least she could give John the money for his house – or the house that would have been his had Arthur not changed his will.

'I know it's what you would do if you were still here,' Pam said to the empty room. 'Yes, I should have consulted Tom before giving that land to Artie. I know it now, but it is too late – and Artie did deserve something, but not all that.' She shook her head. At least the farmhouse and yard would fetch a good bit when she was gone and that would be shared amongst them all; the land being divided between Tom and Artie. The girls had their trust funds, which were equal to John's house. But there was no getting over it, Artie had been given too much. A little thought entered her mind that her son should have shared the money with her when he discovered how much it was worth and that disappointed her in him a little. There was nothing she could do about it now. Artie was settled and at least he was happy – too busy for his own good, but that had been his choice.

She could help John a little and Susan already had the money from her trust fund, but she'd taken her mother's advice and invested it straight back in an account that paid her a modest interest. It was pocket money while she was at college and the money would be there if and when Susan needed it. Angela would have hers when she was eighteen, and, one day Tom would have the fields next to the home farm – but that left George, and Pam had become fond of him since he came to live with her. She had intended to leave her house in Chatteris to the girls, but somehow she would have to find a bit for George.

Returning to the kitchen, Pam arrived in time to see Izzy hurriedly replace her purse on the mantlepiece. The girl turned to look at her, her face hot with embarrassment.

'What were you doing as I came in?' Pam asked her, her suspicions aroused as she remembered that the missing ten shillings when Susan went shopping wasn't the only time there had been less in her purse than she'd thought.

'Nothing...' Izzy stared at her defiantly. 'I didn't take anything...'

'No, because I came too soon, didn't I?' Pam said calmly. 'You have in the past, though, Izzy. I knew small amounts of money were missing, but I thought someone might have borrowed a few shillings or paid the butcher when he delivered – but he hadn't been paid, so I knew that someone had taken money. How long have you been doing it, Izzy?'

Caught out, Izzy's eyes snapped with sudden temper. 'I've only borrowed a bit now and then when I was short. I was going to pay you back...'

'Why didn't you just ask me?' Pam said still in her gentle calm way. 'I would have lent you some money if I could.'

'If?' Izzy scoffed. 'You've got plenty locked away in that desk of yours. Five hundred quid... you found in the attic...'

'What makes you think that, Izzy?' Pam asked, because only she and Tom knew about that money and he wouldn't have told this girl. 'And if I have got a few pounds, don't you think I need it to look after everyone? Things have been hard since my husband died. You only came afterwards so you don't know – but the farm isn't doing as well as it has been.' The look in Izzy's eyes told Pam that the girl didn't care or believe her.

'I suppose you'll want me to leave now,' Izzy said, looking sullen. 'Well, good riddance is what I say – I hate this job. I'm going back to London. I want a bit of life. There's nothing to do round this dead and alive place!'

Pam picked up her purse. There were three one-pound notes in it, which was what should be left, but a few coins had gone. It wasn't worth making a fuss over, so she took out two pounds and handed them to Izzy. 'That is the wages I owe you and another ten shillings. You can keep it to help you until you find another job.'

'Thanks, I don't think,' Izzy said, defiant once more. 'Rotten wages. I can earn far more in town.'

'Well, it's what is due,' Pam told her, refusing to rise to the bait. 'You get thirty shillings plus your keep – and that works out a lot more than you might think, Izzy. When you pay for rent and food, you'll find the difference.'

Izzy threw her a scornful look. 'Not where I'm going,' she said, then turned and marched up the stairs.

Pam heard her banging drawers and slamming doors. She was tempted to check the money in her desk, but in minutes Izzy was back in the kitchen, with her case, and a bag in her hand.

'I'm orf then,' she muttered. 'Thanks for nothing.'

'I'm sorry it ended this way,' Pam replied. 'I wish you good luck, Izzy.'

Izzy sniffed and stormed out, slamming the door behind her.

Pam sat down, her hands trembling as she fought the emotions boiling inside her. She had noticed the small amounts of money disappearing but wondered if one of the girls had paid a tradesman for her, or one of the youngsters had taken some for sweets, Though, when Susan had shown her that ten shillings had gone, she'd wondered for a second if the culprit was one of the land girls, but hadn't wanted to believe that anyone would steal from her.

After a few moments of reflection, Pam went into her sitting room and checked the money in her desk. She discovered with a shock that twenty pounds was missing. Twenty pounds! It hadn't occurred to her to check before, because she'd imagined that only she and Tom knew the five hundred pounds was there. Suddenly, she was furiously angry. That money her husband had so painstakingly saved for her had been stolen by a girl so brazen-faced that she'd been unrepentant when admitting she'd pilfered from Pam's purse.

Realising she'd been a fool to let Izzy just walk off, without checking her desk, Pam felt sick. Twenty pounds was so much money and she could ill afford to lose it. For a moment she felt like weeping. She'd thought no one would find her key in its hiding place, now she knew that Izzy must have searched for it when she was out – perhaps on the rare occasions she went shopping or to visit John. Yes, that was probably when it had gone; Izzy would have known she was safe from discovery then.

Relocking the desk, she put the key in her pocket. She would have to find somewhere safer, or keep it with her – although she didn't think anyone else would try to take money that wasn't theirs.

Artie and Jeanie were in the kitchen when she returned to her work. Jeanie looked at her, stood up and came towards her instantly. 'What's wrong, Mum? You look upset?'

'I am.' Pam told her what had just happened, her hands still trembling a little. 'I should have called the police – but I thought it was just a few shillings.'

'The little thief,' Jeanie exclaimed. 'I knew she was no good – but that is a lot of money to lose, Mum. How will you manage?'

'I have a little bit by me,' Pam replied. 'But if I hadn't caught her touching my purse this morning and challenged her, how much more would she have taken?'

'She's gone then?' Artie said and frowned. 'I know it is for the best, but we shall miss her when it comes to the ploughing, Mum. I doubt there's much chance of getting another girl – but maybe a young lad. I've employed one myself...'

'Oh, good,' Pam said and forced herself to smile. 'Tom is trying for one for me – and we shall need him, because Olive can't do all the work, and you are always so busy on your own land now, Artie. I need someone I can rely on here. The government raised the school-leaving age to fifteen – that means George has another year at school which he will hate. He does as much as he can, but he is only a lad yet.'

Artie had the grace to look ashamed. 'I'll see to things,' he said. 'Don't worry, Mum. I'll be around more once Tom goes back to the Army. I know I've neglected your work for a while, because I... Well, there was more needed doing on that land I bought than I expected. But Jem Googe is a quick learner and he'll be doing tractor work by Christmas, so I'll get yours done on time this year. I promise.'

'Yes, he will,' Jeanie said fiercely. 'I'll make him sorry if he doesn't.'

Artie shot her a look and then got up. 'I'll see you later, Jeanie. I've got some potatoes to deliver – but I'll pick you up on the way back.'

Pam looked at Jeanie after he left. 'Did he bring you down on the tractor and trailer?' Jeanie nodded. 'You must be careful, love. Do you feel all right?'

Jeanie laughed. 'I'm fine, Mum. I got very hot and tired that day when I fainted. Now I just do the housework and a bit of gardening, I am perfectly well.'

'Good. That's what I like to hear.' Pam smiled lovingly at her. 'My family are what matters to me. I was upset over that money, but it is all right. I can manage – and if the crops are as good as Tom says, I'll be fine for next year.'

'She wasn't a nice girl,' Jeanie said. 'I'm sorry she stole your money, Pam – but I am glad she has gone.'

24

Artie caught sight of Izzy on the way back to Sutton. She was sitting on her case at the side of the road, her face a picture of woe, and she'd been crying. He passed her, hesitated, got off his tractor and retraced his steps, standing, looking down at her.

'You stole twenty quid from my mother. I want it back! Or I'll take you to the police – and don't think I won't do it!' He glared at her angrily.

Izzy gave a strangled sob. 'I haven't got it. I've only got the wages your mother gave me.'

'Don't lie to me!'

Izzy looked up at him, a hint of defiance in her woebegone face. 'I sent it to someone. Search me if you want. I don't have it.'

'Why did you do it?' he demanded. Artie had been annoyed with Izzy, because of his own weakness, but seeing her now, he realised that she was just a young girl on her own and, despite what had happened, felt sorry for her. 'If you needed money so badly, you should've asked.'

'What do you care?' Izzy was on her feet suddenly, her face alight with anger. 'I'm just another land girl to you – no one important. You'd like to get in my knickers, but that's all you want – just like all the others,' she cried bitterly. 'Ever since I was fifteen... Men, I hate the lot of you!'

'Yes, I found you attractive, and you did your best to tempt me,' Artie replied and discovered that he felt nothing but compassion for her now. Suddenly, he understood her need for attention and he was curious about what made her that way. He looked at her thoughtfully. 'Why did you need the money so badly, Izzy? You had nothing much to spend it on round here...'

Izzy heard the softer note in his voice and flushed to the roots of her hair. For a moment, she looked as if she would burst into tears, or anger, but then she seemed to sag. She sat down again and started crying. 'It was for her...' The words were indistinct. Artie sat down beside her. 'My little girl...' Izzy raised her head and her greenish-hazel eyes were misty with tears. Artie handed her his not-very-clean handkerchief and she gave a muffled laugh and wiped her face. 'I knew you liked me...'

'I'm married and I love my wife,' Artie told her. 'That doesn't mean I don't like you – if you hadn't been so brazen, we might have been friends.'

'Men only want women for one thing. I thought if we had sex, you would give me money,' Izzy said. She sniffed, raising her head defiantly. 'I have a little girl. She is three and my grandmother looks after her – but Eliza has been ill and she needed an operation and I couldn't afford to pay...'

'Why the hell didn't you tell us?' Artie demanded, staring at her in disbelief. 'We would have helped you. How much did you need?'

'Fifty pounds,' Izzy sniffed and handed him his handkerchief. Artie stuffed it back in his trouser pocket. 'I was desperate – and your mother had so much money in her desk so... I took some and sent it to my mother to pay the doctor's bills.'

'Mum was very angry when she discovered it,' Artie said. He frowned. 'You are lucky she hasn't thought of calling the police.' A look of fright entered Izzy's eyes. 'Don't worry. She won't do that, even though she was very upset.' He stood up. 'Do you want a lift to Sutton? You can get the train from there – to wherever you are going.'

'I am going home,' Izzy told him. 'I've sent the money to my mother and I want to see Eliza – then I'll find another job.' She sniffed and stood up. 'Yes, I'd like a lift to Sutton, thanks – and tell your mum I'm sorry.'

Artie nodded but didn't say anything. He swung her case onto the trailer and helped her in, then glanced back before releasing the brakes. He was thoughtful as he drove to the railway station in Sutton, only speaking as he helped her down and gave her the case.

'I hope your little girl is OK,' he said, and took a ten-shilling note from his pocket, handing it to her. 'It's all I've got on me. Buy something for your daughter.'

Izzy took it and walked off. Artie stood and watched her for a moment, then began to turn away. As he did so, Izzy swung round and looked back at him, an expression of triumph in her eyes. 'There's one born every minute...' she called and ran towards the train that was just about to leave the station, jumping on. She couldn't know where it was going and she had no ticket.

Artie stared. Had he been spun a sob story and fallen for a pack of lies? He stared after the train as it slowly steamed out of the station. He would never know for sure, but she'd made him feel a fool. For a while there he'd been really sorry for her, but now... Anger and bewilderment made him shake his head, but then, he suddenly saw the funny side of it and started to laugh as he climbed back on his tractor.

Izzy was an actress, either way. She could act the strumpet as easily as the lonely, desperate woman. Artie would never know the real Izzy and a feeling of relief came over him. She'd certainly understood how to play him and he was just glad she'd gone. He wouldn't tell anyone that he'd given her a lift to the station, and he certainly wouldn't tell them that he'd given her ten shillings. He'd have to go without cigarettes for the next week, because he'd earned nothing from his land yet, until he got paid for that first crop of early potatoes, and the only money he had was his wages, most of which he gave to Jeanie for her and Winston.

Thankfully, he'd only given Izzy ten shillings, and, all things considered, it was worth that to be rid of her. Deciding she wasn't worth bothering over, he switched his mind to thinking about the work he had to do...

* * *

Jeanie found the handkerchief Artie had given to Izzy to wipe her tears when she was washing his clothes the next Monday. It had a smear of bright red lipstick on it – a colour she never wore.

It was Izzy's colour. She stared at it for several minutes, torn by suspicion and anger, between confronting Artie with it and bursting into tears. In the end, she just put it in the boiler with the other whites, jutting her chin. If she demanded the truth, Artie would either lie or – perhaps worse – tell her that he'd kissed Izzy, or more, and she didn't want to hear either, so she would ignore it. The only alternative was to go home to London. If she knew for certain Artie had cheated on her, she would, but for now she would give him the benefit of the doubt.

The girl had gone and whatever had passed between them was finished. Izzy would never dare to return now she'd been caught stealing. Jeanie frowned. They had none of them really known her, because she hadn't got close to anyone. Was she just bad or was there a good reason for the way she'd behaved? Jeanie suspected she would never know but she was just glad the girl had gone.

25

Tom looked at the last of the wheat sheaves; golden and heavy with kernels, they were stacked in the bottom field and ready for threshing. Working side by side, he and Artie had managed to get all the wheat cut, despite the rain showers that had suddenly arrived out of a sky that had been blue and cloudless for weeks. Just in time, because this was his last day. Tomorrow, he would have to return to his base, and he'd never been as reluctant as he was now, after two months on the farm.

Lizzie was at home when he walked in. She hadn't been to work for the past few days, deciding to take a holiday and leave the salon to the care of her staff. Tom would have liked to spend more time with her, but he was anxious to gather the harvest in for his mother, and Lizzie understood. She'd brought food and cool drinks out to them as they worked, sitting on a blanket with Arthur and watching them, as, stripped to the waist, they tossed the sheaves onto the trailers, skin tanned and glistening with sweat.

'All done?' Lizzie asked with a smile as Tom went to the kitchen sink and splashed cold water over his face and arms. 'It looks to be a good crop.'

'Yes, it is,' Tom agreed, relaxed and happy now the work was done. He wouldn't be here for the threshing, but that wasn't a problem. Olive, George, their new lad – Robbie Fitch – who was big and bony and already showing himself to have a good knowledge of the land, could manage it with Artie's help.

Robbie, the youngest of five, had a sister and three brothers, one of whom worked with their father on their land, which was a smallholding of some fifty acres, meaning the other lads needed to find work elsewhere. Two of his brother were in the Army, both of them professional soldiers, and had been fighting since the start of the war. Miraculously, it seemed, they were both still alive, and neither had been seriously wounded.

* * *

'I'd like to be taking you for a nice holiday now,' Tom admitted, turning to her as he wiped the water from his face and lay down the towel. 'I'm not sure where the time went to, Lizzie. Two months seem to have flown by and we haven't had much of it to ourselves, love.'

'We've all been busy,' she said, smiling as she came to him. 'I've enjoyed having you home, Tom. I wish you could stay, and I know you feel the same, but we've been lucky. You've had this time with us and you have to go back – but perhaps it will soon be over now.'

After years of bitter war, the Allies had entered Paris and it was no longer occupied; the swastika had been taken down from the Eiffel Tower and the newspapers had been filled with pictures of the population celebrating its freedom. People were dancing, calling out to the soldiers, giving them flowers and kissing them. It was a huge victory for the Allies after so many years of wearying conflict, but parts of France still had to be liberated, and elsewhere, the war still raged on. Hitler refused to admit that defeat was coming and was forming an elite home guard for Germany, and there was still fierce fighting in the Philippines and the Low Countries; it wasn't all victories for the Allies and parts of Britain were still suffering from the doodlebugs, the new threat in the skies that were silent until they exploded, bringing terror and destruction where they dropped. Thousands of innocent people had been killed and many more injured by the new menace – and there were rumours of an even deadlier weapon on the way. Tom knew it was imperative those factories were taken out – and taken out soon!

'I keep thinking it can't last forever,' Tom said. 'I know the successful landing in Normandy was the beginning of the end, but Hitler isn't beaten yet – or he won't admit it. He will fight on to the bitter end, so I do have to go back, Lizzie.'

He smiled and kissed her softly, looking into her eyes that were a greenish-brown, more green than brown just now. 'You must promise to take care of yourself and Arthur – don't work too hard, and write to me often. Tell me what you're doing and how much Arthur has grown; it's the little things that mean so much.'

'I shall,' she promised, her arms going round him, holding him as if she would never let go. 'He is growing up fast, Tom. He won't understand why you have to leave, but I'll make sure he knows that you are coming back just as soon as you can. I show him your picture every day and talk about you.'

'And I shall come just as soon as I can,' Tom promised, holding her safe in his arms, nuzzling in her reddish-brown hair that always smelled so sweet and fresh. 'I love you, Lizzie – don't you ever forget that.'

'I shan't,' she promised, looking up at him with love and laughter. 'Go up and see your mum, then we'll have supper and an early night.'

'You're on,' he agreed, his eyes gleaming with mischief. 'Oh, lord! I can hear Arthur. He has just woken up by the sound of it – you'd best see to him, Lizzie. I'll have a chat to Mum and be back before you know it...'

* * *

Pam was cooking when Tom walked in, the kitchen redolent of the rabbit pie in the range oven, the heat of it intense on such a warm day.

'It's very hot in here, Mum,' he said. 'Why don't you have the back door open?'

'I'm used to it,' Pam said, her eyes meeting his. Tom was broad in the shoulder but there wasn't an ounce of fat on him, his features lean and intelligent, eyes piercing, all-seeing as they looked at her. 'I had it open for a while earlier, but the flies come in and I hate that...'

'One of the hazards of living on a farm,' Tom said, observing her flushed face. 'Are you all right, Mum? You look... tired, hot...'

'I'm fine,' Pam replied. 'Yes, a bit hot, but nothing to bother about.'

'Then you've got something on your mind,' Tom said, seeing the lines of worry at the corners of her eyes. 'Anything I can do?'

Pam shook her head, then sat down and gave a little choke of annoyance or anguish. 'It's just things get on top of me at times, love. We've had so much worry and bad luck – and then that girl... a girl I treated like one of the family... stole from us. I know I shouldn't let it bother me, but I can't help it. I've always trusted everyone, left my back door unlocked if I went out...' A shiver went through her. 'She took some of that silver, too, Tom. I had put it in my wardrobe, and a little vase and some of the trinkets have been taken – and the diamond pin your dad bought me for our silver wedding anniversary. I think that has upset me most of all. I only discovered it this morning. It was on my best dress and I was thinking I might have that cleaned, because it doesn't wash well – and when I looked, the pin was gone. It wasn't worth a lot of money, but it meant the world to me...' Pam gave a little sob. 'With your dad gone...'

'The rotten little trickster!' Tom said fiercely. 'You should have let me go to the police, Mum. We might have got some of it back.'

'I doubt it...' Pam sighed. 'I had a letter this morning. I wrote and asked if there was any chance of a new girl, explaining what had happened – and they told me they'd discovered that she'd given them a false name and address when she signed up. She could be anyone, Tom – and she might have gone anywhere. They couldn't trace her. I think it was the fact we'd been duped that upset me.'

Tom nodded, face grim, as he saw the real distress it had caused his mother. 'She isn't worth your tears, Mum. Izzy was a troublemaker. She tried it on with me and with Artie. Just think of the anguish that might have caused if we'd fallen for her tricks! I'm glad she has gone and if a few trinkets were the price we paid to see her go, I'd say it was worthwhile. I am sorry she took Dad's pin, because I know you loved it – not for what it was, but because he bought it for you.'

Pam blew her nose and got up to investigate her vegetables simmering on the stove. 'I know you are right,' she told Tom with an effort to shrug it off. 'It just seemed the last straw.'

'You've had too much to put up with,' he agreed. 'You should have gone on holiday with Susan and the youngsters. Lizzie would have helped out, but Olive is capable of getting herself a meal – she would probably go to the pub for a pie. You need a holiday yourself.'

'Leave you all to get on with it in the middle of harvest?' Pam shook her head. 'I shall be fine, Tom. You just caught me at a bad moment.'

Tom went to her and put an arm about her shoulders. 'I know you've always done your duty, but make time for a little fun, Mum. You and Lizzie could take the small children somewhere for a holiday. Give yourself something to look forward to...'

'Perhaps I shall when Susan gets back,' Pam said. She looked at him, smiling fondly. 'I'd like to go to London for a couple of days, do some shopping, go to the theatre – but we couldn't take the boys there.'

'I suppose the zoo is closed for the duration, and they would be a bit of a burden if you want to shop,' Tom replied. 'Do you think Jeanie could cope with them?'

'It would be too much for her,' Pam said. 'Dot Goodman might have Arthur and Susan could look after Jonny just for a couple of days – but I'll see what Lizzie thinks.'

'You do that,' Tom said, a little surprised that she was considering it. 'It will do you good, Mum.' He hesitated, then, 'I'm leaving early tomorrow. I want to see John again, make sure he has all he needs.'

'You can take him some of that money,' Pam said. 'I've still got just over four hundred pounds, and I'd like to give him half – two hundred pounds. Tell John that I am going to sell the house and the money will be his to help him get started.'

'Yes, all right,' Tom agreed. 'What about the rest of the silver? Do you want me to put it back in the attic before I leave?'

'No. I'll take some of it with me when I go to London, see if I can sell it there. Luckily, Izzy didn't steal part of the tea and coffee set.'

Tom nodded, regarding her with love and compassion. She'd had too much to bear this past few years. 'Yes, that would have made it worth much less – but that would be heavy to carry, Mum – if you want to go shopping...'

'Oh, I'll just take some of the small pieces with me – the service... I thought I would put that in a local sale.'

'Tell you what, I'll ask Lizzie to take it into March when she visits her mother. I think there is a dealer she might be able to sell it to there,' he said and gave her another hug. 'Don't let that bitch get you down, Mum. Put it all behind you – after all, it might have been worse.'

Pam nodded, forcing a smile. Tom grinned and went out, but then the smile dropped. His mother was suffering, though most of the time she put a brave face on things. These past years had been hard on everyone, and she wasn't the only woman to lose loved ones to a devastating war. Tom knew she was still grieving for his father, and for what had happened to John – he was all but lost to her now, since his decision not to come home. She would also have to give up Jonny as soon as John felt able to take on the care of his son, and that would be like cutting out a part of her heart. Tom knew the loss of some money and a few trinkets wasn't the source of her distress, just another straw on the camel's back.

He just hoped she was strong enough not to snap under the weight of it all.

26

Pam was baking, as always in the mornings, when Susan and the youngsters, and Rover, got back from their holiday in St Ives, a small country town not far from Sutton and Earith. The empty kitchen was immediately full of voices and happy laughter and her mood lightened at once as she listened to all the chatter about what they'd done and where they'd been on their holiday. Angela and George almost immediately went off to look at the calves and see how much they'd grown while they were away. Susan had brought Pam some lovely scented soap she'd been lucky enough to find and the children had a little basket of sweets they had bought for her, tied up with pink ribbons and a silk flower; it made Pam smile and realise that she was still very lucky to have so much love about her.

'Did Tom get off all right?' Susan asked as the noise settled. 'We shall miss him, Mum.'

'Yes, I always do, but he was here for weeks this time, and it will seem strange without him,' Pam agreed. She watched as Susan's eyes moved about the room, as if searching for something. 'That new doctor – Doctor Bryant? He called to see if you were all right while you were away. Said something about nearly knocking you off your bike. I told him you had taken the younger ones on holiday. He said to tell you he hopes you have a lovely time.'

'Oh, that was nice of him,' Susan said carelessly, clearly not much interested.

'Oh, I forgot to say, Jeanie was here the day before yesterday. Terry is driving a car now and he brought her down. She asked if you would like to go for tea on Sunday – said to go up about three.'

Susan's smile beamed out immediately and Pam nodded to herself. 'Terry asked after you. He seemed disappointed because you were on holiday, but I told him it was free and the only chance you had to go, so he understood.'

'It was lovely.' Susan sounded slightly defiant. 'The caravan sleeps four, but there isn't much room, and we had to make the beds every night and stack them back in the morning – Rover would get on my bed. We went swimming every day – Angela can swim properly now. George already could – and so can Rover. He loved being in the river, kept shaking himself all over us when he came out. Rover was really good when we hired a motorboat, didn't try to jump off...' Susan laughed at the memory. 'Neither I nor Sally could steer it properly, but George could, so he was in charge – and didn't he love that...'

'He is very good on the tractor, so I suppose a boat is much the same,' Pam agreed. She hesitated, then, 'I promised Jeanie some of my eggs, as her hens aren't laying much at the moment. Do you want to take some up this afternoon for her?'

Susan's eyes lit up. 'Yes, of course, Mum. Do you need any shopping?'

'You can ask the butcher if he has any scraps for the dog – and I might have enough coupons for some sausages...'

'I still have all mine for this week,' Susan told her. 'Sally's dad gave her some extra coupons, and we mostly had fish and chips or paste and salad sandwiches, what we used was for Rover. We managed to buy him some sausages...'

'In that case, bring anything our butcher has got for us.' She went to her purse and gave Susan a pound note. 'If there is any change, you keep it, love. You'll be returning to college in a couple of weeks, Susan. I am going to give you twenty pounds to take with you for pocket money.'

'Oh, Mum! I don't need all that. I really don't,' Susan told her. 'You've already given me lots this holiday – you always do...'

'I know you have a small income from your trust fund money,' Pam replied with a smile. 'But I can manage it – and I want you to have it, love. I've got a pretty diamond brooch for you, too – but I don't think you'd want that at college?'

'No, I wouldn't,' Susan replied. 'I'd be frightened of losing it. Keep it safe for me, Mum – keep it until I get married and I'll wear it on my wedding day...' She gave a wry laugh. 'If I ever do...'

'Oh, you will,' her mother said. 'It's just a case of waiting for the right man...'

'Yes, but... supposing he doesn't love me?' Susan said, a flash of something akin to fear in her eyes.

'Then he isn't the one,' Pam said simply. 'I've been loved by a man I loved, twice – and I can tell you; it is in their eyes. Just be brave enough to look and you will know, my love. Even if he doesn't speak, and he might not for various reasons, he won't be able to hide it in his eyes.' Pam had thought Doctor Bryant might be interested in her lovely daughter, but he didn't stand a chance, because Susan had loved Terry for years.

'Oh, Mum, you know, don't you?' Susan said and a shy smile curved her mouth. 'I've always loved Terry. All the others I went out with were just friends. There was one airman I liked a lot, but he went away before I had time to know if I liked him as much as Terry...'

'You didn't, Susan. If you had, you would have known. True love can happen in an instant, with just one glance – or it can come slowly, unfolding little by little as you get to know someone. I've experienced both; the first with Tom's father and the second with yours. In the end, I think my love for Arthur was the strongest, but we were together longer.'

'You must miss him so much,' Susan said and went to hug her. 'I know I do, too. Dad was always so calm and thoughtful. He didn't say that much, but when he did – well, we all listened.'

'Yes, that is what I miss – him just sitting there with his paper, telling me little bits of news, putting me right – but it is getting easier, Susan.' Pam gave herself a little shake. 'I've got all of you – so I am lucky.' She smiled at her daughter. 'Get some eggs from the pantry and put them in a bowl and then get off, love. I will expect you when I see you...'

'I'll just go up and wash my face and tidy up,' Susan said. 'Thanks, Mum.'

Pam nodded to herself. She hoped that Susan would find what she was looking for. Her daughter was doing well at college and would finish the course come what may – but if she wanted to get married soon after she passed her exams, Pam wouldn't object. She'd had to let John go and his son, her precious Jonny, would go soon – and the others would fly the nest when they were ready. This was the time when she and Arthur ought to have been thinking of the future, of taking things easy, having a bit of fun in their later years.

For perhaps the first time since she'd lost Arthur, Pam began to think about her own future. Tom was right. She needed to have a little fun in her life, because, although she was content in her kitchen, cooking and caring for others, there was an outside world. The war would end one day and then perhaps she might think about what came next. In the meantime, she would take a day off to go to London, shop, eat out and perhaps the theatre. If Lizzie didn't feel up to it – she might ask Dot Goodman. She'd visited a few times since she'd been looking after little Arthur and, like Pam, Dot spent most of her life at home, but she didn't have Pam's large family so was probably lonely. Yes, she thought, if Lizzie couldn't come, she would ask Dot, or she might even go on her own, because she was determined to take a little time for herself from now on.

* * *

Susan visited the butcher on her way through Sutton.

'I've been keeping the bits for you,' he said as he gave her a bag of gristly bits, fat and bones, and winked at her. 'Got to look after my favourite customers.'

He also supplied her with a pound of sausages, ten rashers of bacon and some brisket. Susan knew that her mother could produce all sorts of delicious things from this precious hoard, feeling pleased, and after arranging to pick up her purchases on the way home, she cycled the rest of the way to Jeanie's home.

Her heart was beating very fast as she approached the large old house, its faded red bricks glowing in the afternoon sun. Would Terry be there? Would he look the same? Would she feel the same as she had when she was not yet sixteen and she'd seen him as a gallant war hero, suffering terrible grief after the loss of a leg and his wife?

As she walked up the drive, she could hear the high-pitched screams of laughter coming from inside and then the door opened and a young girl of about six came rushing out, a man hobbling after, a teasing smile on his face. Tina stopped abruptly and looked at Susan, a puzzled look in her eyes, as if she vaguely remembered her but wasn't sure.

'Hello, Tina,' Susan said. 'Do you remember me? I'm Susan... you stayed with us at the farm.'

'Daddy...' Tina said, turning her face into the man as he joined her and clinging to his legs, suddenly shy and uncertain.

Susan's gaze moved from the child to the man's face. Terry looked almost the same. His hair was still that sandy red, lighter than his sister Jeanie but not fair like his mother's. His eyes were greenish-blue and smiling as he looked at her. Susan saw that he wasn't as handsome as she'd remembered, but he had a strong face, and as he moved towards her, holding out his hands to her, her heart leaped. As she took them, feeling the cool firmness of his grip, she knew that it was his character that she'd loved; the essence that was uniquely his, the steady, honest manner when he spoke, and the feeling that here was a man she could trust. It all came rushing back, the days when she'd seen such pain in his eyes, the longing to reach out and help him, the gradual gaining of his trust, and the quiet times when they'd just sat and talked, on their own, often not speaking for ages, but content to be friends, to be together.

Susan's love had remained unspoken, admitted only in the privacy of her own bed. She had never been sure whether he felt more than friendship for her, because he'd been grieving, wrapped up in the pain of loss – and the more physical pain of his wounds.

Realising that they were just staring at each other, Susan blushed. 'How are you – and Tina?' she asked to cover her nerves. 'It is so long since we've seen you both.'

'I know and I'm sorry,' he said, his eyes never leaving hers. 'I meant to come. I've wanted to for a long time but...' He laughed, looking as if he had sloughed off some doubt that had been plaguing him. 'Now I realise that it was stupid. I should have come sooner.' He looked down at Tina, then bent to lift her up so that she was on a level with them. 'Tina – this is Susan. Do you remember how she used to play with you, take you for walks and put you to bed when you stayed at the farm?'

Tina looked at her then, a look of realisation and delight as she began to remember. 'Kittens...' she said and Susan nodded. 'We had kittens...'

'Yes, you did, Tina,' Susan said. 'We had several kittens then – there was a stray cat and she was always producing a new litter.'

'I loved them...' The little girl turned to her father. 'Can I have a kitten, Daddy?'

'It isn't fair to them to keep them shut up where we live, Tina,' Terry told her. 'There's a busy road outside our garden and they get knocked over. You need to live somewhere quiet – like Aunty Jeanie's house – to have kittens safely.'

Tina pouted but didn't persist in her request, looking at Susan intently. 'Have you got kittens now?' she asked.

'No. We have a dog now,' Susan told her. 'It was a stray. My cousin George and my sister Angela found him and brought him home. He is a good dog, but he sometimes chases the hens and if they get upset, they don't lay – which reminds me, I brought some eggs for Jeanie.'

Jeanie had appeared in the doorway. She ushered them all inside and thanked Susan for bringing the eggs. 'Thank you so much. I wanted to make some cake. Tina loves cake and so does Artie. They've eaten all I made earlier between them...'

Laughing, they all trooped back into the big kitchen. A vase of wild flowers was on the table and some used cups and plates. Jeanie gathered them up and placed them in the sink.

'I've got the kettle on,' she said. 'I made some jam tarts this morning – I think there are enough left for one each...'

Terry held a chair for Susan and she sat at the long, scrubbed-pine table, inhaling the faint fragrance of the flowers. 'Your mother said you were having a holiday with a friend and your sister and cousin,' Terry stated as they looked at one another. 'Was it good fun?'

'Yes – we had a chance of a caravan. Sally's father lets it out to friends and family and there was a week free so we went. He'd got it parked near the quay-side in St Ives, and there was quite a bit going on. Boats, swimming – and some ponies that belonged to a riding school. George and Angela enjoyed riding them. Sally and I just watched. We went to the pictures a couple of times, but mostly we were out walking or playing games outside. We didn't want to leave Rover too much, but a friend of Sally's father, who has a caravan there too, looked after him for us so we could go to the cinema.'

'It sounds wonderful,' Terry said. 'Mum and I took Tina to a boarding house at the sea for a week last year. We couldn't go this year, because the government banned all seaside visits unless strictly necessary...'

'That was because of all the secrecy over the D-Day landings,' Susan said, nodding. 'Mum was allowed to go to visit John, because it was on compassionate grounds – and the convalescent home is outside Hastings, so it isn't really on the coast, though he can see the cliffs from his bedroom.'

'Yes, of course.' Terry inclined his head, his eyes focused on her as she talked. 'I was sorry to hear of all your John has been through. I liked John when we met years ago. Mum was really shocked when Jeanie told us – she thinks we got off lightly, considering.'

'Have you recovered completely now?' Susan asked. She'd noticed that he walked much better than when he'd first had a false leg fitted years ago.

'Yes, more or less,' Terry replied. 'My stub was very sore if you recall? I had trouble wearing my leg, because it rubbed the wounds and became infected again – but that all cleared up eventually, and now I hardly notice it. I can drive, walk, do most things I could – but not bricklaying unfortunately. However, that isn't my job any more. These days I do the costing for the bigger jobs and all the bookwork, wages, and the bits and pieces Dad can't manage.'

'Do you enjoy it?' Susan asked him. Their gaze seemed to be magnetic, locked together, neither of them able to look away. 'You were reluctant to return to London I remember.'

'Yes, for more than one reason,' Terry agreed. 'I didn't want to face the memories, but now I am glad I did. The work isn't what I'd planned for my life – but I'm not the only one who has had to change his job because of a war wound, and I shan't be the last.'

'No...' Susan looked at him soberly. 'John has decided to train as an accountant. He was always good at maths but doesn't like it much. Mum says he wants to look after Jonny himself so he has to work.'

'Yes. My parents have been very good, but I have my own house again now. I bought it on a mortgage, so I need to work to keep a proper home for Tina. She is at school now...'

Tina was laughing at something Jeanie was saying to her and they both turned their heads to look at her. 'You haven't... I mean I thought you might get married... Tina needs a mother, doesn't she?' Susan asked and blushed at her own temerity in asking such a question.

'My mother has her a lot of the time,' Terry admitted with a frown. 'She collects her from school and I take her in the mornings. We go to Mum for our Sunday dinner, but I manage at home myself. I won't say it is easy, but we're OK. I think Tina probably needs more attention than I can give her, but she is a good girl – and I won't marry unless it is to the right person.'

'You knew that Faith died?' Terry nodded. 'John was going to marry again to a girl named Lucy – but when he was missing... well, she found someone else. I am not sure if he will marry again, though he is determined to have Jonny.' Susan frowned. 'Mum was very upset over that for a while, but I think she has accepted it now.'

'Yes. I suppose she has to,' Terry said. 'Mum only does part-time midwifery now, because of Tina. She knew I couldn't manage early on, so she cut her hours. She talks of going back full-time, but I'm not sure she will. There's only her and Dad to think about now. Annie is working in a military hospital abroad again. She seems dedicated to her work. Mum says she doesn't think she will ever marry or come home. So she says she ought to go back to work, do something useful – but so far, she hasn't...'

'What are you two looking so serious about?' Jeanie said, coming over to them with a loaded tea tray. 'How much longer have you got before you go back to college, Susan?'

'Just over two weeks,' she replied. 'Tom went back to his unit a couple of days ago, so Mum will have a nearly empty house again.' She bit her tart. 'Oh, lovely, it's blackberry jam – did you make it?'

'Yes. Pam gave me the recipe.' Jeanie nodded, smiling. 'There is a nice film on this weekend at the Ritz Cinema in Ely,' she announced. '*Snow White* and – I think there are cartoons as well. I was telling Terry he should go and take Tina. You could take Angela, unless she has seen it? Terry can pick you up in his car – can't you?' She looked at her brother expectantly.

'Well, yes – if Susan would like to come?' he said. 'I'm not sure if you'd enjoy a children's film?'

'Oh yes, I like all the Disney films,' Susan replied, smiling. 'I've seen several – *Bambi* was my favourite, but I don't think Angela has seen *Snow White*, although that was out before the war. Dad used to take us sometimes.'

'I'll pick you up tomorrow then – about one-thirty?' Terry said and smiled at her.

Tina had been staring at Susan in silence. Now she came to her and pulled at her sleeve. 'I like you,' she said. 'Can I sit on your lap?'

'Of course you can,' Susan said and pushed back her chair to allow her to climb up.

Jeanie poured more tea for Susan and a small glass of milk for Tina. Tina took the glass in both hands and drank from it, the creamy liquid smearing her mouth, which she wiped with the back of her hand.

Terry frowned and leaned over, completing the job with his handkerchief. She looked at him with big brown eyes but said nothing. Then, as he sat back to drink his own tea, she commenced eating her jam tart, once again smearing her mouth with the sweet sticky jam, and evidently enjoying it. Susan sipped her tea, picking up a few crumbs and watching as bits of the tart went flying, and retrieving the edible pieces. Tina munched steadily until it was all gone, then finished her milk.

Terry smiled. 'She is getting spoiled here. Mum doesn't make cake very often. She used to say she didn't get time, but I think the truth is she just isn't a cake maker. So Tina doesn't often get cake or jam tarts, I'm afraid. We have biscuits but seldom cake – and, like me, she has a sweet tooth.'

'I remember when Lizzie stayed with us in London,' Jeanie said. 'She made lovely cakes and you and Dad used to eat them all...' She laughed. 'I couldn't cook them either until Pam taught me. Your mum is a marvellous cook, Susan. My mother has lots of wonderful qualities, but cooking isn't her strongest point.'

Susan laughed; sitting here, relaxing, looking at their happy faces seemed so natural, as if the years between Terry's stay at Blackberry Farm and now had never been.

'I'd best get home,' she said at last. 'I've got to pick some meat up for Mum before the shop shuts. Thanks, Jeanie – and I'll see you and Tina tomorrow.' She smiled as Terry walked outside to where her bicycle was parked.

'I shall look forward to it,' he said, wheeling her bike for her to the gate. 'Take care, Susan – it was lovely to see you again.'

'You, too,' she said, and then, driven by an impulse, she kissed his cheek. He turned his head and their lips touched briefly. She saw the look in his eyes and her heart raced. 'Mum was right,' she whispered, then laughed and shook her head as his eyebrows lifted. 'I'll tell you one day...' Then she got on her bike and pedalled away, turning back once to see him still standing at the gate, watching her.

27

Angela was excited when Terry came to fetch them from the farm that Saturday afternoon. George had been offered the treat, but he'd refused in favour of a game of football in the chestnut fields with other local lads; they were getting a team together and he'd been chosen as a winger, and a Disney film wasn't enough to risk his place for, even though he'd looked a bit regretful as the others drove off.

'I really want to see *Snow White*,' Angela said as she settled in the back seat beside Tina. 'Thank you so much for taking us, Mr Salmons.'

'No, no, you must call me Terry,' he said, looking over his shoulder at the two girls. 'You two played together when I was staying at the farm – do you remember, Tina?'

His daughter nodded shyly. Susan thought she probably didn't remember, but she usually agreed with anything her father said and was smiling happily.

'Good. We are going to have a lovely family time. I've got some bags of sweets for you to share, and afterwards we'll go to a nice little tea shop by the marketplace and have some cakes and lemonade...' He glanced at Susan. 'If that is all right with you?'

'It sounds lovely,' Susan said and laughed. 'I think we both had the same idea. I went to the local shop this morning and used all my sweet coupons. I bought toffees and Tom Thumb Drops – they are tiny so you get a big bag for a quarter pound.'

'Oh, I love those,' Tina said and gave a little giggle of pleasure.

'So do I,' Angela agreed and the girls looked at each other and then put their heads together and started whispering.

Terry glanced in his mirror and saw them, smiling to himself. 'That's a good sign,' he said softly and Susan looked at him.

'Yes...' she replied. 'I'm sure they will be happy together.'

'I certainly am...' Terry was smiling. The country road was empty of traffic as he risked a quick look at her. 'You?'

'I don't think you need to ask,' she said and saw his smile broaden as he returned his attention to an approaching bend in the road. The route through the village of Witcham was twisty and bumpy, fields to either side, except when in the village itself, but hardly any traffic about, apart from two tractors they passed, a lad on a cycle and one rather smart car. Susan caught a glimpse of the driver. 'I think that is our new doctor... hopefully, he hasn't lost his way again...'

Terry asked what she meant and she told him about coming off her bike when the doctor had taken a bend too swiftly and made her veer off. 'You weren't hurt?' he asked and she laughed.

'Only my dignity, but he was so apologetic, poor man.'

'He is supposed to be saving lives, not putting them at risk,' Terry remarked harshly.

Susan nodded. The incident seemed more humorous to her than dangerous now, but she liked the obvious concern in Terry's tone, because it meant he cared about her. Aware of feeling happy, she relaxed in her seat, enjoying the ride to Ely, mostly flat countryside with fields all around, some with cattle grazing, others shorn of their crops and awaiting the cycle of ploughing and sowing once more.

In the back seat, the younger ones chattered and giggled, but she and Terry hardly spoke; they didn't need to, because a shared glance was enough.

* * *

The visit to the cinema was busy, because, as children always will, there were hasty visits to the toilets, shuffling in and out of their seats, and supplying them with ice creams or orange drinks, from the lady who walked round in the interval with a tray around her neck; supported on a wide band, it fitted comfortably on her shoulders so that her hands were free to serve and take money.

It was a family outing, one of many, because the cinema was filled with children and their parents, though in most cases there was only a mother with perhaps another female adult, because all the fathers were away fighting. There were a couple of older men, but Terry was the only young man present, and several curious stares were directed at him when the lights went up, because he wasn't in uniform.

The films were fun, and the cartoons had everyone laughing out loud, so by the time the showing ended, there was a pleasant atmosphere as they all trooped out of the cinema in Ely, the children talking excitedly about what they'd seen.

It was as they paused for a moment in Market Street, getting a breath of fresh air after the rather stuffy confines of the cinema, that Susan overheard one woman say something that made her angry.

'I suppose he is one of those conchies,' a thin, mean-faced woman said in a loud voice that was meant to be heard. 'How she can bear to live with a coward like that I don't know.' She then sniffed and looked straight at Susan.

Susan hesitated. She would have left the woman in ignorance, but when her companion replied, 'Well, I dare say he's got something she likes...' in a sneering way, she suddenly lost her temper.

Marching up to the tall, thin woman, she looked her in the eyes and said in an ice-cold voice, 'You are a nasty woman and should be ashamed. You have no idea what you're talking about. The man you just maligned was in at the very start of the war, so badly wounded that he suffered life-changing injuries in the service of his country, and now can't do the job he loved and has to work in an office.'

'Well, how was I supposed to know...' the woman blustered, her face going red.

'You should have thought before you opened that foul mouth of yours,' Susan said curtly. 'Next time, madam, think before you speak... that's if you have anything to think with!' And she turned on her heel and walked back to Terry, who, bent over Tina as she fussed about something, seemed not to have realised what was going on.

He looked at her as she joined him, 'Something wrong?'

'Oh, no,' Susan replied, feeling as if she wanted to giggle. 'Everything is fine.' And it was, because she was with the man she loved and she was happy.

'Right, tea next,' Terry said. 'Who is hungry – anybody?'

'Me...' both children clamoured and Susan smiled, adding her voice to theirs.

'I hope they've got angel cake. That's my favourite.'

'I like cauliflower cakes,' Tina announced. 'Grandma buys me one at the tea shop on the corner.'

'She means Lyons',' Terry explained. 'They go there for a treat sometimes.'

'What is a cauliflower cake?' Angela asked. 'It sounds horrid...'

'It's lovely,' Tina told her. 'It's white cake in the middle with cream and then marzipan icing on top and green marzipan wrapped round it.'

'Oh, I like marzipan,' Angela said. 'We have it on fruit cake at Christmas, if Mum can get the ingredients. I've never seen one of those cakes you like, Tina.'

'I haven't seen one either,' Susan said. 'I don't think they have them at the tea shops in Ely.'

'They only have them now and then in Lyons,' Terry replied. 'I shouldn't think it is easy to get the almonds for the marzipan. But Tina never forgets what she likes, even if you can't get them often.'

Laughing, talking about their favourite foods, they walked through the passageway from Market Street, past a discreet corsetry shop into the High Street. The tea shop was situated towards the top of the hill, which eventually led to the river. It was run by a baker, who made all their own cakes and bread, including an angel cake that was so soft and moist it just melted in the mouth.

The café part of the shop was busy, but the waitress was an elderly woman who found them a quiet table. From the window at the back of the large room, they had a view of the beautiful old cathedral, its weathered stone looking almost white in the evening sunshine. At the bottom of the hill was Broad Street, and halfway down its length was an entrance to a park, leading up to the back of the King's School and not far from the magnificent building, begun way back in history by Saint Etheldreda. At the top end of the park, the Gallery was a quiet road leading off the busy High Street and people used it to park their cars while they visited the ancient cathedral, or sat on a bench in the green opposite. Across from the green could be seen the rose-red buildings of the Bishop's Palace, and further along was what had once been Oliver Cromwell's house. On a summer afternoon it was a peaceful oasis, away from the hustle of the shops and cinemas.

Cauliflower cake was not on offer, but angel cake was, also madeira and a buttercream sponge. Terry ordered a selection and they all tucked in, enjoying the moist and very tasty treats on offer. It was only when the girls had eaten their fill and retreated to the broad windowsill to sit and gaze out at the view of pigeons flying to and from the ancient church towers that Terry looked at Susan.

'You didn't have to defend my honour to that woman,' he said softly. 'I'm used to remarks like that, because I am not in uniform. I no longer let it bother me.'

'But it was so unfair,' Susan said, a faint flush in her cheeks. 'She had no call to be so rude. You did your share right at the start. It wasn't your fault your wounds prevented you from continuing as a soldier.'

'I don't let it stop me doing much these days,' Terry replied. 'Of course there are things I can't and never will be able to do – but life is OK.'

Susan nodded. 'You would never know,' she agreed. 'You hardly limp at all now, except when you chase after Tina.'

'It took months of practice,' he said and laughed. 'For a long time, I couldn't balance well without a stick, but in the end, I got the hang of it... can't run, though. I take it off to swim in the pool, but sometimes people stare, so I tend not to do it much – unless I go when no one else is around.' His eyes met hers. 'I do have a disability, Susan. I can't change that – and there are times when it gets sore and I have to leave the leg off and use a crutch. Not often, but it happens. And of course it comes off when I bath or go to bed...'

Susan saw the look in his eyes and knew it was significant. 'I know, Terry. I've always known how it was for you. I remember the start of it and the pain it caused you then.' Her eyes widened. 'Did you think it would upset me – that I wouldn't be able to live with your disability? Is that why you didn't visit like you promised?'

He reached out to take her hand, his long fingers curling about hers. 'You were very young, hardly more than a schoolgirl. I understood there was something between us even then, but I wasn't sure – and even though I knew I could love you, I felt it might not be fair to you. You have all your life in front of you and you are beautiful, Susan. I can't give you all the things I'd like to and I can't take you dancing or... lots of things. You are an intelligent girl, Susan. You could find someone far more—'

She reached across and put a finger to his lips. 'What – richer, more famous, stronger, more successful?' Her eyes teased and caressed. 'What makes you think I want any of that?'

'I don't know what you want,' he admitted ruefully.

'Then I'll tell you.'

'Please do...' He smiled into her eyes and her heart gave a little leap of joy.

'First of all, I want to qualify as a teacher. I owe that to my parents for all they've done for me, and for myself. It is a good job that I can always return to. After that, I want love and marriage to the right man. I want a family life, but I also want to have a job and teach – and I'd like to live in a town, I think. I enjoy being in Cambridge and the shops and cinemas... but mainly I just want to be happy.'

'Would London do?' he asked, his eyes never leaving her face. 'Dad talks of coming this way after the war, when the rebuilding starts in earnest, though there will be plenty of work everywhere.'

'To be honest, I don't much mind, if I am with the right person,' Susan said, smiling at him.

'Am I the right person for you?' he asked and she nodded, suddenly shy, her heart racing.

'I've waited a long time for you to ask that,' Susan said. 'The answer is yes and if you ask me to marry you when I've finished my training, the answer will be yes.'

'Then that is what I'll do,' Terry said. 'I'll come down to Cambridge as often as I can meantime and we'll go out – without the children...' There was laughter in his eyes as Tina came hurtling back to them, gabbling about a dog she'd seen go by.

'Can we have a dog?' she asked urgently. 'I'd love a dog to take for walks, Daddy.'

'Perhaps when you're a little older,' Terry said, giving Susan a look of apology. 'We might move to a new house with a bigger garden soon, and then you'd have somewhere to play with him.'

Tina ran off to join Angela, calling out that she was going to have a dog. Angela was talking to the lady behind the cake counter, asking her if she ever had cauliflower cakes, but the assistant shook her head and told them the marzipan was too difficult to get these days.

'Oh, I forgot to mention, you'd have to take on one rather spoiled little girl, into the bargain,' Terry said ruefully, watching them.

'I've always loved her,' Susan replied with a smile. 'She will grow up, Terry. We just have to help her learn discipline as she does, but I understand perfectly why you spoil her.'

'It's Mum more than me,' he replied. 'She says Annie doesn't look as if she'll ever marry and she seldom sees Jeanie's son, so she fusses over Tina.'

'Mum has several grandchildren, but Jonny is the one she fusses over. She will miss him if he goes to live with his father.'

'John won't come home to live then?'

'No, I don't think so. I am not sure what he will do with his life. Mum has been to visit a couple of times, but he asked that the rest of us stayed away. I should like to see him, but not if it makes him unhappy.'

'No, you have to give him the consideration he needs,' Terry replied. 'It took me quite a time to be at home in my own body – but in the end I did...' He smiled as his fingers caressed the back of her hand.

'Yes, you did, and perhaps John will too,' Susan replied and glanced at the girls. 'We'd better go now – they are getting restless.'

Terry nodded, stood up and called them to him. They came running and he looked at Susan. 'What shall we do tomorrow?'

'Take this pair down by the river if you like?' she suggested. 'It's all they keep wanting to do – paddle where the water is shallow.'

'Then that's what we'll do,' he said and reached for her hand. He turned back to the girls. 'Come on, you pair – bet you can't race Angela to the car, Tina.'

'Bet I can,' she said and went flying off with Angela in hot pursuit. 'Tomorrow afternoon then...' Terry said and smiled. 'We'll go back to Jeanie's for now and then I'll take you home in the car. It's a good thing I've been saving my petrol coupons for months...'

* * *

Alone in her bedroom that night, Susan hugged her happiness to herself. She hadn't wanted their day to end, but her sense of responsibility wouldn't let her throw caution to the wind and tell Terry she would marry him now. Her parents had both wanted her to be a teacher, and her father had put some money aside for her so that she could train. So she would finish that training and then, when Terry asked her, she would marry him.

After years of not knowing if she'd imagined his feelings for her, the reality of being loved by the man she loved was overwhelming and lovely. She would tell her mother and Lizzie soon, though her mother would probably know already, just from looking at her, but for the moment, she just wanted to hold the feeling inside. She had a few more months at college, and then a year as a pupil teacher, and then she could apply for a job wherever she wished – but there was plenty of time to plan for the future. Just now it was enough that her dreams had come true.

28

To Pam's surprise and delight, the house in Sutton sold for nine hundred and twenty-five pounds within a month of her putting it up for sale. As soon as the contract was signed, by the father of a new bride, she rang the home to tell John she was coming to visit with Jonny and had some good news. He'd been with the doctors, but Sister Jane had taken the message, telling Pam that it was just a routine visit with the consultant who had done the operation on John's eyelid.

'I'll tell him. He will be pleased to see you.'

'Thank you. I will let him know when as soon as I can.'

Pam planned to visit as soon as she could arrange it, and asked Susan if she'd like to go with her, explaining about the sale of the house.

'I should think he will be delighted with that,' Susan said when Pam told her what she was planning. 'Could I really come, Mum? I should like to see John, even if only for a few minutes. I haven't asked before, but if you think it would be all right...'

'Yes, come with me, love,' Pam said. 'We'll stay at a nice hotel overnight and perhaps go into Hastings to the pictures. They are letting us go to the coast again now – so it would be a nice little trip for us.'

'Terry is back home in London, as you know,' Susan said. 'He will visit now and then, but his petrol coupons have run out, so it will be on the train unless he can get some on the black market. If he does, he might come down on a Saturday afternoon and go back on Sunday.'

'That will be nice, dear.' Her mother looked at her. 'I think you are being very sensible waiting until you've qualified as a teacher – and I don't need to ask if you are sure, because I know you are, love.'

Susan nodded. 'I thought if I told John that Terry and I will marry next year, it might help him to understand that his injuries don't mean no one can love him. I know it is different for John, because Terry's scars don't show – but they are still there.'

'Yes, and I understand what you hope for, Susan, but I'm not sure he will listen – I think John has to make up his own mind. If he feels it isn't right for him to come home, then I shan't try to persuade him.'

'I know you are giving him money,' Susan said. 'But he has to train for a long while before he can be an accountant – how will he live?'

'I think he has a small invalid pension from the Air Force,' Pam replied. 'I am not sure what he intends, in the meantime, but, knowing John, he will have worked it out.'

'Then I hope he will be happy whatever he does.'

'And you're happy now, aren't you?'

'Yes, I am, Mum. Very happy.' Susan looked into her loving eyes. 'I know it won't be all roses. There are things we shall probably never do, despite Terry's determination to live as normal a life as possible – but he is the one I want to spend my life with. I've known it since he stayed with us after he lost his leg. I was only a child then, but I've grown up – and I still feel exactly the same.' She laughed. 'I played the field for a while, and all that taught me was that some men are not to be trusted. I've just been waiting, Mum – waiting for Terry to make some sign that he cares. Now I know and it is all I want.'

'Then all I can say is I wish you a long and happy life together,' Pam replied. 'Hopefully, the war will be over by then and I'll be able to make you a proper cake.'

'Oh, Mum,' Susan said and started laughing. She shook her head but kept on laughing until the tears streamed, but they were tears of mirth and happiness. 'Is that all you're worried about – that I should have a proper cake...'

Pam looked at her and then started to laugh. 'Well, it makes all the difference to a wedding, but I do see why it is funny.'

* * *

John was working in the crafts room when Pam and Susan walked in the following week. He had been making some more models of animals and his hands were thick with clay.

'Sorry about these,' he said, wiping them hastily on a towel before bending to pick Jonny up. 'Hello, Susan. It's nice of you to come and see me.'

'John, it's good to see you.' Susan went to him and kissed his scarred cheek. 'I've wanted to come – and I have some news for you. Terry Salmons and I will be married when I've finished my teacher training.'

'That's good news,' John replied, not seeming in the least surprised. 'I knew you liked him. He is a decent chap, Susan. I am sure you will be very happy.'

'Daddy – what are you making?' Jonny asked, pulling at him. 'I like animals...'

'I am making some horses,' John said. 'They aren't painted or glazed yet – but I had an order for them.'

'Someone wanted to buy some of your models?' Pam asked, interested.

'Yes – just half a dozen, but he also took some of the caricatures,' John replied, meeting her eyes. 'You said they might sell if I made moulds, but he likes the solid models I make and it is the feel of the clay that inspires me. It won't earn me a fortune, but it might just pay the rent on the cottage I am about to move into, at least for a week or two.'

'Oh, that is good,' Pam said. 'Are you ready to leave then, John?'

'Yes, more, or less. I'm going to try it. Jane says I can come back whenever I feel like it – and I can continue to use this room until I am sure I can manage.' He smiled at his son, who was staring at him, finger in mouth. 'I'll have a trial on my own for a couple of weeks – and then, if I'm managing, I'll ask you to bring Jonny to stay with me.' He took Jonny's finger from his mouth. 'Would you like to live with me, Jonny?'

The little boy nodded solemnly. 'Live with Daddy – Gan-gan come, too?'

'No, she won't come,' John said. 'But she might come and visit if we ask her nicely.'

Jonny nodded vigorously. 'Gan-gan come, too,' he repeated.

'I could come for a few days to help you get settled when you take him,' Pam said, surprising them all. 'Someone will cover for me at home – Lizzie or perhaps Dot Goodman.'

'That would be a big help,' John said, accepting her offer without hesitation.

'Thanks, Mum. I'll let you know when I am ready to have him with me. When will he start school?'

'Oh, not for a couple of years or a bit longer,' Pam replied. 'It depends on the policy of the school – but there might be a nursery school where he could go for a while each day, perhaps next year anyway.'

'Oh, I shan't bother with that until he has to go,' John said, looking fondly at his son as he reached for one of the unfinished models. 'That one is wet – take the one next to it.'

Jonny did as he was told, examining the model carefully, turning it in his hands. 'Nice,' he said at last. 'Like Gan-gan's horsey...'

'Well, yes, it is a carthorse,' Jon agreed. 'Have you still got old Dobbin, Mum? He can't still be working?'

'No, he doesn't work,' Pam agreed. 'Artie said I should sell him for dog meat, but George and Angela have a little ride on his back sometimes and so does Jonny. Poor Dobbin doesn't eat much, just a few oats when we can get any, or a carrot – mostly hay or grass, but your father was fond of him. He preferred to work with a horse, but Tom and Artie only use the tractors now.'

'I remember Dad trying to catch him,' John said, laughing. 'He'd run round the field after him, but Dobbin would sheer off at the last and kick up his heels and off he'd go. The only one who could catch him was Tom.'

'Yes, I remember. He comes to George these days, and that boy usually has something special for him.' Pam smiled, because it was lovely to see John smiling. She felt in her bag and brought out the cheque in an envelope and handed it to him.

'What's this, Mum?'

'I sold the house you would have inherited when I go,' Pam told him. 'It fetched nine hundred and twenty-five pounds, and I've made it up to a thousand for you. It will help you to live until you start work.'

'Mum! You shouldn't have done that,' John said. 'Are you sure you don't need the income – you could invest it...'

'I can manage, and I know it is what your father would have done,' Pam told him. 'I want you to have it, John. It should make your life easier.'

'It will help me to set up my business sooner – but I already have a little job, Mum.' John smiled at her. 'Jane spoke to one of the patients' fathers and he wanted someone to help him with his bookwork, wages and things. It is quite easy for me, though not yet actual accountancy, of course – but it will help me put what I'm learning into practice.'

'That is very useful, John,' his mother said. 'But will it be enough?'

'Mr Whiley has a fleet of trucks and I'm recording his wage roster and his expense sheet for him,' he replied. 'I think it will need several hours each week – and the wage he pays is fair. He is my first client, and I think it won't be long before I have others.'

'Yes, we've brought you our accounts, as well,' Pam said a little guiltily. 'If you don't feel able...'

'Don't be daft,' John said and laughed. 'Figures always came easily – I just preferred using my hands.'

'Terry says the same,' Susan put in, making her brother look at her. 'He would much prefer to work out in the fresh air, but he can't, so he works in his father's office; he does the ordering for their materials and keeps the wage book – but they use an accountant for their tax records. I am sure they would use you, once you qualify, if I asked.'

'Well, that is a way off, so wait a bit.' John looked at her thoughtfully. 'I remember, Terry. He liked being on the farm, because of the fresh air – but I expect building work was much the same for him. I loved the artistry of my work, but I've discovered there is a kind of magic in numbers if you bother to look.'

'I hope I am not disturbing you?' Jane's voice sounded from the doorway. 'I came to ask if you would like your tea here or in the garden?'

'I'll wash my hands and we'll go into the garden,' John said. 'Jane – this is my sister, Susan. She came to tell me she is getting married next year – and my mother has just given me a thousand pounds.'

'Goodness me!' Jane said, looking surprised. 'That was very kind of you, Mrs Talbot – and may I congratulate you, Susan? I feel that I should bring out the champagne, but we do not have any.'

'A cup of tea will do very nicely,' Pam said and smiled at her. 'We are lucky to have this mild weather into September, I think.'

'Yes, we are,' Jane replied. 'Shall I show you where we've set the table?' She glanced back at John. 'You can follow when you are ready, but don't start working again...' She smiled at Pam and Susan. 'Sometimes, he forgets all about the time and I have to remind him his dinner is ready or it is time for his exercises...'

'I'm coming,' John said, giving her a look that was filled with affection and, to Pam's eyes, love. 'Promise – just need to wash my hands...'

Pam followed Sister Jane out into the garden, where a little table and chairs were prepared, ready, but Jonny had lingered with his father and came out with him a few minutes later. John was holding his hand, talking to him, showing him flowers, and telling him what they were. Pam's eyes filled with tears; it was lovely to see them together, the child looking up to the man with such trust. How could she ever have thought that she had the right to keep him? He so obviously belonged with his father. Even that first time she'd brought him to visit, his instincts had been to be with John, and it was right and proper that he should be. She felt at peace with herself in that beautiful garden, watching them all talking together. Unusually, Sister Jane had lingered, seeming reluctant to leave the family party, though she obviously had work calling her.

Despite that, she sat with them for a while in the autumn sunshine beneath the sheltering branches of an ancient oak tree, its huge trunk knotted and twisted but still solid and somehow comforting. The easiness of the chatter between them all, and the way John and Sister Jane looked at each other, told Pam all she needed to know. She wasn't sure whether her son had declared his feelings to this woman, but they had an understanding, spoken or not.

Pam came to a decision; looking from John to the smiling woman, upon whose lap Jonny had chosen to sit, she said, 'Susan and I would like to go to a cinema or something this evening – would you be able to keep Jonny with you for a few hours?'

'I don't see why not,' John said, his eyes seeking Sister Jane's for confirmation.

'Actually, it is my afternoon and evening off,' Sister Jane told them, looking pleased. 'I'll be around to help, if you need it, John.'

'I think we can find something to do for a few hours,' John said and grinned. 'It will be good practice...'

'That is what I thought,' Pam nodded, rewarded by the look of delight in both John and Sister Jane's eyes. 'Susan and I never have any time to go out together, so it will be a nice treat for us, too.'

29

'What are you going to do?' Jane asked after Pam and Susan had departed. She had started to clear the used plates and cups to the tray. 'Stay in the garden for a while or go back to the craft room?'

'I thought we'd have a while playing in the garden,' John told her, watching her capable hands as she finished loading her tray. A lock of her fine hair had come down, trailing in her neck. 'Would you stay with us, Jane – if you don't have to rush away?'

'I don't have to do anything, unless there is an emergency,' Jane replied and sat down. 'Have you thought about what you'll play with?'

'Yes. I have a football in my room,' John replied. 'It has been in my kitbag for a while, so may need pumping up a bit, but we can have a kick around until the light starts to fade. Then we'll come in... I don't have any children's books yet. I need to buy some things for him...'

'I think I have a colouring book and pencils somewhere,' Jane said. 'Why don't you take Jonny to your room and fetch your ball, and I'll take the tray in and come out and join you in a little while.'

John agreed, and taking his son by the hand, they walked into the house. Jane carried the tray round to the kitchens at the back, where she was met by the smiling woman who ran the kitchen for them.

'Lawks a'mercy, Sister Jane,' she cried. 'Why didn't you ask one of the maids to bring the tray in? There's no call for you to be doing that, lass.'

'Oh, it was no trouble, Rita,' Jane replied. 'I am going up to change now. I'm off duty – so unless it is desperate, you don't know where I am...'

'I shan't tell a soul,' Rita promised. 'Not that I know where you're going.'

Jane laughed but didn't reply. She was free to take the evening off, go into town and visit the theatre or have a meal out if she chose, but she seldom took her free time and was usually around if needed. As she went to her small apartment at the back of the main house, she was smiling, thinking about what she should wear for a game of football, finally deciding on a pair of cream linen slacks, a white blouse and a red cardigan slung over her shoulders. Slipping off the heavy black shoes she habitually wore for work, she put on a pair of flat-heeled sandals. A glance in the mirror, and a brush through her long fair hair and she was ready.

* * *

John and his son were in the garden, playing football when Jane approached. They were enjoying themselves, the little boy laughing and giggling as John showed him how to kick the ball, then to keep it on the end of his toe, kicking it into the air several times before it fell out of reach. Intent on their game they hadn't noticed her, and then John looked up and the world suddenly seemed to spin.

'Jane...' he breathed, feeling as if everything had turned upside down. 'You look... wonderful.' It was as if he'd seen her for the first time and he realised that he hadn't ever witnessed the feminine glory of her out of uniform until now. All at once, she was a lovely curvaceous woman and not the caring, consci-entious nurse he knew and loved, and his chest felt tight as he struggled for breath. Yes, he'd come to realise he loved her before this, but he hadn't actually felt the need to make love to her until this moment. He'd forgotten how good it could be, how much it was possible to want a woman in a purely physical way, not just to silently adore her for being a ministering angel. John became really, tinglingly alive for the first time since the crash. It was as if he was the only man in the world and she was the only woman – a moment of intense joy and plea-sure that he felt down to the end of his toes and fingertips.

The spell was broken as Jonny ran to her, pulling at her slacks with eager and slightly grubby hands. 'Come and play with us, Janey,' he pleaded.

'Yes,' John spoke as he found he could breathe again. 'Come and play, Janey.'

His eyes met hers and had he known it, a very different meaning to those simple words was being conveyed.

Jane laughed – a joyous sound that made John's heart beat faster – and, in her eyes, he read the answer to his unspoken question.

'And what am I required to do?' she asked teasingly. 'I expect you want me in goal, don't you?'

'How did you know?' John asked, laughing.

'Because I had male cousins and friends, and girls always get to be the goalkeeper.'

'The right and proper way,' John remarked, his eyes meeting hers. 'Looks as if we've got a team then?'

Jane nodded, smiling, but didn't reply – until much later that evening.

* * *

It was much, much later, after Pam and Susan had called to collect a very sleepy but contented little boy that they were finally alone. They had retired to Jane's apartment after the football had worn them all out. Jane had made tea and hot buttered toast with jam for Jonny and grated, melted cheese for them.

Jonny had been using crayons to ruin a perfectly good colouring book for an hour or so, but became very sleepy and had made no objection when Susan carried him out to the waiting taxi.

'We decided to spoil ourselves and use a taxi,' Susan had told them. 'Mum has had a really good time – and you'd never believe it. She nearly got picked up...' A giggle broke from her. 'This man kept staring at us in a cinema foyer – and then he came over and told Mum she was beautiful and he wanted to paint her.'

'Never!' John was indignant. 'The cheek of him – she said no, of course.'

'She apologised and said she lived too far away,' Susan had said. 'He looked so disappointed – but fancy that. It made Mum laugh after we left him.'

'Your mother is lovely,' Jane had said. 'I can see why someone might want to paint her portrait – she has a very wise and serene look at times.'

'Yes, I suppose she does...' John had agreed. 'I hadn't thought about it.'

'We'll pop in again for a little while in the morning,' Susan had told John. 'Goodnight, Sister Jane. It was lovely to meet you.'

'Please, call me Jane...'

'Yes, I shall...' Susan had kissed her impulsively and then her brother. 'Take care of yourselves – both of you.'

'Thank you for coming,' John had said. 'It was good to see you – and give my love to Angela.'

Susan had promised she would and took Jonny out to her mother, who was still sitting in the taxi.

After it had driven off and the door was closed, Jane turned to John with a smile of inquiry. 'So, how did it feel, being a father?'

'It felt good...' John smiled wryly. 'He has a lot of energy.'

'Are you able to cope with it?'

'Yes – yes, I shall,' John replied. 'To be honest, I can't wait.'

'You don't think you'd like a bit of help?' Jane looked at him. He stared at her, not quite understanding. She shook her head at him. 'I'm asking if you want me to move in with you when the cottage is ready? If you'd like that... for us to take care of Jonny together...'

'Jane – are you saying...?' He hesitated, then took an uncertain step towards her. 'I—'

'The looks you've been giving me all evening seemed to say you'd like us to be together,' Jane said with an exasperated sigh. 'For goodness' sake, John! Do I have to beg?'

'Oh, my God, no!' He moved quickly towards her, taking her into his arms and holding her close, looking down at her. 'I love you – want you, Jane. I was just... afraid to ask, because I knew you cared for me, but you care for all your patients.'

'Not the way I care for you, believe me,' Jane said and looked up at him. 'Well, are you going to kiss me and show me how much you love me?'

She didn't have to ask twice. John's kiss was full of passion and long-denied need, the ache of his loneliness and despair melting away as the kiss went on and on until they were forced to break away by the need to breathe.

'I love you so much,' John told her then, his scarred hands touching her face, cradling it as he kissed forehead, nose, eyelids and then lips but softly, lightly with reverence. 'I knew you felt something for me and I knew I wanted to ask you to marry me, but I kept getting cold feet – I couldn't believe that you could feel the way I do. I want you, need you, so much, Jane. I want to touch you, make love to you – but more – I want you in my life, beside me when I wake up in the mornings and when we sleep.'

'And I shall be,' she promised. 'I'll continue my work here, but I shall cut my hours so that I can help with taking Jonny to school – and so that we can have time together.'

'We'll be a family,' John told her. 'We might have more children – would you like that, Jane?'

'If it happens, but it might not; I think I might not be able to – and if it doesn't, I shall be happy looking after you and little Jonny.'

'Thank you, my dearest,' he said softly, kissing her again. 'Shall we... Do you think we might...'

'Oh yes,' Jane said and took him by the hand, leading him to her bedroom. 'I definitely do...'

'I'm not sure...' he began, but she put a finger to his lips.

'We'll start slowly, and whatever happens, it will be good, because we are together – but there's nothing wrong with you in that way, John. I should know. I washed you all over for weeks.' She gave a gurgle of throaty laughter. 'There are no secrets between us, my love – or only for you to discover...' Her eyes looked up at him, bright with love, teasing and promising all. 'If you want to...'

He did, and they did, and it was wonderful. In each other's arms, they forgot the war, they forgot the pain, and they forgot so many months of unhappiness and worry when it had seemed nothing would be right again. It had all turned full circle and for them it was the beginning of a love that burned bright.

30

Tom's new batch of recruits were fresh-faced, eager and brimming with energy, as different from the last as chalk from cheese. Most of them were under twenty years of age, some straight from college or the Army cadets. His heart had sunk when he'd first seen them, because the thought of sending these boys on what could be a suicide mission was appalling – but his protest to Major Carlton had fallen on deaf ears.

'They are all volunteers,' he'd told Tom, looking as if he'd won first prize on the football pools. 'They heard about us somehow and wanted to be a part of it, Gilbert. You won't find them trying to stick a knife in your back because you pissed them off. They are willing to die for their country – and they all think you are the bees' knees.'

Tom had stared at him in disbelief. 'I doubt they'd heard my name until they arrived here – and once I've had them training for a while, they will want to murder me. I felt that way about my training officer.'

'Well, whether you credit it or not, you've become something of a hero,' Major Carlton had laughed. 'I know they need their romantic nonsense knocked out of them, Gilbert – but you're the man to do it.'

'I'll do my best, sir,' Tom had promised, but he felt uneasy. The last batch of men had been sent on a dangerous mission, and so far, none of them had made it back, though they'd been successful, and it might be that some of them would turn up eventually. Tom hoped so. These youngsters should be planning a bright future; careers, homes, families, not training for a mission that might be the end of their lives.

'Oh – and Tom...' Major Carlton had frowned and Tom stiffened in response. When his officer dropped the formality, he knew something unpleasant was coming. 'I need to warn you – that fellow Regan... he escaped while being transferred from one prison to another.'

'Regan escaped custody...?' Tom had stared at him in disbelief. He'd expected the man to be court-martialled for treason and shot by this time. 'How did that happen?'

'I'm not sure,' Major Carlton had replied, frowning heavily. 'He was set to be court-martialled, as you know – but then an order came through that they wanted him sent to London. He was to be questioned, because someone somewhere decided he might have some useful information – and en route, the van stopped to clear something blocking the road, and somehow, he jumped out of the back and ran off. He is being searched for, but so far without result.'

'Do you think it was planned? Someone wanted him free?' Tom had frowned because it sounded that way; it shouldn't be possible to escape from a prison vehicle. 'Why – and who?'

'We simply don't know,' Major Carlton had sighed. 'It isn't as if Regan was the main spy – he just worked for Connors, at least that's what we believed.'

'I picked him at random from a prison, as I was instructed. As far as I was concerned, he wasn't important... just a man who had turned traitor for money.'

Major Carlton had nodded. 'That is what we all believed and perhaps it was just a lucky accident for him that he escaped – but why did someone on high want to question him?'

'Where did the order for the transfer come from?'

'Somewhere in the War Office, or so we believed – but as yet we've had no conformation.' Major Carlton had cleared his throat. 'He is probably just a nasty little criminal who got lucky – but he hates you. I just wanted you to be aware, in case.'

'You think he might try to revenge himself on me?' Tom had found that idea incredulous. 'Surely not? If he has any sense, he'll find some way to leave the country.'

'Let's hope he does.' Major Carlton had looked grim. 'We don't want his sort here. I know you can handle him, Gilbert – but I thought you should know.'

'Thank you, sir. I doubt he'll come looking for me – but if he does, I'll be ready.'

Major Carlton had nodded. 'You're looking very fit. Life on the farm suits you then?'

'Yes, it does. Actually, the exercise has done me a lot of good.' Tom had flexed his right arm and smiled, because it was so much stronger again, the nerves seeming to have healed, despite his being told by doctors they never would. 'Can't wait to get back there, if I'm honest, sir.'

'No thought of becoming professional Army when it is all over then? Pity – we could do with men like you, Gilbert. You would make a fine officer and Army life is very different in peacetime. I know most of the men will be disbanded when we finally beat that bastard, and we're close to it, now. I can feel it in my bones. We shall still need good men. There will be a lot of clearing up to do after this little show is over.'

'I imagine so, sir,' Tom had agreed. 'But no, it isn't for me. I have a home and family waiting – and I'm needed on the farm.'

'Well, you've more than done your duty, so I shan't try to persuade you. Carry on, soldier!' He'd saluted and Tom had known the interview was over.

Walking away from the major's office, he'd mulled over the information. He'd told Artie that Regan would soon be dead, shot as a traitor, but now it looked as if he'd got away, and that made Tom slightly uneasy. It was unlikely that Regan would come looking for him, but he might, because he probably blamed Tom for bringing him here. So, in his criminal mind, he likely wanted to get even... yet how probable was it that he would come back here where he would be recognised? If he was seen entering the camp, he would be arrested.

Tom shrugged his shoulders, pushing the memory of that interview from his mind. He didn't think Regan could get to him here – and in the meantime, he had a new batch of recruits to train.

'Right then, you lot,' he called the men to attention. Unlike most of their predecessors, they came to attention smartly, saluting him, young faces eager, eyes alight with excitement. 'Now then, I suppose you idiots think this is all an adventure, glamourous and exciting? Well, I am here to tell you that it is not – blood, sweat and tears is what you'll get in the next few weeks and months of your training. And by the end of it you'll hate my guts – so if anyone wants to change his mind, now is the time to do it.'

Tom waited expectantly, but no one slunk away, instead their eyes were fixed on his face as if drawn by some invisible magnet. He shook his head, half amused by their innocent eagerness, half torn by grief at their likely end.

'Right. I think we'll start you off nice and gently then,' he said. 'Just a five-mile run today, lads. I'll be with you on the bike, watching for slackers...' Not that he imagined any of them would slack or falter. He would probably have had a job to keep up with this lot, even if his leg didn't have a permanent limp.

The warm summer weather had finally broken, dark clouds gathering overhead. It was probably going to rain and rain hard before they got back and they would all get soaked through, including Tom. At least he could wear his thick jacket; they would all be wearing just trousers and vests, and their Army boots. Tom made them run in their boots, because it was how they would need to run if on a mission. No good in training them to run in plimsolls when they would be in full Army gear, whatever they were sent to do, and he was pretty sure he knew where they were headed when the time came.

Those miracle weapons of Hitler's needed to be destroyed, because unless they were, he might succeed in keeping the war going for much longer – and it was time that it came to an end. Everyone was sick of the death and destruction, Tom as much as the next man. Like these youngsters, he'd been eager to do his bit once, but now he just wanted it all over so that he could go home to his wife and family.

31

'I wish I didn't have to go back to London,' Terry said that afternoon. He'd managed to fill up with petrol and come down for a long weekend with his sister and had spent most of the time with Susan. His car was loaded, a basket of fresh food, including a big seed cake, and some eggs, to take back to London. Tina was being fussed over by her Aunty Jeanie, kissed, with promises of another visit soon. He sighed as he looked at Susan and reached for her hands. 'You have to go back to college, too – but I'll visit when I can.'

'Good,' Susan replied and leaned in so that he could kiss her. It was just a brief kiss on the lips, a regretful promise, but neither of them felt like going into a passionate embrace in front of his sister and daughter. 'I'll write – and you must, too.'

'I'm not much of a letter writer, but I'll try,' he promised. 'Just remember I love you – with all those glamorous college students around.'

'Not interested,' Susan replied. 'Most of them are serious academics, or too young for the Army – all the eligible men joined up. I've not bothered with any of them since I started there.' Susan smiled as he swung Tina up to kiss her goodbye. 'I shall see you soon, love. Be a good girl for your daddy.'

'Bye. Love you.' Tina clung to her for a moment. Then she was in the car, in the front seat next to her father, leaning over the back of it precariously, to wave at her auntie.

Terry pressed Susan's hands. 'Thank you for loving us,' he said. 'We'll see you very soon, my dearest girl…'

Susan felt a sudden strange panic and threw herself at him, kissing him with all the passion in her. 'I love you,' she said. 'Don't forget. I always shall love you…'

'I adore you,' Terry whispered. 'Be down as soon as I can…'

Susan watched until the car was out of sight, waving, her cheeks wet with tears. She became aware of Jeanie beside her and dashed a hand over her cheek. 'Sorry, Jeanie. It was just hard to part with him… We've only just found out how we feel. I've been aware of my feelings for years and so has he – but we never acknowledged it.'

'I know,' Jeanie said, putting an arm around her waist. 'He told me – he'd felt something for you when he stayed at the farm, but he'd lost his leg and his wife, and I suppose he couldn't even think of a new relationship then, and you were very young. In London, he says he found himself thinking about you a lot, wanting to write or visit, but he wasn't sure you'd felt anything for him, so he just left it and did nothing…'

Susan nodded, because she knew that was how it had been. 'I wasn't sure then. I knew I liked him a lot and I missed him. We used to have quite a few airmen to tea a year or two ago, as you know – and I went out with lots of them. I liked one, but he went away. So I wasn't even sure in my own mind whether my feelings for Terry were just a young girl's fancy… a sort of made-up dream that I'd invented. Then you told me he was coming to stay and…' She laughed. 'It seems as if it happened in an instant – but actually, it has been simmering for years.'

'And I'm glad,' Jeanie told her and hugged her. 'I've worried about Terry for a long time, but I know he will be happy with you, Susan – and it keeps our family together.'

'Yes, it does,' Susan replied. She smiled. 'I have such a lot to look forward to now…'

'Yes, we all do – your mum thinks John might marry his nurse. Did you meet her last weekend?'

'Yes, I did,' Susan said, smiling. 'She is really nice, Jeanie. A bit older than John – but he has changed so much, and I don't mean his scars. He is all grown up now – a man, not the young lad he was when he went away to war.' She sighed, her smile disappearing. 'That all seems a lifetime ago, Jeanie – Faith, them getting together, then she had the baby and they weren't married – and then Mum stepped in and looked after Jonny. It doesn't seem possible it is only a few years, does it?'

'A lot has happened to our family,' Jeanie agreed. She shivered as a cold wind swept across the fenland. 'I think it might rain soon. Do you want to get off, Susan – or come in for a cup of tea?'

'I'll get off,' Susan replied, glancing up at the heavy sky. 'It does look like rain. I might get soaked – but I've got to start getting my stuff together for next term. After that, I'll be working as a pupil teacher – and after a year of that, I can apply for a proper teaching position.'

'Where will you apply?' Jeanie asked, knowing that Susan would be sent to an appointed school for her final year of training, but after that she could apply where she wanted. 'London?'

'I expect so,' Susan replied. 'I am sure Terry will go on working for your father – but it really depends on what he decides. I'll go wherever he leads.'

'Love's sweet dream,' Jeanie teased, but there was a look in her eyes that made Susan wonder. She was about to ask if anything was wrong when a rumble of thunder made up her mind. 'I'd better go. Mum will worry if the storm is bad.'

'Terry should have put your bike on the car and run you home...' Jeanie said shaking her head. 'Be careful, love. If there is lightning, get off the bike and shelter for a while.'

'Yes, I shall,' Susan promised, got on her bike and pedalled off for all she was worth.

Jeanie stood for a moment. Then, hearing a cry from her son in the house, she turned and went in, just as the heavens opened and the rain started to sheet down.

* * *

Susan was soaked to the skin when she got in. Pam took one look at her and banished her upstairs. 'Strip those wet things off and I'll run you a hot bath,' she told her daughter. 'Why didn't you wait until the storm was over, love?'

Susan shook her head and ran upstairs. She stripped off her clothes, then put on a warm dressing gown and made her way to the bathroom. Pam was just turning the water off; it was above the Plimsoll line.

'I've given you my share as well as yours,' she told Susan. 'A wash in the morning does me – and this will warm you up, love. We don't want you catching a chill, do we?'

Susan smiled at her, slipped off her robe and was about to step into the bath when she felt a shudder. It was as if something hit her in the chest and she gasped, doubling over for a moment.

'What's wrong, love?' Pam asked her, looking at her anxiously. 'Are you in pain?'

'No...' Susan looked at her in bewilderment. 'I don't know – it was odd... as if something hit me, knocked the breath right out of me...' She shook her head. 'I'm fine, Mum. It must have been a stitch or something...'

'Yes, I expect so...' Pam gave her another anxious glance and left her to her bath.

Susan settled back in the warm water, eyes closed, thinking about the future. It was all going to be wonderful. She knew that, but try as she might, she couldn't picture herself with Terry in their future home. After a few moments, she became aware that her cheeks were wet with tears, but she had no idea why she was crying.

* * *

Susan spent the next day catching up on some revision for her college work, and packing her case ready to return the next week. Her nose felt a bit sniffly and she had to wipe it a few times, which was a nuisance, because she really didn't need a cold when she was so close to returning to college.

She spent a restless night, and when she woke, her throat was sore and her eyes were streaming. Pam took one look at her when she went down to break-fast and sent her straight back to bed.

'I'll make you a hot drink,' she told her daughter. 'I've got half a bottle of brandy I keep for winter colds – with some sugar and hot water, it will make you feel much better.'

Susan nodded, accepting her mother's fussing without argument, because she really did feel unwell. Her head was going round and round and she had started to feel very hot. When her mother gave her the warm drink, she swallowed it down as swiftly as she could and lay back, her head so dizzy that she hardly knew what to say when Pam asked how she felt.

'Should I ring for the doctor?' Pam inquired, but Susan shook her head. 'Only a cold – better soon,' she said and promptly fell asleep.

* * *

However, it wasn't just a cold and Susan did not get better; she got worse the next day and was delirious. Worried out of her mind, Pam rang for the doctor. He came and it was their new young doctor. He introduced himself and was taken to the patient, immediately concerned as he examined her.

'She is very ill,' he told Pam. 'She must be kept as quiet as possible. Are you able to nurse her yourself? I think you may need help if you have other commitments. Is there anyone available?'

'I'm not sure – both my daughters-in-law are pregnant and I wouldn't want to risk them,' she said. 'We are busy on the farm – but I will manage.'

'No, that isn't good enough,' he told her. 'Susan either has to go to hospital or we get you a nurse who can live in until the patient is better.'

'Well, Dot Goodman might come...' Pam suggested and saw his approval.

'I know Mrs Goodman,' he said. 'She has a little experience of these fevers, because she nursed her mother and her father before she married. Yes, I will call and ask her myself. If she says no, I shall send an ambulance to collect Susan.' He saw her anxiety and touched her arm lightly. 'She will live, Mrs Talbot. I'll come every day and if need be, we will have her in hospital...'

'It isn't just her illness...' Pam hesitated. 'Can she hear?'

'I expect so – sort of...'

Pam nodded. 'I will speak to you downstairs...'

In the kitchen, Doctor Bryant looked at her expectantly. 'Something else is wrong?'

'Artie came and told me this morning. They had a phone call from Jeanie's mother... and Jeanie has gone up to London to be with her parents...'

'Bad news?' he asked, his eyes seeking hers in concern.

Gulping back her tears, Pam said, 'Susan was practically engaged to a young man she'd known some years ago. He has a little girl...' She swallowed hard, and a tear trickled down her cheek. 'Terry had been down on a visit last weekend. He was driving home in that thunderstorm two days ago and something happened – either he swerved or misjudged a bend – the car overturned and went into a deep ditch and...' Pam gasped and sat down hard; the colour leaving her face. 'They were both killed – Terry and the child. I don't know what it will do to Susan, doctor. She was so happy, planning the future for after she finishes her teacher training... now this terrible tragedy. Tina was such a little darling and Terry was a lovely man.' Pam was trembling, her shoulders bowed as if this last grief was just one too many for her to bear. 'It is too awful...'

'Terrible – an awful thing to happen... Susan will be distressed.'

Looking up, Pam saw that the doctor too was pale; he looked as if he'd been hit in the face, but he did a sort of blink and then nodded.

'I am so very sorry,' he said. 'I met Susan briefly a while ago – but I had no idea she was engaged. That is a real tragedy, Mrs Talbot. You must all be devastated.'

'We are,' Pam agreed. 'His sister Jeanie can't stop crying and I can't think how his poor mother feels. I shall ring her soon, but I don't want to intrude on her grief. When Jeanie is with her, I will, but saying how sorry we are doesn't help.' Pam sniffed and wiped her eyes. 'Terry lost a leg early in the war, was just getting over it and planning a happy future – and now... that little girl too... and Jeanie. It must have been a terrible shock. I just pray it doesn't affect the baby.' She shook her head as the enormity of what had happened drained all the life from her and, for a moment, she felt she might faint.

'Do not faint, Mrs Talbot!' The young doctor's stern voice brought her back from the brink. 'Susan needs you now more than ever in her life. You have got to be the strong one here. I know you lost your husband quite recently, and your younger son was badly burned – but you came through, and you have to do it again. For Susan, and your family. Who is going to look after them all, if you don't?'

Pam raised her head and looked at him, the sympathy in his face reaching through the wall of her misery. He was strong and kind and, somehow, she felt that strength helping her, pulling her back to the real world.

'I am sorry,' she said and dashed the tears from her eyes. 'Thank you for reminding me of my duty. For a moment, it all seemed too much... but I do know that I have to be strong and carry on.'

'Think of it this way, you still have Susan. Had she been in that car you might have lost her too. She is still alive and we shall nurse her back to health.'

'Yes, that is true. If Terry had decided to bring Susan home because of the storm she might also have been killed; I must count my blessings.'

'That's right,' he said and smiled at her. 'You are going to have a hard job, because Susan is very ill and when she gets better – and I shall see she does – then she will be in such need of you, Mrs Talbot.'

'Please,' she said. 'My name is Pam.'

'Yes, I've heard,' he told her. 'My name is Stephen... and I can see we shall be friends.' He went over to her kitchen sink and washed his hands. Pam hurried to give him a clean tea cloth to wipe them. He smiled at her. 'I must go now – but I shall call again after surgery hours this evening. And I shall speak to Mrs Goodman for you. Can you manage for now? Just try to keep her as cool as possible – you may need to sponge her with warm water if she becomes too hot.'

'Yes, I know,' Pam agreed. 'Thank you so much. I feel better because of your understanding.'

He nodded, picked up his bag and went out.

Pam splashed her face in cold water and dried it, then went back upstairs to her sick daughter. As she looked down at Susan's feverish face, she felt a great sadness. Her lovely, generous, kind daughter was going to take the news of Terry's and Tina's deaths hard. She would have to keep it from her, until she was out of danger – and then, somehow, she would find a way to tell Susan the terrible truth.

32

Tom received two letters on the same day; the first was from John, telling him about his plans to marry in two months, when his cottage would be ready for them to move into. He asked if Tom could get leave and be his best man at the wedding, which was intended to be a simple church ceremony, with just a few friends and relations present. The second letter, from his wife, told Tom of the tragic deaths of their friend and his little daughter, and of Susan's illness.

Lizzie wrote:

It is all so awful here, Tom. Susan is very ill. She and Terry had just got together and planned to marry in a year or so when Susan had finished her training. She doesn't know of the accident that killed them both, because she went down with a severe chill the day after he returned to London, which the doctor fears may have turned to pneumonia. Susan is desperately ill, Tom. I know you are doing important work and may not be able to get away, but please try for some leave if you possibly can. Your mum is coping, just. Dot goes there for several hours a day, and I take Arthur there in the evenings. We sleep there and sit with your sister for some hours of the night so that Pam can get a little rest, but I'm not sure she sleeps. She looks grey with fatigue and I'm not sure she could go on if anything happens to Susan.

Tom took the letter straight to Major Carlton and requested compassionate leave. His commanding officer was silent for a moment, looking annoyed.

'You've not long returned from leave,' he said, frowning. 'Your men will be needed very soon – I can't have you disappearing for two or three weeks at this crucial time.'

'I understand, but I am only asking for a few days, sir. My corporal will keep them training.'

'Three days,' the major barked. 'And see you get back on time or you might find yourself in the cooler for real.'

Tom saluted smartly and left swiftly with his pass. He stopped to speak with his corporal, giving him brief orders to carry on with the exercises they'd been doing. Then he returned to his barracks, made sure he had his pay book, which every soldier was required to carry at all times, enough money to get him home and his seventy-two-hour pass. He knew he was in his superior officer's bad books now, but after that letter from Lizzie, he had to go – even if he'd gone AWOL.

* * *

Tom took one look at his mother's face and knew he'd done the right thing. For all the trouble she'd had these past years, he had never seen her looking so pale and ill. Her eyes were red and had dark shadows beneath them and the depth of her fear and misery cut Tom to the heart. He took two strides towards her, catching her in his arms and holding her tight. Her body shook with the force of her emotion as the tears she'd been holding back flowed.

'I can't lose her, too,' she choked. 'Oh, Tom, she is so ill...'

'I know, Lizzie told me,' he said. 'I have only a few hours, Mum – but I'm going to sit with Susan. You have to rest and you must sleep...' He looked at her as she would have denied him. 'Have you got any of that brandy left?'

'Yes, some...'

'Then I'll make you a drink. Go and get in bed, Mum. I will bring it up to you and you can tell me what to do for Susan...'

Tom was too forceful, too much used to command to be denied and Pam caved in. She couldn't have done anything else, because her son would have carried her there if she'd tried to deny him.

In bed, she explained how they'd been treating Susan, keeping her cool and dry. 'Her sheets need changing all the time, because she has terrible sweats and they get soaked. She mustn't turn cold, Tom. She has to be warm but not hot. I shouldn't leave her...'

'I can do all that, probably easier than you,' Tom said. 'Swallow that brandy and let yourself sleep, Mum. Susan isn't going to die on my watch.'

'I know... I'm foolish...' Pam sighed and closed her eyes, overcome by tiredness.

Tom slipped from the room and went to his sister's room. It smelled of sickness and he opened the window just a crack, then went to look down at her pale face. Her hair was streaked with sweat and his heart caught with sudden grief, because she was his little sister and he didn't want her to be like this; he wanted her to be full of life and beautiful, as he'd last seen her.

A jug of lukewarm water was on the washing stand. Tom poured some into a bowl his mother had put ready, then he pulled back the sheets, which were already damp, removed Susan's nightgown and bathed her all over. He then dried her and dressed her in a clean nightdress, lifted her into the armchair next to the bed while he stripped the damp sheets and replaced them with fresh white ones. He then lifted her carefully back and covered her just with the sheet and one thin blanket. As he turned away to empty the bowl, he heard a murmur or gasp behind him, and turned.

Susan's eyes were open and she was looking at him, a puzzled expression in her eyes. 'Tom?' she croaked in a voice hardly above a whisper. He replaced the bowl on the stand and went to the bed. She gazed up at him. 'Am I dreaming or did you just wash me?'

'You aren't dreaming,' Tom said and smiled. 'You've been in a fever for a while, love. Mum was exhausted looking after you, so I did it for you. Did it make you feel better?'

'Yes, it did,' she said and closed her eyes. Tom put his hand on her forehead. It felt quite cool and dry to him. 'Why did you come home? Have I been so ill?'

'Yes, pretty bad, so they tell me. I only arrived a couple of hours ago.'

'And now I'm better...' Susan gave a weak laugh. 'It must be you, Tom – the fever knew when it was beaten.'

'Looks like it,' Tom murmured. 'I didn't do much, love. Mum has been nursing you for more than a week. I came as soon as I got Lizzie's letter.'

'Dear Lizzie,' Susan said and closed her eyes.

Tom touched her again, half afraid that something was wrong and she'd gone, but was reassured by her pulse, which was steady enough now. He closed his eyes in thankfulness that she'd turned the corner and sat down in the chair beside her. His mother would want him to watch until she woke and so he would. However, after he'd been sitting there for perhaps half an hour, he heard someone enter the kitchen and a male voice asking something. He thought it was Olive that answered, though he hadn't heard her come in earlier.

A few seconds later, a man's footsteps came up the stairs, someone knocked softly at Susan's door, and then a man entered. 'Hello, I'm Susan's doctor,' he said. 'I think you must be her brother Tom...'

'Yes, I am,' Tom said. 'She seems better now. She was sweating and I gave her a wash and she woke up for a while.'

'Did she know you?'

'Yes.' Tom laughed. 'She said it must be because of me she was feeling better and then went to sleep.'

'Thank God for that,' Doctor Bryant said and felt Susan's pulse. 'I thought we might lose her a couple of days ago. Your mother was desperately tired from nursing her – have you sent her to bed?'

'Yes. Unfortunately, I only have three days – at least one of which has already gone.' Tom frowned. 'Will Susan be all right now? My wife thought she might have pneumonia?'

'I thought so too at one time. Fortunately, I think it was just a virulent fever – but it certainly seems to have waned for the moment. It might return, but hopefully it won't. Tell your mother she is to send for me at once if Susan has a relapse.'

'Yes, I will, but I am sure she would anyway,' Tom said. 'Thank you for coming. Lizzie said you've been visiting at least twice a day – that was good of you, doctor.'

'Please, call me Stephen,' he said and offered his hand to Tom. 'I will call again tomorrow morning. Someone should continue to sit with her all the time for now, though I hope and believe she has somehow turned the corner.' They shook hands and the doctor left. Tom resumed his seat by the bed.

Ten minutes later, someone came up the stairs; the door opened and Lizzie peeped round. 'Can I come in? Is she sleeping? The doctor says she is better...'

'Yes, she is,' Tom agreed and smiled. 'Come in, but we mustn't wake her.' He smiled as she came to him and kissed her softly. 'I only have a few hours, Lizzie.

I won't be able to spend much time with you and Arthur. I need to help Mum –
it's what I came for and I had a job to wangle that…'

'It doesn't matter,' Lizzie said. 'We could none of us get Pam to sleep. She
would go for an hour and lie down and then come back; it was wearing her out
and I was frightened she might become ill, too. I know I shouldn't have asked
you to come.'

'Yes, you should,' Tom told her. 'This is my place when things are desperate,
Lizzie. I wish I could just say to Hell with the lot of them and stay, but I can't –
but if Mum has a good sleep, she will feel better – and if Susan is on the mend it
will help.' He frowned as he looked at his sleeping sister. 'Does she know yet?'

'No, Pam won't tell her until she is stronger. I think it will break her heart,
Tom. She was so happy for a few days – and she went to see John.'

'He told me. He said her visit helped him to make up his mind to ask Jane to
marry him – it's in two months' time. We are both invited; you must go if I can't,
Lizzie. I doubt I'll get leave again, unless… well, if my present job ends…'

'I know – and John will understand. We haven't told him about this other
business yet, but I shall write once I know Susan is over this illness.'

'Yes, do that,' Tom agreed. He smiled at her. 'I could murder a cup of tea and
a sandwich, love.'

Lizzie laughed softly. 'I'll bring you some food and drinks up on a tray,' she
promised. 'When you're tired, I'll take your place for a while, Tom.'

'You've been doing your share,' Tom replied. 'Get me that tray, then go and
rest, Lizzie. I think I can manage a few hours on watch…'

* * *

It was past seven the next morning when Pam came to Susan's room, wearing
her old dressing gown, slippers on her feet. She exclaimed as she saw Tom
sitting by the bed, leaning his head back, his eyes closed.

'It's all right, Mum,' he said and opened them. 'I've been watching her all
night and Lizzie was with me some of the time – she brought drinks and food.
Susan has slept most of the night, like you. We helped her use the chamber pot
once, but then she went straight back to sleep. She had some of your home-
made lemonade, then slept again.'

'Dot got me the lemons,' Pam said, looking down at Susan's peaceful face.

'She asked the man on the market and he'd got four hidden under the counter and he let her have the lot for nothing, because she told him how ill Susan was.'

'That was kind,' Tom said and smiled. 'You look and sound better, Mum.'

'I am, thanks to you,' she replied. 'I couldn't leave her, Tom. I couldn't rest if I did – but when you came, then I knew she would be all right.'

'It's funny, but Susan said much the same,' he told her. 'You have to rest, Mum. Susan has turned a corner, but I don't think she will be going back to college just yet. She will still need nursing – so you have to let others take their turn. What about Artie and Jeanie?'

'They went to London for...' Pam glanced at the bed. 'I think Artie is back, but I haven't seen him. Olive said he gave her instructions and disappeared back to Sutton. I imagine Jeanie is still in London with her mother...'

'Why is Jeanie in London with her mother?' Susan opened her eyes and looked at them.

'She went to visit her and buy some baby things,' Pam replied swiftly.

Tom looked at her but didn't interfere. He would do what he could to help in the short time he had left, but he wasn't at all sure that his mother was right to withhold the news of the tragic deaths. Susan would have to know at some time and he just hoped she didn't blame her mother for not telling her sooner.

* * *

It was hardly any time before Tom was on the train heading back to his base. He slept most of the way, exhausted after two nights without sleep, but his mother was looking and feeling better and Susan was over the dangerous period. She was still weak and a little fractious, but she would improve – and her devoted doctor was still visiting her every day.

When Tom arrived back at camp, he was told by six people that Major Carlton wanted to see him the moment he returned. He frowned as he strode towards his commanding officer's room, suspecting he was in trouble, though he'd made it on time, by travelling throughout the night – fifteen minutes early, as it happened.

Major Carlton sprang to his feet as Tom entered the office. 'Just the man I want to see. Two things, Talbot. Firstly, your men are needed urgently – by next week. Can you have them ready by then?'

'Yes, sir,' Tom replied, because he knew in his heart that this bunch were the best he'd ever trained.

'You are certain? This mission is important – if it succeeds in destroying the target where air raids have failed, it could shorten the war by months.' Tom knew that the men were destined for a mission behind enemy lines, because the V2 rockets had to be destroyed on the ground, at the factory that was turning them out in such numbers they were causing serious problems. It wasn't said in so many words, but they both knew what had to be done.

'We all want that, sir – and the men are ready. They were ready to go when they got here and the training has gone better than I expected.'

'Good...' Some of the tension went out of Major Carlton's face.

'And the second thing, sir?' Tom asked.

'The second... Oh, yes, a couple of bits of good news for once. Some of your men from the last mission have reported back, Sergeant Zeeman for one. And Regan was apprehended and shot on sight. He is dead now, Tom. You can relax and forget him. And, once this batch of men have gone, you could put in your application for a medical discharge. I could recommend it if you wish.'

'That is good news, sir.' Tom saluted smartly. 'I'll go and tell the men they are off soon and take them on their last hike, because they need a bit of relaxation before they go – if I have your permission, sir?'

'Yes, of course – and how was your sister, Talbot?'

'Thankfully the fever has broken at last, and my mother finally got some sleep while I watched over Susan.'

Major Carlton nodded. 'Don't think I don't understand, Tom. My daughter suffered too much when Shorty died; she loved him very much – and I don't think she is over it yet, though she tries to carry on. I dare say your sister will take a long time to get over the deaths of her fiancé and his daughter.'

'Yes, I expect so,' Tom replied. 'Thank you, sir.'

'Dismissed, Talbot.' Major Carlton saluted, Tom did the same and left.

Tom was smiling as he walked away – the old devil had some human compassion after all! He couldn't wait to ring Lizzie and tell her he would soon be putting in for his discharge, but first of all he had a hike to go on – and he wanted to talk to Sergeant Zeeman, too. Ask him how the mission went and how many of them had made it back...

33

Susan returned to a semblance of normality very slowly. Still weak and shaken from the first serious illness she'd ever had, she couldn't think much about anything other than the effort it took to get herself sitting up, then to the bathroom. Day by day, she improved just a little, able now to summon a smile for her visitors, and it was only after a week or so of convalescence that she began to sense something was wrong. Her mother was trying hard to be normal, but she wasn't – nor was Lizzie, and neither Jeanie nor Artie had been to see her. Angela visited her sickroom once, but was so obviously under orders not to distress or worry her that she hardly spoke, just sat and stared at her sister with thinly veiled tears in her eyes.

'What's wrong, Angela?' Susan asked eight days after Tom returned to his base. She was sitting propped up against her pillows, some of her college books on the bed, though she hadn't read much, because she felt too tired. 'I know something is – you are all tiptoeing round me as if I were made of bone china. Why don't you tell me?'

'Mum said I mustn't, because it will upset you – but I am upset, too, and she doesn't think how it worries me,' Angela sniffed, because she knew she mustn't tell her sister the big secret, but she also knew she would. Susan wanted to know and someone had to tell her one day.

'I know something is wrong,' Susan's voice nagged at her, like a magpie relentlessly picking at the skull of a young nestling it had killed. 'You may as well tell me now. I shall keep asking you.'

'I'm not supposed to and it's horrid,' Angela blurted out, tears popping into her eyes. 'I liked Tina and her daddy and it isn't fair... Ohh!' She clamped her hand over her mouth and ran shrieking for her mother, out of the room and down the stairs.

Susan lay back against the pile of feather pillows, her head swimming as terrible thoughts filled her mind. She'd known for days that something was wrong; her mother's avoidance of her questions about letters for her, the way she always had an easy explanation ready, and the strange lack of visits from Jeanie and Artie. Vaguely, she recalled hearing someone say Jeanie was in London with her mother; she'd been told it was for a visit and to buy baby clothes, but she would surely not still be there for that reason. Only one thing might keep Jeanie with her mother, away from Artie and the farm – and that was the death of a member of her family – Terry or Tina.

Susan tried to remember the moment of their parting, but found she couldn't. That day was lost somewhere in the mists of her fever, just out of grasp. Why had she been so ill? She seemed to recall cycling home in a thunderstorm and getting soaked. The lightning had turned the sky a strange white colour as it zigzagged across the fens and she'd seen it strike something – a tree she'd thought, but the rain had prevented her from seeing what had been hit. Then she'd got home, soaked through. Hurried into a warm bath by her mother, she'd gone to bed and to sleep – but that storm had raged on its destructive way causing mayhem and what...?

In her mind's eye, Susan saw Terry's car, his little daughter sitting beside him, kneeling up to look back and wave at them – and she saw him glance at the child, telling her to sit back properly in her seat. Now, Susan saw her, wilfully disobeying her father, then falling back across him as he swerved to avoid some creature on the road; saw him losing control, and the car spinning round in a circle, hit by an oncoming vehicle and tossed over and over into a steep dyke. She saw the windscreen shatter and the jagged glass pierce flesh, and she screamed. Again and again, she screamed, until her mother came rushing into the room.

'Susan, are you ill?' she asked, seeming shocked and unlike her capable self.

'He is dead, isn't he?' Susan said, but it wasn't a question, because she knew with awful certainty that she was right. 'Tina and Terry are both dead. Killed in an accident. I know it, so don't try to deny it.'

'Did Angela tell you?' her mother asked, still seeming too shocked to offer comfort. Not that anything could offer comfort for this overwhelming sense of loss and grief. Susan had cried for her brothers when they were wounded and she'd cried for her father's death, but she hadn't felt as if the world had ended. As it had for her, she realised, as the sobs began to break from her. All those secret dreams of Terry coming for her one day – dreams that had seemed to come true – were gone now and there was nothing left. Nothing to plan or hope for. Nothing. He was gone and she wanted him. She wanted him so badly that it was a physical pain in her breast.

Lying back against the pillows, she closed her eyes and willed herself to die. She didn't want to get well if Terry was gone from her. Much easier to die and put an end to this agony.

'Susan, I am sorry.' Her mother's voice seemed to come from a long way off. 'I thought it best not to tell you until you were stronger. There was nothing any of us could do... they said it was instantaneous. They couldn't have known much...'

To Susan's ears her mother sounded as if she was trying to placate a child for a nagging toothache. 'Stop it! Stop lying to me!' she shouted, her voice loud and shocking in the small room. 'Do you think I don't know... I saw it in my head, saw the accident, saw them die, and it wasn't like that... I know it was terrible. You are all so shocked, trying to hide it from me... but I know how it must have been.'

To Susan's horror, her mother flopped down in the chair next to the bed and burst into tears. She was clearly close to breaking down, her shoulders hunched and defenceless, as if all her strength had drained away just like that. 'I am sorry,' she choked. 'I just thought with you so ill, it was best not to tell you.'

'Not your fault,' Susan said, closing her eyes. She knew her mother needed more, a show of love or forgiveness, but she just couldn't make the effort. It was hardly worth trying to speak or think when all she truly wanted was to sleep and never wake up again.

* * *

For several days, Susan lay in a blur of pain, as much mental as physical, not caring whether she ate or drank, wanting only to be left alone, sunk in the agony of knowing that all her dreams had been shattered by a wet road and some kind of accident. No one had told her exactly what had happened and she wasn't certain she wanted to know, because it must have been horrific to kill them both just like that.

Angela crept into her room like a mouse. She sat weeping at her bedside.

'I'm sorry... so sorry,' she said over and over. 'I didn't mean to upset you. Don't die, Susan, please don't – Mum will blame me. She will never forgive me.'

Susan murmured that it wasn't her fault, but Angela kept on crying until Susan asked her to go away. Her sister's grief was intruding into her world of pain and she didn't want that, because it pricked her, making her conscious of life still flowing about her when all she wanted was to let go and never feel hurt again, but they would keep coming: her mother with hot drinks and food, her sister with her tears, her dear Lizzie with Arthur and her loving touch, Olive with her entreaties to think of her mother – and then, at last, Jeanie.

'You have to get better,' Jeanie told her and her voice was firm and harsh. 'You have to, because we can't take any more grief, Susan. This family has had enough. My mother was devastated, because her life revolved around those two – but she knows she has to go on, and so do you. Don't hurt us again, Susan – none of us can bear it.'

'You don't understand,' Susan told her tiredly. 'He was my dream and it had all come true.'

'Dreams shatter all the time,' Jeanie replied in a dull flat tone. 'I love your brother, but he isn't always the man of my dreams; he can be thoughtless and inconsiderate – and he may have been unfaithful...'

Susan's eyes opened at that, and she pushed her way up the pillows, looking at her sister-in-law. 'Artie wouldn't – surely you don't think that, Jeanie? I know what he can be like, but he loves you. I thought you were so happy together?'

'Sometimes we are,' Jeanie agreed. 'Not always. I almost stayed on with my mother, because she needed me – but she made me come home. If you marry a man you have to stick to him, whatever he does – that's what she told me and it's true. Mum wants to come and see you. I told her you were planning to marry – and that made her happy; the thought that Terry's last days with you were the happiest he'd had for a long time, picked her up, gave her the strength to carry on. She's lost him and Tina – don't make her go through that again, because she's thinking of you as a daughter now.' Jeanie leaned forward, giving her a little shake of the shoulder. 'Don't you think Pam has had enough grief to last three lifetimes? Are you going to break her now?'

'What do you mean?' Susan looked at her, puzzled. 'It isn't Mum's fault – how could it be? I don't blame her for anything...'

'She blames herself for not telling you before Angela did – and it is killing her, Susan. If you let go now, if you die, after she fought to bring you through that awful illness – well, I think she may just give up altogether. She has been saying she thinks her family is cursed. We are all anxious about her...'

Susan stared at her. 'Mum is ill? I've been too miserable to notice. I just wanted to drift away so it stops hurting but... I don't want Mum to be ill or die because of me.'

'Don't you know how much she loves you? How much we all love you? You were my sister-in-law because I married Artie, but when you and Terry... well, then you became my sister. You will always be special to me, Susan, because he loved you – and, God knows, it broke my heart when they told me what had happened to him and Tina. I couldn't believe it and I've been crying for weeks, but I have a husband and son, and another baby on the way. I have to put my grief away in a corner of my heart and go on living, for their sakes. You were not the only one to lose someone very special, Susan. Don't leave me alone with my grief, please. I need you to help me – and Pam needs you to get better.'

Susan looked at her, eyes filled with tears. 'I've only been thinking of me and what I lost, but you and your parents, and Annie, you all loved them. I'm sorry, Jeanie. I just couldn't bear to think of them...' She closed her eyes for a moment. 'I need to ask – where they badly cut... mutilated...?'

'Oh, Susan, have you been thinking the unthinkable?' Jeanie reached for her hands and held them. 'I went to identify them. Tina had a bruise on her forehead but was otherwise untouched; she must have gone instantaneously. Terry's hands and face were bruised and scratched – but an artery in his leg was severed and they couldn't stop the bleeding; he died on the way to hospital. There was no terrible mutilation, I promise.'

Susan nodded, brushing her hand across her cheek. 'I kept seeing jagged glass... in their faces...' She choked with relief. 'So they didn't suffer for a long time? I couldn't bear it if they did.'

'Tina must have died instantly, a heavy bang on the head can do that to a child – and Terry was unconscious so...' Jeanie wiped the tears from her own cheeks. 'The police told me that they've seen much worse – but they still don't know why the car swerved.'

'Tina was kneeling up in her seat when they drove off. I thought perhaps she might have fallen against his arm or...' Susan sighed. 'I suppose we shall never know.'

'Children are best in the back seats, unless on a rein or something; they will fidget and climb about, so it may have been as you've seen it in your mind – but, as you say, we will never know. It was just an accident, Susan, and they happen however hard you try to prevent them.'

'Yes, I know.' Susan gave her a wan look and pressed her hand. 'I kept wondering. If I'd asked him to take me home first – would it have been avoided? Was there something I could have done?'

'No one could have prevented it,' Jeanie replied. 'Except perhaps Terry. If it was because Tina distracted him: he did tend to spoil her and... But that is a useless thing to say, because we don't know that happened. It could have been an animal crossing the road, anything... The police say they don't think another vehicle was involved. Artie says the roads might have been greasy – mud on the road and then a thunderstorm.'

Susan was sitting up now. Jeanie's arguments had got through to her where her mother's constant apologies and fussing had not. 'Is Mum really making herself ill over me?'

'Yes, she has been. Tom came home for two nights and that was the only time she slept properly. I've been in London, but I've told Artie I am going to stay for a few days to look after you and Pam. It really frightened me when I saw how drained she looks.'

'That's my fault,' Susan said. 'I'm sorry. I never thought of anyone else...'

'You were entitled,' Jeanie replied. 'Pam said there was a time when they all thought you would die, but then that new doctor came and gave you a different medicine and that helped. She reckons his visits saved your life when you had the fever – but then you seemed as if you wanted to throw all that away.'

'I did want to die...'

'But you don't now?' Jeanie asked anxiously.

'No, I know that would be selfish,' Susan replied. 'I'll carry on, because it would hurt others if I just refused to live...' She smiled as Jeanie got to her feet with a groan. 'You look as if you should be resting yourself – how long before the baby is born?'

Jeanie put her hands to her back. 'Another six weeks or so, the doctor says, but it could be any time. Babies come when they're ready.'

'I'll try to get up later,' Susan told her. 'I wouldn't mind something to eat now – but send George up with it. I haven't seen him since...'

'He wouldn't come near you, because he said he didn't want to make you worse, so he stayed away, but he's been doing the work of a man on the farm, feeding the calves, mucking out – and he missed two weeks of school, because he wouldn't go, said he had to look after Pam. His headmaster came to see Pam, so he's going back on Monday...'

'What day is it?' Susan asked. 'I've lost all sense of time.'

'You should have been back at college two weeks ago,' Jeanie said and smiled at her. 'You'll have to catch up. They might let you do some of your coursework at home in the circumstances – otherwise, you'll need to do an extra term, I should think.'

'Yes, I suppose so,' Susan replied. 'It doesn't seem to matter much at the moment, Jeanie.'

'No, of course not, but it will in time. You want to teach and you'll find happiness doing the things you enjoy, love. Not just yet, but one day in the future it will come right.'

'Perhaps...' Susan sighed, the doubts in her eyes.

'Look at what John has lost,' Jeanie reminded her. 'He lost Faith and then Lucy let him down – but now he is going to marry his nurse and he is retraining for a job he will probably hate.'

'John is braver than me,' Susan said. 'I am very pleased he is to marry Jane. I hoped he would – but...' She gave a little shake of her head. 'I know I have to go on living, Jeanie, but at the moment I can't imagine ever being happy again.'

'Then dedicate your life to teaching – and give children who really need it a better start in life than they might get if you weren't around,' Jeanie told her. 'Don't sit and be miserable and waste your life, Susan. Terry would hate that. He loved you, and for him, loving was wanting those he cared for to be happy. Live for him and have a good life. It's what he would tell you if he could.'

'Oh, Jeanie,' Susan's tears were fresh but healing now. 'Oh, Jeanie. I loved him so much.'

'Go on loving him,' Jeanie advised. 'Make everything you do a tribute to the man you loved. He doesn't have to be dead to you, Susan; he can live on in your heart and mind. Keep him close and be a better person, because he loved you.'

Susan gulped, her head coming up, as she realised Jeanie had shown her the way forward. 'Yes, I shall,' she said and a look of determination entered her eyes. 'I will do something special with my life – and it will be for them, Terry and Tina.'

Jeanie leaned forward and kissed her. 'That's lovely, Susan. You do that – make him proud.'

She went from the room, her body moving slowly, heavy with child. Susan watched her and wondered how she could cope, because her grief must have been terrible, too.

Sitting back against her pillows, Susan decided she would fight to get her strength back; she would apologise to her mother, and make sure Angela knew there was no reason to cry. Her grief was like a cold stone inside her, but she knew she had to go on. Susan was young, with all her life in front of her. She could make of it what she would – and she decided to dedicate it to children who needed extra care. She would dedicate her life to helping others – and she would keep Terry and Tina close in her memory. She would, as Jeanie had suggested, make them proud of her.

34

'When are you coming home?' Artie asked Jeanie two weeks later. 'It was good of you to stop when Mum was so worn out, but now that Susan is getting up and making progress, she is much better. I miss you being at ours...'

'Are you sure you want me to?' Jeanie asked, giving him a straight look. 'I could always go back to London. Mum would love to have me there – and it would leave you free to get on with your own life, Artie.'

'What do you mean?' He knew a moment of panic. Was she thinking of leaving him? He'd believed she would come back when she was ready. It had been a time of turmoil for both families, but, surely, she wanted her own home? 'My life is with you and the kids – isn't it?'

'I thought you might be bored with married life, with the tie of kids and a pregnant wife? I know you fancied Izzy, Artie. She wasn't the sort I'd think you need, but if you'd rather be free – to go with who you like, as you did before we got together...'

'Oh damn it!' Artie cried, running his fingers through his thick dark hair, thoroughly disturbed now. 'I know I was a bloody fool – but she threw herself at me and you were tired, and that isn't an excuse. I am sorry if I hurt you. I never meant to – and nothing happened, honestly. I was tempted a couple of times, but I didn't – please believe me.'

'I found a handkerchief in your pocket after she quit working for us,' Jeanie said quietly. 'It had her lipstick on it...'

'Impossible!' he cried indignantly, then, 'Oh, I remember. After I left you and Mum that day, I found her sitting on the grass down the Witcham Road. I questioned her about the money she stole. She spun me a tale about a child that needed an operation. She was crying and I believed her, felt sorry for her – so I gave her my hanky and took her to the station in Sutton – gave her ten bob, actually...' He made a wry face. 'She ran to catch a train standing in the station, and as she jumped on, she called out something... sounded like, "There's one born every minute," so I think I was had. She was a troublemaker and a thief and I swear I never touched her.'

Jeanie looked at him for a moment and then laughed. 'Oh, Artie. Surely you didn't let her swindle you out of another ten bob – after what she stole from your mum?'

'I was an idiot,' he said ruefully. 'I believed her story about the kid and felt sorry for her. Yes, she was attractive and she flaunted herself at me, but I never would have, because I love you, Jeanie. You are the only woman I want. You are beautiful and loving and I adore you, and I want to make love to you, just you. You are my wife, the mother of my children. I've never wanted to spend my life with anyone else. You make me laugh; you make me happy. You have to believe me. You are the only one for me.'

'Promise?'

'Promise.'

Jeanie nodded, smiling now. 'Then do something for me to prove it, Artie.'

'Anything,' he said.

Jeanie raised her eyes to his. 'Go and see John. Make up any quarrels you had with him. He's getting married. You should at least visit – maybe take a present from us.'

Artie frowned. 'I would go. I've wanted to, believe me – but I am not certain he would see me.'

'Just try, please,' Jeanie said earnestly. 'It might not change his mind about coming home – but perhaps he might come with Jonny now and then, and that would make so much difference to your mum, Artie.'

Artie was silent for a few seconds, then he looked at her and she saw the glimmer of tears in his eyes. 'What did I do to deserve you, Jeanie?' he asked. 'It's what I ought to have done a while back, but I kept telling myself I was too busy.'

'Well, the treadmill of work will all start again soon. Go now, this weekend, and say what you need to, Artie. I think you owe it to him, to your mother – and to yourself.'

'All right, I will,' he said. 'You'll stay with Mum until I get back?' He looked at her anxiously. 'I think he might come any day now.' His eyes lingered on her large bump under the loose smock she wore, and she stroked it protectively.

'Doctor says not,' Jeanie smiled. 'Don't worry. I shall wait for you to get back. And I think this one might be a girl.'

'Don't care as long as you are both all right,' he said and then took her in his arms and kissed her. 'I love you, Jeanie Talbot. I'll love you until the end of my life.'

'Even when I've got six kids and I'm as round as a barrel?' she teased and laughed as he couldn't hide his look of alarm. 'Don't worry. I'm going to try not to have any more just yet after this one. The nurse told me about something I could try – and it doesn't interfere with our love life.'

'I'm not sure I can afford six just yet,' he said and smiled wryly.

'Well, we'll have what we have,' Jeanie told him. 'Mum had three and she never got fat, so maybe we'll stop there.'

'You're a minx,' Artie told her. 'You do know that I love you?'

'Of course. I always did – and, for my sins, I love you, Artie Talbot, but just remember if you stray, I'll make you very sorry...'

Artie laughed, but there was just enough menace in her voice to let him know she meant it.

'I'll visit John on Sunday,' he said. 'Go down on the late train Saturday night and come back Sunday afternoon.'

* * *

'How did you get him to agree to that?' Pam asked when Artie had announced he was going to visit John that weekend, then gone off for a pint at the pub, leaving them to their knitting and a comfortable gossip. 'I suggested it weeks ago and he just said he was too busy.'

'Well, he was then, but he isn't so much now; the new lads have been a big help, Mum – and I have my ways.' Jeanie's eyes twinkled and Pam looked at her and then started chuckling.

'You minx! I reckon you know how to handle him. He's always been moody and unpredictable. One minute he's laughing and joking, then the next he's quiet and hardly a word to say. How do you put up with him?'

'I love him, Mum. I always will, but I know him for what he is – and so far, we're doing all right.' Pam nodded. 'What about you, Mum?' Jeanie was serious now. 'Are you feeling better in yourself? We were very worried about you, both of us.'

Pam's laughter left her and she closed her eyes for a moment, then, 'I was near breaking point,' she admitted. 'It wasn't just the work that got on top of me; I can cope with work – but I truly felt there was a curse on me and my family were suffering because of it...' She gave herself a little shake. 'It's stupid – and I hadn't thought of it for years – but I was cursed once, by a gypsy. I wouldn't give her sixpence for her lucky heather, so she put a curse on me.'

Jeanie giggled. 'Oh, Mum! As if she could. Had she the power, she would be the queen and the world would turn upside down.'

Pam looked at her and then started laughing. 'Yes, I know it is daft – but, oh, Jeanie. We've had so much bad luck as a family. Tom was wounded – John twice and nearly died – my lovely Arthur died much too soon... Then there was Faith, and...' She stopped, looking at Jeanie with tears in her eyes.

'Terry and Tina,' Jeanie said with sadness in her pretty face. 'My mother is devastated, too. She told me she intends to go back to full-time midwifery – and Dad... well, we don't know how he feels, because he won't speak about it. He won't allow anyone to say Terry's name. I think he feels that everything he worked for has gone now that his son is dead – but he won't say a word. Just eats his meals and goes off to work. I don't know how Mum can stand it.'

'Oh, poor Vera,' Pam said and wiped her eyes. 'I wonder if she would like to come for a little visit when she's ready. I had no idea how bad it was for her. Of course I understood she was suffering terribly – but your father must be out of his mind with grief, poor man.'

'Yes, it is awful there,' Jeanie replied. 'It's why I stopped as long as I did – but then Mum told me to come home. She said if I wanted my husband, I should go home and look after him, and leave her to cope with hers.'

'What about Annie? Does she know how your mother is suffering?'

'Annie came home for two days and then went back to work,' Jeanie said. 'I don't know whether she realises what is going on at home – but she is only interested in nursing these days.'

'No sign of a romance then?'

'Not that she tells us,' Jeanie replied. 'I know there was someone – a doctor, but either he didn't want her or he had a wife... She never really told us.' Jeanie blinked hard and sniffed. Pam handed her a handkerchief and she dabbed her eyes. 'The war changed Annie. She used to be fun and we shared lots of stuff – but now... well, I am closer to you and Lizzie than my own sister.'

'That's a shame,' Pam said. 'Perhaps, when the war is over, she will think about things and come to find you again.'

'I have my own family now,' Jeanie replied with a shrug. 'Please tell me you will be all right, Pam. I don't think I could bear to lose you. This family would fall apart without you.'

'Daft talk,' Pam said. 'Anyway, I'm not going anywhere, so no call for such nonsense.' Something struck her as ironic and she laughed wryly. 'I was all set to take some time off. To have a little fun – and then all that drama with Izzy and then Susan's illness and your dear brother...' She shook her head. 'I must think myself lucky I didn't lose Susan, because it came close...'

'Yes, I know. Artie told me how ill she was and that was when I decided to come home – but she is getting better now, Mum.'

'Yes, she is,' Pam smiled. Lizzie had taken Susan home with her that evening and was giving her a new hairstyle and a manicure. 'She is trying, poor little love...' Pam sighed. 'I don't know when she will get back to college. They've sent some work for her to do, but she hasn't looked at it yet.'

'Give her time, Mum,' Jeanie said and looked up as Artie walked in. True to his word, he hadn't been long. She yawned, then, looking at her husband, 'Had a good chat, love?'

He nodded. 'I think I shall go up – you coming, Jeanie?'

'Yes. Goodnight, Mum. I hope Susan doesn't come back with green hair...' They both smiled at the memory of one of Susan's experiments with colouring her hair and then went up the stairs, leaving Pam to sit and think while she waited for Susan to come home.

Having Jeanie and Artie stay was almost like old times, but they would go home soon, and, with luck, Susan would return to college – and then it would just be the young ones and her again. Before she could dwell on it, the door opened and Susan entered, her hair waved and curled about her face – that was still much too thin – and she had white-blonde streaks in her hair.

'Oh, that looks nice, love,' Pam said, giving her a warm smile. 'Did you want a hot drink before you go up?'

'No, I had tea with Lizzie,' Susan replied and sat down, looking at her. 'Mum, I've talked it over with Lizzie – and I've decided not to continue my teaching course – at least for a while. I can go back to it later, if I want to...'

Pam's heart sank as she looked at her. 'What do you want to do then?' she asked, knowing she hadn't the heart to argue.

'I am going to look after children, disadvantaged, disabled children,' Susan told her. 'I've thought it over carefully, Mum. I'm sorry if it disappoints you, and I can finish my college education and go for pupil-teaching at a later date, because I've asked – but for the moment... Well, I just want to do this and...'

'I think that is a wonderful idea, Susan,' Pam said and, to her surprise, she really did. 'Do you know how to start... when you are well enough, that is?'

'I think I'm nearly ready, Mum,' Susan said. 'I get a bit tired, but... well, it will take a few weeks. I expect I'll need special training. I thought I would ask Doctor Bryant. He might know where I should start, don't you think?'

'You are not talking about nursing?' Pam asked and Susan shook her head. 'I'm not sure he would know then – but one of the nurses might...'

'Lizzie says there is a place in Ely that cares for them. I might go and ask there if they need help – but I think I need training first.'

'Yes, I expect so. Speak to someone at the doctor's first, and then go into Ely. I know where it is – on the Palace Green... I've seen those poor children in the town with their carers. They are all in wheelchairs, but they look happy, so I think the girls take good care of them.'

'Yes, I know,' Susan replied. 'I'm sorry if you think I'm letting you and Dad down, Mum, but I need this – even if it is only for a while.'

'Don't be daft, love. I want you to find contentment, Susan – and to be happy again. If this helps you, I'm all for it.'

Susan rushed and hugged her and was kissed in reply. 'It means I'll be living at home if I get a job locally.'

'That is a bonus,' Pam said and smiled. 'Lizzie has done your hair lovely, Susan. It really suits you. I'm going up now – are you coming?'

'No, not yet. You go up and I'll make sure everywhere is locked,' Susan told her.

'Yes, all right,' Pam said and left her. Susan had left childhood behind. She was a woman in her own right now, and Pam could only be glad that she still wanted her approval. She felt a little glow of pride in her eldest daughter – in all her family.

Yes, they had been through tough times, but they were still a family. She smiled a little wearily. 'What next, Arthur?' she murmured as she prepared for bed. 'What will they throw at us next?'

It had been one thing after another these past years, but, somehow, they had weathered it. When you thought about it, there was a lot to look forward to – John's wedding, two new babies in the family – Susan's recovery and the life she had chosen for herself. Pam's dream of her being a teacher might have slipped away, but Susan seemed to have found something she wanted for herself and that was even better. Life changed and yet it didn't. The cycle of work on the farm remained the same, and once Artie returned from his visit to John, it would begin again.

She wondered briefly how that would go – John hadn't wanted to see Artie but he'd been fine with Susan, and surely it was better that they meet and talk – settle old differences. As a mother she'd known the two had never really got on. John preferred Tom. It was a pity he wouldn't come back to the area and make his home near them, but he was determined and it wasn't her place to change his mind.

She would be losing her dearest Jonny soon. That was going to hurt, but it had to happen, and Pam had forced herself to accept it. Jonny wanted to be with his father and that was right and proper.

'Having a family isn't easy, Arthur,' she murmured as she settled to sleep.

'It never was, old girl,' his voice, reassuring and steady, was in her mind, just as real as if he'd been beside her. In all honesty, he'd never left her and she guessed he never would. She might face loneliness in the future, because most widows did; children couldn't visit all the time, but in her heart, she knew she wasn't truly alone.

'You're with me,' she whispered and promptly fell asleep.

35

John was studying in the craft room when a nurse came to tell him his brother had arrived to visit. He often used the room for his studies, because hardly anyone else ever came near. Most of the men preferred the sports and outdoors pursuits available to them, so he found it peaceful to work here, and the light from the long windows was good.

'Tom here?' John was surprised as he looked up from his books. Then his eyes went past her to the man standing just behind in the doorway and his expression froze. 'Artie – I didn't expect to see you...' he said as the nurse left them.

'Probably didn't want to,' Artie said, hesitating before advancing awkwardly into the room. 'Nice place this – must have been a lovely home once...'

'It still is,' John replied. 'To many rather than just a few.'

'You know what I meant,' Artie said. He looked at John's face and his feelings showed, whether or not he intended it. 'Sorry about what happened to you, John. I wanted to tell you – to say... if I hurt or offended you over Faith, I didn't mean it. I've said a lot of things I didn't mean...' He shuffled his feet, clearly uncomfortable. 'I'm sorry. I wasn't the best of brothers. I suppose I was always jealous, because you were Mum's favourite – daft because she loves us all. Jeanie says I'm an idiot and I probably am – but don't let me be the cause of your not coming to the farm. I don't live there now and I wouldn't say anything nasty about... well, your face. I'm not that cruel.'

John looked at his brother in astonishment. Being humble didn't suit Artie and, in all honesty, John didn't need this. 'Don't be such a stupid bugger,' he said and laughed. 'Do you truly imagine it was all about you? Yes, I did dread that look on your face when you saw mine, but it no longer matters. I don't give a damn about what you or anyone else thinks of my looks. I am me and you can all take me or leave me, as you please. I can't come back, because the memory of what happened to Faith still haunts me – and because I no longer belong there. I've moved on, Artie. It's what I want and nothing to do with you...'

'Jeanie thought you might visit more if I made things right...' Artie stared at him, John's words ignored. 'Don't you care that it will hurt Mum when you take Jonny away? She has looked after him like a son since Faith died...'

'I know that – but he is my son, and she understands.' John looked at Artie and knew he didn't like him. They were chalk and cheese and always had been. 'I think it best if you leave, Artie. We really don't have a lot in common – but thank you for the thought and the visit. It was kind of Jeanie to make you try.'

'You little bastard!' Artie said and issued several profanities under his breath. 'Well, that is the last time I try to make peace with you.'

John met his eyes. 'You made my childhood on the farm hell with your mockery and your careless use of words,' he said. 'But it no longer matters – just as the scars no longer matter. I have a life of my own and people I love. Tell Jeanie she is invited to the wedding – you can come or don't, as you please.'

'I wouldn't bloody come if you paid me,' Artie said, turned and stalked out of the room.

John started laughing. He laughed until the tears ran, only stopping when Jane walked in. 'What's the matter?' she asked, looking at him anxiously. 'You look strange, John – and that laughter wasn't like you...'

'I just paid back years of slights from my brother,' John said.

'Artie was here?' She needed no telling which brother he meant, because he had nothing but praise for Tom.

'He thought I was afraid to go back to the farm because of him,' John said and the laughter had gone. 'The damned cheek of him! You know why I want to start a new life away from all that...'

'Yes, I know,' she said. 'Perhaps he was trying to be kind, John.'

'In his way, I suppose he was,' John replied. 'I thanked him for the visit but asked him to leave. You would have too, had you seen the look on his face when he saw mine – he was struggling with his revulsion, his pity and his superiority.'

'Then you did the right thing,' Jane said. 'Forget him, John. You won't have to see him again.'

'I doubt I ever shall. What I said was probably a bit strong, Jane – but it just came out, after years of repression, of being hurt by the things he said without thinking – and suddenly it didn't matter a jot and I told him so.'

'Unfortunately, brothers are sometimes enemies,' Jane said. 'It is a shame, because he came a long way to be told to bugger off.' Her eyes twinkled at him and he laughed once more. She smiled to see that his look of suppressed anger had gone, understanding that the sensitive, shy soul that lived within this man had suffered more than most at the jibes of a thoughtless brother for many years. It wasn't that Artie was deliberately cruel; like many others, he just didn't think how his sharp words could hurt. A jeer that someone with a tough skin could throw off, sometimes pierced those with thinner skins to the heart. 'It isn't important now, John.'

'No, it isn't,' he murmured and moved forward to capture her hands and hold them up to be kissed, finger by finger. 'You matter and Jonny – and my family, but Artie can't hurt me again.'

'So I can cross him off the wedding list?' Jane twinkled up at him.

'He said he wouldn't bloody come if I paid him,' John said. 'I was pretty rotten to him – but it was irresistible. He looked as if he thought I should be so grateful for his apology. Probably thought I would fall on his neck in tears... he's just so damned arrogant.'

'It might be that it is the unconscious arrogance of the strong.' Jane looked thoughtful as she went on, 'I've seen it before with men in uniform. Some of them just give off this air of superiority, as if they know they are better than all the others.'

'That is Artie!' John told her. 'He was always tall, dark and handsome and the girls swooned over him. He could have any one of them he wanted at the flick of his fingers – and I think it irked him that Faith was so beautiful and preferred me. He made constant digs at us... but that is over now. I have put it behind me, Jane – just as the scars are no longer important. I know what I am and I know my limitations. I can't be strong or athletic or do the work I once did, but I'm getting the hang of this accountancy thing, and I think I'll do all right.' John smiled down at her. 'Why wouldn't I, now I have you, my wonderful Jane?'

'Oh, John, I'm just very ordinary,' Jane said, looking up at him with love. 'You are brave and strong, and exceptional, don't you know that? You won a medal for your bravery, and you fought for life when many men would have given in, and you won – surely that is enough?'

'It is more than enough,' he agreed and laughed. 'I forgot about the medal. I think I threw it away when it came.'

'You did, but I rescued it,' she said and laughed. 'I've got it hidden away safe and one day I will show it to your family.'

'Artie will say they gave them to everyone...'

'Not this one, they don't,' Jane said. 'It's the King George Cross. Next time – if ever – he says something slighting, I'll show him.'

'You would too,' John replied and laughed. He glanced at his watch. 'Is it time for dinner? I'm hungry...'

'We're having fish and chips this evening – all the men are,' Jane replied. She took his hand in hers. 'Let's take a stroll in the garden first...'

* * *

Artie caught the first train home. It was late in the evening and he wouldn't get home before mid-morning, but he could sleep on the train. He was damned if he was going to waste money on a hotel room for the night! He had already wasted time coming here.

Artie was fuming as he lit a cigarette and sat staring moodily out of the window, waiting for the journey home to start. John really was a smug bastard, just as he'd always been... his mother's favourite, pale-faced, and couldn't say boo to a goose. He'd never been able to understand why his mother would favour the little runt!

Inhaling the smoke, he sat back as the train engine chugged, and the wheels began to rattle on the track, leaving the rather dirty, old-fashioned railway station behind. For two pins he could have murdered the bugger! He was still smarting at the laughter in John's eyes. What was so bloody funny? He'd gone all that way to apologise, against his better judgement – and John had practically told him to clear off...

It rankled and, surprising Artie, it hurt. He knew that he'd upset John by mocking him about being a virgin, and then some rather smutty remarks about his relationship with Faith. It had been a joke but one that the sensitive John had hated. Artie was used to such talk amongst the lads he'd gone around with – and he'd never taken any notice of such mockery, giving back as good as he'd got. He'd never understood why John was different. It had annoyed him.

Since Faith's death and John's horrific injuries, Artie had regretted the breach between them. He'd genuinely wanted to apologise – to make it easier for John to come home, if he wanted, but his attempt to make friends had been thrown back in his face, and it had made him angry.

Leaning his head back against the padded seat, Artie closed his eyes, giving his thoughts free rein. He'd been furious when he'd stalked off, but now he was sorry – sorry he'd failed, because he didn't want a rift in the family, or not one that he'd caused. Yes, he was thoughtless at times, and he supposed he might seem a bit arrogant, but it wasn't something he'd cultivated; it was just a part of him – the way he was.

The two of them were so different, but they were brothers and Artie wished their relationship might have been otherwise. John had been through such agony and it took a whole lot of courage to face up to the tragic things that had happened to him. It was odd, but when John had told him to bugger off – though not in those words – he'd respected him for the first time.

John wasn't the little coward Artie had always thought him. It had angered him as the older brother that John never fought back but looked as if he'd been stabbed to the heart when something careless was said. Artie had always stood up to Tom, his elder half-brother, and they'd had both physical and verbal fights all their life, and though they often fell out, they were still friends. He would be glad when Tom got his discharge and came home. He actually missed having him around, despite the fact that they often crossed swords.

Artie wanted to be friends with John, too, but he supposed it would never happen. He'd clearly made John hate him, though none of it had been said with real malice, but perhaps Artie didn't always think before he spoke. Maybe he should try being a bit more diplomatic in future, the way Jeanie was often telling him.

Artie opened his eyes, picked up his newspaper and began to read. The Allies were surging into Europe, the fighting fierce as Hitler threw all he had at them, and it didn't look as if the war would end any time soon. Oh, well, there wasn't much he could do about it – he was the one who stayed home while his brothers went to war.

Some folk might think he was the coward, but Artie knew that the farm would have gone under if his parents had needed to rely on just the land girls, though Olive was a big help. He hoped she wouldn't get married and leave just yet, though she was courting steady. George was a big help and his cheeky smile appealed to Artie. If John had been more like him, they would never have fallen out.

Sighing, he contemplated the mountain of work that would be his in the coming months. He'd been a fool to grab all the land he could get. One school-leaver wasn't going to be enough if he wanted any time at home with his family. He would have to advertise, see if he could get more help – even some of those prisoners of war. He'd heard that some folk had Italians working on their farms. Yes, he would make inquiries, see what was on offer, because he wasn't going to sell his land, but he had to look after Blackberry Farm, too. He couldn't neglect it, as he had earlier that year. His mother needed him, and he was sorry he'd let her down a bit. Once his land began to pay, he'd give her some of his profit, because he knew she'd given him far too much.

Artie folded his paper. He wasn't really reading it. His mind was too busy with plans for the future. The anger had faded now, a feeling of justice taking its place. John had hit back and for once he'd made it hurt, and now that he could think clearly, it made Artie grin. His little brother was no longer the meek and mild lad he'd teased unmercifully; he'd toughened up, just the way Artie had wanted. All the mockery had been to one purpose, to make John tougher, to enable him to cope with the realities of life. The war had done that far more effectively, and John was going to need to be tough once he returned to normal life – with that face he'd get a lot of stares, and he'd have to ignore them, the pity, and the whispers, if he wanted to go out into the real world.

Artie smiled to himself. 'You gave me my own – well done, little brother,' he said aloud, and then he began to laugh. He laughed, because he was glad that John had come through it all and was tough enough to tell him to get lost – and he laughed because he knew that he, Artie, was the lucky one. He'd got it all; he was simply better than all the rest – and be damned to them! He was going to show them all – just wait and see. The future was there for the taking and Artie was the one to reach out and grab it!

✳ ✳ ✳

MORE FROM ROSIE CLARKE

The next book in the Blackberry Farm series from Rosie Clarke is available to order now here:

https://mybook.to/BlackberryFarm6

ABOUT THE AUTHOR

Rosie Clarke is a #1 bestselling saga writer whose books include *Welcome to Harpers Emporium* and The Mulberry Lane series. She has written over 100 novels under different pseudonyms and is a RNA Award winner. She lives in Cambridgeshire.

Download your exclusive bonus content from Rosie Clarke here:

Visit Rosie's website: www.lindasole.co.uk

Follow Rosie on social media here:

f facebook.com/Rosie-clarke-119457351778432
X x.com/AnneHerries
BB bookbub.com/authors/rosie-clarke

ALSO BY ROSIE CLARKE

Welcome to Harpers Emporium Series

The Shop Girls of Harpers

Love and Marriage at Harpers

Rainy Days for the Harpers Girls

Harpers Heroes

Wartime Blues for the Harpers Girls

Victory Bells For The Harpers Girls

Changing Times at Harpers

Heartbreak at Harpers

Troubled Times at Harpers

The Mulberry Lane Series

A Reunion at Mulberry Lane

Stormy Days On Mulberry Lane

A New Dawn Over Mulberry Lane

Life and Love at Mulberry Lane

Last Orders at Mulberry Lane

Blackberry Farm Series

War Clouds Over Blackberry Farm

Heartache at Blackberry Farm

Love and Duty at Blackberry Farm

Family Matters at Blackberry Farm

Tears and Fears at Blackberry Farm

The Trenwith Trilogy

Sarah's Choice

Louise's War

Rose's Fight

Dressmakers' Alley

Dangerous Times on Dressmakers' Alley

Dark Secrets on Dressmakers' Alley

Better Days on Dressmakers' Alley

The Family Feud Series

A Family at War

A Family Secret

A Family Fortune

Standalone Novels

Nellie's Heartbreak

A Mother's Shame

A Sister's Destiny

Sixpence Stories

Introducing Sixpence Stories!

Discover page-turning historical novels from your favourite authors, meet new friends and be transported back in time.

Join our book club
Facebook group

https://bit.ly/SixpenceGroup

Sign up to our
newsletter

https://bit.ly/SixpenceNews

Boldwood

Boldwood Books is an award-winning fiction publishing company seeking out the best stories from around the world.

Find out more at www.boldwoodbooks.com

Join our reader community for brilliant books, competitions and offers!

Follow us

@BoldwoodBooks

@TheBoldBookClub

Sign up to our weekly deals newsletter

https://bit.ly/BoldwoodBNewsletter